Daughters of January

E.Z. Rinsky

Also by E.Z. Rinsky:

Lamb and Lavagnino Mysteries

Palindrome

The Binding

To Mom and Dad

Daughters of January

Part 1
The Face of the Waters

1

Rosalyn Carson opened her eyes. For a moment, she thought she was in her sunny bedroom in her house on Polo Drive, engulfed in a Rosalyn-shaped sinkhole in her memory foam mattress, trying to ignore her snoring husband.

Scott's snoring had always been awful. It was obvious to Rosalyn that he had sleep apnea, but for years he'd resisted doing a sleep study to confirm the diagnosis. Every night there'd be several moments when he'd go completely silent, and then wake up gasping for air. How many times had they had the same conversation at breakfast?

You have to see someone, Scott. Last night wasn't snoring. It was a fight for life...

A fire in Rosalyn's chest jerked her into the wretched present. She was choking. Her cheeks and sinuses were throbbing in pain, like she was at the bottom of a swimming pool. She could hardly breathe.

It was the gas mask. The mask had saved her life, but seemed to have turned on her. She tried inhaling hard to unclog the filter, but it was no use. She wasn't getting enough air.

She had no choice. She unfastened the strap, stuck two fingers in between the collar and her neck, and peeled the rubber lobster off her face. She half-expected to choke on diseased air, and when she didn't she gulped down fresh breaths hungrily.

For a few minutes she just sat in bed savoring the feeling of blood rushing back to her face. She touched her cheeks and nose for the first time in a week. Everything looked so vivid; she hadn't realized just how grimy and cloudy the visor of her mask had become.

Slowly she took stock of her situation. She was in a cabin on a ship. Somewhere below her, the engines–not Scott–were rumbling. Through the porthole beside her bed she saw nothing but open sea. She wasn't sure if it was still her eyes adjusting from the dirty visor, but the colors seemed off: the sky was hazy yellow and the sea looked like a frothy cappuccino. The planet was dead, and she was a still-living cell trapped inside its decaying corpse.

She suddenly remembered last night's sprint to the coast. Between the darkness and the cloudy visor of the gas mask, she'd been nearly blind, and forced to crawl on her knees over the rubble and bodies.

The stagnant air in the cabin was hot and wet, and she was sucking it down too fast. The relief of getting the mask off was giving way to panic as she processed her new reality. She dug her nails into her thighs. Her vision was narrowing, clammy hands shaking...

Instinctively she turned to the mantra she'd used since she was first assaulted by this horrible feeling thirty years ago, in a middle school gymnasium darkened for a Sadie Hawkins dance:

This isn't real. Nothing is real.

For a few minutes Rosalyn just concentrated on slowing her breathing and unclenching her shoulders and fists. She was relieved when her heart finally stopped threatening to burst from her chest. She'd managed to keep the monster at bay.

Carefully she prioritized her needs, to decide on a course of action.

She was thirsty. That was the most pressing concern: water.

No, she realized as she checked her watch. Water was the second most urgent issue. It was a bit past eleven in the morning, which meant it had been roughly seven hours since she'd collapsed. Most urgent was to turn off the engines before the ship ran out of fuel and was left floating, stranded in the middle of the Atlantic.

Rosalyn stood up, and nearly lost her balance as the blue carpet seemed to shift beneath her feet. She took a moment to collect herself, pulled on her soiled linen shirt, and then exited out of the cabin door.

"Hello?" the words left her throat as a warbled groan.

She was in a narrow hall. The floor was the same coarse blue carpet. If it weren't for the metal pipes overhead, the slight rocking of the ship, and the growl of the engines, she could just as well be in a cheap motel. Keeping one hand on the wall to steady herself, Rosalyn made her way toward the door at the end of the hallway.

"Hello?" she tried again. Her voice sounded pitiful echoing down the narrow hall. Why wasn't anyone responding?

The thought made her chest clench all over again: was she alone on this boat?

No, it couldn't be. There had been others last night, hadn't there? Someone had helped her up the gangplank; a large man with hands the size of bear paws. She remembered that moment clearly: crawling up onto the lip of the ship, the night sky ignited by phosphorescent explosions and mountains of fire. There'd been a woman crying next to her too. At least one.

Rosalyn's hiking boots smacked against the metal stairs as she climbed. One flight up there was a swinging door labeled *Deck*. The door opened into a hallway that smelled like disinfectant, and ended in another identical swinging door. She put her shoulder into the far door and stumbled into blinding light.

Wet air slapped her cheeks. Her vision was slow to return, and she groped forward to make sure she wouldn't run into anything. The deck beneath her boots was slippery with ocean spray. She could feel the glow of the fierce sun on her face, and hear the hiss of waves and steady thump of the engines.

"Hello?" she cried. "Hello?"

As her eyes adjusted to the light she found herself surrounded by containers. The containers were the colors of sun-bleached Skittles, and each was large enough to hold a car. They were stacked seven or eight high, and formed walls that blocked her view of the ocean from three directions. If it hadn't been close to high noon, the walls of this maze might have blotted out the sun entirely.

Behind her though, there weren't any containers. Instead there was open deck filled with crates, ropes, railings, and barrels. And beyond this bleak array was a metal stairway leading up to a glass-enclosed tower. She rushed toward the base of the stairs.

"Hello!" she shouted, as loudly as she could.

This time a voice replied, from above.

"Hey!"

There was a man sitting on a step about halfway up.

She looked up and shielded her eyes from the glare. The sky was the color of overripe banana flesh.

"Hold up!" the man shot to his feet. "I'm coming down."

The man sprinting down to the steps was short and skinny, with burnt caramel skin. He jumped off the last step to meet her.

He placed a hand on Rosalyn's shoulder. He was only about a half inch taller than her.

"Hey there, hey, are you okay?" he asked.

"Yes I'm fine, thanks. You?"

"Lung cancer. Will be dead in a month. Kidding, kidding. I'm fine." He showed a mouthful of impossibly straight teeth. "Greg," he said.

"Hi," she tried to smile. "I'm Rosalyn."

His hand was still on her shoulder, and now he stared deep into her eyes and asked again, "Are you okay?"

Greg's face, framed by the dirty sky, was a picture of serious concern. He had kind green eyes and excellent posture. He wore a purple polo shirt and khaki shorts. He was attractive in a daytime soap sort of way, his only blemishes some deep indentations on his nose and neck, surely from his own gas mask. "Are you hurt?"

"I'm fine. A bit thirsty…"

"Of course you are. Of course you are." He offered her a blue plastic container he was holding with the hand that wasn't resting on her shoulder. "Here."

When Greg handed her the jug, Rosalyn was seized by something primal. She tilted her head back and chugged. The tepid water tasted like plastic, but her body screamed for it. Every corner of her was flooded with relief as it gushed down her parched throat.

"Wow," Greg smiled. "Save some for the fish."

Rosalyn finally lowered the jug, panting. She could swear colors were brighter now as if, in addition to the dirty mask, her eyesight had been dulled by dehydration. Greg's purple polo shirt was particularly striking.

"So, you must be pretty wiped. Feel free to rest up." Greg sat down on one of the metal steps. "Me and Sammy are taking care of everything. We'll gather everyone for a meeting in a few hours maybe."

"Everyone? How many people are there on board?"

"Not sure. A dozen maybe? Everything last night was pretty rushed, you know."

Rosalyn licked her wet lips.

"Let's go up to the bridge."

A grimace passed over Greg's handsome face, then he forced himself into a strained smile.

"Let's just hold tight for now. Big Sammy is down in the engine room. He'll be up in a few minutes and we'll take care of everything."

This was the second time this lanky man had used that expression–*take care of everything*–as if he was a concierge reassuring an unsatisfied guest.

"I'm going up."

"Listen," Greg took a deep breath. "There's a really creepy guy sitting up there on the bridge. I just think it's probably safer to go in with Sammy. That's why I was waiting on the stairs."

"A creepy guy?" she asked, shielding her eyes and peering up dubiously at the bridge

"Yeah."

She frowned. It struck her as slightly strange that this man who she'd known for about three minutes was calling someone else a creep. For all she knew, Greg himself was a psychopathic rapist. Not that this was her impression of him. He didn't seem dangerous. At the same time though, his presence wasn't exactly putting her at ease.

"If this creepy guy was going to murder us, wouldn't he just come down and do it now?"

"Well," Greg chuckled uncomfortably. "He can't. He's kind of, um, secured?"

Rosalyn's adrenaline spiked.

"You tied someone up?"

Greg seemed aghast at the suggestion.

"No, no, no. We, well, the truth is we found him like that last night."

Rosalyn was losing her patience.

"Well, creepy guy or not, we have to go turn off the engines. I'm going up there."

"Turn off the engines?" Greg's face shifted into a mask of curiosity."Why?"

"Because we're just going to burn up all our fuel."

"Hmmm," Greg stood up, put his hands on his hips and frowned in a way Rosalyn found slightly demeaning. The posture also had the convenient effect of obstructing her way up the stairs. Was he hiding something?

"Do you even know which direction we're going?"

He scratched his neck and pursed his lips.

"Well away from the east coast so…" his smile wavered for an instant. "East?"

"Someone's going to have to deal with this 'creepy guy' sooner or later. I'm going to go up and explain to him that we're just burning fuel. We don't have a destination, so let's just turn off the engines and figure out a plan."

In the east, eventually, was Southern Europe or maybe North Africa, but anyone who'd watched the news in the past week knew these regions were as barren as the devastation they'd just left behind in Savannah. Air infused with poison, disease, nuclear fallout, and whatever other plagues the Daughters of January had unleashed.

"Do you want more water?" Greg asked. "You probably don't even know how dehydrated you are."

"I'm going up there," Rosalyn said. She took a step toward him, and was relieved when he immediately moved aside to let her pass. "We're just burning fuel."

"Right," Greg nodded, first slowly and then rapidly enough to make Rosalyn slightly unsettled. "Right, right, right. Okay, just don't get too close to him."

"Uh huh." At this point she was pretty sure that this boogeyman was just Greg's tactic to keep her out of the bridge for whatever reason.

She pushed past Greg and climbed up the stairs to the bridge, gripping the railing tightly to steady herself against the rocking of the ship. She stepped inside, through the ajar sliding door. It wasn't exactly the shining tower on the hill she'd imagined from below–just a few rows of desks, monitors, panels, swivel seats, and buttons, all enclosed by dirty glass.

There was one other person on the bridge, sitting on one of several swivel seats. The creepy guy. Immediately, Rosalyn understood that Greg had been genuine. Over the past ten days, Rosalyn had witnessed unspeakable destruction and pain, things she never would have thought possible. Waking nightmares. Still, the strangeness of this scene shook her in a totally new way. The young man gazed at her with wide, confused eyes.

"Can you please untie me?" he pleaded. "I have to use the bathroom."

2

I need a cigarette. That was the thought that roused Vic from a deep, dreamless sleep. He hadn't had a cigarette for five days, and woke up wanting one more than he'd ever wanted anything in his life.

He'd had a pack of Camels in his car. They were in his glove compartment–along with his lighter–when he pulled over to the side of a dirt road at three in the morning to take a leak. He'd been wearing only his blue swimming trunks and a pair of pink Crocs he'd pulled off a corpse near the Georgia border. By the time he'd finished relieving himself–just in time to see the door of his Ford Bronco slam shut, smell burning rubber, and watch the taillights of his car recede into the inky night–his Crocs, swimsuit, and phone were his only worldly possessions.

For perhaps the thousandth time since then, four nights ago, he cursed the faceless bastard who'd stolen his car and cigarettes, and he cursed himself as well for being an impatient fool and leaving the car running while he peed. It was a small solace that the thief was almost certainly dead by now; Vic would be more satisfied to know that the thief had died before getting a chance to enjoy those Camels. They were unfiltered Camels: twice as rich, with twice the head high, of the loose-leaf cigarettes he usually rolled; a luxury Vic had decided to indulge once the news announced that California had ceased to exist.

He sat up in bed and rubbed his temples. Or rather, he tried to, because he was still wearing the damn mask. Enough with this, he thought. If he died, he died. He'd lived a pretty full life. Though, he considered as he unfastened the neck strap and yanked the mask off his face, he would have liked to have been famous.

The mask was off and he could breathe; there were no diseased spores in the air. He could now focus on the fierce pounding in his head. The sensory inputs in the cabin were an immediate source of irritation: the harsh morning light through the porthole glass, and the snoring of the man on the floor beside his bed. Notably absent, however, was the churning of the engines. Somebody must have turned them off.

Vic rubbed his bleary eyes and stared down at his roommate. He only vaguely remembered last night; by the time Vic had climbed aboard he'd been bone tired, running on his last dregs of adrenaline. He had absolutely no recollection of this man being here when he went to sleep.

The man wasn't snoring exactly, Vic realized. He was moaning, his face buried in the blue carpet. A throaty, phlegmy sound muffled by his mask.

"Hello?" Vic said. "Sir?"

When the man ignored him, Vic reached down and patted the quaking mass on the back of the shoulder. Instantly the crying stopped, and the man rolled over onto his back so his opaque visor was facing Vic.

"You can take off the mask," Vic said, pointing to his own face. "I'm okay."

Very slowly, as if suspicious this was all an elaborate trick, the swarthy man undid his own neck clasp, and pulled off his mask. He groaned with pleasure at the fresh air, and rubbed his face as if confirming it was still there. He was an older man, maybe sixty-five. He had an enormous gut, stubby limbs, and strong meaty hands. He reminded Vic of a toy hippopotamus he'd had as a child.

"Sir?" Vic said.

The man looked at him.

"Hello. What's your name? I am Victor. Fournier."

The man remained mute. He just stared up at Vic.

"Sir?"

Nothing. Vic tried his native French.

"Monsieur? Je m'appelle Victor Fournier. Comment tu t'appelles?"

When this too failed to elicit a response, Vic gave up. He climbed out of bed, leaving the rotund man stomach-up—like a flipped beetle —and went to the bathroom. It was only once he entered the cabin bathroom, a cramped cell lit by a yellow tube over the sink, that Vic realized that, in addition to needing a cigarette, he was also very thirsty. He turned on the tap. A hiss of air and then, a few seconds later, a thin dribble of water. He formed a cup with his hands, filled them, drank deeply several times, and then splashed a few more handfuls on his face. Vic poked his head out of the bathroom and saw his roommate hadn't moved, though the man had lifted his head up and was observing Vic intently.

"Hey," Vic called. "There's water in here. *L'eau.* Aren't you thirsty?"

Vic mimed drinking from his hands and gestured for the man to join him. The man considered the offer for a long moment, still breathing hard, and then tentatively sat up. Keeping both eyes on Vic, the man then grunted and pushed himself up to his feet. Standing, Vic saw that he was built like a bowling ball. His gut was threatening to burst the buttons of his threadbare shirt

"Man mariz hastam," he muttered, under his breath. The man located a wool jeff cap near his feet. He bent over, retrieved the hat, slapped it onto his completely bald head, and waddled cautiously toward Vic.

"There's water in there–"

The man pushed past Vic into the bathroom and turned on the tap. He was too impatient to use both hands as a cup. Instead he leaned in as close to the tap as he could, but his head was too wide for his lips to reach the stream. Once he accepted that his head would preclude direct access, he opened his mouth and smacked at the running water with a flat palm, frantically trying to guide as many droplets as he could into his eager maw.

Vic watched the man go at it for perhaps two full minutes, wondering if there was any less efficient way to drink from a sink.

Finally sated, the man leaned back and closed the tap. He sighed and smiled, a toothy smile that only reinforced Vic's association with the hippopotamus toy.

"Khobtar. Khobtar."

What was this guttural language? Arabic? Or whatever they spoke in India… Indian?

"Vic," he said, placing a hand on his chest. "I'm Vic."

The man squinted in confusion.

"Vic," he tried again. "Vic. You?"

"Mmm," the man nodded and placed a thick hand on his own chest. "Bahram."

"Bahram," Vic repeated.

"Bahram."

"Vic."

"Bahram."

Vic was about to figure out a way to excuse himself from this exchange when a crackly voice suddenly filled the room, making both men jump.

"Hello everyone and anyone aboard. Good morning!" There was a speaker over the bed, Vic saw. An on-board PA system. *"A few of us are up here on the bridge. Why doesn't everyone come up and we can all have a little powwow."*

Vic stared at the speaker in disbelief. Who could possibly be so peppy this morning? And what the fuck was there to discuss? They were on a boat. If God, or fate, willed it, they'd be rescued. But that was a long shot. Most likely the reward for their persistence–or sheer luck, really–in getting to this ship would be a few days of reflection before eventually succumbing to starvation. So why did this guy sound like a summer camp counselor trying to get his kids out of their bunks?

A click, and the man's smooth baritone was replaced by a woman's nasal drone.

"Please nobody shower. We don't know how much water we have so don't waste it. We'll meet up here in fifteen minutes."

Bahram was utterly confused, of course. The announcement must have just sounded like gibberish to him.

"Cheh?" he asked Vic, pointing to the speaker. *"Anja keest?"*

"We're going up," Vic said, pointing to the ceiling. Then he had a thought. He made a V with his fingers and held them to his lips. "Cigarettes. Bahram. Do you have cigarettes?"

Bahram mirrored the motion.

"Siggar-Est," he repeated, then pointed at the speaker over the bed. *"Siggar-Est?"*

Vic again stroked his throbbing temples. He sympathized with Bahram; Vic's English was passable, but nowhere close to perfect, and since he'd moved to the States he'd often felt confused, frustrated, or isolated because of his linguistic handicap. But he didn't have the patience to deal with this now. Especially if Bahram didn't have anything to smoke.

Vic's poor English, in fact, was the only reason he was on board. Once it was clear this was the end, by the time every TV station was nothing but Daughters of January videos and red-eyed anchormen grappling with the unthinkable sentences sliding up the teleprompter, Vic hopped in his Bronco and headed south. His destination was obvious: Natalie Chandler, the girl who'd kissed him seven years ago, just two weeks after he'd moved to America. When she shoved her tongue into his mouth and groped him over his pants in a public bar, he couldn't believe that this magical new world had already managed to surpass even his most wild fantasies. The land of opportunity, indeed. Streets paved with gold. A chicken in every pot and a sultry vixen in every dive bar.

He saw Natalie three more times, and then she moved to some city in Georgia called Macon, Two hundred fifty miles west of Charleston. When he pledged to come visit her on weekends, she frowned, put her hand on his shoulder and just said, *That's sweet.*

He hadn't seen her in the seven years since. When he called she was always busy, and eventually he got the idea. He hadn't kissed another girl in the meantime, but not for lack of trying. There was no question, then, of how he wanted to spend his final days on the planet: in the sweet comfort of Natalie Chandler's bed.

She didn't pick up her phone, but that didn't mean anything; a lot of people's phones already weren't working. He had her address saved in his notes app. He'd looked it up years ago, with the thought of driving down to surprise her in a grand romantic gesture, but never summoned the courage.

It was very slow going, over back roads and sometimes over no roads at all. But the highways were at a standstill by then, bumper to bumper, many cars already abandoned. He had GPS on his phone, but no reception–phone infrastructure must have been destroyed–forcing him to navigate with a map he plundered from an abandoned gas station.

When his Bronco was stolen, with map and cigarettes inside, he estimated that he was forty miles east of Natalie's town, but since the road he'd been taking wasn't on the map, he didn't have much confidence in his assessment. He decided to follow the dirt road south until he either found an east-west road, or at least until the forest and brush thinned out so he could make his way west more easily.

It was three in the morning, but the road and forest were illuminated by fires on the horizon. The flames must have been taller than skyscrapers, and they bathed the pine trees and dry dirt in orange–an eerie facsimile of dusk. His camera had been in his Bronco, stolen along with everything else. He snapped a few photos with his phone, then felt silly; who was he going to send them to?

After walking for a few hours, he reached an intersection. Sitting to the side of the intersection was a man whose face was wrapped in a heavy black gas mask that made him look like a human fly. By this point, Vic was well aware of the possibility that Natalie was dead. He'd already driven through many towns that had been completely reduced to rubble, and bypassed several that were swallowed in flame. With each passing day he'd seen fewer and fewer living people, and those he did were maimed half-souls, trudging slowly, aimlessly. But at this point Vic had no Plan B. What else could he do? Where else did he have to go? It was Natalie Chandler or bust.

So Vic stopped in front of the hunched figure and asked which direction was west. The road he'd been walking on had taken several sharp curves, and Vic felt totally turned around. Adding to the confusion were the fires. All night the horizon had glowed dirty yellow, and yesterday the sky was so smoky and murky with ash that it was impossible to tell with certainty where the sun was in the sky, or even if it was day or night.

Excuse me, sir? Vic pointed at what might have been the sun. *Is that east?* And then Vic pointed behind him, *And that's west?*

The masked man looked up and fixed his visor on Vic. He was wearing a military uniform. Heavy black boots and camouflage. Then the mask looked over Vic's shoulder, toward the possible sun, and uttered a sentence that was heavily muffled by his mask. Vic's English was usually okay, but he struggled with comprehension in the presence of complications, for instance when on the phone, or in a loud bar. The man's voice through the mask came through like he was underwater. The last word he uttered though, Vic was pretty sure was 'east'.

That's east? Vic confirmed, pointing toward the splotch that might indeed be the morning sun.

The man nodded.

East, Vic repeated, pointing. And this time he heard the man's reply clearly:

Yes. That way.

Thank you very much.

Vic turned, about to walk in the completely wrong direction, when the man barked something through his mask and Vic swung around. The man had risen to his feet and was extending to him a rubber mask, like his own. He gestured aggressively for Vic to take it from him and to put it on. Mostly because he didn't want to be rude, Vic obliged; there was smoke in the air, but so far he hadn't had much trouble breathing. He slid on the mask. The world turned grey. Vic could hear his blood in his ears, and it felt like his brain was being squeezed in his skull.

The man said something, mimed taking off his own mask, then put his hands on his neck and pretended to be choking.

Vic grabbed the mask at the neck, to pull it off and demonstrate to the man that the air was obviously just fine, since he'd been breathing it a second ago. But the man seized Vic and pulled him close with astonishing strength.

Don't take it off. Plague. Plague is coming in the air.

Vic nodded, and the man released his grip.

D'accord. Thank you.

Then Vic turned and walked due east, toward the Port of Savannah. Only once he emerged from the thick woods, hours or days later–he had no way of knowing–weak with hunger and thirst, did he stop and replay his exchange with that man, considering for the first time that the word 'east' in French is *'est'*, pronounced with a soft vowel sound, so that the French equivalents of *both* 'east' and 'west' rhyme with the English word 'west', and that furthermore, Vic, like many Europeans, was so revolted by the harsh American *ee* sound, of words like 'bead', or 'seed', that he tended to soften these words until they sounded nearly like 'bed' and 'said', respectively, which usually wasn't a problem because of context. Usually.

So by all rights, Vic thought, he should be dead. His presence on this boat was a strange post-script, like after giving two weeks notice at a job and then just going through the motions. He should be dead, but wasn't. He should have been exhilarated but instead felt only profoundly irritable.

"Bahram," Bahram repeated, tapping his chest, then pointed at the speaker over the bed. *"Siggar-Est."*

3

Elissa McClure stopped halfway up the external staircase to catch her breath. She could hear at least three voices coming from the bridge above. She leaned on the railing, a little lightheaded–weak from hunger and the brutal morning sun. Stairs themselves had become difficult for her over the past couple years, but she would never admit that.

She listened to the voices. Were they arguing with each other? A pit opened in her stomach as she considered that her shipmates might well be savages: ruthless and hell-bent on personal survival. Practically speaking, that was the persona most likely to have made it onto this ship.

Elissa laughed to herself. Probably most of the people who knew her would use similar adjectives to describe her managerial style: ruthless, cunning, hell-bent on the bottom line. Maybe, she mused, these strangers should be scared of *her*.

She grabbed the railing tightly and half-pulled herself up the remaining stairs. The glass sliding door was open, but the four people inside–three standing, one sitting–were so engrossed in their conversation that they didn't notice her standing in the doorway.

"Greg, he's clearly harmless," said a man dressed in traditional Jewish garb, with a thick black beard.

A slender man in a purple polo shirt, presumably Greg, snorted indignantly.

"Have you thought maybe he's tied up for a *reason*?"

Elissa stood up as straight as she could and cleared her throat.

"Hello all," she announced and smiled.

The four strangers immediately swung to size up the new arrival.

In addition to the Jewish man and Greg, were a mousy woman of about forty-five wearing a brown linen shirt, and a young man seated on a swivel chair, shirtless…

Elissa inhaled sharply, and attempted to understand what she was looking at. The young man's shoulders, chest, abdomen, and forearms were covered in a series of deep burns. At first the burns appeared to be a random web of slashes. But then a sort of pattern emerged. They were characters, written in raised pink flesh. It was backwards writing; numbers written across his chest in mirror-image. And on his sternum, above the numbers, was an image she knew well. The hairs on the back of Elissa's neck pricked up. Burned onto his chest were two profiles, facing away from each other. The two heads of Janus, the appropriated logo of the Daughters of January.

Elissa tried to maintain her composure, even as her mind raced wildly. Were these three terrorists–members of the DOJ? Had they mutilated this young man? She ignored her initial revulsion, and tried to analyze the situation without bias.

There was little doubt that these burns were the work of the DOJ; in the past months even the normally sober news sources Elissa favored had become hysterical over the bizarre graffiti popping up around the country: a forty-mile stretch of highway in rural Iowa stained in neon orange and green, a recurring pattern so that drivers were forced to read the words *you've been poisoned* thousands of times over the stretch; every window of the twenty-five-story Wells Fargo building in Denver spray-painted through a stencil, such that every office occupant arrived to the message *money is a fiction* obscuring their view; a cornfield in Indiana set ablaze at three in the morning with what a fire marshal said was enough homemade napalm to raze Vietnam all over again, flames tinted green with phosphorus, and only once a news helicopter arrived on the scene was the message written in green, size-million font discernible: *it's too late.*

Then came the so-called 'human graffiti': shirtless men and women, chests tattooed with similarly perturbing sentiments, wearing sacks over their heads. They loitered just outside the gates of university campuses, sat on public sidewalks, and stood deathly still in dark corners of packed concerts. All their chests, like this young man's, were signed with the two faces of Janus. Most of the time the police didn't touch these people–they were usually careful not to actually break any laws–but those times when they arrested them on the pretense of disturbing the peace they'd turn out to be teenagers or drug addicts who'd been communing with the Daughters in the darkest corners of the internet, and manipulated or brainwashed into making themselves human message boards.

But this young man sure didn't look like he was here of his own accord. His ankle was tied to the base of his stool with a length of steel coil that was fastened with a small padlock. He was squeezing his knees together and squirming desperately.

"Please," he croaked, "I have to use the bathroom."

Elissa took a deep breath. Her impulse was to flee before these people tied her up too. But, of course, there was nowhere to run. So she planted her feet, stared hard at these strangers, and braced for the worst.

"Why did you do this?" she asked them softly.

All three of them seemed horrified by the accusation. The Jewish man's eyes flew wide open.

"My goodness. No, no. We came up here and found him like this, just like you."

"Well, Greg found him like this," the woman spoke for the first time. Her voice was nasal and monotonic, giving her a sort of dopey, detached affect. Her complexion was grey and her face seemed locked in a perpetual frown. "He was tied up even before we all came aboard, presumably."

Greg nodded in furious agreement, rubbing both hands through his thick brown hair.

"That's right. You can ask Sammy when he comes back up. This guy was here last night, just sitting there."

"But we found the key. It was just here, in one of the drawers," the Jewish man said, then to Greg: "So we can unlock him."

The seated young man seemed overwhelmed and bewildered by this whole scene.

"Yes, please," he said, voice hoarse, looking only at Elissa this time. "Please. I have to use the bathroom."

Now Elissa began to understand the dilemma. Assuming these people were telling the truth about finding the young man mutilated and tied up (and frankly, they didn't initially strike her as being sadistic or psychotic enough to hurt someone like this), there was the issue of whether the boy himself was dangerous.

Elissa approached the seated man.

"Hi," she said to him gently. "I'm Elissa, what's your name?"

The young man studied her warily. He seemed even more confused about what was happening than she was.

"I…" he hesitated, then glanced down, and together they read the burns on his forearms. On the left was written the word *Adam*. He displayed the burn to her and smiled weakly. "Adam," he said, without much confidence. On the right, she saw, was the word *Island*, followed by an arrow that trailed up his bicep and pointed to the numbers on his chest.

"Who did this to you?"

"I…" Adam grimaced and shook his head. He was on the verge of tears. "I don't know. I don't know. I'm sorry. I just have to use the bathroom. Please."

"Let's wait for Sammy," Greg said behind her. "He's huge. You know, in case anything happens."

Elissa sat down herself, a few feet away from Adam. She was a little dizzy, probably from the sun. She now noticed for the first time that a cheap mirror had been fastened to the window opposite Adam. So he could read the numbers on his chest? This was too much for her to deal with at the moment.

"Just unlock him," Elissa said, leaning discreetly against one of the panels to steady herself. She didn't want to show the others how close she was to fainting. "He's fine."

"Sam will be up in just a few minutes," said Greg.

The mousy woman nodded.

"Just a few minutes," she said. "It's not worth the risk."

The Jewish man frowned but didn't argue. The issue was apparently settled, and Elissa didn't have the strength to argue. The Jew and the mousy woman both sat down as well, subtly choosing seats that would be out of Adam's reach. An uncomfortable silence descended, punctuated only by Adam's soft whimpering. Elissa felt awful. Greg was still standing, hands on his hips, staring at Adam, lips pulled back in a smile of extreme discomfort.

The Jewish man cleared his throat and turned to Elissa.

"I'm Mel," he said.

"Elissa."

"Rosalyn Carson," said the mousy woman.

"Hello."

Rosalyn was an odd person, was Elissa's first impression. Reasonable though. All three of them in fact–Mel, Rosalyn, and Greg– were behaving pretty reasonably in a situation that could have easily prompted hysteria, and Elissa appreciated that very much. Perhaps, she considered, it wasn't ruthlessness which was the competitive advantage that delivered a handful of souls to this salvation while billions asphyxiated back on the mainland, but rather the ability to keep a level head amid chaos. A world in which the ultimate sign of fitness was clear-headed, reasonable thinking... In some ways Elissa had been longing for that her whole life.

There was a gentle pitter-patter, and for a moment she thought it was raining, until she saw a thin stream running down Adam's thigh and dripping onto the linoleum floor. Mel lowered his head in shame. Rosalyn's frown deepened. Greg's pearly smile remained, but his eyebrows shot up so high they looked like they were trying to escape from his head.

4

Art Roselli crossed his legs and tried to make himself comfortable in the stiff chair. He couldn't remember ever feeling this awful. His lower back was killing him, his head felt like a tetherball on a playground full of kindergarteners, and his body was peppered with innumerable bruises from last night's pitch-black marathon to the port. How had he done that? It had been years since he'd dropped his gym membership in favor of a second pack a day.

He looked around the table at the others. Initially he tried not to be too conspicuous about staring, but everyone was doing the same thing. Sizing each other up. There were eight of them, including Art. They sat around a big oak table in heavy silence, all of them undoubtedly as hungry and miserable as he was. In the middle of the table was a blue plastic water jug, and everyone helped themselves liberally to Dixie cups full of the stuff. There was also a modest pile of food: a few cans of corn, beans, and spaghetti-Os, a box of cinnamon-raisin Power Bars, and some bags of nuts and dried fruit. Theoretically, this was all the food they'd brought on board last night, though Art was sure everyone was holding something in reserve. He'd personally stashed half his supply of prunes under the mattress in his cabin.

It smelled like carpet cleaner in here, and maybe mold. The "captain's lounge" was the maritime equivalent of a bank lobby: nice enough if you squint, but soul-crushingly generic and sterile to anyone who has to spend any serious time there. A bookcase behind Art's head held what looked like a series of Italian sailing manuals and encyclopedias. A ship-in-a-bottle straight out of Hobby Lobby. Shitty carpet in navy blue… seriously? You don't see enough blue out here?

The skinny man at the head of the table broke the silence:

"Just waiting for Sam. The big fella. He'll be here soon with Adam."

The skinny man smiled knowingly, as if everyone sitting around the table was familiar with both Sam and Adam. To fill the silence that followed he added, "I'm Greg, by the way." He gestured to the blue water jug. "Everyone get enough? It's really important to stay hydrated. The sun is super strong at sea."

Art suppressed an eye roll.

Vague nods from the others. A few tried halfheartedly to match Greg's good humor with their body language, and failed. Art realized the Asian woman next to him had been sobbing into her palms since he'd arrived, but was trying to hide it. Art rubbed his temples, but this only intensified the pulsing lights in the corners of his vision.

Silence in the hot air of the lounge, save the muffled sobs of the woman to his left. Art wished he had a kerchief to offer her. He considered a few different ways he might try to comfort her, but envisioned all of them coming off the wrong way.

A guy who was either an Orthodox Jew, or had a really weird sense of style, stood up from the table to study the thermostat near the door. He was surely desperate for some AC; the back of his white button-down shirt was literally transparent with sweat.

"The generator probably runs off the engines," Art said. "So there's not gonna be power when we're just floating."

The Jew frowned.

"That doesn't make sense. There must be a battery."

"I'll bet there is, yeah," Art nodded. "But it's like a car you know. Since we turned off the engines it can't recharge, so who knows how long it can run for? Seems unwise to just turn on the battery."

Art expected an argument, on account of the Jew's beard being soaked with sweat to the point that it resembled a wet poodle, but the guy just nodded and sat back down.

Across the table, a shirtless man with a wild shock of sunflower-colored hair rubbed his thumb and index finger together in a well-practiced motion that Art recognized instantly. Art shot the shirtless man a sympathetic smile, like to show he was also dying for a cigarette, but the man didn't notice; he was staring intently at his hands, as if a rolling paper and pinch of loose-leaf American Spirit might materialize at any moment.

Art was starting to get agitated just sitting here. Why weren't they already scouring the boat for something to eat? There were thousands of containers, maybe one would have some food. They only had enough on the table to feed themselves for *maybe* a day or two. He'd give it ten minutes, he decided. If they weren't searching for food by then, he'd say something.

"Is anybody hurt?" said a woman to the right of Greg. A plain looking woman of about forty with a sharp nose, and ears that were slightly too big for her head. She wore a brown linen shirt. "I'm sure everyone is rattled, but does anybody have any serious injuries? I'm a doctor and I'm happy to help. Let me know if you need anything. My name is Rosalyn. Carson."

"I think I've got a migraine coming on," Art said. "Advil would be great, but a cigarette would be even better."

The blond guy jerked up at the mention of tobacco.

"You have one?" he asked Art, in a thick French accent. He must not have understood completely.

"Tell you what, amigo," Art smiled. "If I get my hands on some smokes you'll be the first one I sell them to okay?"

The blond guy smiled weakly.

"Well I don't have any painkillers," Rosalyn said. Her voice was slightly nasal, which Art found incredibly grating in his current condition. "But I'm hopeful we'll be able to find a first aid kit on board." She forced a quick smile, then her face reverted to a frown that Art imagined was her resting state.

The door to the lounge swung open and three people entered. The trio looked like a circus act. In the middle was a man built like a tank. Huge, spherical head, biceps as wide as Art's torso, hands like baseball mitts. He had a pudgy nose, wide-set eyes, and buzzed hair. A football player, perhaps. He nearly had to duck just to get in the doorway. This must be 'the big fella'–Sam.

To Sam's left was a young, unshaven man with dark circles under his eyes. He had torn a neck hole in a white bed sheet, and it formed a tent that covered his arms and upper body. Must be for protection from the sun, Art thought.

On Sam's right was a beautiful twenty-something brunette in a tight tank top. Her arms were folded across her chest–an obviously defensive posture–exposing a small tattoo of a heart on her left wrist.

Greg stared at the girl. The Frenchman's interest was also clearly piqued, and at least for a moment he abandoned his imaginary cigarette.

"So now that we're all here, should we introduce ourselves?" Greg said, directly to the brunette.

Art could take it no more.

"Listen. This isn't the first day of high school, kid," he snapped. "there will be plenty of time for chitchat later. But I gotta say I'm getting a little peckish, and I'm guessing you all are too. So let's talk food. I say we split up and scour this ship top to bottom. Otherwise we're just going to have to head back to shore and take our chances with radiation poisoning, that disease, and the Daughters of January."

Art cleared his throat and tried to gauge how his little outburst went over. It might have been a bit aggressive, for a first impression. As a concession to civility he added: "And I'm Arthur. Roselli. My friends call me Art. So all of you can call me Arthur."

Nobody laughed. Bunch of stiffs, he thought.

"Arthur, you're absolutely right," said Greg. "Sam, why don't you three sit down. I just, I thought—well never mind. Take a seat and let's just get everything sorted out ASAP."

The yellow haired Frenchman across from Art emitted an indignant snort.

"Yes, yes," he said, waving his hand dramatically in the air. "Please, fix everything."

Greg smiled pleasantly.

"I'm sorry?" he said.

"I am saying…" The blond guy leaned back in his chair, revealing that his bare chest was covered in curls the same color as the yellow mop on his head. "I am saying to you my friends, *les carrots son cuis.* We have earned ourselves a few days, and the right to die in peace. Let's just relax now. Take a swim. There's nothing to sort out but our illuming deaths."

The Asian woman to Art's left, who had been sobbing this whole time, now redoubled her efforts. The Frenchman stole a glance at the brunette, perhaps checking if his rebellious monologue had impressed her.

"Looming," said Art, stomach growling. "I don't think 'illuming' is a word."

The blond shrugged.

"As you like."

Beside the French blond, the Jew sat with a certain peacefulness, as if he'd already come to terms with the heat and their new ocean-bound reality.

"What is your name?" The Jew asked the blond man.

"I am Victor–Vic–Fournier." Vic extended his hand to his neighbor. The Jewish man took Vic's hand.

"Mel Glazer. Vic, I'm afraid that, respectfully, I must disagree with you. We all made it to the coast, to this boat, because we are survivors. And I suggest we continue to think in that vein."

Vic laughed and turned his palms to the ceiling.

"My friend, to what end? We are only pushing off what is *inévitable*."

"Enough of this, please," Sam stood halfway out of his chair and placed his palms on the tabletop. The mere shifting of his weight tilted the opposite end of the table a few inches off the floor, tipping over the now-empty plastic water jug and everybody's Dixie cups. Everyone froze in their chairs and stared at the giant. Sam now noticed the overturned water jug and eased his palms off of the table, clumsily letting it drop back into the blue carpet. He flushed a bit, embarrassed by this accidental display of mass. "I'm sorry to interrupt," he said. He wasn't angry, rather his face was sad and pleading. He shook his head helplessly. "But I'm going to get hungry very soon, and we have enough food on board for maybe one good meal. And—no offense mister—but I didn't bike across two state lines, fight off four armed looters with my bare hands, eat mouse, and escape from gas and bombs just to die from starvation in the middle of the ocean. So if you all want to curl up and die that's fine with me—" Sam's voice crescendoed. Art stared in disbelief as the slight escalation in Sam's blood pressure caused a network of pulsing veins to pop, Hulk like, from his tree trunk wrists—"but I'm going to find something to *eat*."

Sam sat back down in his chair, his last deep syllable hanging in the air like an ominous gas.

"I agree. Very sensible," an old woman to the left of Vic spoke for the first time. Art had hardly noticed her; if you didn't look closely she could just be a loose black dress draped over a heap of twigs. Like many aging women, her face had the quality of a wax bird melting in the sun on a hot day. But she held her chin up when she spoke, and her gaze was defiant, as if daring someone to judge her based on her age and size. "My name is Elissa McClure" she said, holding up a wrinkled hand in greeting. "I agree with Sam, Mel, and Arthur. We should split up and look for food in just a moment. But that's not all. Someone needs to stay on the bridge to send out distress signals on the radio. The coast guard or Navy may be out there looking for survivors. Furthermore, we may be able to save ourselves some time searching for food. I imagine a shipping vessel like this has some sort of cargo manifest. I'm happy to volunteer to see if there's such a document somewhere in–" Elissa stopped to cough, and everyone waited patiently for her to finish and recover. Obviously nobody else had considered the existence of a manifest. She'd thought things through better than any of them, and Art for one was relieved to have someone competent taking control of the situation. "Excuse me," she continued. "On the bridge or below deck. But there's also the issue of this young man here, Adam." She gestured to the guy wearing a bed sheet over his upper body. He was unshaven, with bloodshot eyes. Probably in his mid-twenties. He looked completely bewildered. Almost stoned. He'd never sat down with everyone else. He was still standing in the doorway to the lounge. "Adam, could you please…" she indicated he should pull the sheet off. "Show us what happened to you?"

Adam blinked. Then nodded slowly, and removed the sheet to reveal his upper body.

The Asian woman beside Art stopped sobbing to gasp in horror. Vic went pale and mumbled something in French. Art swallowed. No wonder Adam looked so out of it; someone had really done a number on this kid.

In the far corner of the lounge, a round man who had thus far stayed silent, shot up from his chair, face bright red, and stabbed a finger in Adam's direction. He yelled something in a language Art didn't recognize:

"Be uh khatar jam namitavan shud!"

It took Sam, Art and Greg a few minutes to get the man to return to his chair, sandwiched between Rosalyn and Vic. And even then, he continued babbling, half to himself, half to his neighbors. Rosalyn was listening politely with a strained smile. Vic still seemed mostly interested in the brunette. Elissa walked to the front of the room to stand beside Adam.

"As I was saying. After we all came aboard last night, Sam and Greg found Adam on the bridge. His ankle was tied to a chair with a steel cable, and locked with a padlock. We found the key in a drawer, just out of his reach. Greg and Sam say that near Adam's feet were one of the blue water containers, totally full, and a bag filled with a few boxes of cinnamon-raisin Power Bars. As you can see, he has recently been badly burned."

Elissa took a deep breath. Cinnamon-raisin Power Bars, Art thought. Someone really wanted this kid to suffer.

"There are four parts to the burns. Here across his chest and torso are numbers written in mirror image. Above, on his sternum, this two-faced icon I'm sure you all recognize as the symbol of the terrorist group, the Daughters of January. On each arm is burned a single word. On the left, 'Adam'. On the right 'Island.'"

Art squinted at the backwards numbers. Two rows of eight characters each:

34 40.161 N 40 57.422 W

"Now, I know his appearance may be disturbing to some of us," Elissa continued, now leaning on the table for balance. She was clearly struggling physically. "It's quite a terrible thing that's been done to him—he's been made into one of these strange pieces of human graffiti that the Daughters of January encouraged. In all likelihood, some brainwashed sympathizer did this to him, and left him on the boat for god knows what reason. Point being, let's treat him with respect and kindness. As much as we've each been through, it's quite possible he's been through even worse. He doesn't even seem to be able to remember how he got here."

Seven digits North, seven digits West. GPS coordinates, thought Art.

"Uh. Well or maybe he's a nut-job brain-washed sympathizer himself," the Asian woman beside Art spoke for the first time. "Or just a terrorist. Look. He has their sign right on his chest. Come on. He doesn't *remember*? That's bullshit."

Everyone, including Elissa, looked at Adam, as if to ask him whether this accusation had legs. In response, he only stared back at them glassy-eyed, somewhat bewildered, as if studying a peculiar Escher sketch.

"It's not implausible that he has some sort of PTSD," said the doctor, Rosalyn Carson. "Receiving these burns was surely very traumatic. He may well have blocked the whole event from his memory."

"Well, I'm sorry," replied the Asian woman. "But I think he's gonna have to explain what the fuck happened, or else... Well I mean. What, we're just going to let a terrorist run around on board?"

Adam finally spoke.

"I'm not a terrorist," he said, slowly. His voice was hoarse. "I'm not a terrorist."

"So who are you?" The woman insisted. "How did you get all those burns? What are they?"

"I..." the man looked down, to study his own torso and arms. "I... I'm sorry. I'm sorry."

"*Be uh khatar jam namitavan shud!*" The foreign man was getting wound up again in the back. He pointed at Adam, his voice more pleading than angry. "*Bimani,*" he said, motioning to his own torso and arms. "*Bimani!*"

"Pal, we don't understand," said Greg, laughing nervously.

"Let him talk," Mel said. "He's obviously trying to tell us something."

"It's useless," sighed Vic. "In a half hour this morning I only managed to learn his name."

"He's probably trying to tell us that this dude is a *terrorist.*"

"Look at him? Does he look like a terrorist?"

"Uh. Yeah actually."

Art stood up.

"Hey. Guys. Guys!" he shouted. "Guys. Please! I know who did this to him!"

This finally got them to shut up. Art had their attention. He took a deep breath.

"Well, not *who,*" Art said. "But it's obvious to me *why* they did it. Elissa, I'm sorry but you're wrong. This wasn't some arts and crafts project. Everything is written for Adam himself to read. They wanted him to navigate to an island, which apparently is to be found at the GPS coordinates written on his chest. "

"What?" Vic squinted.

"The numbers inscribed on his chest. Those are clearly GPS coordinates, written backwards. And there was a mirror in front of him so he could read them and navigate the ship there."

Elissa frowned.

"I agree they look like coordinates. But let's not jump to conclusions about their purpose."

"Let's check if he has an ass tattoo," said the Asian woman. "It could be a treasure map."

"Enough!" Sam slammed the table with his fist. "I'm hungry. We're looking for food. Now."

5

If one of these douchebags tries to touch me, Jennifer thought, I'm going to put this screwdriver through their skull.

It would happen too, she was pretty sure. Maybe they'd find food among these hundreds of crates. But then what? The men would just want to play Monopoly until they got rescued?

She hadn't liked the way those guys had looked at her before. Art, Greg, and the shirtless Frenchman whose name she couldn't recall, had all been salivating like dogs. She'd thought about saying something, telling the doctor maybe. But what could she do? Call the authorities and submit the appropriate paperwork?

The men were of far greater concern to her than the guy–Adam– they'd found on the bridge. Sure, he was weird and confusing, but his temperament seemed pretty gentle. He didn't strike her as dangerous. He seemed more frightened that someone would hurt *him*.

There were mostly huge metal containers on board, but there was also a small section of wooden crates near the rear of the ship that could be opened relatively quickly. Sam had led one group farther toward the rear of the ship, where they were hacking the locks off of the metal freight containers with fire axes, while these four busted through the wood crates. Jennifer had volunteered for crate opening duty with Lily Chen, Mel Glazer, and Bahram, mostly because they seemed like three of the less obnoxious individuals on board.

Bahram kept to himself out of necessity. Didn't speak a word of English. Could be a calculus professor, or the most popular guitarist in the Middle East, for all Jennifer knew. She was only able to communicate with him through pantomime. He'd settled down after his outburst in the meeting–or maybe just given up after failing to convey whatever it was he'd had to say about the burns on Adam's chest–and wholeheartedly embraced the search for food. He was working dutifully and tirelessly on deconstructing the crates. Unlike the other men, she hadn't once noticed him checking her out. He was completely enraptured with plying nails from wood.

But just because she hadn't caught Bahram ogling her didn't mean she should let her defenses down around him. Jennifer gripped her screwdriver tighter. She'd made it to this boat while thousands of others had tried and failed, mostly because she hadn't made any stupid mistakes, like taking off her gas mask prematurely. The biggest mistake she could make now, she thought, would be to prematurely assume any of these people were trustworthy.

She'd once talked to an ex-marine at a frat party who told her if she was ever being attacked she should just act totally fucking crazy. Turn the tables. Be like *Yeah, okay, let's rumble.* To even bite your own arm and draw blood just to show how totally bonkers you were. Seemed like solid advice. Maybe after a few days on board she wouldn't even have to pretend.

They worked with tools they'd found in the engine room. Jennifer had a flathead screwdriver to pull the nails out of the wooden crates. Bahram used the claw of a hammer. Sweat streamed down his face. He wasn't even drinking water as he worked. He was fat and round. He was built, in fact, almost exactly like a classic three-ball snowman.

Opening the crates turned out to be much slower work than they'd assumed. In a few hours they'd only opened and combed through nine.

One box was full of watercolor landscapes. Another with a variety of expensive-looking bike parts. One with pleather purses. One with an enormous Xerox machine.

Jennifer and Bahram were about halfway through dismantling a tenth crate, working in silence. This in sharp contrast to Lily, who's abrasiveness Jennifer had badly misjudged when volunteering for crate duty. Lily's emotional compass had done a one-eighty about an hour ago. She'd finally stopped sobbing, but now wouldn't shut up.

The recipient of Lily's sudden exuberance was Mel, who was working in his white button-down shirt, black pants, and loafers despite the merciless sun. Jennifer had told him he was going to get heatstroke dressed like that. He'd just frowned slightly in the direction of her tank top and shorts and muttered something about being used to it.

She thought about what that lecher–Art–said to her as they were filing out of the "meeting", the two of them a few paces behind Mel and Lily.

"If you had to eat one of them, which would you choose?" he'd whispered to her, winking. "Pastrami on rye? Or Peking Duck?"

"That burned guy is so creepy," Lily was saying to Mel, wiping sweat off her face. "Fine, maybe he's not a terrorist. But there's definitely something wrong with him. I'm not saying that in a mean way. Like, something *actually* wrong with him. Like a brain injury."

Lily put down her screwdriver and stretched. Observing her, Jennifer involuntarily considered that Lily would be tastier than Mel. Mel would be all bone and sinew, while Lily was a bit plump; a slight gut stretched the fabric of her red shirt. Her cheeks were puffy, a bit chipmunky.

"I mean, I hate to say it, but somebody like that is probably going to go bonkers and hurt all of us eventually. If he's really *crazy*, you know. And I'm the last person to say something like this, but I think we need to seriously consider tying him to a bed or something. For his own good. And also so he can't hurt anybody! I hate to be the one to say it, but I'm just stating the facts here."

Mel continued working for a moment, as if to confirm that Lily had truly finished speaking, and then said:

"We're not tying anybody up. Can you please help me with these nails?"

Jennifer suddenly craved pastrami. She hadn't eaten meat for eight years. But she also hadn't been this hungry for eight years. That place her parents always wanted to eat whenever they visited Miami... They'd stack the sandwiches so high you needed those special toothpicks to keep the top layer of bread on. She'd slather hers in spicy mustard...

Her parents were certainly dead now. And as Jennifer considered this fact, for perhaps the hundredth time since the first bomb fell, she again felt absolutely nothing.

"I'm just trying to be helpful here," Lily said to Mel. "Excuse me for trying to be helpful."

These two were pathetic, Jennifer decided. Lily was obviously unhinged; she'd cracked from the strain of the last weeks. Fine, whatever, but keep it together. To Jennifer, Lily's earlier sobbing presented as a kind of narcissism: you think you're the only one who's dealing with shit right now?

And Mel was risking heatstroke because he believed in a higher power. A higher power who had no problem slaughtering a few billion people, but was really concerned about him continuing to wear long sleeves. A different sort of narcissism.

Karen, from the Task Force, had always said that believing in invisible men in the sky consistently led to terrible things. But Karen wouldn't call Mel a moron. That wasn't going to affect any change. Her bottom line: be proactive. She'd say something like: *You just need to have a dialogue with him.* That was what had initially appealed to Karen about the Daughters of January videos and forums.

Look, Jennifer. These people have real ideas and they're doing something about them!

That must have been about a year ago, sitting in Karen's dorm room, watching a person of indeterminate gender (mask and voice alteration) on her laptop, explain how Nero Entertainment–a conglomerate that operated several huge casino hotels in Atlantic City and Vegas–was the primary investor in a certain chemicals company, which was just a front for a massive arms manufacturing and distribution operation. These weapons were killing people. In order to save lives, the person on the screen explained, the Daughters of January would launch a cyberattack that would disable power to these casinos, until they pledged to divest.

See Jennifer. That's the kind of stuff we should be doing for Najaf, instead of just writing letters and protesting.

Karen had even signed up to give a monthly recurring donation to the DOJ (through heavily encrypted channels, of course). It was hard to blame Karen. Those were the early days of the DOJ, and nobody had understood where this movement was headed, perhaps not even the DOJ themselves.

"Please," Mel pleaded. "Pry out those nails."

"Maybe you should try actually listening to what I'm saying," Lily said.

Jennifer caught Bahram's gaze. She wondered what he heard—did Lily just sound like a scratchy record to him?

Bahram was probably in his mid-sixties. His dark arms and legs were covered in thick grey hair. He wore a tattered black top and cutoff shorts that he'd obviously made himself by taking a knife to a cheap button-down shirt and pair of Levis respectively. On his head was a plaid golfing hat. He smiled a sad, toothy grin and rubbed his ample gut in the universal sign for hunger. They'd all treated themselves to a snack from their collective food before this, so they'd have the strength to search. Jennifer had gotten a third of a Power Bar and two spoonfuls of creamed corn. She wished she could convey to Bahram that everyone had agreed to have a "dinner" this evening, as soon as it got dark. Instead she just smiled back weakly, then the two returned their attention to their work.

Lily was sitting with her back against the crate she was supposed to be deconstructing. Her eyes were still puffy from her earlier crying session.

"It's just like, it would be a shame for us to all make it here onto this boat, and then to all die because of some insane terrorist. Hacked to death or something. That's all I'm saying. Just think about it. What if he tied himself up there, just to fool all of us into thinking he's harmless? We have to think about this."

"Please stop," said Mel, putting down his hammer and looking at her, exasperated.

Bahram finally turned his head to see what all the fuss was about. Even as he did, his hands kept working.

"Excuse me for being *practical!* I'm trying to figure out what's best for all of us!"

"Probably the most practical thing to do now is to unpack these crates as quickly as possible."

"Why don't you just pray to your god to just give us food?" Lily said "Or is he too busy killing everyone?"

Jennifer could be silent no more.

"I know you're upset," she called to Lily. "But the number one priority now is opening crates to see if there's food on board."

Bahram finally lowered his hammer and watched.

Lily swiveled to face Jennifer, frowning as if noticing her for the first time.

"Mind your own business. Don't eavesdrop on our conversation."

Mel scratched his bearded cheek and said, "I'm not sure you could call this a conversation."

"Eavesdrop?" Jennifer said. "I'm just trying to work over here. Believe me, I would love nothing more than to tune out your whining."

Lily's jaw dropped open in disbelief.

"My *whining?*" she gasped, while her thin eyebrows arched into trembling bows. "Well pardon me for being *upset,* you haughty *bitch.* It just so happens that every person I've ever known died last week, and I'm stuck on a boat with a terrorist, and a fucking *whore!* Where do you get off dressing like that! Have some goddamn *respect!* You think I want to see your fucking tits? Half of your goddamn ass is hanging out of your slut-pants. You think I want to have to look at that shit?"

Jennifer gaped at this crazy woman, her face flushed from sun and fury. Jennifer couldn't recall anybody ever speaking to her this way.

"Listen," she said, "You're obviously not in a very good place. That's understandable. But stay the hell away from me."

This was little consolation to Lily, who crouched slightly, as if physically gearing up for the retort from hell, only to suddenly drop her screwdriver, crumple to the slippery ship deck, and devolve into a fit of sobs.

Jennifer stared at the wretched heap that was Lily, suddenly like a de-winged moth writhing in agony. Jennifer came over and joined Mel, standing over her. Lily had her palms over her eyes, bawling so violently that she was struggling for breath.

Finally Mel knelt beside her.

"Lily," he said softly. "Lily, listen, it's been a very hard week. For all of us. Me too. It's okay to cry."

"It's just… Everything's gone. Every*one* is gone."

"I know," said Mel. "But you have to believe everything is for the best. That everything happens for a reason."

Jennifer shook her head. How could anyone possibly say that now?

Lily's crying was interrupted by the crack of wood. Bahram had pulled out enough nails to pry open one side of a tenth crate. With singular determination he ripped the planks off, then stuck his head and arms inside. Jennifer, Mel, and Lily—looking up from the deck—watched in anticipation as he first extracted a few layers of plastic sheeting and bubble wrap. Then he plunged his upper body back in, lingered for a few tantalizing seconds, and returned with a promising looking cardboard box.

He threw the box to the ground and feverishly ripped away the packing tape with the claw of his hammer. Jennifer held her breath.

Please be Honey Bunches of Oats, she thought.

They didn't even need to see inside the box; the disappointment on Bahram's face was all too clear.

He yelled in frustration and dumped the contents of the box all over the damp deck.

"*Kuss! Kuss amack!*" he bellowed.

They were books. All identical. Jennifer knelt and picked one up. It seemed someone across the Atlantic had ordered a whole bunch of copies of **The Five-Hour Work Week: How to escape the daily grind,**

*work from home, and have plenty of time left to enjoy the lifestyle
you've always dreamed of.*

Jennifer threw a copy as hard as she could, and watched it arc over
the railing and disappear into the endless blue.

6

After the meeting, Elissa McClure went straight to the bridge. There
was a lot of work to do and, at least for the moment, half a Power Bar
had her feeling like her usual self. Most urgently, of course, was to
figure out the radio. Surely there were other people out there who had
managed to escape on ships. Or, even more likely, military vessels that
had been out in the water anyway. It just wouldn't make sense that ten
civilians–eleven if you counted Adam–would be the only survivors
floating offshore.

All the equipment was old; this ship was probably built in the
eighties or early nineties. The panels had the bulky analog look of
technology from the days of cassette tapes and car phones, the days
when you had to wait until six to see news about the Gulf War, and a
cell phone was only for making calls. The radio, PA system, and GPS-
assisted auto-pilot were the only systems that had power now that
they'd turned off the engines. These ran off a separate battery, which
made sense for situations exactly like this: if the engines broke and you
couldn't recharge the central battery, you could still call for help, and
use the GPS to relay your location to the coast guard.

All the labels to the radio were in Italian–this was apparently an
Italian vessel–but using the radio was intuitive enough. It was already
configured with several preset maritime frequencies, which Elissa now
clicked through, finding nothing but dead air. Someone would have to
monitor this at all times, shifting through the preset frequencies in case
anyone was out there looking for survivors, and also sending out their
own periodic SOS calls.

She began searching all the cabinets for a ship manifest, interrupting
her work every few minutes to change the radio channel. The bridge
was absolutely packed with papers. and she quickly realized the job
would be even more difficult than she'd thought. Though most of the
user manuals had sections in English, all the documents in the file
cabinets–the records pertaining to cargo–were only in Italian

Elissa had two years of college Latin and a bit of conversational Spanish, but it would be much easier for a native French speaker to decode the Italian; Elissa recalled that the vocabulary overlap between the two languages was something like eighty percent. Vic would have to do this. She was liable to miss something important in there–a single note perhaps which specified a container that was carrying food.

She picked up the PA handset.

"Hello all, this is Elissa on the bridge. Vic, do you think you could come up to the bridge and help me? I need your language skills. Thanks."

While she waited for Vic, she inspected the GPS-assisted autopilot. It took her a few minutes of reading to understand that you couldn't control the engines from here–that was done in the engine room below. This machine just controlled steering. If the engines were on, you could input a destination and this would navigate you there, recalibrating the course every five minutes based on the new GPS location and turning the rudders accordingly.

It would be nice to know exactly where they were–how many miles precisely from the coast. But the GPS was an old system and there was no visual map display, only a readout giving the ship's current coordinates, which were meaningless to her without a map. So she found an atlas in a cabinet, alongside the user manuals for the GPS and autopilot. Then she looked up the coordinates displayed on the GPS system. It appeared they were fifty to sixty miles off the coast of Georgia.

Her eye caught the chair where Adam had been tied. The steel coil was still on the ground, around one of the legs. She rubbed her forehead. The whole thing was so strange it was hard to wrap her head around.

Was Art's hypothesis plausible? That someone locked Adam there and wanted him to navigate to the numbers on his chest? In support of Art's hypothesis:

1a) Adam had been tied up with a stack of Power Bars and a water container at his feet, and close enough to the autopilot system that he could reach it. So, theoretically, Adam could sit here, eating and drinking (and soiling himself), while periodically confirming that the autopilot was set to the GPS coordinates burned onto him.

2a) The numbers on his stomach did indeed appear to be GPS coordinates: seven digits North and seven digits West. There was really no other way to interpret them.

3a) Writing the digits in mirror image and placing a mirror in front of him was pretty indicative of the fact that the burns were intended for Adam's use. The whole thing was done very, very, deliberately.

Against Art's hypothesis:

1b) When they'd all climbed aboard, the engines hadn't been running, and, as Elissa had just discovered, the engines couldn't be turned on from the bridge. So if nobody had shown up, Adam would have just eventually died from dehydration in Savannah port. If the plan was for Adam to navigate the ship to some island, someone had missed a very crucial detail.

2b) Whether it was the Daughters of January who'd done this, or some sympathizer who believed there was some kind of island... why wouldn't they still be on board? Why tie someone up and have him self-navigate? Why not just sail there yourselves?

3b) There wasn't an island anywhere close to those GPS coordinates.

(3b) was easily confirmed by studying the atlas. She was no cartographer, but it only took her five minutes to locate the quadrant described by those longitude and latitude coordinates, and it contained nothing but blue. (2b) raised the unsettling thought that, as Elissa had initially assumed, one or more of the people on board had done this to Adam. Those people would likely be Sam and Greg, who claimed to have found him in this state last night. Co-conspirators. Or, Elissa considered, theoretically someone else could have mutilated Adam, left the ship, and then returned posing as a civilian... but to what end? That was an absurdly complicated scenario and Elissa couldn't imagine any possible motive to justify that behavior.

So that was that. Occam's razor: amid all the craziness of the last week, some DOJ sympathizer went bananas and did something totally nonsensical, while in a fanatical, delusional state.

The other panels on the bridge were mostly for navigation: a standard magnetic compass, a gyro compass, radar, and a rudder-angle indicator to assist with steering. Like the lights and HVAC system, all of these machines were automatically switched off when the engines and generator weren't running, to conserve power in the central battery. Elissa poked, prodded, and studied the inert equipment with the fastidiousness of an autopsist. It was a compulsion: she couldn't bear to be in environments she didn't understand, or situations without clearly defined parameters. The past thirteen years she'd run an entire equities department–eight trading desks–and known every single thing that happened on her floor.

She'd known before anyone else on the floor when Eric Lowenson, the clean shaven kid from U of Chicago, got engaged. First thing in the morning she called a floor-wide meeting, gave him a bottle of thirty-year Lagavulin, and told him to take the next three days off. She knew that Martin Kosakowski was calling her a bitch behind her back for making him close his short position on some alternative energy company he swore was on the cusp of bankruptcy. She called Martin into her office and said he had a day to put together a report showing her why he should have kept the position open, and he did, and she absolutely tore it apart, coldly deconstructing his logic piece by piece until the man was practically weeping. She knew that everyone talked shit about Louis Forrester and thought he'd been coasting on his reputation for years. She agreed with this assessment, but also knew that a team needed somebody to talk shit about, and if it wasn't Louis it would be someone else, and Louis was a good choice–he was so oblivious that the ongoing slander was actually a pretty stable situation. True, Louis' performance wasn't great, but he didn't have a reckless bone in his body, which counted for a lot in Elissa's book.

She needed to make notes of everything she was learning about the ship controls. She found a clipboard and a pen. There were no blank notebooks, but there was a long ream of double-perforated printing paper, the kind she hadn't seen for maybe thirty years. She ripped off a few lengths to write on. She didn't mind that she'd have to write by hand; when everyone at WhiteBridge was given their own personal tablet, she'd left hers in the box and gave it to the doorman. She was no luddite; she had no nostalgia for the days before the markets were digitized, and fraud was a million times easier to pull off. Nor did she long for the days when you had to check your ticker symbols every morning in the paper (unless you happened to live in lower Manhattan). Although, Elissa supposed, there had been something ever so slightly romantic about it when she traveled: reading Barron's at her niece's house in Poughkeepsie, monitoring the pulse of the free world over a hot coffee, snow falling outside.

No. Who was she kidding. Those days at her niece's house were a stir-crazy nightmare. Spending all day trapped with her niece, grand-nieces and -nephews in that god-forsaken upstate suburb, horribly aware of the possibility that there was a crisis unfolding on her trading floor at that very moment. This angst was only partially mitigated by the validation, every time some kid threw up or screamed, of her decision to not have children.

Vic eventually came up to join her on the bridge. She showed him the file cabinet that contained all the documents in Italian, and then how to operate the radio. She explained that as he searched for anything that hinted about the location of food he also had to keep monitoring the radio, and switching between the preset frequencies in case someone sent out a broadcast. She didn't have much faith in the Frenchman's multi-tasking ability–he seemed somewhat disengaged– but she needed to survey the rest of the ship, and see what kind of documents were below in the engine room.

So she left Vic there and climbed down the external stairwell, then followed a narrow path between containers to a few stairs that led down to the half-corridor that ran around the perimeter of the ship. Gripping the railing to protect against the mild rocking of the sea, she made her way to the bow of the ship.

Besides the bridge, which rose two stories higher than the top of the container stacks, there were two above-water decks. The top level supported the brightly-colored containers, stacked seven or eight high and arranged with admirable efficiency. There were narrow walkways between some of the stacks, and you could squeeze by on the sides, but generally this deck was not a human-friendly area. Between the tip of the ship and the bridge, which was about a third of the length of the ship, Elissa estimated there were three hundred stacks of containers. Times seven high, meant about two thousand containers in the front of the ship, and if there were indeed double in the rear that was about six thousand total containers. It seemed inconceivable that not a single one of them would have food.

This perimeter walkway was the only open-air space that really seemed intended for humans. The railing between her and the ocean was just waist high, which seemed insufficient. It would be remarkably easy for somebody emotionally unstable–say that boy, Adam, who was either shell-shocked, on the autism spectrum, or both–to simply climb over the railing and plunge down into the brine. Were there any rope ladders around here in case something like that happened? Elissa made a note to herself to check. By way of this perimeter walkway, the very front tip of the boat was accessible. At this apex, the walkway opened into a wider space, where there were the type of folding lounge chairs you could rent at public swimming pools. At least, that was what Elissa remembered from the last time she'd been at a public swimming pool, about a half century ago. There was also an anchor of unbelievable scale. It was the size of a small car, and suspended just beyond the railing by a thick steel coil, which was rolled around a winch that looked like an enormous manual paper towel dispenser. It was motorized; there was no way that a team of sailors could pull that anchor back up from the ocean floor.

Every morning as of market open she'd known the extent to which each of her desks was leveraged, the variance of their underlying assets, and the correlation between each desk's underlying assets and every other desk on the floor. And from this, every morning, she calculated her ninety-nine percent value at risk: if the day that followed would be iterated one hundred times, what would be the worst loss they would incur? If this was an unacceptably large loss she would be walking from door to door by ten-thirty, thermos of iced coffee in hand, telling her traders to change their positions.

Nobody ran their equity division like that. Monthly VAR was something you'd have an intern calculate a couple of times a year. Daily VAR was an exercise in masochism. Investors and C-levels didn't want to see worst case scenarios, they wanted profit projections. But Elissa only ran profit projections when a higher-up twisted her arm. She only projected losses. She told her traders they could manage their upside however they wanted–she was only concerned with avoiding the downside. It was a culture of astounding pessimism. There had been a couple of meatheads when she took over the desk–cocaine-snorting, ass-slapping monkeys who'd asked to transfer to a different department once they realized what a buzzkill their new manager was. Over the years her moribund outlook began to infect her employees. Her equities division was increasingly home to a very specific sort of sharp-eyed, soft-spoken man, the kind who thought about the philosophy of the markets, and spent his annual bonus on vacations to places of historical significance.

Elissa now made her way to the aft of the ship via the walkway on the other side. There were emergency fire hoses built into the wall at regular intervals. She recalled hearing something years ago about how these high-powered hoses were also used as weapons to keep pirates from boarding. She looked over the railing and imagined how long of a ladder a group of pirates in a sea-level craft would need to board. It was at least a twenty-foot drop. She completed a lap around the perimeter of the ship. The only notables besides the hoses were two bright orange inflatable emergency rafts compressed into packages,

two of the rope ladders she'd been hoping for, and one actual lifeboat–
a micro craft with a diesel engine. The capacity was supposed to be six,
but after she poked her head in, she decided all eleven of them could
theoretically squeeze in here if the boat was sinking.

She returned to midship and the main stairwell. There was nothing
of interest on C-deck; just the cabins where everyone had slept last
night, and a small gym with dumbbells and a Smith machine.

D-deck, one floor down, was still slightly above ocean level. Here
was the mess hall: a sad dining room with three long cafeteria-style
benches, all the sadder because somebody had made an effort to
spruce things up by placing plastic, flowery tablecloths on the tables.
D-deck was close enough to the surface of the water that the windows
here got splashed by the bigger waves. The mess led into a very
modest kitchen. Elissa took an inventory of all cooking utensils; these
could potentially be useful tools. There was a knife set which gave her
pause. It was an expensive set; all the knives fit perfectly into notches
in a polished wood block. Most worrisome were a massive cheese
knife and a butcher's cleaver. She didn't like the idea of these just
sitting out here. She was thinking mainly of Adam. If he really was
disturbed, he could hurt himself or someone else.

She searched for a good place to stash the knives out of sight. There
was a walk-in freezer off the kitchen, but it was totally empty, and
there'd be nowhere in there to hide them. The pantry, too, was
completely bare, and the empty shelves offered no hiding spots.
Eventually she decided to take the knives out of their wood holder,
wrap them all together in a dishtowel, and hide them in a metal
cabinet under the sink. She then gathered a few more towels and threw
them on top of the bundle. She was fairly satisfied that nobody would
give the mound a second glance.

She took her clipboard and notes and headed down to E-deck: the
engine room. All of the other doors she'd seen on board were made of
wood. The door to the engine room was thick steel and could be triple
bolted from the inside. Elissa supposed this was the last line of defense
against pirates. Though the only entrance to the engine room was from
E-deck, it was a cavernous space that descended deep into the ship.
There were three levels in here. Elissa began her methodic survey on
the top level, which was home to perhaps a dozen primitive-looking
machines that evoked memories of the "super-computers" from the
eighties, the kind that took up an entire room. The floor was

vulcanized rubber and, like all the machines, the color of pea soup. Elissa appreciated the absolute lack of regard for aesthetics.

The complexity of this ship was astounding. She laughed softly to herself. She'd naively assumed the engine room would be a single dial with which you could simply adjust the speed of the craft, plus maybe a gauge to tell you how much fuel was left. Elissa was impressed that Greg and Sam had figured enough out to get them away from the coast last night. A thick binder with a green cover that they must have consulted for instructions was still open atop one of the machines. Elissa left it for the moment, and did a full lap of this top level of the engine room, through a maze of these crude machines outfitted with clumsy monitors, red dials, gauges, and slots for giving paper printouts. The machines seemed somehow oafish. They reminded her of a stock broker she'd apprenticed for in the seventies. He was a huge, clownish man who wobbled when he walked and always had an expression of deep confusion. Each of these machines seemed to wear that same confusion on their blank stupid screens.

Well, she thought, who's really the stupid one? The machines? Or you, the one who doesn't understand a damn thing about them?

There was a desk in the corner of this floor, and beside it a steel bookcase with twenty more binders. She opened one. Laminated pages outlined the functionality of every square inch of this ship, in both Italian and English. She checked her watch, then laughed out loud at herself. Was time really a concern? There was no opening bell, no lunch break, no appointments…

She sat down at the desk and began with one of the green binders, annotating and underlining. It was silent in here since the engines were off, and she felt a kind of calm she hadn't in a long, long time. Perhaps it was because she'd spent so long obsessing over the worst case scenario that there was a certain relief now that it had finally arrived.

7

Combing through hundreds of folders looking for a ship manifest was crude, mindless work. Especially because Vic Fournier was sure it didn't exist—the few documents he'd pulled from the file cabinet only referenced cargo from past journeys and were dated years prior.

Clearly the ship hadn't been fully loaded or ready to sail when the bombs started to fall.

Vic left the papers and relabeled a couple of buttons on one of the navigation panels–finding Italian words with close French counterparts, and then translating them into English. After a few minutes he collapsed from boredom. And hunger, perhaps.

This work was beneath him. And futile. Even if they found food, it would just buy them a few weeks or months. It wouldn't change anything fundamental about their situation.

He reclined in one of the stiff rotating chairs and swiveled languidly. He slowly ran a hand through his thick chest hair and looked out on the water. The sky directly above was blueish, but in the west, the direction of the shore, there was a sickly orange and yellow haze so thick that the circular outline of the sun was barely noticeable. Poison, ash, radiation, who knew what else.

Everything would have been simpler if he'd reached Natalie, and they'd crawled into bed together; made love until being vaporized as a tangle of intertwined limbs, melded together for eternity.

He stretched his beefy arms back over his head and yawned. There was a bit of a breeze trickling in through the open door to the bridge, but it was still fairly stifling in here. The glass walls might be creating a bit of an *effect de serre*. What was the English term? The effect of the green foyer? He switched the radio to the next frequency, as Elissa had instructed him to do every few minutes. More dead air.

He considered whether the healthy girl in the tight tank top would be a suitable proxy for Natalie. He wished the bridge afforded a view of the crates where she was working. He would enjoy watching her apricot skin glisten with sweat. He thought about how in the meeting earlier her breasts had bulged against the tight cotton of her shirt; how they'd seemed to possess a sort of magical upward propulsion, as if those mythical fruits were actively trying to escape the confines of her brassiere.

Vic had been at work, in the Walmart Superstore in Charlotte, at the beginning of the end. He was in the darkroom developing photos of newborns, as he'd done six days a week for the last four years. The pictures were so silly. He understood parents wanting photographs of their babies, but he couldn't wrap his head around the props. Each day at work he was simply stunned by how many parents pushed their carriages up to his counter in the rear of the store. Most of them already knew what they wanted–they'd seen their friend's album and wanted the same thing: their baby sleeping on a tree stump; dressed in some American superhero costume Vic didn't recognize; dressed as a cherub; dressed as a Christmas elf sitting in fake snow beside a diorama of reindeer.

For the first months at the Superstore, Vic had tried to add an artistic flair to the photos, like offering to use lighting techniques he'd learned during his online MFA program. The parents were never interested in this. They'd point to the sample photos hanging on the wall and say, *Just make it look exactly like this.* Once, Vic had replied *Fine but you know* that *baby is a model, right?* and he'd nearly been fired. So he was in the darkroom–perhaps the last functional darrooms on earth existed solely for natal photography, the nostalgia aspect demanding real, physical photographs–when someone poked their head in and said *Vic, get out here.*

The entire store was silent. They'd turned off the Superstore background music for the first time Vic could remember. Everyone– employees and shoppers– were pressed shoulder to shoulder in the TV aisle watching a CNN anchor struggle to explain what had happened to California:

We're still trying to piece together the details. What we do know is that two hours ago, at ten-fourteen this morning Eastern Time, all Russian broadcasting advised citizens in Moscow and surrounding areas to seek immediate shelter, underground if possible.

At the time, Vic wasn't aware of losing anyone. His parents were still in France, and he hardly ever talked to them anyway. As he watched the only footage CNN had managed to obtain–a five-second loop of destruction that could easily have come from a Japanese monster movie–he didn't feel much of anything.

At ten-nineteen, Israeli intelligence detected an unauthorized Russian aircraft breaching their airspace. At ten-twenty-one, the President authorized a cruiser to fire at an Iranian vessel in the South China Sea.

People were crying all around him, and he supposed this was a reasonable response to the news. He sort of wished he felt sad, but he didn't. He turned away from the dozens of screens and pushed his way through the crowd, until escaping through the sliding doors of the Walmart for the last time, already scrolling through his contacts for Natalie Chandler.

On the deck now, he inspected his phone. The phone still had life– he'd been able to charge it during the drive to the coast–but without service it was mostly a nostalgia piece, filled with correspondences and photos of the dead. What to do with the last eighteen percent of his battery? He had some videos he'd downloaded for the occasional *session après-midi* in the employee bathroom, when he'd summon far more concentration and passion than he ever devoted to his day job. Vic scrolled through the videos looking for his favorite. Seventeen percent.

At ten-twenty-five, our network received a video from a heavily encrypted source claiming to be a representative of the fringe group known as the Daughters of January. Unlike other networks, our editorial board has made the decision not to screen the video. However, we have noted that the clip seems to accurately predict attacks on several population centers along the West Coast, which didn't occur until over an hour after we received the file.

By the time he found the video he'd wanted, the battery of his phone had already dipped to fourteen percent.

"Merde," he muttered, and pulled his hand out of his swimsuit. He suddenly knew he couldn't in good conscience use the last dregs of battery of what was possibly the last working smartphone on earth to watch an oiled up actress explore alternate methods of payment with her taxi driver.

He cracked his knuckles and frowned. He was embarrassed to have even considered doing that here and now. He tried to distract himself by flipping through one of the manuals he'd found in a drawer beneath a control panel and decoding what he could of the Italian. Emergency procedures. All obvious... if there's a fire on board there are hoses on every deck that can pump salt water... blah blah... procedures for maneuvering in strong winds... no wind now... what to do in case of power outage... boring... emergency codes to call the coast guard for help... no longer applicable...

Vic tossed the manual onto the warm linoleum and stretched his arms. He stood up and walked a few laps around the bridge, then looked out one of the dirty windows facing the rear of the ship hoping to catch a glimpse of the girl in the tank top, but her team was concealed by a column of containers. What he could see was the others: the doctor, the man in the purple shirt, Art, and Sam. Mostly Sam, the ogre, gripping a fire axe and hacking with frightening desperation.

The daunting reams of cargo documents that Elissa had showed him were still waiting in those file cabinets. Hours and hours of tedious work. He supposed he had no choice but to sift through them, even though he truly believed what he'd said earlier to everyone: escape to this boat was just a prelude to death. They'd managed to buy themselves another few days. Maybe weeks if they ended up finding food. Still, Vic had to admit these people's persistence was inspiring. He certainly respected them more than he had his dead-eyed coworkers at Walmart. And *much* more than the parents who'd brought their newborns to be photographed beside a wicker basket filled with Easter eggs.

Vic turned to look out over the sea again, back in the direction of the shore and the pumpkin-colored horizon. It was late afternoon, and the sun was descending into a hazy shroud. Had he not known what the clouds represented, he might say they were beautiful. Especially the reflection on the sea, which painted the water with a spectrum of autumnal browns, oranges, yellows, and reds . He pulled his phone back out of his pocket. Thirteen percent battery. He hit the camera button, then bent over and steadied himself against the railing. He fit the sun, clouds, and sea into the frame. Vic imagined God working in the Walmart photo center, setting up these apocalyptic conditions in the same way Vic once arranged plush reindeer and superhero dioramas. He tapped the shutter button to take a picture, then pulled the phone back to study his handiwork. Not bad.

8

"Dinner" was a low-key affair. They divided up some of the food people had thrown on the table this morning. Each person got six almonds, four salted crackers, and a protein shake. Doctor Rosalyn suggested they save the remaining canned food for tomorrow and nobody argued.

The mood in the poorly lit mess hall was grim. They'd managed to open and sort through thirteen thirty-foot containers today, as well as about twenty wooden crates, and hadn't found any food. Sam wanted to keep working through the night but the on-deck lighting, like the air conditioning and indoor lighting, ran off the battery when the engines weren't running. Elissa declared that it was okay to use some indoor lights, but was concerned that AC and on-deck lighting would deplete the battery within a few days.

Everyone had quickly agreed to eat a bit and then rest until dawn.

The mess hall contained three long parallel tables, enough space to sit thirty, but it felt small and cramped because the ceiling was low and the windows that looked out onto the sea were dark.

Mel Glazer collected his dinner from Elissa, and sat down at the end of a hard metal bench. He held a cracker to his dry lips and closed his eyes.

"Blessed are you Lord, King of the Universe," he whispered to himself, "for creating all the grains of the earth." He sighed and ignored his growling stomach, wanting to make sure he amply relished what could be one of his last opportunities to make a blessing over food. Neither the crackers nor the protein had been labeled with a certificate of *kashrut*, but there was no question that one was permitted to eat non-kosher food in order to survive. Mel allowed the tiniest bit of the cracker to enter his mouth, savored the crystals of salt melting on his tongue, and swallowed.

"This seat taken?"

Before Mel could answer, Arthur Roselli sat down across from him. Art was probably ten years older than Mel's fifty-two, and looked like he'd spent a lot of time in the sun over the years. He wore a faded green t-shirt, the silk-screened image of someone playing guitar just barely visible on his chest, and a worn baseball cap with a logo Mel didn't recognize.

"How you feeling, Rabbi?"

Mel spread his palms.

"I'm not a rabbi. And... I'm fine I suppose. Given the circumstances."

Art cracked his knuckles expectantly, then popped a whole cracker into his mouth and scarfed it down, Mel thought, like a dog.

"Magnificent," Art smiled. "Notes of cedar and raspberries. Recommended pairing: tepid lead-infused water."

Art drained his Dixie cup, then eyed Mel with curiosity.

"What, you're not eating, Rabbi?"

"What's the rush?"

Art grinned. "That's the fucking truth."

"Attention? Guys?" Greg was standing in the middle of the dining room, knocking a fist on the metal table to get everyone's attention. "I just wanted to say, I know we didn't find anything in the crates today, but good work everyone. Don't be discouraged. I've got a good feeling about tomorrow."

"This guy..." Art whispered to Mel, shaking his head.

But Greg wasn't done: "I also was just realizing, I'm not sure I really got to know everyone properly. Maybe we could take the opportunity to go around and say something interesting about ourselves?"

Art's hand immediately shot up. "I'll go first. My name's Arthur Roselli and I'm stranded on a cargo ship."

This got a bitter laugh from Jennifer, the pretty young woman in the immodest tank top.

"Really, Greg," Doctor Rosalyn said. "It's a nice idea. But we're all pretty beat."

"Well, I–" Greg laughed nervously. His left eye twitched in a way Mel recognized from the study halls of his youth–a tic developed by some of the more obsessive students who became agitated when they felt they were unable to grasp a difficult passage of Talmud. But the man didn't relent. "I'm sorry but I really think this is important. We're all going to have to work together here to survive, and it's best if we're not strangers."

"Not everyone is present, *mon ami*," said Vic, arms folded across his bare chest. "We're missing the young man we found chained above."

Mel glanced around. He hadn't noticed but yes, Adam was missing. Didn't he want to eat?

"Well…" Greg affected a weird nasal voice, *"Can't please everyone!"*

"Hey!" Sam bellowed, nearly shooting out of his chair. "You're Greg *Pink*. I can't believe I didn't recognize you. You were in that movie…"

"No, no," Greg gave a dismissive hand gesture. "I mean, yes, that was me, that's me, but it's not important."

"With the prisoners playing basketball, right? *Chain Net?*"

"Oh my god," Lily was suddenly flushed. "That was *hilarious.*"

Greg sighed in mock helplessness.

"Guilty as charged."

"Wow man," said Vic, "I'm also seeing this movie. Very amusing."

Mel had no idea what these people were talking about.

"Thanks guys, really, that means so much to me."

"So you met Ryan Grant?" asked Lily, eyes glowing. "What is he like in person? Is he hilarious?"

"He's—"

"Dead," Art snapped. "Real dead."

"Thank you for that, Arthur," Doctor Rosalyn stood up, glaring at him. "Just to continue what we were discussing this morning while we have everyone–nearly everyone–here: I think we should search for food for two more days, and if nothing turns up, head south. Maybe we can find some island in the Caribbean that doesn't have the virus in the air."

Greg nodded as if he appreciated this feedback, as if this sort of declaration was exactly what he'd been hoping for.

"Anybody else?" Greg asked, as Rosalyn sat back down.

"Well, hi everyone, I'm Lily Chen," said Lily standing, and forcing herself to smile. She tossed her dark black hair back. Mel couldn't help but feel a sort of loathing for her. He considered himself a patient person, but he'd had a headache all day from the sun and hunger, and working with Lily this afternoon had been unbearable. "I guess you could say I wear a lot of hats. I used to be in customer service, but was really concentrating on a line of artisanal salad dressings. All organic and super healthy. My most popular was made with tahini and orange zest–they actually sold it in the Whole Foods in Louisville–eek sorry, I shouldn't be talking about food now! Anyways I just wanted to say sorry about getting upset today. As some of you may have noticed, I can be a little emotional sometimes and if I offended anyone I'm sorry–" she looked apologetically at Jennifer, then at Mel. He nodded at her as if to say all was forgiven, and immediately felt terrible for judging her so harshly. She continued: "Also, I guess I feel the same way as Doctor Roz. If we don't find food within a couple days we gotta go back to shore somewhere."

She sat down quickly.

Greg crossed his arms and surveyed the rest of the crew like a schoolteacher patiently waiting for one of them to answer his question.

This man is an imbecile, Mel thought. A complete moron. Of all the people to survive… Mel stopped himself. He was judging again. Everyone here had lost everything.

Mel felt a twisting in his gut. There was that thought he'd been dancing with the past week or so. On dry land he'd managed to fend it off; he'd been able to distract himself with the job of survival. But since waking up this morning he'd felt it bubbling up. Pretty soon he was going to have to ask himself, ask the Holy One…

He pushed it away and concentrated on what Elissa was saying. It was shocking how loud her voice was considering her size.

"–wanted to second Greg. I think it's very important that we communicate with each other. Now. I'd like to point out that if we're all down here, nobody is sitting on the bridge monitoring the radio. We need to make sure we have someone there at *all times*, checking shortwave frequencies in case another ship puts out a signal, as well as broadcasting our location–about fifty miles off the coast of Savannah. This is our best chance of survival. As for heading back to shore: North America is out of the question. The radiation is dangerous, and the airborne plague is certain death. Gas masks aren't built to work indefinitely. We've probably gotten all the use we can out of them. I agree that the Caribbean–" she glanced at Doctor Rosalyn, "–is probably our best bet."

"The plague is all over the Caribbean by now too, I'm sure," Art said. "If just a couple of spores blew out there and reached some plants, that would be enough to spread the plague."

"Arthur please don't call it that–" Rosalyn said. "We're not sure exactly what it was. The only reason we have to think there was a disease being spread via spores was the Daughters of January videos, not exactly a credible source."

"You're talking about the plant thing?" Sam asked.

The doctor looked exasperated.

"Please let's not go down that road."

"There's something in the air, and plants, that's for sure," said Sam. "I saw things happen to trees and plants I never saw before."

"We don't know the facts. Please, let's not speculate."

"With all due respect," Elissa said, "if someone has something to say, I think it's important to say it. Everyone's opinion will be valued–"

"Alright then," Art said. "I got something to say."

Elissa appeared upset at the interruption, but couldn't object without contradicting herself.

Art rose from his seat. He appeared strong for a man of his age. He had skin the color of leather, and large features: big nose, big eyes, big ears. His lined face suggested to Mel that he was a man who's kindness had been taken advantage of, to the point that he'd grown bitter and packed it away. "Are we just going to ignore what somebody did to that kid? Adam? What if there really is an island at those coordinates? I mean, can we really afford to just dismiss that possibility out of hand?"

"We're not dismissing it out of hand," Elissa said. "I looked in the atlas. There's nothing there."

"Yeah, well..." Art was clearly caught off guard by this development. "Still though. Maybe we should try to talk to the kid a little more. See if we can jog his memory. I'm just saying, our two options right now are either die out here waiting for the Navy to spot us, or go back to shore and die there from radiation and infected spores."

"Talk to him?" said Lily. "I'm worried about getting *stabbed* by him!"

"Hey, hey," Art said. "That's not fair. There's no reason to think he's dangerous."

"He didn't come join us for dinner after Elissa made the announcement on the PA," Jennifer said. She sounded a little nervous, Mel thought. Maybe because she was so much younger than everyone else. "I think he's just sitting alone in his room. That's a little worrisome."

Art said, "So here's a crazy idea: let's bring some food down to his cabin and schmooze."

"There's not enough food as it is," Sam said, "Why should we waste it on someone who doesn't want it?"

This statement from Sam provoked a flurry of smaller conflicts. Art crossed the room to argue with Lily face to face. Doctor Rosalyn was speaking to Sam. From what Mel could overhear, the doctor was explaining how mental illness could lead to lack of appetite. Greg and Vic were talking about something which Vic seemed to find amusing.

Only he, Mel, remained seated. No, scratch that. Bahram, the Persian gentleman had been sitting in the far corner this whole time. Mel made eye contact with him. Bahram shrugged, bewildered. Mel considered how difficult this whole ordeal was for him, given that he couldn't communicate with anyone. Bahram he had sympathy for. But these other people…

Anger bubbled in Mel's chest. He tugged on his beard and tried to compose himself. He started on another cracker to distract himself. Sam was speaking, but Mel could hardly make out the giant's words. His hands trembled on the tabletop.

"Okay, okay," Elissa was shouting over the rest, but her voice sounded very far away to Mel.

How could the Holy One deem these people worthy of saving, and just let Shoshana, Rueben, Tsipora…

"There's nothing to discuss right now," Elissa said. "Everyone agrees we're looking for food tomorrow right?"

"What's wrong with just *talking* to him?" pleaded Art.

"Fine, *you* go talk to him," someone retorted.

Mel's vision went a little red.

And why me, God? Mel thought. *You should have let me die with the rest of my family. Why keep me alive in this cruel purgatory? Is it a punishment? If so please, please tell me what I did to deserve this?*

"Mel?"

He felt Doctor Rosalyn's warm hand on his elbow. It was the first touch of a woman not his wife that he'd felt in a very long time; for religious reasons he didn't even shake hands with women. But he didn't protest. She asked: "Are you alright?"

Mel exhaled. Nodded and smiled.

"Yes," he whispered. "Just fine. Thank God."

9

Rosalyn Carson left the mess hall before everyone else. She was exhausted and needed to be alone. She was heading back to her cabin when someone tapped her upper arm.

She turned, startled. Sam had followed her out of the mess.

"Hey. Can we talk?" he asked.

"Okay."

"Let's go to my room."

Rosalyn stiffened.

Since the brief, uncomfortable interaction with Greg this morning, she'd managed to avoid any one-on-one situations with men. Not that any of them seemed particularly ill-intentioned, but she wasn't stupid: there were no police or laws out here. Every single person on board had experienced horrible trauma over the past weeks, plus there was the very real possibility that they didn't have much longer to live. Under these sorts of conditions, all bets were off.

Before she could respond, Sam took a step toward her, practically pinning her against the wall. She was trapped, and he weighed at least twice as much as her. Neither fight nor flight was an option. Her back was flat against the wall, heart hammering, hands shaking.

"I need some privacy," he whispered.

"Back away or I'll scream," she said, voice trembling.

Sam blinked, uncomprehending, and then suddenly his eyes widened in horror. He drew back and shook his head. "Oh gosh. I'm so sorry. No, no. I'm so sorry. I just... I just wanted to ask you a question. You're a Dermatist right?'

Sam seemed legitimately rattled by the misunderstanding. She exhaled.

"Dermatologist," she said. "A skin doctor."

"Yeah well, I have a problem, and I wanted your advice. But, never mind. I apologize."

Rosalyn's pulse slowly trickled down toward baseline. He wanted medical advice. What could it be? Her best guess was he'd gotten some kind of cut and hadn't cleaned it properly. Could he be worried about tetanus? That would be bad. If he'd never had a tetanus shot, there was nothing she could do other than help him die comfortably.

And the truth was if this enormous man actually planned on assaulting her, she'd be utterly powerless. Hell, everyone else on board combined would probably be unable to subdue him. He didn't need to lure her back to his cabin under false pretenses.

"What's going on?"

Sam gave her a weak, pleading smile, and then peeled up the bottom of his wife beater. His pale torso was covered in reddish-brown hair that matched his buzz cut. He pointed to a spot just below his waistline.

"It hurts here. Really, really bad. And it's not just a pulled muscle or something. I've had those before. I'm worried it might be, well… Look I heard what you just said back there, about stuff just being speculation. But like I said, I saw the way the trees looked in places where there was gas. And there was a video too I saw online a couple days ago when I got wifi for a few minutes. It showed Paris from the air. Some of the buildings were fine, they hadn't been bombed, but there was nobody moving below. Then the same thing in Mexico City. So it wasn't from explosions. I heard it on a news report too, that there were diseases in the air and anybody within five miles of a tree that inhaled this stuff would start bleeding from the inside, from their stomach and eyes.

"I don't know a whole lot about science, I can't say how these things work. I'm just telling you what I saw. I saw trees that usually have green leaves turning dark purple, and plant stalks oozing some kind of clear paste. And they said in one of the videos I saw that the Russians had terrible things stashed in their embassies around the world, ever since the Cold War. Diseases that spread through the soil, infecting plants, which spread it through their seeds floating in the air."

"A Daughters of January video, you mean?"

Sam grimaced, and then nodded quickly.

"And that's the thing. I'm worried that I got infected." He pointed again to the top of his groin. "I think, well, I saw the thing on the video about bleeding from the inside and..." he bit his lip. "I think it's happening to me. And I'm scared. It could also be a tumor that grew super fast because of radiation. But I'm even more scared that it's the disease and maybe I'm infecting all of you on board. I didn't think about it till this morning. I didn't make the connection until I was working on the containers, with the axe, and it started fucking *killing*, excuse my language–"

"Okay, okay, settle down. It's not a tumor. I can tell you that right now."

Rosalyn was feeling reenergized, better than she had in weeks. This was her bread and butter. Helping people was wonderful of course, but the most gratifying aspect of being a doctor for her was the satisfaction of solving a complex problem. It was why she'd chosen dermatology: you didn't have to rely on the patient's vague description of symptoms; the clues were all there in clear view, waiting to be deciphered, like hieroglyphics written in flesh.

"Let's go to the captain's lounge. I think I know what's going on."

"Thanks Rosalyn. Thanks so much."

He eagerly led her down the corridor, to the gangway door. He brushing aside the swinging door like he was swatting off a fly, then held it open for her. Then he climbed the metal steps two at a time. Rosalyn followed.

The captain's lounge, where they'd had their first gathering this morning, was empty. Sam turned on the two reading lamps beside the bookcase and soft light reflected off the circular window that looked out onto the nighttime sea.

"Show me where it hurts," she said. Sam took her hand in his much larger one and placed it on his stomach. Her hand found the bulge. It felt like a rubber ball. This was almost certainly a hernia.

"You said it hurt worse when you were swinging the axe?"

He nodded.

"I thought maybe it could be a burst appendix," he said. "I had a cousin who that happened to."

"Sam stop. If your appendix burst you wouldn't be standing here talking to me. Is the pain generally worse when you're active?"

"Oh yeah. Way worse."

"Lie down," she ordered. "Flat on your back."

He eased himself to the carpeted floor.

"You feel okay now right?" she asked. "No pain?"

"I, um, yeah I guess not actually."

"And can you still feel the lump?"

"Yeah, but it's a lot smaller now. Weird. I never noticed that."

She knelt beside him, pulled down the waist of his shorts and probed his groin. Once her diagnosis was confirmed, she got to her feet, and moved to a leather chair.

"You can stand up," Rosalyn said. "You have an inguinal hernia. You probably got it from overexertion during the past week."

Sam didn't budge.

"I'm just gonna lie here for a while," he said. "It's kind of a relief. So how do I fix the hernia?"

"The only real cure for this is surgical, but that's obviously not an option now. The important thing is that you don't do anything strenuous, like heavy lifting, and exacerbate it. "

"No lifting?" he said, looking up at her from the floor. "I have to swing with the axe though. To bust through the containers."

"Absolutely not. A hernia is a muscle tear, and that kind of exertion and lifting can widen the tear."

"I have to swing the axe. I can break the locks faster than anyone else. A lot faster."

"You asked for my help. That's the advice I'm giving you. Obviously I can't stop you if you want to hurt yourself."

Sam shook his head slowly, but said nothing for a moment.

"I was positive I was going to die. I'm such an idiot..." he turned to face her again, "Listen, Doctor Rosalyn, anything you need. Let me know. I dunno, if anyone gives you any trouble or anything. I'm gonna look out for you."

She was surprised at how much this primitive offer–which sounded like a recruitment pitch from a prison gang–affected her. For just a moment, her chest swelled. How sweet it would be to just let someone else worry about everything for once. For him to wrap her tightly in arms as thick as logs, like she was an infant, and tell her everything would be okay, even though that was clearly nonsense.

Rosalyn came back to earth. She suppressed the childish thought.

"It's kinda weird," Sam continued. "When I was out there, driving to the coast through all the destruction, scavenging for food, not even sleeping in case someone killed me and stole my food... I wasn't scared at all. But now that we're here, and things are quiet, now I'm scared as hell."

"I know. I feel the same, actually," she said.

"Are you glad you made it to this boat?" he asked her.

Rosalyn blinked. She almost asked him to explain the question, but the truth was she knew exactly what he meant.

"I don't know," she answered. "What about you?"

He shrugged.

"Same, I guess."

They sat in silence for another moment.

Still splayed on his back, Sam reached to touch the spot on his midriff, and shook his head, like he still couldn't believe something as simple as lying down could make it go away.

"There's something I always say to myself when I'm getting anxious," Rosalyn said. "I just repeat to myself: 'This isn't real. Nothing is real.' until I settle down. It usually works. Maybe try it."

"'This isn't real. Nothing is real," he repeated.

She nodded, suddenly feeling sheepish. Her mantra sounded so silly when she said it out loud.

"Why does that calm you down?" he asked.

"Well…"

She'd never told Scott this. They'd been married for sixteen years. And now she was about to explain her mantra to a man she'd known for about ten hours. "It's the idea that whatever it is that's bothering you is almost definitely a stupid human construct that we decided to take seriously."

Sam looked confused.

"I don't get it."

"Well as an example… I remember being maybe fifteen, sitting in the stands of a high school basketball game. I wasn't such a big sports fan but my friends and I went to the games. Everyone in school did. With ten seconds left in the game our team was down one, with the ball, and called a timeout. I was so nervous. So nervous it made no sense. My hands were sweaty and my heart was beating fast. I was physically uncomfortable. And I looked around the gym and everyone was frozen. The emotion on their faces was just outrageous–it looked like they were preparing to watch an execution. And then suddenly I realized I couldn't care less about the game. Because it was all fake. The game of basketball itself, while sometimes elegant, I admit, is just something we made up. The rules and the drama are artificial. There's not, fundamentally, such a thing as a three-point shot, for example. Someone just drew that line and decided anything from here out is worth three points. And once you start thinking like that, how can you be nervous about who wins this totally arbitrary game?"

Sam mulled this for a while.

"But that's sports. Maybe sports are kinda random. But–"

"No but that's the thing. Once you start thinking like that, you realize it's *everything*. We're all just pretending!

"I'm a dermatologist, and for years I've been prescribing coal tar–it's a black liquid which is a byproduct of coal production. Every dermatologist prescribes it. Why? Because a hundred years ago in London they realized that kids who were chimney sweeps, who were covered in charcoal dust all day, didn't suffer from certain common skin ailments. If someone came into my office with dermatitis, it was my go-to remedy. It works quite well, but *nobody knows why*. There are dozens or hundreds of chemicals in coal tar, and I, as a dermatologist who prescribed this for years and years, don't know which single chemical made the rash go away. We pretend we understand things, but even modern medicine isn't much more sophisticated than bloodletting with leeches..."

She trailed off. Was Sam even listening? It felt like all of that had gushed out more for her own benefit than for his. They were both silent for a moment, in fact she thought maybe Sam had fallen asleep on the carpet. But then after a long time he said:

"I wonder if there will ever be another basketball game."

10

Jennifer lay wide awake in her cabin. She was too wired to sleep. Dinner had satiated her for a few hours, but now her stomach was growling again.

The mattress was comfortable and the sheets crisp and clean, but it was ungodly hot in here. The wet air was constricting and oppressive. Were it not for the past week, she might have complained or felt sorry for herself, but this was heaven, relatively.

She considered the odds of her winding up here on this boat. The combination of lucky breaks and survival instincts that had to go her way: that she'd been in her car, driving up the coast to her parent's house for summer break, when Tampa went up. The fact that she hadn't yet made it to Orlando when it went up too—in light so blinding that she'd crashed into the guard rail. That she'd had half a tank of gas at the time and her car was still functional. Hell, that she'd even decided to road trip back to her parents in Baltimore in the first place, instead of just flying. That she'd decided to reroute to Jacksonville, realizing that water was the only escape.

That Jacksonville had thus far survived, and that she'd been among the first to receive a gas mask from the National Guard. That the gas mask was an M40, the only model that ultimately ended up being effective. (She knew she'd only gotten an M40 because the guy from the national guard thought she was cute, implications of which were too unpleasant to dwell on.) That she'd affixed said gas mask properly and—being a little compulsive about it—didn't take it off, and just sucked down liquids through the built-in straw, even as her stomach rumbled and she feared she might faint from hunger. That something told her to get out of Jacksonville, and that she'd listened and left just hours before the city was swallowed by a firestorm. That she'd happened to catch the broadcast on 87.8 AM just minutes before the radio station was gassed: a clerk for a shipping company called in, advising people to head for Savannah port, where there was a partially fueled ship.

That she'd summoned the fortitude to make her away through a wading-pool of corpses—many still wearing their ineffective masks–to the ship, just in time to watch the dark horizon shattered by a new wave of mushroom clouds.

She felt a little proud of herself. She was ashamed to feel that way; it was a ridiculous reaction to all of this. But she couldn't help it. She kept thinking about the first months at Tampa, how pathetic and confused she'd felt. Her intro to psych lecture had over two hundred people in it, so when she got lost it wasn't like she could raise her hand and ask a question. And she'd never been a phenomenal student. Average intelligence–that was usually how she thought of herself. Hell, she didn't even know what she was doing in a psychology lecture. Was she interested in psychology? Not really. During her consultation with her high school guidance counselor, when the older woman had asked her what she was interested in, Jennifer hadn't known how to answer.

Do you have any hobbies? How do you spend your time outside of school?
You know. Hanging out with friends. Going to concerts and stuff.

It was true. She might not have been a great student, but she'd had tons of friends. Though, honestly, lying here in the darkness, she struggled to remember what she'd liked about those people.

Jennifer had been middle of the pack in high school academically, and those first few months at Tampa she'd been terrified that she was going to flunk out of college. And then what would she do? It would have been so embarrassing; Tampa wasn't exactly a campus of overachievers.

She went out with the girls on her hall three or four nights a week. She took a little comfort in thinking that they were as confused and lost as she was. She'd never know if that was actually true.

She didn't even like drinking that much, but it couldn't be avoided. She wasn't an idiot—she never got so trashed she had to be carried back to the dorm or anything—but she drank a lot. Bacardi and Diet Coke. How many Bacardi and Diet Cokes did she drink freshman year? How many pictures were posted of her with her arms around the shoulders of the other girls, wearing too much eyeshadow and trying to look like she was enjoying herself? How many men—no, boys—had shouted in her ear, to be heard over the blaring top-40 playlist, asking her name? Once, freshman year, she'd allowed one to come back to her dorm room. Had she wanted him? Hard to say.

He was muscular and had pretty brown eyes. She refused to take off her bra. The guy was frustrated that she just wanted to make out. He kept trying to grope her through her underwear. She got nervous and told him she was tired, and to get out. He didn't budge from the bed. She flung open the door to her dorm room, even though they were both half-naked. If she hadn't done that, would he have left peacefully?

Despite herself, she'd gotten fine grades her first semester. Not great, but fine. This was weird: she hadn't worked very hard and knew she wasn't smart enough to coast. It felt like she'd tricked someone into giving her fine grades. The grades helped her relax. She stopped having anxiety dreams about unexpected final exams. The fine grades encouraged her to stick with psychology.

Sophomore year, a girl named Karen who was a year older invited Jennifer to an on-campus political rally. Someone handed Jennifer a sign that said *Free Najaf,* and Jennifer waved it around for an hour. Later the situation was explained to her: there were violent militant extremists in Najaf—a city in Iraq—committing human rights violations against the peaceful, religiously-moderate majority. A man with a well-curated beard, who everyone called 'Gear', gave Jennifer reading material and she surprised herself by reading all of it. The more she read about the situation in Najaf the more she couldn't believe something like this was happening in the same world as Tampa Bay, Florida. The treatment of the women especially got her. It was horrible. Raped in the streets if they went out without proper attire; punished for crimes their husbands committed, all in the name of a god who they probably didn't believe in.

Finally, Jennifer Presley had an answer for her high school guidance counselor: she was interested in helping the oppressed people–particularly the women–of Najaf. She stopped going to parties, and instead sat in her dorm room writing letters to her congressmen. She volunteered with the group, joining Karen and the Gear. They organized both rabid protests and "die-ins"–where you got students to lie on campus walkways pretending to be dead–to raise awareness of the situation in Najaf.

Jennifer was shocked to discover that not everyone shared her outrage for the deteriorating situation. Many students couldn't even find Najaf on a map. *It's in southern Iraq*, she explained. Sometimes that didn't help.

Some students even opposed her:

The situation isn't so simple. You're distilling a centuries-old regional conflict into black and white. Do you even understand the history of Shiites and Sunnis? Do you have a practical solution to the problem? If you remove the current regime you'll create a power vacuum which will likely be filled with something even worse. Do you know that twelve years ago the situation was basically reversed?

Are you even listening to yourself, she'd reply. *People are being raped and killed. Who cares about the history of the conflict. These are* people.

The righteous indignation gave her a sense of purpose she'd never felt before. Everything was framed in terms of the situation in Najaf. She didn't abandon her school work, but it was a distant second, priority-wise. Her parents didn't get it.

Of course it's terrible, honey. But it's on the other side of the world. Let those people work it out for themselves.

As the months wore on, she was dismayed to see even Karen and Gear losing their enthusiasm.

The issue isn't getting any attention in the press anymore, which means our chances of getting the House to approve military intervention are close to zero.

What about the sanctions we've been pushing so hard for?

At this point, even if you get another layer of sanctions, it's just going to trickle down and hurt the people more than the regime.

But, Karen had offered hopefully, the situation in Venezuela was getting pretty bad. There might be some actual chance of preventing bloodshed, if they acted fast.

The whole experience left Jennifer feeling pretty low. Shattered, even. Questioning the purity of her own motives. She returned to the parties, finding they'd changed very little during her hiatus. She drank Bacardi and Diet Cokes, sat in the corner, and gazed around the room, glassy-eyed, loathing her fellow students. When boys came to sit next to her she told them to fuck off.

And that, she realized, staring at the ceiling of her cabin, was why she felt a little proud of herself. Of all the people at those parties, only she'd made it. Karen, Gear, all the kids in her intro to psychology class that she'd thought were so much smarter than her, the older students who'd told her she was oversimplifying the conflict in Najaf, the professors, her parents who thought she should *let those people work it out for themselves…* They hadn't made it. She had.

A knock on her cabin door snapped her back to reality. She rubbed her eyes, sat up in the darkness and walked barefoot to the door. She looked through the peephole and saw Greg Pink standing in the dark hallway, flashlight in hand. She'd never admit it, but she'd recognized him from the start and pretended she hadn't. She didn't want to be a fangirl. Well, she *wasn't* a fangirl. But she'd seen one of his movies and yeah, she had to admit his stupid self-degrading character was pretty lovable, and she'd laughed a few times.

"What time is it?" she asked.

"Almost eleven," came Greg's muffled voice. "I just wanted… Can I come in for a second?"

Greg Pink is asking to come into my cabin, she thought. Who saw this coming three weeks ago?

"What do you want?" she asked.

"I couldn't sleep," Greg hesitated. "I just… Want a drink?" He held a two-shot bottle of some cheap Russian vodka up to the peephole.

Something melted in Jennifer as she stared at the tiny bottle. She was exhausted and sorely tempted by the promise of drugged sleep.

When she didn't say anything, Greg added:

"I found it on the bridge. Captain's secret stash I guess."

In the hall, Greg half-smiled.

Jennifer bit her lip, then fished her filthy tank top off the dresser, pulled it on, and—before unlocking the door—slipped the screwdriver she'd been using that morning into the back waist of her shorts.

Greg smiled and stepped in.

"Thanks," he said. He walked past her and sat down on the edge of her bed. She made sure the door would stay open on its own, pulled the desk chair out, and sat facing him.

"So?" she said, greedily eyeing the bottle in Greg's hand.

He shrugged. His green eyes were misty and desperate—a very different look than he'd had at this morning's meeting. He started to speak, and then gesticulated helplessly, as if words were both insufficient and unnecessary. Instead he opened the cap of the bottle and offered Jennifer the first pull. She let half the vodka gurgle down her gullet and then gasped from pain. On a near empty stomach, the vodka burned all the way down. Her eyes watered as she handed the bottle back to Greg, who took a gulp.

"How many bottles did you find?"

"Just this…" said Greg. "Is it wrong, you think? For us to drink it alone?" His tone told Jennifer that he'd already decided it was, but didn't particularly care.

"Probably doing them a favor. This will dehydrate us in this heat."

Greg nodded halfheartedly. He finished the bottle and coughed.

Then he lowered his head between his knees and groaned, took a deep breath, and then sat up perfectly straight: spine rigid, shoulders pulled back.

"Quite a thing, isn't it?" he said. "Being on this boat."

She nodded.

"Yeah," she said, unsure what else to add.

"Tell me about yourself," he said. "What were you doing before all of this? A student, someone said?"

"Yeah. At University of Tampa."

"Studying what?" he smiled.

"Psych but…" she shrugged. "Who knows if that's what I would have stuck with."

"Totally," he laughed, like she'd cracked a great joke. "Boy I remember college. Willlld times, that's for sure."

"You studied acting?" It felt like what she was supposed to ask.

"No, no," he waved his hand. "Didn't get into that until later. Actually I was doing pre-law. Thought I wanted to be a lawyer. Can you imagine? Me? *A lawyer?"* Greg chuckled again. She wasn't sure why that was funny.

"I'm–"

Greg leaned in and tried to kiss her. She recoiled so violently she tweaked her neck.

"Um," she said, heart pounding. "I'm going to try to get some sleep."

Greg sat back in his chair.

"What's wrong?" Greg smiled.

"I'm just tired."

"C'mon don't be ridiculous."

She stood up and pulled her screwdriver from her shorts, then pointed it at the door.

"Please leave," she said.

"Jenny…" Greg remained seated, ignoring her weapon. "We probably won't find food, you know. This might be our last chance to enjoy ourselves."

She felt her resolve weakening. It was true, they might well die in a few days, so what was the difference? And why did she have her screwdriver out? He hadn't threatened any violence.

"I'm going to try to get some sleep," she repeated, voice wavering. She felt if he pushed back just one more time she might buckle and submit.

But he didn't. He stood up and sighed.

"Whatever you say."

He walked briskly out into the hall without even looking at her, as if he'd already lost interest.

Jennifer closed and locked her door, then sat back down on her bed. Why had she pulled out her screwdriver? She felt so stupid.

She scooted over to look out the porthole window. It was totally dark, of course; all the lights on the deck were turned off. Miles and miles of dark water. Could she really blame Greg? The magnitude of the darkness, how far it extended in all directions; left, right, up, down, was enough to make a man do much worse.

11

To his growing mental list of material comforts he'd give a finger for, Art added sunglasses. Even on the beach in Miami he'd hardly ever worn them, but on the deck of the ship at noon, sunlight was reflected from every direction. Looking at his feet was blinding; the surface of the deck in the cargo area was some type of synthetic rubber lacquered in a water-protective white finish, which reflected sunlight like a mirror when it was wet, which it always was. At dawn there'd been ample shade thanks to the cartons—stacked as tall as a two-story house—but now the sun hammered down from directly above. Art wondered how many other survivors around the world were looking up at the sun at this moment. Was it possible that the sun had risen today only for the eleven people on board?

Art took off his Dolphins hat and wiped some sweat off his forehead. This should have been siesta time, but to waste daylight hours seemed foolish.

The sheer quantity of cargo on board was staggering. There was no way of knowing if this was even the ship's full capacity; the crew could have been halfway through loading it up when the harbor area was gassed. Yesterday they'd successfully hacked the locks off of thirteen crates at ground level. This morning they'd done five. Only several thousand to go.

They'd found furniture, expensive tiles, a deconstructed grand piano, a couple refrigerators, antiques, kitchenware, car parts…

No food.

"Well, big fella," Art asked, shielding his eyes as he looked up at Sam. "Feeling lucky? Wanna choose the next one?"

Sam was belly-up on the deck like a dead cockroach, and he seemed to have abandoned hope of squeezing his whole frame into the sliver of shade afforded by the carton wall behind him. His face was bright red. He shook his head.

"Lily, you choose."

Art's shoulder was killing him from swinging the axe, and he was even weaker today for hunger, but he liked working. It was good to feel like he was doing something productive.

The three of them—Art, Sam and Lily—comprised one team of container openers. Greg, Mel, Jennifer, and Roz were hacking locks off containers on the other side of the ship with the second of the two fire axes they'd found on board. Vic was on the bridge, still looking for the manifest that could conclusively tell them this was all a lost cause. Bahram was opening wooden crates solo. Elissa had wanted to help, but everyone insisted she rest; she'd been getting a little wobbly from hunger and nobody wanted her to faint or something. And who knew what Adam was doing. Nobody had even tried to recruit him to help.

"This one," Lily said, and before the men could respond she snatched the axe from Art and began hacking at the rusty lock that secured the green storage container nearest them.

Lily's red shirt was soaked through with sweat, and with every swing she emitted a ferocious cry.

Art shot a look at Sam:

Not bad.

The giant didn't notice. His eyes were unfocused, staring straight up, his entire head wet with sweat. One of his hands clutched his lower abdomen. Art wondered what this guy had been doing a month ago. If he had to bet, he'd say middle school football coach. A good guy. Beloved by all the kids, but considered a meathead by the rest of the faculty.

"You feeling alright, big fella?" Art asked him.

It took Sam a few seconds to respond.

"Fine."

Art watched Lily work for a few minutes, hacking at the lock like it was a cheating ex-boyfriend. She was ambitious, but ineffective. Finally Sam sat up, perched himself on one knee, and, with what appeared enormous effort, pushed himself to his feet. He seemed to swallow a groan, still clutching his stomach, then stumbled to Lily and gestured for her to hand him the axe.

She took a few steps back and wiped sweat off her brow as she and Art admired Sam's craft. The sheer power of his thick arms and broad back was astonishing. He brought the axe down again and again on the lock, each repetition culminating in a clang, a spark or two, and a warbled cry. It was almost frightening, Art thought, to see the power Sam was capable of generating.

Lily plopped down next to Art in the shade and they watched Sam work. For a moment, at least, she seemed too exhausted to speak.

Sam was like a machine. There was a surprising grace in the fluidity of his movements. What was most impressive, Art thought, was how he showed no signs of fatigue. There was no pause at the bottom of the swing to gather his strength for another whack at the lock; rather one swing led straight into the next, as if he was a flywheel being cranked by some invisible source. This sort of single-minded act could only come from desperation so encompassing that Sam was unable to think about anything else. You could see the emptiness in his eyes. His world had been boiled down to a very simple directive: get food.

Art was hungry too. Everyone had only had a few bites of cinnamon-raisin Powerbar for breakfast.

But so what, he thought. You're hungry, so you get food so you don't feel that way. Then what? He suddenly found it hilarious that everyone had agreed to search for food, without first discussing whether it was even worth it.

"I know it sounds stupid," Lily said, interrupting his train of thought. "But I'd give anything to be in Nordstrom right now."

Yes, Art thought. That sounds stupid.

"Not because I wanna buy clothes. But the AC. The AC in those stores is so good."

"I'll give you that," he said. "I could definitely go for some big box store air conditioning. "

"And the one in Lexington had a guy in a suit playing a grand piano. And there was a café inside the store that had the best Caprese salad. I'd go there sometimes on Sundays for like an hour and just eat in the cafe and listen to the piano. I never even bought anything. It was too expensive. All the deals are at Nordstrom *Rack*. But that store isn't nearly as nice."

Art noted her use of the present tense but decided to let it slide.

"Where would you be?" she asked.

"You talked me into Nordstrom."

Sam landed a particularly impressive swing. Maybe he'd polish it off before Art had to put his shoulder through more stress.

"Hey."

Adam was standing a few feet away from Art and Lily. The sun beat down on the white sheet he was wearing over his scarred torso. The kid didn't smell great, but none of them did. He had soft almond eyes, and well-shaped cheek bones; a kind of beautiful face if you could look past the scraggly hairs hanging off his chin, his yellow teeth, and pimples.

"Hey kid," Art said, and nodded in the direction of Sam, who was still hacking with abandon. "Wanna take a few swings?"

Adam squinted at Sam, then turned back to Art.

"Do any of you know when lunch is? I'm famished."

Lily scoffed.

"Are you serious? Can't you see we're out here looking for food? Maybe you could actually *help*?"

"Oh. I'm sorry. Yes, tell me how to help," he said, finally joining them in the shade. He forced himself to smile, but something was clearly bothering him.

"What have you even been doing all morning?" Lily demanded. "You think you don't have to help out like everyone else?"

Adam looked terrified and confused by the accusation. "What is this," he said weakly, "the Spanish Inquisition?"

"The line is: 'Nobody expects the Spanish Inquisition,'" Art said

"Right," Adam, wiped some sweat from his face with a corner of the sheet, seeming to grow more and more distraught as this exchange progressed. "Now I remember."

"So maybe you also remember how you ended up on the bridge with all those burns?" Lily asked. "Or you still conveniently can't recall?"

"What?" Now his face melted into a puddle of utter confusion and he backed away from them. "Sorry. I'm sorry to have interrupted."

He disappeared around the corner of a stack of containers.

"Wow," Lily said. "What the hell. Something's seriously wrong with him."

"Reminds me of a guy who lived across the hall from me in Hell's Kitchen for a few months," Art replied. "Vietnam vet, I think. Not a bad guy, just a little detached. No sense of time and place. You can tell he's seeing everything different than you and me. That's all."

Art didn't see any need to mention to Lily that one night he got back late and his neighbor was waiting for him in the hall. In apparent seriousness, the Vietnam vet had threatened to devour Art's soul.

A powerful swing from Sam split the lock. A piece of metal clanged to the deck at Sam's feet. He turned to Art and Lily and gave a weary thumbs up. His face was a picture of agony.

"You're getting good at this, Sam," Art said. "Too good. We should let you do all the swinging."

"Sure," Sam said, breathing hard. He dropped the axe on the deck. "Art, you have the screwdriver?"

Art fished the flathead out of his pocket and tossed it to Sam, who snatched it out of the air with a meaty fist. Then the beast went to work prying the unlocked container door open.

"We can help..." said Lily. Sam dismissed her with his hand.

"It's fine," he muttered.

Art stood up, bent over, and tried to touch the tips of his Reeboks. He made it to his ankles, then straightened up, earning a gratifying pop.

"You believe in God, Lily?" he asked.

She shrugged.

"Could you ask Him for some vacuum-packed minute steaks, and maybe something from Pepperidge Farm for dessert?" Art asked jutting his chin in the direction of Sam, working in a slavish frenzy to access the contents of the green container. "I'd ask myself, but not sure my credit history's good enough to ask for a loan right now."

Sam heaved, and the crate door slid a few feet, opening up the dark entrance to the box.

"You guys go in," he wheezed. "I need some water."

The red-faced giant staggered to them, and collapsed against the side of a crate. Art handed Sam a blue water jug, and he sucked on it for a solid fifteen seconds.

"Are you okay?" Lily asked.

"Check the crate," he said between breaths. Sweat poured down his blocky face in rivulets.

Lily got the flashlight. Art pulled off his t-shirt in preparation for the stuffy crate.

"Sorry about the view guys," he said, gesturing toward his wrinkly gut and flabby chest, then headed into the crate. He stuck his head in. As expected, the inside was like a furnace. The still air smelled like plastic. Lily shined the flashlight over Art's right shoulder, illuminating an impenetrable wall of hollow white discs stacked from top to bottom, shielded by transparent plastic sheeting. Each disk was about three inches in diameter.

"What the hell is that?" she asked.

Art tore off enough plastic sheeting to reach his hand in. He recognized the texture from twenty-something years ago, when he'd created a piece that was half art installation, half fully functional thirty-foot bong.

"No food," he sighed, as he and Lily backed out of the crate. "PVC pipe. Great for plumbing, not for eating."

Sam's legs were splayed out on the deck. He looked at them despondent, already knowing the answer.

"Plastic pipes," said Art. "No go. Onto the next. I'll hack."

Sam clutched the axe to his chest.

"I'll do it," he said, but didn't sit up. "Art, wanna choose?"

Art almost laughed. Sam asked as if there was skill involved in the decision. The crates were all identical besides their color. It was like people thinking hard about roulette numbers. Except in this case, they weren't even sure there was a single winning option.

"I don't know," Art sighed. "I'm starting to realize, if we just find food, but no tobacco, I'm not sure I even want to go on anyway–"

They were interrupted by what Art initially took for a high-pitched scream. His adrenaline spiked and his shoulders stiffened.

It was a cheer. Whoops of delight. Applause. The three of them looked at each other. Were they hearing right or was this some sort of communal hallucination? Because it sure sounded like Mel was shouting: "Food! We found food!"

12

"Okay!" Mel burst into the captain's lounge wielding two steaming trays. Behind him came Vic carrying another two. Mel deposited the plates of food onto the oak tabletop, face flushed pink. He'd had to cook the food downstairs in the kitchen and carry it up, but nobody wanted to eat in that stuffy mess hall right now.

Elissa McClure leaned in for a whiff along with all the others. It smelled delightful. She looked from face to face, at her companions squeezed around the oak table, all smiling widely. There was energy in the room, the sort of manic camaraderie, that she'd seen in Friday meetings following an exceptionally good trading week. Enemies would clap each other on the back and laugh. All was forgiven until the market turned down again. And this was their on-board equivalent of a market surge: a container filled with sealed aluminum food packets, rations presumably bound for some third-world country.

At the head of the table, Lily shrieked in delight upon seeing the steaming spread. Art shook his head in disbelief of this turn of fortune. Bahram rubbed his hands together in anticipation.

"Fantastic," Doctor Rosalyn murmured.

"There's polenta and lentil daal," Mel explained. "Somebody liked yellow foods. Frankly there wasn't much cooking to do. All I really did was heat them up on the propane stove."

"Mel, don't be so humble!" laughed Greg. "You're a wizard!"

"I'm not..." Mel sighed. "Anyway. Enjoy."

Bahram instantly lunged for serving spoons. Art raised his hand and said.

"Wait, wait. Just a sec."

Bahram pulled back and gave Art a pleading look. Vic already had a pile of daal on his plate, and gripped his fork tightly as Art spoke.

"Before we dig in, let's give credit where credit is due. Greg—I don't know how the hell you spotted that Red Cross logo four containers up, but you might have just saved our lives."

Elissa nodded in agreement. "Really phenomenal, Greg."

Greg shrugged sheepishly.

"I got lucky, that's all."

"Greg is our hero!" declared Vic, pumping his fist.

Lily put her hand on Greg's chest. "Really amazing," she said, scarcely able to contain her glowing admiration.

Jennifer frowned. Something was bothering her.

"Guys!" Greg laughed. "We were all working out there. Anybody could have noticed it. It's no big deal! Enough of this. Let's eat!"

"Well, well, wait," Elissa said, "Maybe our local clergyman–" she nodded to Mel, "–would lead us in a quick grace before meals."

Elissa wasn't religious herself. She never prayed. But if there was ever a situation that called for it…

Mel cleared his throat.

"Alright."

Elissa sat down and extended her open palms to those on either side of her. Rosalyn's hands were coarse, and trembling from either anticipation or weakness. Bahram's were sweaty and strong.

Mel?" Elissa smiled. Mel was at the other head of the table, opposite her. He closed his eyes and in a deep, impassioned voice said:

"Blessed are You Lord, King of the Universe, who has provided us with this miraculous feast. Who has snatched us from the jaws of certain death, to deliver us to plenty…"

Elissa saw Vic biting his lip in agitation and gazing down at the daal already on his plate. This only reinforced to her the importance of this moment.

"…like *manna* in the desert to the unworthy Israelites, so we have been provided for—for no reason save Your abundant kindness. Blessed are You, Lord, King of the Universe, who has brought us to this day."

"Amen!" said Art, tickled pink. "Thanks, Rabbi."

Vic tentatively picked up the serving spoon.

"So can we…"

"Go ahead," said Elissa.

"*Avec plaisir*," Vic said. Those were the last words spoken for at least fifteen minutes.

Elissa waited while everyone else took food–a habit from years of corporate lunches. The men had always shown their weakness by rushing the buffet table. Millionaires acting like they hadn't eaten in days.

Just as she had then, she now sat with her arms folded, and waited patiently until she wouldn't have to compete for a serving utensil.

But in the end, Greg noticed that her plate was still empty, and ladled her out a portion of polenta and daal. Elissa smiled at him. Her heart was warmed. The people on board weren't perfect, but ultimately they were kind and generous. What else could you ask for?

And when she finally took a bite of polenta she almost cried from happiness. Had a forkful of food ever tasted so good?

Elissa was satisfied after just a few bites. She looked around the table at her companions. Vic chewed with his mouth open, and his exposed chest hair was already peppered with spilled yellow flecks.

Beside her, Bahram was crying tears of joy as he shoveled polenta into the slot between his jowls. Mel ate slowly and deliberately. Lily's appetite was astonishing. Jennifer, like Mel, ate slowly. But she wasn't savoring the food; she was more like a wary hyena on the savannah, looking up between bites to scan the horizon for rivals coming to butt in on her fresh kill.

Even Adam seemed to be happy. She looked at him from across the table until she got his attention, and smiled kindly. He seemed taken aback by this gesture. Suspicious. Elissa gave him a thumbs up and finally, with some discomfort, he pulled back his lips and bared his teeth in an approximation of a smile.

The cramped lounge was filled only with the sounds of heavy mastication and the clink of silverware–everyone too busy to talk. Vic continued to stuff his face with abandon.

Eventually Jennifer broke the spell. She'd had enough to eat and sat back in her chair clutching her stomach.

"About the grace before meals," she said. "Let's not make a habit of that please. Mel, I of course respect your right to do whatever you like on your own. But I have to say it makes me a little uncomfortable. I feel religious extremism was a big part of what led to everything."

Mel swallowed, seemed to consider arguing, but just nodded.

"Well. Something to think about," he said quietly.

Another few minutes of eating passed. The pace slowed, as everyone filled up. Elissa realized she should have cautioned everyone not to overdo it. On an empty stomach you could hurt yourself by eating too much. Once the meal seemed to be drawing to a close, Bahram wrapped his knuckles on the table and stood up.

He waited patiently until he had everyone's attention, then he put a hand on his chest.

"Bahram," he said.

Vic rolled his eyes and groaned. Bahram noticed and slammed his fist on the table, and barked something at the Frenchman. Then he took a deep breath, obviously willing himself to be calm. He had something to say, that was clear, and was trying a new approach.

"Bahram," he repeated, hand on his chest, "Afghani*stan*." He gestured to all the others: "*Amaireeka*," then again: "Afghani*stan*."

Elissa nodded dutifully, to show Bahram that she understood. He smiled, then continued.

"*Ad-um*," he pointed at Adam, who perked up suddenly, like he'd been caught sleeping in class. Then Bahram pretended to write on his own chest. "*Ad-um*."

Elissa tried to figure out what Bahram was saying–that Adam had numbers on his chest? Wasn't much of an insight.

Then Bahram launched into a furious, inscrutable pantomime. He kneeled behind a leather chair, peeked around the room, rushed to a wall and pushed himself flat against it pretending to struggle as if he was tied up.

"*Ad-um*," he repeated.

He rushed around, assuming awkward poses, each supplemented with an indecipherable word or two. It was impossible to follow. He was terrible at this.

"Bahram…" Jennifer said., "Can you slow down?"

Elissa waved to get Bahram's attention. If he had something to tell them about Adam, it was important that they understand.

"Bahram," she said. Then motioned with her hands: *easy, easy*.

He froze mid-pose, kneeling, pretending to struggle with a heavy object–and gazed at his deeply confused audience.

"*Man Hamarah Bidam*," he said, then insisted: "*Man Hamarah Bidam*."

"What language is he speaking?" asked Sam. "Arab?"

"Most people in Afghanistan speak Dari. It's a Persian language," said Elissa.

"Man Hamarah Bidam."

Elissa shook her head helplessly. Bahram stood up straight, looking around, realizing that nobody had absorbed a single thing. He clenched his teeth and clutched the sides of his bowling ball head so hard it looked like he might twist it off.

"Man Hamarah Bidam!" he pleaded, *"Man Hamarah Bidam. Psaray Sta Buse Ad-um."*

Vic sighed.

"I'm going to get some rest."

"Psaray. Psar…" Bahram repeated, seized by yet another level of anguish.   Voice cracking, he now gestured to his genitals, and repeated. *"Psar."*

Rosalyn grimaced. "Is he talking about Adam soiling himself?"

"No, no, he's not. He's gesturing to his loins. I know this word…" Mel closed his eyes and tugged furiously on his beard. Elissa imagined Mel walking the long corridors of his mind, searching for one little dusty book among millions. Then his eyes flew open. He'd found it. *"Ibn?* Is that what you're trying to say? *Ibn?"*

"Balee!" Bahram responded, more relieved than pleased. *"Abnay. Abnay. Abnay."*

Everyone turned to Mel, confused.

"You speak his language?" asked Greg. "Persian or whatever?"

"No. But I know a handful of words in Arabic, because of the overlap with Aramaic. And Bahram seems to as well."

"Abnay! Abnay!" Bahram repeated forcefully.

"So what the hell is he saying?" asked Art.

"Abnay means 'my son' in Arabic," Mel said.

Art raised an eyebrow

"What about his son?"

Mel shrugged.

"Your guess is as good as mine."

13

"I don't know which one creeps me out more," Lily said. "Adam, the terrorist, or the Arab guy. He seems super unsteady right?"

Greg rubbed his biceps. Lily and Vic were in his cabin. They'd followed him in instead of going into their own rooms, as if the three of them were old friends. Christ almighty. He'd known them for less than forty-eight hours. He wanted them gone. He wanted to be alone.

Did he though? Sometimes having company was better. Being alone for the last week had been bad too. He shuddered.

"It seems like the Arab guy and Adam are in on something together. And why are we just pretending like it's no big deal about those burns? It's a *huge* deal!"

Lily's yammering was like a jackhammer in his ear. She was possibly even worse than Allison Gregory, who'd been referred to as Allison *Gagory* by almost everyone she'd ever worked with. It was never clear whether that meant she was so obnoxious that she made you gag, or that she was so obnoxious you wanted to gag her into silence.

When they were together on the set of *Loony Bin*, she kept making jokes about how if they got married he could change his name and be Greg Gregory. That girl had the worst fucking sense of humor he'd ever seen. And when he was banging her in his trailer she made the weirdest sounds. That whole thing was a nightmare. Afterwards he'd felt so dirty he sat on the floor of the shower for what felt like an hour. He'd felt sick. Actually, he felt kind of sick right now. And now he couldn't stop thinking about Allison Gregory's flushed face looking up at him with some kind of admiration or worship, like she was having a spiritual experience on the couch of his trailer in the twenty-minute break between takes, and it was making him *sick* and he wanted to be alone.

I'm also disturbed by the young man's burns," Vic said. "But he's small and harmless."

"Harmless? He might be one of them, Vic. He's got their logo on his chest!"

Greg's heart was beating too fast and the room was spinning a little. He needed to lie down. Why wouldn't they leave him alone?

"Heh," Greg heard himself chuckle. "Definitely quite a weird one. But I'm sure we'll figure it out."

There were no rules on this ship. Greg hadn't really thought about that before, when they were all hungry, but now he was thinking about it. It was weird. He could do all sorts of things without consequences. He could steal someone's shoes. He could smack Jennifer on the ass. He could pee on the carpet in the captain's lounge. He didn't *want* to do any of these things–he was a good guy–but it was weird to think that he could. The only real potential consequence of anything was that Sam could decide to hurt you. When it came down to it, whatever Sam said was law because he could crush the skull of anyone on board with one hand.

Skull.

Greg thought about the family he'd seen in that restaurant. That was an even worse image than Allison Gregory in the throes of ecstasy. What used to be a family inside what used to be a restaurant. But everything was burnt. Everything in the whole restaurant was cooked to a crisp, including the family of four. But they hadn't fallen out of their chairs. The four of them were still sitting around what was left of the table, like they were wondering when their food was gonna come.

"What if Adam tries to poison us?" Lily said. "The kitchen is right there in the open!"

"That kid's nuttier than Mister Goodbar on crack," Greg said. It was a line from *Lawn Elves* that hadn't made the final cut. Nobody would recognize it.

Vic laughed.

"Crack, wow," he said. "Listen, Lily. I understand why you're concerned, but look at him: he's no terrorist. He's confused and scared."

Vic and Lily were here, Greg realized, because they didn't want to be alone.

Oh fuck. That was the worst part. He did it a second time. For a whole week Greg had avoided Allison's eyes, except when the script called for it. Then, after he'd had a couple shots of Jack in his hotel room he called her and asked where she was, then drove to *her* hotel and knocked on the door with a bottle of expensive champagne. Why?? He *hated* her! She let him in and asked tentatively if it was going to be like last time where he just zipped up and ignored her after, and he'd put his hand on her shoulder and been like *I'm so sorry about that…*

"Oh my god. You're so naive," Lily said. "I'm telling you we gotta keep an eye on that weirdo day and night. What happens when someone murders their whole family? The neighbor always says the same thing: 'he was quiet and kept to himself, seemed like a nice guy.' Guess what–I think that guy's a *ticking fucking time bomb*. It's like Greg said: maybe he was tied up for a *reason?*"

Vic pursed his dry lips.

"Perhaps we'll discuss it tomorrow morning. At breakfast."

"Greg?" Lily demanded. "What do you say?"

"Greg," Vic said. "Surely you agree to proceed patiently?"

Who *were* these people? They were like puppets, and someone offstage was doing the voices, alternating between a thick French accent and Lily's skull-shattering mosquito whine.

That family was probably still sitting there. Most of their skin had burned off, but one of the little boys had had enough of a mouth left for it to look like he was kind of smiling.

"One hundred percent," Greg said, not even recalling the question.

Vic nodded knowingly.

Lily was sitting next to him on the bed and their thighs were touching. How long had that been happening? The truth was Greg never liked to be touched, even though he acted like he did. When Allison Gregory opened his belt buckle in that hotel room during their second tryst and settled any uncertainty about her moniker, Greg had to resist the urge to squirm uncomfortably. Then he was back on top of her and… Yes, that was what had bothered him so much: the expression on her face was *exactly the same* as it had been in the trailer. Mouth a little O, eyebrows high, like she both feared and revered him, like she was looking up into the face of God… But it was a *sham*! He'd had the overwhelming sensation that he was banging a silicone sex doll, with preprogrammed pleasure expressions. And the Allison Gregory doll had misinterpreted what must have been an expression of distaste on his face and, ironically, vamped up her performance, wrapping her skinny legs around his ass, and making those weird sounds again, only strengthening his suspicion that she wasn't a real person, just a hyper-realistic replicant.

"Well I still think we should really tie him up," Lily declared. "Like chain him to a bed."

What a relief it had been to peel himself off Allison Gregory and excuse himself to go into the bathroom.

Are you okay Greg?

Never better!

Well hurry back and spoon me.

He'd sat on the floor of the hotel room shower with the water as hot it would go, to burn off her chemical smells and synthetic fluids. He stuck his fingers in his ears to drown out the sound of her knocking on the bathroom door, asking if everything was okay. He was trapped in that bathroom… He absolutely, positively, could not go back out there and pretend everything was cool and spoon her. The thought of touching her made him sick. Sick, sick, *sick*. Now he was really dizzy.

"Guys, I'm going to close my eyes for a few hours," Greg said. "Let's talk in the morning."

Vic stood up. "Of course."

Lily didn't move. Her thigh was still touching him.

Please, please, please leave.

If she didn't stop touching him he was going to explode.

"Lily?" he smiled. "Mind if I get a little peace and quiet?"

"Oh, right," she blushed and stood up. Tried to compose herself.

"Ciao guys!" Greg said.

"Sleep peacefully," Vic said.

Lily took one last look at Greg, then turned and reluctantly followed Vic out of the cabin, closing the door behind her.

Greg exhaled. He finally had space. Although now his room felt cramped. And beyond this room, he was trapped on this boat with ten insane puppets. None of this made sense. How did these people manage to get on board while millions of others died? How did the Arab guy get here? He didn't speak a word of English. It made *no sense!*

Greg laughed out loud as something occurred to him: it was all a setup. Everyone else was in on it. He was like Harry in *Harry Down the Chimney Tonight,* in the scene towards the end where he finds out that he never really lost his job as manager at an insurance company, that actually all his friends, family, boss, and coworkers were in cahoots to make him think that he had, so he'd be forced to dress up as Santa and deliver presents to sick kids, and learn a valuable lesson about the importance of family.

The room was so hot it seemed possible that the mattress he was sitting on was melting.

He'd never liked the way Harry acted in that final scene, laughing with relief and hugging everyone. Greg always thought if he'd really been Harry–not just playing him–he'd have gone ballistic. Especially because after something like that, how could you ever be sure you weren't in another similar scenario? What if he got fired again? Would he take it seriously? He'd have to wonder if *everything* that happened to him from then on was just another elaborate prank.

Greg felt ill. What if the world was fine? Everything was normal. The family in the restaurant had just been CGI or something, and now they were all out on this boat thinking the world had ended.

Or everybody else on the boat was also in on it. He wasn't sure which way made more sense.

Another croaky laugh gurgled from his throat. He couldn't tell if he was joking with himself or not. The family in the restaurant. Allison Gregory. Greg, as Harry, trudging through the blinding snow to the hospital, wondering what he'd done to deserve every single aspect of his life suddenly falling apart.

Despite the heat, Greg wrapped his head in a blanket to block out the light from the window.

14

Bahram Nasim sat with the young woman with brown hair. Her long name was like a slippery candy he couldn't quite keep on his tongue: *Yenfor*.

They were in the mess hall at a lunch table. He was exhausted from fruitless hours attempting to communicate with these people–the man with the funny black skullcap and beard, the old woman. It turned out the bearded man only knew maybe a dozen words in Arabic besides *Abn*, and things had only gotten more frustrating after that small revelation. Bahram provided them with hours of pantomime, but they were too dense or stubborn to internalize the most obvious of movements. It was useless and aggravating beyond measure.

So he abandoned hope of explaining the very strange things he'd seen over the past month and concentrated on just explaining what his son, Azzami, had told him about Adam:

He needs to be tied to something at all times.

Like an animal?

No, no. More like a blade of grass. If it is not connected to the earth, it will just blow away.

I don't understand.

It's okay, Father. Just… don't even try to interact with him. He's not like us. He belongs to another world.

But these Americans were thick. They couldn't even grasp that it was important to keep Adam secured, and Bahram soon felt like he was explaining arithmetic to a herd of donkeys. And he could tell that when he got even a bit worked up, they became dismissive; wrote him off as hysterical. Eventually Bahram had seen no choice but to take Adam by the elbow, intending to lead him back to the bridge and show the others that they should re-anchor him to the stool. This really

                                    E.Z. Rinsky

spooked the donkeys. They hadn't allowed him to touch Adam since, and he could see in their eyes that they were starting to suspect he was a madman.

But who was really mad? How long did the donkeys intend to keep floating out here in the middle of the sea? He knew there'd been some kind of war, and so it made sense to wait it out a bit–but for how long? Bahram was getting worried. As happy as he was to have food in his belly, finding those packets only meant it would be that much longer until they got to this place that his son, Azzami, had told him about, and from there perhaps he could finally get back to his family and friends in Afghanistan.

The memories of his lost son and wife, Keti, were twin knots in his stomach. Perhaps the hardest part was that he was unable to mourn them properly, with a feast and the rest of the family. And he'd never had a chance to call anyone back home to tell them what was happening...

"Bahram?" said *Yenfor*.

He was very tired. When she'd interrupted his nap before he assumed it was for something urgent–maybe Adam had gone berserk, and the donkeys realized they owed him an apology. But the only emergency was dragging him down to the dining room for another unpromising attempt at communication, this time by drawing images on a piece of paper.

"Bahram?" she repeated, and handed him the pencil. She'd drawn a simple smiling face and, it seemed, wanted him to do the same. Fine. He'd give it a try, though he couldn't remember the last time he'd drawn anything; certainly not since he stopped his formal education at the age of twelve. His only use for pencils for at least five decades was tallying inventory and sales of carpets. Bahram tried to replicate her illustration. She frowned at his attempt. Bahram had to admit it was quite poor.

Yenfor gave him an encouraging smile, like he was a small child. Bahram considered that there was something fundamental about America which generated a unique brand of donkey-headed arrogance.

Then she drew the image that was on Adam's sternum: the two faces looking away from each other, and gazed at Bahram meaningfully, as if hoping he could explain it to her.

"*Abnay?*" she asked.

He looked up at her, into her green eyes. He nodded. Was she starting to understand?

Five weeks ago he'd stepped foot in America for the first time in his life. He landed in JFK International Airport with his wife, Keti, and was greeted at baggage claim by his second oldest son, Azzami. He pulled his son into an embrace, kissed him on both cheeks, barely able to contain his tears of joy. It was the first time he'd seen Azzami in nine years.

Keti made no effort to control herself. She dried her tears on the sleeve of her son's shiny jacket. Strange American clothing, Bahram thought. He rubbed the slippery sleeve of his son's jacket between his fingers.

What is this? It looks like what they wear in space.

It's actually made in Japan. They make the best clothing.

And then it was time to dispatch with the small talk.

So, where is she? Where is this woman—your fiancée? You didn't bring her?

Azzami's smile wavered for a moment.

Come. I'm parked outside. I'll explain everything.

Keti looked at Bahram, worried. In retrospect, his wife had realized just how wrong everything was much sooner than he had.

Azzami led them to a beautiful blue car with leather seats. Bahram and Keti sat in the back together. Bahram couldn't stop running his hands over the rich leather. He loved America already.

Azzami. Aren't you going to ask your father how his business is going?

I'm sorry. Father, how is business at your carpet store?

Very difficult. I'm struggling to keep up with demand!

Bahram laughed and slapped his knee. These days, he was lucky to sell a carpet every two months. Nobody wanted to buy carpets anymore. His son didn't laugh at the joke.

Wonderful to hear.

Azzami was distracted, distant. Keti squeezed Bahram's arm tighter. He knew she was worried. Why wasn't Azzami telling them about his fiancée? About the wedding arrangements? They drove for over an hour in silence. This was how a son treated his parents, after nine years without a visit?

This is New York?

Yes.

Bahram had seen New York a few times on TV, but nothing could have prepared him for this. The tops of the buildings were so high that he lost them in the sun. Glowing signs everywhere with words Bahram wished he could read.

Perhaps most shocking were the people. Their dress was fantastic: plumed hats, skirts made–like Azzami's jacket–of wondrous materials he'd never seen before, boots with pointed heels as long as his forearm. People of all colors too. White people, he expected. But not so many Blacks and Chinamen.

Azzami? I thought the Blacks lived in the south of America.

In the front seat, his son made a strange sound.

No, Father.

They kept driving, until the buildings grew more modest. Factories and parking lots.

This is still New York, Azzami?

Azzami didn't respond to his mother. Bahram felt a rush of rage. Had his son forgotten all of his manners? Had this country stripped him of the values Bahram had drilled into all eight of his children: respect for elders, hard work, modesty…

He suddenly decided that in fact he hated this country. Behind all the glitz and noise, this place was empty.

It had been three hours since they left the airport, and it was almost evening. Something was wrong. Why were they still driving? Was New York this big? Keti asked him:

Azzami, we've been driving so long. Can you stop so I can refresh myself?

No response. Rage stirred again in Bahram's chest.

Azzami, did you hear your mother? Take us somewhere she can wash!

Wordlessly, Azzami pulled the car off the main road, into a petrol station unlike any Bahram had ever seen. In addition to the pumps there was a brightly-lit night market. Azzami turned off the ignition.

I'll take you inside, Mother. I'm sure there's a washroom in there.

Bahram sat alone in the silent car for a few moments, watching his son and wife inside of the night market. Then Azzami returned to the car, to wait while Keti finished. Again, his son was quiet. Did he really have nothing to say to his father after all this time? He hadn't said a single word about his fiancée.

When will we meet her, Azzami? From everything you said on the phone, she sounds so lovely.

Azzami tapped his slender fingers on the steering wheel. He'd always had such delicate hands. His mother's hands.

Father, there is no fiancée. There's no wedding. Please don't tell Mother yet. It will make her so upset.

Bahram felt like he'd been punched in the stomach.

What? She broke the engagement?

A long silence.

No. Nothing like that.

Bahram was about to demand answers when Keti emerged from the washroom inside, looking disoriented.

Go help your mother. We'll discuss this soon.

Azzami rushed inside to help Keti, and when they returned to the car Azzami was cradling a few bottles of water, and some brightly colored bags.

Here, try these.

His son was smiling purely for the first time since meeting them at the airport. For just an instant Bahram recognized his second oldest son, the boy he'd thought most likely to one day take over the carpet store. The boy had a good heart, but had always been troubled. Mathematics and reading were struggles for him. He was clumsy at sports, often outmaneuvered even by his younger brothers when they played football. He'd shown a fleeting interest in cooking, but Keti and his sisters didn't have patience for his frequent mistakes.

So Bahram decided Azzami would be the one to take over the family business. He'd patiently taught the boy to restore old beautiful carpets by mending the fringes, scraping off oil stains, gently rubbing a mixture of boiling water and vinegar to clean and reinvigorate. But even at this, the boy was useless, and he ruined several fine pieces before Bahram decided to stop the lessons.

So it hadn't been a surprise to Bahram–in fact it had been something of a relief–when Azzami announced to them that he was moving to America. He'd met an American at a restaurant in town who offered him a job doing construction in New York, and promised he would even arrange lodging. He had no illusions that it would be glamorous work, Azzami assured his parents, but it would be a good opportunity. Maybe something would come of it. Keti too, had been obviously relieved. Finally Azzami had found something to do with himself.

They had a sending off party for him. Bahram took him off to the side at some point and kissed him on the forehead. He told his son that he was very proud of him, that hard work was good for the spirit, and that fate had sent this American to their city to show Azzami his way.

They spoke on the phone. More at the beginning, and then less and less. Bahram took this as a hopeful sign: it meant his son was busy. And when finally Azzami called and told them he was getting married, and he was going to pay for his parents to come to America to meet his fiancée, Bahram and Keti hugged and wept with joy. They'd never worried about their other children like they had about Azzami. And now that he'd be wed, a great weight had been lifted from their chests.

Barham's son was smiling as he handed him a colorful foil bag he'd bought from the night market.

Try these Father. You're going to love them.

It's not sweets is it? You know I don't like sweets.

I know.

Bahram opened the bag.

Are they potato chips?

Not quite.

They were small tubular bits of dough dusted in some sort of yellow-green powder. Bahram tentatively popped one into his mouth. He closed his eyes and bit in. In an instant, all the anger at his son, at this god-forsaken country, melted away.

What are they?

Pretzels. Honey-mustard flavor.

Bahram gripped his son by the collar.

My Son. This is the most delicious thing I've ever tasted.

They drove many more hours. Bahram drifted in and out of sleep, as did Keti beside him. This whole thing was very strange. There was no fiancée, but what could they do? Neither of them spoke a word of English, or had any idea where they were. Besides, they trusted their son.

Azzami tapped his parents awake. It was the middle of the night, and he'd parked outside some sort of residence.

Father, Mother. Come, we're sleeping in this hotel. You can have a real bed.

Azzami took their bags for them, and they wordlessly followed him into the building. They watched him converse with a woman behind a counter, not understanding a word. Then he gave her some bills, and the woman gave him a key.

Azzami picked the bags back up, and they followed him out of reception, up an exterior staircase, into a drab room with a single queen size bed.

I'm sorry, I need to save my money so I only took one room tonight. I will sleep on the floor of course.

Keti could stand it no more. She took a step toward her son, and touched his shoulder.

Azzami, what's going on here? Where is your fiancée? Why are we staying in some hotel? I thought you had an apartment!

Suddenly, unexpectedly, Azzami sat down on the edge of the bed and burst into tears.

Keti sad beside him, putting her arms around him.

You can tell us darling. Whatever it is. We're your parents. We love you.

He shook his head, sniffing.

Something very bad is going to happen.

Keti furrowed her brow

What do you mean, dear? What's going to happen?

Azzami's eyes were red.

There will be a war soon. Destruction like you cannot imagine.

What? Son, I don't understand.

I know, I know. You don't have to. All you have to know is I'm taking you two somewhere where you'll be safe. The only place. Now, get some rest.

I don't understand. Where is your fiancée?

Azzami stood up.

I'm not getting married. I'm sorry I lied to you, Mother. It was the only way you would come to America.

Keti shook her head, shocked, unable to speak, but Bahram put a steadying hand on his wife's shoulder. No good would come of pushing their son now, he could see.

I'm sure whatever Azzami did, he had a good reason. Let's just sleep, like he suggested.

Keti and Bahram crawled into bed, both too exhausted to take off their clothes. They heard Azzami in the bathroom, washing his face, spitting. Keti's eyes were wide and sad.

What's happening Bahram? Do you understand?

No. I don't.

Is he unwell? Should we tell somebody? Get him some help?

How? We don't even know how to call the police in this country. And even if we did, we couldn't talk to them.

Keti started to cry softly. Bahram patted her on the back.

It's okay. He's our son. I trust him.

Azzami emerged from the bathroom. He'd taken off his shirt. Before he flicked off the lamp Bahram saw that there was some kind of burn or tattoo on his son's chest. An image of two faces looking away from each other.

15

"By my estimation," Elissa said, "there's enough food in that container to last us four to five months. However, water is a different story. I inspected the water tanks this morning. Now there *is* a desalination system, meaning we can convert ocean water into drinking water, but it requires a lot of energy, so it can only run when the engines are on. Currently there are roughly six hundred liters of water in the tank. So, assuming no desalination, and a liter and a half per person per day, which isn't much in this heat, we have about thirty-eight days of potable water."

"We can desalinate ourselves," Rosalyn said. "It won't be efficient– but we can set something up using the metal bowls, and make a fire I think."

"A short term fix," Mel replied. "We'll have to keep finding things to burn."

"Everything now is a short term fix," Jennifer said.

Elissa bit her lip.

"Desalinating ourselves can work, but we'll still need the alkaline system that adds minerals to the water after it's purified," she said. "Plain desalinated seawater doesn't have any of the salts or minerals you need, and eventually it can actually dehydrate you. We'll cross that bridge when we get to it, I suppose. In the meantime, we'll just continue sending out distress signals on the radio, and monitoring all the channels."

Sam Arnold leaned back further in the leather chair, until he hit an angle where his hernia stopped throbbing. These four had been discussing the autopilot system, water, food, fuel supply, and even the weather. It seemed to Sam like they were purposely avoiding the most urgent issue: how to deal with Adam? It was obvious to Sam what had happened: Adam was in the DOJ and had done something bad like snitched. Burning him and tying him up on the bridge was his punishment.

"I don't know if a liter and a half a day is enough," Mel said.

Sam was growing weary of this chitchat. He was a man of action, not words. And the worst kind of words were when people beat around the bush. Just say what you want to say! This impatience was one reason he'd lasted only a week as a waiter at Café Roma, a restaurant the Cincinnati Enquirer once described as 'decent fare for the price'.

How is the veal parmesan?

It's really good.

So you recommend it?

Yes.

How's the chicken cacciatore?

Not good. I ate it last week for dinner and felt really sick after. Do you want the veal?

So they moved Sam to the kitchen. He spent the next year bent over the sink at Café Roma, listening to the three guys on the food prep line make the same jokes every hour of every day.

You see the brunette at table six?

Oh yeah. I'm gonna make her Alfredo extra creamy.

It was like the food prep guys' mouths just moved on their own, spewing mindless drivel on autopilot. One day, finally, he bought a pair of headphones, thinking he could at least retreat into some Pink Floyd while his face and hands were blasted with that wretched amalgam of steam, soap, and flecks of unfinished Italian food. His shift manager hadn't approved.

No headphones on the job

Why?

We're a team Sam. We need all communication channels to be open.

But Sam hardly communicated with anyone in that kitchen. The busboys stacked the soiled dishes in the queue to his left, and Sam scraped them, sprayed them with a high-powered nozzle, dunked them in a mix of hot water and cleaning solution, a cool bath for a rinse, then out to the fourteen-year old boy on his right who dried them with a towel and stacked them for reuse. Sam didn't argue though; if he got fired he was screwed. Instead for a month he imagined that every plate was the shift manager's head, and when he dunked it in the hot water he was drowning him.

"I think a liter and a half a day is sufficient," Elissa said. "Especially if we get on a schedule where we take siestas and rest during the hotter hours–"

"–What about Adam?" Sam blurted. Elissa, Mel, Rosalyn and Jennifer turned to him. He felt himself blushing. "I mean. Look, we gotta talk about him. And I'm just saying our food and water would last longer if there were only ten of us–"

"Sam..." Mel started.

"Now let me finish," Sam said, starting to feel a little confidence. "I'm just talking about justice here. Because I figure that guy is a member of the organization that blew up my home town, and everyone in it. So I'm having a hard time seeing why we should be sharing our food and water with him."

Doctor Rosalyn looked at him with something like disappointment, which was an ice pick in Sam's heart. He wanted her to like him. She wasn't beautiful or anything. There was nothing physically exceptional about her narrow face, short brown hair, slightly ruddy complexion, or average build. It was the way she talked. She had confidence in herself. Every woman Sam had ever been with had eventually ended up admitting, one way or another, that they thought of themselves as a piece of trash. Those were the women he ended up with. The charity cases. He'd convince them to stop taking painkillers, and he'd get close with their kids, and help them apply to jobs, and by the time he'd want to break it off they needed him so badly that he didn't feel like he could. It would drag on for months, him feeling horrible every time he looked at the kid he was about to abandon.

"Let's not go down that road," Doctor Rosalyn said.

Mel nodded. "Personally, I very much doubt that he was an actual member of a terrorist organization. As Elissa mentioned, the DOJ regularly engaged in this sort of human graffiti on civilians. He's almost certainly a victim."

"The Daughters of January were very sophisticated," Elissa added. "Quite honestly, Adam doesn't seem to have the wherewithal to have been a member of an elite terrorist organization."

"Honestly, you suggesting we should kill someone is more disturbing than anything Adam's done," said Jennifer.

"I'm not saying he should *die*," Sam pleaded, really regretting opening his stupid mouth. He leaned forward in the chair, momentarily forgetting about his hernia. Something folded the wrong way and a sharp pain shot through his abdomen. "Just, well look at it this way. Every drop of water we give him is one we're taking out of somebody else's mouth."

"Not giving him food and water," Mel replied calmly, "is morally indistinguishable from executing him."

"Yeah, well..." Sam didn't know what to say. He felt his face burning. He wasn't smart enough to convince them of anything and, moreover, he wasn't even sure he believed what he'd said. The more he thought about his theory that Adam was a high-level terrorist, the stupider it sounded. This always happened to him. He always said stuff he wished he could take back.

"Sam, the Daughters of January didn't bomb your hometown. You have to educate yourself a little about what really happened," Jennifer said, smiling like it was funny how little Sam knew. "They didn't actually kill a single person. All they did was mess with a Russian radar, to make the Russians think there were missiles headed for Moscow. All the bombs, gas, and plant stuff were made by the Russians, Chinese, and yeah, guess what: the US Government. If you're going to talk about *justice*–"

"Dear, I don't think that's an entirely accurate portrayal of how it unfolded," Elissa said gently, in the same sort of patronizing tone Jennifer had just taken when talking to Sam. He was relieved the attention had momentarily shifted away from him. "First of all, the Daughters of January are a splinter group of Green Future, which despite their innocuous name, were labeled an eco-terrorist organization by the US Department of Defense. Three years ago, Green Future attempted to hack into the Nasdaq's backend to manipulate stock prices. If they'd succeeded they would have done unspeakable harm. They would have destroyed *billions* or even *trillions* of dollars worth of value."

"Yeah I know about that," Jennifer snapped. "And whatever. Who cares. A stock price is just a number on a screen that represents the ungodly profits of some corrupt company, and the people hurt would have been millionaire traders trying to make even more money for their billionaire tax-evading clients. And everyone knows the prices would have been corrected within like an hour anyway. It was a statement about corporate greed which I happen to agree with."

Sam was losing this thread, specifically who agreed with him about splitting the food ten ways instead of eleven.

Elissa peered at Jennifer over the top of her glasses. Her eyes were cold and sharp.

"I don't think you understand very much about economics, finance, or the world in general, dear. That's forgivable. You're young. I don't think you understand that the New York Stock Exchange may well be–have been, I should say–mankind's greatest creation. It was the engine of nearly two centuries of unprecedented innovation. It was the beating heart that kept the American Dream alive–that with the click of a mouse you could buy a *share* of someone else's venture, become their partner, even vote in their quarterly meetings." Elissa paused to cough. "But it was all built on an illusion. Castles in the sky, the great economist John Maynard Keyes observed. Built on mutual trust and trust in the institution, that if you buy a share you'll still own that share tomorrow. That's what made it such a phenomenon, it was all built on people *trusting each other*. And what Green Future attempted to do was to destroy that trust. It was an attempted attack on much more than a number on a screen. It would have threatened the bedrock of America. The fallout would have been disastrous. Now–" Elissa again paused, this time to take a sip of water. Jennifer looked irritated by all of this, but didn't jump in to interrupt. Maybe because she didn't have a good retort. Or maybe, like Sam, she didn't quite follow anything Elissa was saying.

"Now," Elissa resumed. "Now we were talking about the Daughters of January. The group that splintered off from Green Future because the latter was *too conservative*. They took it a step further. While Green Future simply wanted to reform capitalism–their attack was presumably an attempt to redistribute wealth, to shift power back to the worker, to ensure that industry was moving in an environmentally friendly direction–the DOJ wanted to *destroy* all of this. I saw one of their videos. Their rhetoric was so extreme it was practically laughable, at the time. And I find it irrelevant that the weapons eventually used were developed by governments for defense. It was the DOJ's intent to provoke precisely this type of disaster, and they succeeded. They instigated a chain of events that would lead to absolute destruction. For all intents and purposes, they *were* the ones who dropped the bombs on Sam's hometown."

Sam waited a moment to make sure she was done, and then said:

"You guys are right about Adam. I didn't really think it through. Sorry. How do you know all that stuff about stocks?" he asked Elissa. "Were you a stock broker?"

Elissa seemed amused by this question.

"Sort of," she said. "I was at WhiteBridge for twenty-three years. Most recently I was running an equities floor."

"WhiteBridge?" Sam asked.

Jennifer answered: "It's a big soul-sucking corporate entity that made rich people richer, and empowered the white Christian patriarchy."

Elissa chuckled.

"I don't recall ever getting a call from the patriarchy asking for help."

Sam turned gingerly to look out the window of the lounge. Based on the position of the sun, it was probably about two in the afternoon. The heat of the day. He agreed it would probably be wise to get in the habit of taking siestas.

And then what?

The prospect of tomorrow suddenly terrified him. He'd wake up and there would be thirty-seven days of water instead of thirty-eight and he'd sit around all day thinking about what they'd do after that. He could hack the locks off of containers. Best case he'd find more food and water, which would extend their deadline, but not really change anything fundamental about their situation. He was already restless after just a few hours of inactivity. He'd fought to get to this ship, pushed his body to its absolute limit–past that limit, in fact. And only now he thought to ask: why?

16

Art Roselli sat at the bow of the ship alone.

He'd used a fire axe to take some chunks out of one of the wood crates. The cheap pine wasn't ideal for whittling, and the fruit knife he found in the kitchen wasn't as fine as it should be. But his hands still moved dexterously, shaving off thin slivers, spinning the block in his hand. A blur of action. He barely even had to watch his fingers.

He took a deep breath of salty air. He thought he might taste a hint of smoke on it, but that could easily be his imagination.

The piece of pine in his hands was starting to look like a bishop–the last of the pieces he needed. The moment Mel mentioned that he used to play chess, Art sprang into action. He'd been working for four or five hours now. He hoped Mel was decent. A good opponent would go a long way toward passing the time. If Mel disappointed, further prospects were dreary. Elissa was sharp. She was probably the next best bet. Bahram probably grew up with backgammon, not chess. Adam? Art laughed softly to himself. He'd actually played chess a few times with that neighbor in Hell's Kitchen–the Vietnam vet. What was his name? Edgar? He was a good player during his more lucid moments. But too often he'd lose his concentration and talk nonsense, or make illegal moves as "jokes" and ruin the game. Then, of course, he'd offered to devour Art's soul, and that felt like an effective declaration that he wasn't interested in any further chess sessions. Edgar had been arrested for indecent exposure a few weeks later anyway.

Art was shocked by how quick his shipmates were to dismiss the GPS coordinates burned onto Adam's chest as nonsense. Considering their lack of any solid options, it sure seemed silly not to at least try to learn more about how those burns got there.

His hands worked without thinking. The piece was already taking shape. He wondered if he could reasonably play chess against himself–maybe taking enough time between moves to forget what his strategy had been for the other side.

Art sighed. Was that it? Was he giving up? Just gonna spend the last few weeks of his life trying to outsmart himself? He'd worked like a maniac getting to the coast. The moment he saw the news anchor's face he knew what they were dealing with. And at age sixty-two, he'd felt that rush for the first time in decades. The drive for survival. He was shocked to watch himself tear through his Miami penthouse with abandon, ripping oil paintings off the wall to find the concealed safe he hadn't opened for years. How had he immediately understood he'd never see his apartment again? Suddenly the designer furniture–a Burtini couch he'd bought from a collector for five figures, a teak table he'd had flown in from Peru–just looked ridiculous to him. How could he have a million dollars worth of furniture in his house, and no canned food or bottled water?

Even in his trance, he recalled the combination to the safe with ease. 17-11-37-2. The numbers of the two horses–*Gravy Train* and *Abigail's Dream* respectively–and the odds against for a first and second place finish for the two of them. 372/1. You don't forget numbers like that.

He took the three gold bars and the cash, stuffed them into a burlap sack, and rushed out of the apartment, not even bothering to lock it. Down three floors were boring old Larry and Barbara Coleman. Art beat on the door. Fucking Barbara took forever to shuffle over.

Who is it?

 Art saw the peephole go dark.

Arthur Roselli. The queen from upstairs.

Is everything alright?

You think I'd actually visit you two stiffs if everything was alright?

Yeah. Everything's great. Just wanted to talk.

Barbara took what felt like an eternity to undo all the locks. Someone across the hall had the TV on loudly, and though Art couldn't make out the words, the tone confirmed that he was making the right call here.

Arthur! What a pleasant surprise. Come on in. Can I get you something to drink? Larry is out at the club at the moment.

Art opened the burlap sack and pulled out a wad of hundreds. Trying to sound as reasonable as he could, he explained that he wanted to buy her Range Rover on the spot. In cash. She seemed confused.

I don't understand what you're talking about.

This isn't complicated. That car costs eighty grand brand new. I'm offering you ninety in cash. How much gas is in the tank? I'll give you ninety-five if you have a full tank of gas.

Our car? Arthur is this some kind of joke?

No joke. How much gas is in the tank?

I... I filled it up yesterday. But... Arthur this is very unusual. I'll have to speak to Larry of course.

This offer expires in exactly one minute.

Arthur, you're scaring me. What's going on?

That was when Art realized her TV wasn't on. She hadn't seen the news. She didn't know that California had ceased to exist, nor that the United States was already retaliating. This was ethically dubious territory. Art hadn't checked, but it was a fair bet that as of ten minutes ago, the US dollar was a less reliable store of value than beef jerky, condoms, or gasoline. In a sense, he was offering her worthless paper for the chance to get to some kind of fallout shelter. On one hand, it was sort of theft. On the other hand, asymmetrical information is pretty common in many sorts of business transactions: when a coffee shop sells someone an iced coffee for four bucks, they are under no obligation to disclose that it cost them twenty cents to produce it.

Also, Art had never really cared for Barbara Coleman.

I'll make it one-twenty. One hundred twenty thousand dollars cash. Here. Look. These are hundreds.

I...

Plus a gold bar. This is worth 10k. I'm nearly doubling the value of your car. You can go buy a new one tomorrow and have a fortune left over.

The dumb bird was paralyzed. His eyes swiveled to the counter. The car keys were there, in a bowl. Obviously he could just overpower her and take the keys. He knew exactly where the Coleman's parking spot was downstairs in the garage. But he had rules. He'd sold neckties to Wall Street traders, sold his sculptures on the street, realized he could sell his sculptures to art galleries if he posed as a dealer selling his client's work, used the capital to take sports bets from friends until he was running a thirty-man bookie operation, sold the bookie business a month before the cops cracked down…

His whole life he'd cut hard deals, he'd paid for people to tell him things they shouldn't, he'd convinced people they could afford things that they couldn't. But he never stole. He could always look his customer straight in the eye the day after and say *Hey, you agreed.*

You hand me the keys to your Jeep, I'll give you one hundred and fifty thousand dollars for your car. Do you realize how ludicrously good my offer is?

He stared hard at Barbara Coleman.

You have ten seconds to decide. Then I'm leaving with my money.

On deck, Art turned the finished chess piece around in his palm, admiring what his hands had created seemingly independently of him. Four bishops–two smooth, two scratched with lines around their spires. The pawns were basically just nubs, the kings just crosses, the knights jagged upside-down Ls. But the bishops actually looked like real chessmen.

He looked out beyond the ship's edge. The sun was hovering about an hour above the horizon, but looked like no sunset he'd ever seen. It was a white disk painted on a dark red canvas. He could comfortably stare directly at the sun for a few seconds, thanks to the filter of smoke, ash, and god knows what else. The sea took on the color of the sky, a pool of black blood.

It was suddenly too hard to look at. The scope of devastation was simply overwhelming. He stood up, took off his shirt, and used it as a sack for the forty pieces. Then he walked to the stairwell and brought his new chess set down to C-deck. He started down the hall, intending to knock on Mel's door, when he passed Adam's room. The door was open and Adam, shirtless, was sitting in a chair reading an Italian maritime encyclopedia Art recognized from the captain's lounge. Art stopped and observed him for a moment. The young man's almond eyes were riveted to the page. Art watched him read for a few minutes, trying to imagine him without burns all over his scrawny upper body. What had he been doing a month ago? Maybe a steel beam had knocked his marbles loose just last week, and before that he'd been finishing a masters in linguistics, or making cappuccinos in a hipster cafe.

"Hey, kid, do you know how to play chess?"

Adam looked up from the book. Blinked. He hadn't been getting a masters, Art decided. There was some kind of emptiness or hunger in the young man's eyes, something unequivocally *off*, that made it impossible to imagine that he'd recently been a productive member of society.

"Yeah," Adam answered.

Art cautioned himself against being too hopeful. The odds of the kid being competent were still long.

"I made a set. Want to play?"

Adam licked his dry lips.

"I mean, might as well kill some time right?" Art said.

Adam looked around the cabin, as if to check if anything pressing required his attention, but said nothing.

"I'm inviting myself in."

Art placed the board (drawn on printer paper) on the coffee table, and dropped the pieces on top. He was encouraged when Adam picked up the smooth pieces and set them up in proper formation.

"Ready?" Art asked.

His opponent nodded.

Art moved first. Pushed his king's pawn, very standard. Adam responded with his knight's pawn up two–a very weird move. And that was how the game went. Adam made moves that, while legal, appeared totally nonsensical.

Each time after Art moved he caught Adam staring off into space, or looking back down into the maritime encyclopedia. Art had to remind Adam that it was his turn, and then the young man would look back at the board and study the position anew. He had seemingly no strategy. There was little cohesion between any two moves. But the kid definitely remembered the rules. He castled correctly, and understood that he couldn't move pieces that were pinned to his king.

Art won eventually, but had to admit it was made slightly difficult by Adam's style, since he couldn't count on the boy defending in any reasonable way.

"Good game," Art said, when he finally checkmated Adam. The young man looked at the board again, then seemed to lose interest. He sat back in his chair, baring the burns on his chest. The two heads of Janus and the numbers.

"So what's the deal with those?" Art asked, pointing to Adam's sternum. Adam didn't seem to understand what Art was referencing, and when he looked down at his own chest he looked shocked at what he saw. He looked back up at Art, mouth agape, literally speechless. His face was white. His lips wriggled like worms drying out in the sun.

"What?" Art asked. "Did they change or something?"

"I… What… What did you do to me?"

Adam swallowed. He was breathing fast. His eyes were wide with bewilderment. He turned to look at his surroundings, then back at Art with a look of utter confusion.

"We're on a boat. You don't remember coming on board?"

"Who are you?" Adam asked. "Where did you take me? What have you done to me?"

"I'm Art. Roselli. Relax, Adam, we just had a perfectly nice game of chess together."

Adam looked down at the board, his checkmated position. He studied it for a long, long time. Too long. And when he finally looked back up he had relaxed somewhat.

"Good game," he said, smiling. "I don't know how I let myself fall for that."

Art shifted uncomfortably. What exactly was he dealing with here?

"So what's the deal with the burns?"

Adam scratched his cheek.

"Let's play again."

"Do you remember who gave them to you? Who tied you to the stool?"

Adam swallowed.

"Let's play again," he repeated.

"What about me. You remember my name?"

Adam smiled, but said nothing.

The hairs on the back of Art's neck stood up.

"Let me show you a magic trick," Art said, and enclosed a white pawn with his left hand, and a black one with his right. "Watch them carefully, okay?" Art didn't move his fists, just let time pass, counting seconds in his head. After about fifteen seconds, Adam looked at him like he was an idiot.

"What's the trick?" he said.

"Just a sec," Art said. Once he got to thirty, he said, "Okay. Which one has the black and which the white?"

Adam rolled his eyes and laughed.

"Come on."

"Alright then," Art smiled. "Tell me."

Adam looked down at Art's fists, and suddenly grew hesitant. Hesitancy gave way to that same look of bewilderment. Adam looked up at Art

"Come on. This is a game for kids," Adam said.

"What year is it?" Art asked.

Adam shook his head, laughing deliriously.

"What is this, the Spanish Inquisition?"

Art exhaled slowly. Adam was smiling at him, an impossibly light smile. Smiling from fear, like Barbara Coleman had been in the doorway.

One hundred and sixty thousand dollars, Barbara. You have ten seconds to decide.

You're really frightening me Arthur. Let me call Larry. This is a big decision.

Nine, eight, seven…

Okay, okay. Lord above, I… okay. Here. Here's the key.

The old bird wouldn't have had much of a chance anyway, even with the car; she wasn't exactly American Gladiator material. But still, Art didn't like thinking about what her last moments might have looked like: prone on her couch–either suffocating from disease-laden spores, choking on gas, or withering from radiation– replaying her negotiation with her sketchy upstairs neighbor, finally understanding what had happened. Art rarely felt guilty after a deal if he'd been faithful to his own rules, but he'd really swindled Barbara Coleman.

On the other hand, the tank to her Range Rover had only been half full.

17

There is an obscure commandment in the Old Testament–in fact it's the very last of the six hundred and thirteen–which says that every Jew should write an entire Torah scroll themselves. Even the most pious admit this is kind of a stretch. By law, a Torah scroll must be written by hand, on parchment made of cow skin, with absolute precision. It's a craft that takes years to perfect, and even a skilled scribe can't write an entire scroll in under a year. It's simply unreasonable to expect everyone to devote a half decade to this single *mitzvah*.

So it hadn't bothered Mel that he'd probably never write a scroll himself. But now, on board, not only did he have nothing but time on his hands, but for the first time in… maybe ever?… there was a real urgency to this commandment.

Mel was quite sure that the spores thing was true. Whether it was the Chinese, the Russians, or the United States who'd developed and released that weapon, he couldn't know. But he'd seen things on his nine-day journey down the East Coast that were difficult to explain any other way. He'd driven through a town somewhere in North Carolina that was untouched by fire. The lawns were green, the window trim on the A-frame houses crisp. When he pulled the car over and stepped out onto the empty street, he saw that the sidewalk was littered with dead sparrows.

He approached a blue house and rang the doorbell. Waited patiently for a few minutes, then tried the handle. It was unlocked, and he entered to look for something to drink.

The interior was so benign that he unthinkingly started peeling off his gas mask, before just barely catching himself. It looked like a family still lived here. There were kids toys scattered all over the carpet. A chenille couch faced a big flatscreen TV.

Hello? Mel called, his voice muffled and alien, distorted by the mask filters. Was he just being paranoid, keeping it on? It was so uncomfortable.

Only the memory of visiting a cousin in Israel during the uncertain months following the Gulf War, when his cousin gave him a tour of the bomb shelter in his house, made him scared to take it off.

If you're here, and God forbid there's a siren, his cousin had explained, *put this on, and don't take it off until you're sure it's okay. You might want to shave off your beard. It can ruin the seal.*

How do you know when it's okay to take the mask off?

If other people did it and are fine… Never be the first one to take it off.

Three days before, Mel had hastily shaved his neck and chin area before putting on the mask, and each moment since cursed himself for not just taking off the whole damn thing. As if it wasn't hot enough inside the mask, he also had a carpet of sweaty insulation between his cheeks and the rubber.

There was a straw built into the mask for water. Mel had been risking drinking apple juice through the straw. He didn't want to clog up the straw but he needed the calories. Hoping to find more juices, Mel wandered into the kitchen of the blue house. He opened the fridge, and was glad he couldn't smell through the mask. The power was out, of course. There were ribeye steaks coated in blue fur, a bowl of pasta that appeared to have grown a protective mineral shell, and a plastic container bursting with angry green moss. No juice.

They had a generous pantry, inside which he was pleased to find a few two-liter bottles of bright-red Hawaiian Punch.

This was before he'd heard the broadcast about the boats in Savannah, so he was in no rush. He drank a quarter bottle of Punch and lay down on the sofa to close his eyes.

He'd been thirty miles south of Baltimore, visiting his fish guy, trying some new samples, when the bomb fell. Shlomo was one of his secrets. Everyone knew Mel's deli had the best kosher fish in Baltimore, but nobody knew where it came from. Most assumed that Mel made it in-house, and he did nothing to dissuade that belief.

The moment was etched into Mel's mind with astonishing clarity. Shlomo grinning as he plucked a jar from his fridge, twisted off the top, and speared a fatty slab with a toothpick.

This is the best creamed herring I've ever made

He handed Mel the impaled chunk of carp. It dripped pickling fluid all over Shlomo's floor, but the fishmonger didn't seem to care.

I can give you only twenty pounds of this. It's a small batch.

Mel took the toothpick and smelled it before tasting. Wine sauce, onion, and brine. He put the fish to his lips, and the entire store shook. The windows blew in, and the shock wave threw the two men to the floor. Mel's whole body seemed to be vibrating, perhaps from shock. Then the light. He turned his head and saw nothing but a sheet of yellow. He shielded his eyes. There was no noise. Perhaps that was the strangest thing: silence and light.

Mel first drove back in the direction of the city. It was where Shoshana, Rueben, and Tsiporah were.

But after a few miles he could fool himself no longer. The city was ash. Sodom.

And now what? He was on a couch in some town called Brevard in North Carolina. He was well aware that staying on the move was just a distraction from the unspeakable. He sat up on the sofa. He saw a backyard through a screen door. In a daze, he left the bottles of Punch on the floor, slid open the door, and stepped out onto the patio. There were two rocking chairs and a big wooden swing bench that could fit four, which was anchored to the wood beams overhead by thick chains.

Movement caught Mel's eye. There was a large shed in the backyard, behind a garden. There was a hole in the side of the shed, and something protruding. The something was moving. Jerking. It was someone's hand. Somebody was alive in the shed.

Mel rushed to the door of the shed and tried to pull it open, but it was locked. The person was locked in.

Hold on! he said, through his mask.

The shed's walls were just wood. He could break through if he had some kind of tool.

He rushed back into the house. An axe or crowbar would be ideal, but he didn't expect to be that lucky. Mel found a poker next to the fireplace, and took it back to the shed. The hand was still moving.

Mel hacked at a side wall of the shed, opposite the hand. The boards relented with more ease than he'd expected. He pried out enough boards to see inside. But before he could, the hole was filled with the face of a woman. Her skin was green, eyes red as cherry tomatoes. She had some kind of sweater tied over her mouth and nose. She was making sounds like a cat that had just been hit by a car, dying on the pavement.

I can't understand you.

She unwound the fabric that was over the lower half of her face. Her nose was clogged with thick yellow mucus. She tried to speak, and Mel realized she could hardly breathe; her throat was constricted.

What happened?

She couldn't get words out. He kept clearing out boards, to help her out of the shed. By the time she could step out, she just collapsed on the grass, shivering. When Mel looked inside the shed he saw a dead man, surrounded by three dead children, one of which was a baby. Within ten minutes, the woman died too.

There was a shovel in the shed. Mel dug them graves in the backyard. It took hours. He wrapped his hands in ziplock bags from the kitchen, sealed with rubber bands around the wrist, so that he wouldn't have to touch them directly. By the time he filled their graves with dirt, it was getting dark.

He kneeled, and sang *El Malei Rachamim*—God Full of Mercy—the prayer traditionally chanted at funerals. The ancient syllables echoed inside his mask. Back in the house he forced himself to drink a half liter of Hawaiian Punch, and then collapsed on the couch. Before he fell asleep he wondered if every house on this block, in this city, had been similarly afflicted. He thought of the night of Passover in Egypt, when God had killed the first born son in every Egyptian household, passing over the Israelite's houses, which were marked by the blood on the lintel.

He'd thanked God that his family hadn't had to suffer like this one had. They must have been in the center of the blast. Killed instantly, probably. He hoped.

So the plant thing, the spores, there was no doubt in his mind. And even if it wasn't exactly as he'd heard described–that anyone within five miles of a tree would die of the sickness he'd seen–there was certainly *some* horrible plague they'd left behind on dry land. Which meant there was a very real chance that the people on this boat were among a very small number of survivors. And, from around the globe, did any survivor happen to have a Torah with them? Probably not. It wasn't hubris, it was simply fact: he was likely the last surviving Jew on earth, or at least the only one with enough knowledge to preserve the tradition.

Obviously there was no parchment on board, so Mel settled for a roll of printing paper he'd found on the bridge. He had to write from memory. Under normal circumstances, that would be totally unacceptable. But he had no choice; it was memory or nothing. Luckily, he'd studied for so many years as a boy that he knew many sections by heart. For the other passages, he'd try his best, and annotate explaining that his transcription could be inaccurate. It was imperfect, but if he didn't do this, there was a very real possibility that five thousand years of Jewish knowledge would be lost.

The first couple of pages would be easy enough. He unrolled the beginning of the paper roll, weighed it down with pieces of wood from one of the crates so it wouldn't move around, and started writing with a ballpoint pen:

In the beginning God created the heavens and the earth. And the earth was without form, and void; and darkness was upon the face of the deep. And the spirit of God was hovering upon the face of the waters.

Part 2

Without Form, and Void

18

It had been six days since they climbed onto the boat. Vic Fournier lay in bed, twirling his chest hair around his index finger. It was probably around noon and he had yet to leave his cabin. Soon he'd go down to the mess to grab a foil packet of slop, then do a lap around the boat hoping to run into Jennifer Presley. He'd avoid the midship, behind the bridge, where some people were still hacking the locks off containers. He didn't want to be roped into participating.

He was upset with himself that he still hadn't managed to say a single word to Jennifer since coming aboard, but blamed it mostly on the language barrier. If he could speak to her in French, he had no doubt that the seduction would be complete by now.

When Vic wandered around the ship, he hoped to run into Greg Pink almost as much as he did Jennifer. Greg was hilarious, and entertainment was in short supply aboard. Vic smiled just thinking about Greg's impersonation of some famous American comedian. That was how good the impression was: Vic had no idea who he was impersonating, but found Greg's rendition brilliant.

No respect! I tell you, I get no respect!

Classic.

Vic considered again whether he should seduce Lily. She wasn't exactly attractive, but she also wasn't bad looking. There was just something very off-putting about Lily. Perhaps it was the desperation, which oozed from her like perspiration. And like sweat on the brow, the more she tried to hide it the more she called attention to it.

There was some English idiom that captured this idea of ironic recursiveness. The cat being out of the bag? No. That didn't make any sense.

English was so complex. And each passing day it seemed less and less important.

He was just letting his eyes close again, falling into a nice little nap, when the speaker in his room buzzed to life. He was so startled to hear Elissa's scratchy voice in his cabin that he nearly fell out of bed.

"Hello all. It's Elissa. I'd like to call a meeting. There are some things we all need to discuss. We'll be meeting in the captain's lounge in ten minutes. If you don't attend, you will lose your opportunity to make your voice heard."

Vic sat up in bed. *Thing we all need to discuss.* He found himself intrigued by the drama. Any break in routine at this point was exciting.

He pulled on his underwear and shorts, both reeking of sweat and mildew. His shirt had been in the Bronco when it was stolen. He hoped one of these days someone would find some shirts in one of the containers.

Vic unlocked his cabin door and walked out into the hall. Adam's cabin was directly across from his. The door was open and Adam sat on the floor staring into his maritime encyclopedia. The young man had a pen beside him, and a bunch of the double striated printing paper from the bridge. In the days since they first saw his burns, even Lily had conceded that the young man was totally harmless. He didn't seem interested in doing anything other than just sitting here. Even though Vic was probably only five years older than Adam, Vic thought of him as a boy. That was how he'd come to understand this strange being: a child inhabiting an adult's body.

"Would you like to come up to the meeting?" Vic asked him.

Adam looked up, forehead crinkled in confusion. This sort of response was typical. It was the way a toddler might respond to a question; you were never sure if he understood what you were saying. Adam then turned to the stack of papers beside him. He scanned a few lines of what–presumably–he'd written, and frowned, clearly in distress.

"Mon ami?" Vic sighed. "I am going now. Are you joining?"

"Um, no thank you."

"D'accord."

Vic continued down the hall. Rosalyn was just leaving her cabin as well. She'd lost some weight, and had dark bags under her eyes.

"How are you, Vic?" she asked, as they walked shoulder to shoulder to the stairway leading up to the bridge and lounge.

"I'm great. How are you, Doctor?"

They climbed two flights of metal stairs.

"Good," she said. She sounded exhausted. Her brown linen shirt had faded from the sun. "I've been working on opening more containers."

"Oh?" he said. "Interesting."

They passed through the bridge. The glass windows had accumulated a layer of oily grime over the past week. The green binders filled with documents were in the corner where Vic had left them a week ago.

Vic and Rosalyn entered the captain's lounge. Elissa, Greg, Jennifer, Mel, and Bahram were already sitting around the oak table.

Vic's heart sped up at the sight of Jennifer. Everyone else looked haggard and worn, but not her. She really was beautiful. Her glowing bronze skin… like the sun, you could only safely observe her in your peripheral vision. Vic sat down next to Bahram, across from Jennifer, so he could steal looks at her. He turned to the Afghani.

"*Bonjour,*" he said.

Bahram nodded tiredly.

"Hello," he responded. "How. Are. You."

Vic raised an eyebrow.

"I've been teaching him some English," Jennifer said, beaming. "And we can communicate a little now with pictures."

"How. Are. You."

Vic was happy to have an excuse to talk to Jennifer.

"Do you understand what he's been saying now about the boy? Adam?"

"I'm getting closer I think."

Bahram grumbled something and picked at his hairy ear. He probably wasn't looking forward to another meeting that he wouldn't understand.

"Hello Vic, Doctor Rosalyn," Elissa smiled coldly. There were a few Dixie cups filled with water already on the table, like hors d'oeuvres.

Vic helped himself to a cup of water, drained it, then took another.

"So? What is the news?" he asked.

"Just waiting a moment for anyone else who wants to attend," Elissa said. Her hands were clasped behind her back and she was still standing. Her gaze was fierce and directed at nobody in particular. Vic imagined that if she stared long enough at a flower like this, it might turn its head away to avoid her intensity.

"Hi Greg," Vic said.

"Vicky boy!" Greg smiled, like he was noticing him for the first time. "Where you been hiding yourself?"

"C-deck," Vic said, already buoyed by Greg's energy. "Same as you. Come visit my room."

"I will, I will."

Art came in.

"Hey everyone," he said and sat down. "Is this our one week reunion? Where are they now? Mel Glazer! I had you down for most likely to succeed."

Vic had no idea what Art was talking about.

Sam entered the lounge.

"Hi," he said, and grunted with relief as he transferred the burden of his mass to one of the big leather chairs on the side.

Lily rushed into the lounge.

"Hey, so sorry. Am I the last? Were you waiting for me? Sorry."

She sat down next to Art.

"You're not the last. There's still Adam," Sam said.

"I spoke to the boy," Vic said, emptying his third Dixie cup. "He won't be joining."

Elissa frowned.

"Is he doing alright?"

Vic shrugged. "He seems content."

"He's an interesting fella," Art said. "I've been schmoozing with him a lot actually."

Lily shook her head.

"Why?"

"Well, once I got sick of the on-board casino, saw all the Broadway shows, and swam a few laps in the pool," Art said, leaning forward in his chair, "I got a little bored. I gotta say, he's not a bad conversationalist, in thirty-second increments. But we're not here to talk about that," he looked at Elissa. "Chairwoman, you convened this meeting?"

Elissa didn't give him the smile he was obviously seeking.

"Yes," she said. "We have a few issues to discuss communally. The first, most pressing, is water. As you know, last week we all agreed on an honor system with respect to water. Everyone is entitled to a liter and a half per day. However, I checked the potable water tank yesterday, and it seems that we're exceeding that pace. By a *lot*."

Vic had been reaching for a fourth cup, but now stopped himself mid-lunge and instead pretended to examine his fingernails. He hadn't even been measuring how much water he drank each day.

"The honor system isn't working," Elissa continued. "So we'll have to change. Someone will have to be in charge of water distribution, and ensure nobody goes over their allotted amount."

She paused a moment to see if anybody would raise an objection to this. Vic decided not to voice his opinion on the matter, namely: who gives a shit?

"How would this work?" Mel asked her. "He or she would patrol the halls all day, making sure nobody is gorging themselves? We're not children. Let's just agree to be more careful."

"We *did* agree to be more careful," Elissa replied icily. "And it didn't work. In the engine room there are controls to turn on and off water flow to different spigots. I suggest we turn off all water flow besides the one in the engine room itself. One person will go into the engine room two or three times a day, get water, and then dole it out to everyone."

Jennifer scoffed, and Vic seized the opportunity to look at her.

"That sounds a little fascist," she said. "I suppose you're thinking that the person who distributes water will be you. How do we know *you* won't double your own portion?"

Elissa seemed unperturbed by this attack on her character.

"First of all, I wouldn't do this job. It wouldn't be appropriate, given that this is my idea. You're absolutely right about that. And second, water remaining in the tank is very easy to check. All of us could go down there and check together whenever we like. So if we're exceeding our pace, then we know exactly who to blame. Accountability. That's all we need."

"Elissa..." Mel frowned, stroking his bushy beard. "This really does sound a little... *extreme*."

"I strongly disagree," she replied, pushing up the bridge of her glasses, only for them to immediately fall back down to rest on the tip of her thin nose. "I think it's *folly* to cut our chances of survival. What if the extra water means ten days? And what if those ten days are when we finally get someone on the radio to come help?"

"I'm not necessarily against the idea," Art said. "I just think we need to have a serious talk about our options here. It's been a week and there hasn't been a blip on the radio. I'm starting to think that continuing to just sit here might be 'folly'."

"Interesting point of view," Elissa cleared her throat. "That relates to the second item I wanted to discuss. Over the past few days, some of you have come up to the bridge to take shifts monitoring the radio, and sending out distress signals. Thank you for that. However. I sat next to the radio from eight in the evening yesterday until ten this morning, when I finally called you all up here. Fourteen straight hours. I'm happy to do my part, but I'm just exhausted. I can't be put in a position again where I have to do that."

Everyone fell silent. Again, Vic inspected his fingernails closely. He hadn't really been on the bridge since his halfhearted search for a ship manifest.

After a moment, Sam said, "I'm sorry, Elissa. That's not right." Reluctant nods and murmurs of agreement rose from around the table like bubbles from a bog.

"I'm not angry," she said. "My point again is that we need structure. I propose a schedule: everyone will do a three-hour shift every day, and we'll alternate who gets the bad night shifts. If there are no objections, I'll write up such a schedule this afternoon on the whiteboard on the bridge."

Everyone nodded in the affirmative. No objections to a schedule.

"Wonderful. Mel–I assume you prefer not to work on Saturdays. I'll work around that."

"Listen, the schedule is a great idea," Art said, "and Elissa, I apologize as well for putting you in that position. But–" he cleared his throat, "–and I ask this in all seriousness: why do you think another boat would even help us? I'm not saying we shouldn't monitor the radio but... they'd have the same issues as us. Limited food, limited water."

Vic nodded. Finally, it sounded like someone else was willing to just accept their communal fate.

"So what Art?" Lily said. "You want to just curl up in a ball and die?"

"Well I think what Arthur is saying is, what's the endgame here if ultimately we can't go back to shore?" Mel said. "And we can't. Given the airborne disease. We all agree that our gas masks are almost certainly ineffective at this point. And I think we also agree that the Caribbean islands are infected by the same biological agents as the mainland."

Art nodded.

"Yes. And I'd like to raise something I've been looking into. As I mentioned, I've been spending some time with Adam–"

Lily groaned.

"Listen," Art said, raising his palms defensively. "Here's the atlas we have on board." Art had brought the tattered book with him, and he now unfolded one of the maps on the table. "Elissa was right, there's no island at the coordinates listed on Adam's chest," he pointed to a quadrant with his index finger. "But–"

"–Arthur…" Rosalyn said, the first words Vic had heard from her since they entered the lounge together. She looked weak and unwell. Maybe she was seasick "Please let's not get started with th–"

"Let me finish!" he said. The room gave a communal shrug like, get it over with. Then Art turned to the bookcase, scrolled through the Italian titles, until finding the one he was looking for. He slammed it on the table, then opened it to a page he'd earmarked. "I found this yesterday. No–I don't read Italian, but I'm pretty sure I got the idea. Vic–what do you understand from this entry?"

Vic sighed and pulled the encyclopedia closer. Most of the words he could figure out based on French and English.

"It's about a small island near Iceland called Surtsey," he said. "Very small. One and a half square kilometers. It was made as a result of em…" Vic searched for the English, and came up empty. "*Éruption volcanique.*"

"A volcanic eruption," Art nodded. "And when did that happen?

"1967," Vic said.

"Art…" Rosalyn sighed.

"And guess what, Surtsey isn't in this Atlas!" Art cried. "Look," he turned to a different page and jabbed a finger. "Nada. That island is too small and new. This atlas is from the seventies. If any other island popped up as a result of volcanic activity, it wouldn't be in this atlas. So we don't know. Maybe there *is* something at those coordinates on Adam's chest. And I mean, come on. Someone wrote GPS coordinates on his chest in mirror image, put a mirror in front of him, and tied him next to an autopilot system that takes GPS coordinates. How much more circumstantial evidence do you guys want?"

Sam opened his mouth as if to argue, but he said nothing.

"I assume it would take most of our fuel to find out?" said Mel softly.

Art took a deep breath.

"I'm not sure. We have around half a tank of fuel. This ship's home port is in Italy, so it probably sailed from there to Savannah with a full tank, and then was going to sail back, and refuel once it returned to Italy. If we sail to those coordinates and find nothing, I'm quite confident we'd have enough fuel to continue on to the Azores islands, and if they've been hit then Portugal or Morocco."

Elissa shook her head slowly, like she was sad this conversation was happening at all.

"I called you up here to deal with two serious issues," she said. "This is nonsense."

Art slammed the table with his fist. "It's not nonsense!" he shouted. "Nonsense is sitting here waiting to die."

"Let's have a vote on what I proposed," Elissa replied calmly. "Choosing someone to monitor our water usage."

Art's cheeks were red with frustration, but for the moment he bit his tongue.

"All in favor of us choosing a water monitor, raise your hand," she said, and raised her hand.

Lily put her hand high in the air. Then Greg. Then, with some hesitation, Mel. Bahram looked around and raised his as well.

"Bahram's vote shouldn't be counted," Vic said. "He doesn't know what we're talking about."

Elissa looked at Bahram, who appeared confused to find his own hand in the air. She grimaced.

"Very well. That's four. Okay, all against my motion?"

Vic raised his hand. Then Jennifer. He grinned at her. The smile she returned looked forced, and Vic felt himself blush.

Stupide! Stupide!

"Four to two," Elissa said.

"Rosalyn? Art? Sam?" Jennifer said. "You aren't going to vote?"

Rosalyn shook her head with exasperation.

"I don't know… What you're saying makes sense, Elissa, but maybe we can think of a different way to fix the problem."

"Then vote against," Elissa said. "Simple."

Rosalyn hesitated for a second, then raised her hand against. Sam then raised his hand, like he'd been waiting to see what Rosalyn would do.

"Arthur?" Elissa asked patiently. "I suppose you're our tiebreaker."

"What are the rules here, Chairwoman?" Art asked stonily. "Anyone can just put forward a motion and force everyone to vote for it?"

Elissa sniffed.

"I suppose so. Democracy. Makes sense to me."

"Democracy is okay," Art said. "But there are alternatives. Are we sure we don't want to go with dictatorship?"

"Don't be a smartass," said Lily. "Just vote. One way or another."

"No, I'm being serious here," Art said. "If we're having a vote on this, then after I want to have a vote about going to Adam's island. Alright?"

"Sounds fair to me," said Mel.

Elissa sighed, "Very well."

"Okay, then I vote for the motion," said Art. "And I think Sammy should be our water guard, on account of nobody's going to be able to threaten another couple drops out of him."

"Wonderful," Elissa said. "And I agree, I think Sam is an excellent choice."

Everyone turned to look at the giant. His hand was clasped over his lower stomach.

He shook his head. "I haven't been feeling well. Greg, you should do it," he said. "We all trust you."

Lily said: "I agree."

Vic nodded. "Seems good," he said. If someone had to be in charge of distributing water, Greg was a good choice. Now each time Vic wanted to find Greg to hang out, he'd have an excuse.

Greg spread his hands and shrugged.

"I guess I'll do it if you guys want."

Jennifer suddenly looked like she was sucking on a lime.

"This is wrong," she said. "Just because a majority of people on board want to do something doesn't make it okay. What if five of you decided we're going to start eating each other?"

Mel said, "The young lady has a point."

Greg's left eye started to twitch.

"What," Vic asked. "You don't trust–"

"–Guys," Greg shook his head. He seemed like he was in great pain, but forcing himself to smile."Look, you want me to do it, I'll do it. If not, no biggie."

Mel took a long breath out.

"Alright," he said.

"I don't want to have to beg this guy every time I want a drink," Jennifer said. "This is bullshit." She stood up as if to leave.

"Beg?" Greg half-laughed in confusion. He looked at Vic like *what is she talking about?*

Vic shrugged and smiled. *Women. What can you do?*

"Wait, wait," Art said. "First the island vote?"

Jennifer didn't sit back down.

"Fine. I vote no," she raised her hand. "I vote not to use most of our fuel confirming that whoever did this to him is probably a terrorist and almost certainly insane. Anyone else?"

"That Icelandic island proves nothing, I'm sorry to say. I vote no," Elissa said, raising her hand. "It's not prudent."

"Art, be reasonable," Greg said, raising his hand.

Vic voted no, and everyone else followed, except Art.

Jennifer looked around. "So we're done here?"

"You people are not thinking clearly," Art said quietly. "If we just sit here, we're going to die. The Navy isn't coming. The coast guard isn't coming. Maybe there's something out there at those coordinates, maybe not. *Probably* not. But we have to take a gamble at some point, because staying here is guaranteed death."

This last syllable stung the room with silence. Vic smiled to himself. Finally, they were all realizing that he'd been right all along. They should be enjoying their last moments, instead of arguing about nonsense.

Rosalyn broke the silence.

"Why *that* gamble though?" she said. "Why not gamble that we can find something in the Caribbean, maybe an island that wasn't bombed or poisoned?"

"It's delusional to think we could find an untouched island in the Caribbean," Art said. "They're close enough to the mainland that even if they weren't hit directly, the wind will carry those spores. If even one of those spores makes its way to an island with trees or bushes, the whole thing will get contaminated. If there are plants growing, only an island thousands of miles away from anything will be safe."

Lily looked a little ill.

"And Cuba definitely got hit with something," Sam said quietly. "I remember that."

Elissa stared at Art.

"It's insanity to even consider this possibility."

"On the contrary, Ma'am," His voice was steely. "It's insanity not to."

"Who's thirsty?" asked Greg.

19

Bahram pointed to the drawing of the stick figure with the faces burned onto his shoulder, the one *Yenfor* now understood represented his son, Azzami. She nodded in comprehension. She was growing more patient, Bahram thought. Or maybe it was just that she had nothing else to do. Either way, she wasn't the knucklehead he'd initially taken her for. If she agreed to dress modestly, he would even consider bringing her back to Afghanistan to introduce her to one of his less promising grandsons.

"*Abn,*" she confirmed.

Bahram then tried, for the first time, to draw the strange building his son had taken him and Keti to. The building, unsettling in its plainness, that he'd watched through the car window and wondered what evil lay inside.

Their second day in America they drove from morning to night, stopping only twice to briefly refresh themselves in public restrooms, and for Azzami to refill the car with gas. They spoke very little. Keti was scared, Bahram could see. But they were in a strange country whose rules they didn't understand, surrounded by people they couldn't speak to. There was nothing to do but trust their son.

Around noon, Azzami's phone started ringing and didn't stop. Bahram's son seemed upset at whoever was calling, and each time he would hit a button on the side of the phone to silence it. Finally, sometime toward evening he relented and answered. He had what seemed like a heated conversation in English. At some point he yelled so loudly that he strained his voice. Keti squeezed Bahram's elbow. Azzami hung up his phone and threw it onto the passenger seat beside him. From behind, they saw that his shoulders were hunched up anxiously and the back of his neck was covered in hot sweat.

At night they stopped at a place so similar to the previous night's motel that Bahram initially thought they'd spent all day driving in one big circle. Even the layout of the room was nearly identical. Bahram and Keti sat on the bed while Azzami stepped outside to speak on the phone again. When he came back into the room he was a little pale and his hands were clenched into tight fists.

Azzami. Please explain what's happening. Why have you brought us here?

His son's eyes were red and misty.

It's hard to explain.

It's okay, Son. Whatever it is. We're listening.

Azzami clenched his teeth. He sat down on the floor and rubbed his index finger in a circle around his mouth, a nervous habit Bahram recognized from his son's childhood, and Bahram found it strangely comforting to see there were remnants of that boy in this grown man.

I never worked for a construction company. When I came here the job turned out to be something different.

What was it?

A kind of group... It's difficult to explain. I like them. They always treated me well, and paid very generously. They are good people. But they've made a kind of mistake, I think, and something very bad is going to happen. I've brought you here to save you.

Bahram shook his head, confused.

Save us? We were perfectly fine at home.

Azzami was silent for a moment.

Let's get some sleep. There's a lot I have to do tomorrow. Don't worry, everything will be okay.

The next day they were on the road again. Endless rows of trees, most of a variety Bahram had never seen, with wings of purple-blue needles instead of leaves and branches. Azzami was following directions from his phone. At mid-noon the highway led into a town. The people here were whiter than in New York. And fatter. They reminded Bahram of the cheese-filled pastries his mother used to buy sometimes as a treat. At the edge of town, Azzami pulled into a driveway in front of a building. Two women with wild hair sat on a bench outside, completely still, staring at nothing. A man in white pajamas stood nearby, with his hands clasped behind his back.

In the front seat, Azzami was breathing hard. Then he opened the glove compartment and pulled out a pistol and a glossy photo of a smiling young man.

Keti shrieked.

What are you doing?

Relax, Mother. I'm not going to hurt anyone. I promise.

Son—

Wait here. His son was suddenly stern. *Do not leave this car. I'll be back in five minutes. Don't leave this car, swear you won't.*

Keti was sobbing softly into his shoulder. Bahram could do nothing but agree.

Azzami took a moment to stare at the glossy photo, then he folded it up and shoved it in his jacket pocket. Without turning off the engine, he climbed out of the car, concealing the pistol in his jacket. They watched him pass the sitting women and the man in pajamas, and walk straight into the front entrance of the building.

The minutes that followed felt interminable. Keti wiped her eyes and asked Bahram what was happening, as if he had any clue himself. He briefly considered breaking his promise to his son and leaving the car. But what would he do? Tell the man with pajamas that his son had a gun? Maybe nobody would even care. He'd heard there were places in America that were just like Kabul, where ordinary men walked through the streets with rifles strapped to their backs.

Then Azzami emerged from the building. He held the pistol in one hand and with his other he led the young man Bahram recognized from the picture. The young man wore light-yellow pajama bottoms and was bare chested.

The man in the white pajamas approached the two of them and Azzami menaced the gun at him and barked some kind of threat. The man was terrified, and stood back to let Azzami and the dazed young man pass. Azzami ripped open the passenger side door, shoved the young man inside, then rushed around to hop in the driver's seat, throw the transmission into reverse, and shoot them back out of the driveway. As they pulled away, Bahram saw more men in pajamas rushing outside, shouting and pointing at them. Azzami was driving and swerving around corners so fast that Bahram and Keti, in the back, were tossed around like rag dolls.

Only once they left the town, and returned to a highway, did Azzami's shoulders relax ever so slightly. He said something to their new passenger, and then handed him a bottle of water. The young man drank eagerly, then turned back to look at Bahram and Keti for the first time. He was unshaven and had bad skin. His brown eyes were kind, Bahram thought, but also slightly wrong somehow, as if they were perfect glass replicas of eyes. He smiled weakly at them.

Don't talk to him, Azzami said.

Who is he?

Azzami was silent for a moment. Bahram noticed how tightly his son clenched the steering wheel.

He is an Adam. A special soul, untainted by memory.

Keti and Bahram exchanged a confused look.

I don't understand, Son.

Azzami was still breathing hard from before.

The world is sick, Mother. Too sick to heal. And anyone with memories of it carries the infection. Only the Adams and Eves, those unburdened by these memories, have a chance of making a new, healthier world.

Keti shook her head, confused and frightened to hear her son speaking in such a strange way. Bahram put a hand on her leg to comfort her.

Night fell and they pulled into yet another motel. Azzami gave Bahram a room key.

I'll be in the room across the hall with the Adam if you need anything.

Bahram and Keti lay together in the motel bed for a long time, neither close to sleep.

Do you understand what our son was saying, Bahram?

Bahram shook his head helplessly.

I'm very frightened, she said.

He's our son. Remember that.

I'm hungry. We didn't have dinner.

Bahram nodded. He was hungry too.

I'll go to Azzami's room to ask for food.

Bahram put on his pants, shirt, and hat and walked out into the hall. He knocked on Azzami's door, first softly, then louder. Footsteps, then his son opened the door, fully dressed; he hadn't been sleeping either.

Your mother is hungry. We haven't eaten since breakfast.

Azzami winced.

I'm very sorry. You're right. I'll order some food for us. American Pizza. There's nothing better.

Bahram nodded.

Good.

Over Azzami's shoulder he saw the young man, in his yellow pajama bottoms, sitting in chair in the corner of the room. His wrist was tied to the radiator with a length of steel cable.

20

"I'm thinking about the future here, Lily," Elissa explained. The two women sat on the bridge next to the silent radio. The afternoon air was so humid that it was making Lily Chen a little claustrophobic. She fanned herself with a few pages ripped from *The Five-Hour Work Week*, and rocked from side to side in the swivel chair. It was her shift, but Elissa was joining, either out of the goodness of her heart, boredom, or probably because she didn't trust Lily to monitor the radio properly.

"Yeah," Lily said.

"It's not just about the water. Obviously the water is a critical issue, but I'm thinking beyond that," Elissa took off her glasses and rubbed them with the fabric of her blouse. "No matter what happens, whether we get picked up by someone else, or take our chances back on shore… we need structure. What if there are no survivors on the mainland? Or very few? We may very well be founding our own society. To this end you'll be able to contribute much more than me."

Lily frowned.

"You mean like, having babies?"

Elissa nodded.

"Precisely."

Lily was thirty-four, but for the last few years when she thought about her age it was more like a countdown clock. A countdown to the age when her reproductive chances would fall to near zero. She'd been open about her desire to find a husband and settle down relatively early in life. Other women said they wanted to first take time to focus on their careers, to travel… Lily found this attitude impossibly self-centered. Yes, she had her own passions. She was always experimenting with new recipes–which was how her line of salad dressings had been born–and she loved studying interior architecture and design (she'd toyed with the idea of going back to school for a design degree of some kind). But she was consumed by the twin, inseparable drives of finding a life partner and having children. She assumed most women her age were as well, but did a better job of hiding it.

When she was thirty she took the plunge and joined an online dating site called SoulConnect. She had her friend Amanda come over and take a million pictures of her, then she chose the best ones. Was that a little disingenuous? Of course. But let's be honest, dating is like Risk, a game everyone starts with the noblest intentions, but which quickly devolves into a strange pastiche of cut-throat competitiveness and boredom, until eventually the objective becomes less to win, than to end the game with your ego intact.

Lily had assumed that the principle obstacle would be working up the courage to join the site. That once she joined she'd be bombarded by suitors, and from there the main challenge would be sifting through all of the amazing people out there to find The One. Lily was big on that concept: The One. Well, she used to be big on it. After countless iterations of a frighteningly consistent pattern, she'd grown a bit jaded. The pre-SoulConnect pattern was this: she'd meet a guy–before online dating she mostly met them at house parties, or trendy bars in NuLu– and the guy would hit on her. He'd buy her drinks and loiter around her all night. Sometimes the men would be charming, sometimes not. Either way Lily would usually be lukewarm on them at this stage. They'd ask for her number, she'd comply, then they would text or call a few days later asking if they could take her out.

In the early days, before she'd amassed enough dating data to grow suspicious of the recurring pattern, she'd been kinda flattered at this stage. Sometimes she'd be at lunch with a friend when one of them called or texted and she'd roll her eyes and say something like *Jeez, these guys*, like she was getting so much male attention that it was becoming a burden for her.

So she'd go out with them, and one of exactly two things would happen. One: she'd immediately realize this guy wasn't The One, that this was a wasted evening, and she'd be out of there in under an hour. Two: she'd be smitten. The guy would be perfect. Her vision would get bright with laughter and drink, the butterflies in her stomach would partner up and tango. She'd finally found him! She'd say something like *I'm having a great time.* He'd smile and say something like *Me too.* If they were sitting at the bar then by this point their knees were touching. A few times he would escalate here, and actually touch her thigh, shoulder, or lower back.

It was always a bar. Never dinner. Lily always ate hurriedly before the date to avoid drinking on an empty stomach. But she'd be so nervous that she'd only manage to get a few bites down, so by eleven, after three or four white wines, she was usually pretty hammered. That's right around when, in scenario two, the guy would lean in and they'd start hardcore making out. But then, because he was perfect, he wouldn't push it. He'd stop after like thirty seconds, pull back and smile. He'd say something softly that sent a shiver down Lily's spine.

Her heart would feel ready to burst. She wouldn't be able to stop grinning and she'd feel the heat on her face. In the car, he might put his hand back on her thigh, but not in an intrusive way.

Her room was always immaculate, because she'd cleaned it for hours in anticipation of scenario two. She'd lead him quickly to her room, so he wouldn't see her roommate (Mona, Heather, or briefly, a sublet named Pria), both because Lily was self-conscious about still having a roommate, and also because Mona, Heather, and Pria were all prettier than her.

Usually he'd take her from behind, which was just fine with Lily. She liked feeling his strong hands on her hips, hearing him grunt over her shoulder, while she grabbed her headboard. Sometimes he'd grab her black ponytail–this was before she went shoulder-length–and pull it, as if he was struggling to keep astride a steed. Sometimes he'd push her head down into the mattress to improve the angle. It was disturbing, only in retrospect, how reliably he'd comment on her vice-like anatomy and imply that it was a function of her race.

Sometimes he slept over, and sometimes not. If he did, he would usually couple again in the morning. Her employment over this period of her life was intermittent. When she was working as a sales support representative, her shifts usually didn't start until late afternoon, so she'd have time to make the guy breakfast if he wanted; by this point she was comfortable risking an encounter with her roommate. Usually he had to go straight to the office though. So, after a kiss goodbye, Lily would eat breakfast by herself. In the early days these solo breakfasts were joyous occasions. She'd channel the elation from the night's events into a really fancy omelette, with ham, spinach, and cheddar, maybe make herself pancakes, and sometimes even squeeze her own orange juice. She'd sit at her kitchen table and eat, unable to wipe the stupid smile off her face. She'd text him something like **Can't wait to see you again.** When she thought about the naiveté of these texts she wanted to die.

It would only take a few hours for her world to turn upside down. The worst case was he wouldn't respond at all, which would set off alarm bells: *If he liked me, wouldn't he respond right away? Everyone sees texts right away. If he's not responding, he's purposely ignoring me. What the fuck. Does he not remember what happened last night?*

She'd try to hold out, but usually couldn't help herself from following up. Something referencing the discussion they'd had at the bar the night before.

*I looked it up. Humans **are** considered a great ape. You owe me a drink.*

If he hadn't responded by the time her shift was going to start, she'd usually have to call in sick, which by this point was hardly even a lie. She'd be prone on the couch, or in her bed, staring at her phone, willing him to reply. By the time he did, the sun was likely sinking, and Lily's mind, too, was going to a very dark place.

Hey! Sorry just saw this.

She wouldn't even know how to feel, seeing these words on the screen. Because even in the early days of this routine, she knew in her heart of hearts that it was over. No, not over. It had never even begun. A stillbirth.

No problem! What are you up to?

Most of the time, a one or two word reply here:

Chilling

Lily's heart would be beating fast now.

What are you doing tomorrow?

Umm, gotta check.

Wanna go out for dinner?

Yeah lemme get back to u about if that works.

And it was over.

Then came SoulConnect, the nuclear option. Looking back, her optimism when joining the site was nothing short of heartbreaking.

"I always wanted to have kids," Lily said, still fanning herself furiously. Elissa, she noticed, hardly sweated at all. She was the only one on board who actually seemed pretty comfortable in this heat.

"I didn't," the older woman replied. "Never appealed to me."

Lily hadn't believed in the concept of The One for a long time now. It was sort of tautological: the older she got without The One in her life, the more the theory, apparently, was invalid. Unless it applied to nearly everyone except for her, but this was too painful of a thought to entertain for long. Since climbing onto the boat, though, she'd started to consider an amazing new possibility: not only was The One a real thing, but it was *such* a thing that fate had pulled out all the stops. The Daughters of January had provoked the Russians into unleashing a lethal plague just to unite Lily with her soulmate.

Lily pretended that she was just now considering what Elissa was saying, about repopulating the earth, but in truth she'd spent the last week thinking about it obsessively, growing more and more excited and convinced: this was destiny. How could it not be? She was stranded in the middle of the ocean with *Greg Pink.*

21

The toilets on the ship were pretty primitive. There was a central tank for waste, located on the lowest floor of the engine room. In order to ensure that whatever mess you left in your cabin's toilet was ushered through the sewage pipes into the tank, you first had to toggle a black lever next to the toilet, which enabled the flow of water into the bowl. Then you had to pump a second lever a few times to stimulate this flow. Finally, there was *another* pump, which–nobody was quite sure of the inner workings of this–but it felt like you were pumping air out of the sewage tube in order to create a vacuum, so the diluted waste would be sucked down violently, like the greedy tank below was slurping it up through a straw.

All the men decided quickly that this production wasn't worth the trouble if they were just going to pee, so they just let loose over the side into God's great blue toilet. Jennifer wasn't sure if any of the other women were adventurous enough to try that, but personally she'd been content with the pumping –especially because each cabin had its own bathroom so she could do it all in guaranteed privacy.

Prior to the meeting, Jennifer had considered the private bathrooms, and the fact that the cabin doors could lock from the inside, the only even mildly compelling evidence of a benevolent post-apocalyptic higher power. In the days following the discovery of food, Jennifer spent a lot of time alone, locked in her room. A few times she went up around daybreak to help Sam and Art open containers, and every day she spent at least an hour with Bahram, trying to teach him English and understand whatever he had to say about Adam and his son. But besides that she liked to be alone. She'd even take her food from the mess and bring it back to her cabin to eat in isolation.

The meeting changed her routine. She was now obligated to spend three hours a day on the bridge flipping through radio frequencies and broadcasting their location. She didn't begrudge it; fair was fair. She was, however, livid about the water situation. And not just because she now had to wait for Greg's "water hours" to collect her drinking ration–though, to be sure, that was bad too; when she arrived at the engine room entrance with her cup and smiled cursorily at him he'd fill up the cup without saying a word. It was beyond awkward. It would have been infinitely better if he either 1) just pretended everything was cool–that nothing had happened–which was what she'd expected from him, or 2) was straight up about it, like said directly let's just forget about the other night. But instead he completely disengaged. Jennifer didn't know what to do. She wasn't going to apologize; she had absolutely nothing to apologize for. But the palpable discomfort of this routine was such that she was starting to think it might be worth giving him a phony apology, just for her own sake. Twice now she'd skipped her water ration because she didn't want to deal with him. Other times she'd sit on the stairs next to the engine room, waiting for someone else to come for their ration so she wouldn't have to face him alone.

But the whole ordeal with Greg wasn't the worst part of the new water rules. The worst part was that as part of the rationing, they'd turned off all the faucets in the cabin bathrooms. And it turned out that when you switched off the tap to the bathroom sink–which was connected to the potable water tank–you also had to shut off the plumbing–the "grey water" system. She could still pee in the dry toilet, but fecal matter without a flushing mechanism was a problem. When this issue was discovered, Elissa, instead of backing off of her rationing initiative, proposed an inhumane solution:

There was a nearly-full tank of sea water in the engine room, filled by pumps the last time the ship was at sea. This water was used both for the grey water in the plumbing, and also went to the desalination mechanism to be converted into potable water when the engine was running. At Elissa's suggestion, Greg quickly and heartily agreed to fill up two big blue containers with salt water twice a day and carry them to the mess hall. You could then come down and use the public three-stall bathroom off of the mess hall. You'd bring one of the containers in with you, pour the salt water on your fecal matter, and use the pumping mechanism. You could also use the salt water for "brushing" your teeth with a finger, or even bathing, but that was pretty gross.

Theoretically, you could carry sea water back up to your own private cabin and bathroom, but that was risky. The flushing didn't go nearly as smoothly when you poured in your own water instead of using the internal grey water system, and, though there was no way to confirm this, it sure smelled like with their new method, a lot of the sewage wasn't making it all the way through the pipes into the tank. So if you wanted to go in your own cabin you risked it starting to smell like a rotten egg soufflé, which had already happened to the three-stall bathroom on D-deck.

Greg arrived in the mess every morning at seven bearing two heavy tanks full of ocean water. Jennifer woke up with the sun every morning having to poop. But she didn't want to see Greg, and figured that after Greg brought the tanks of water he loitered in the mess for a while, making stupid jokes while people filed in and picked up a tank: *Enjoy! It's not how you start, it's how you finish!*

For the first three mornings after this system was implemented, Jennifer held off as long as she possibly could, then rushed down to D-deck to relieve herself, and was successful in avoiding Greg.

Each of those three mornings she knocked on the bathroom door to see if it was occupied by a man or men, and Rosalyn called out in response: *Just me.*

The first morning Jennifer tried waiting for Rosalyn to leave. It was nicer to have the whole bathroom to yourself. Also, being around Rosalyn in particular made Jennifer uncomfortable. The doctor was so awkward. Not like funny awkward. Painful awkward. Yesterday, when they ran into each other in the lounge, Rosalyn gave Jennifer an honest-to-god handshake. And Jennifer knew she couldn't say something like *Well that was awkward*, because the doctor was so unaware of how awkward she was acting that she'd probably just cock her head and say something excruciatingly awkward like *What do you mean? Should we have a chat?*

People should just act normal, Jennifer thought. Rosalyn's behavior gave her the same unsettled feeling she'd had whenever she had to walk past this grungy guy at Tampa who stood on a chair doing "slam poetry" in front of the door of the rec center. She felt so embarrassed for him. She always wanted to do that guy a favor and tell him, *Dude, everyone thinks you're a freak.*

Pooping next to Rosalyn was, obviously, awkward.

On the fourth morning since the meeting, the smell in the bathroom was unspeakable. Jennifer had only smelled anything remotely close to this in zoos and nursing homes. She wondered if she'd be better off trying to shit off the deck into the sea. But no. Anyone could stumble upon her. Greg could stumble upon her. Mel, the fanatic, or creepy old Art could stumble upon her.

Rosalyn was sitting in the middle of the three stalls, as she had the previous three mornings, which was absurd and selfish. Jennifer entered the stall at the far end, trying not to breathe. The smell wasn't

Rosalyn's fault, of course, but because her's were the only feet Jennifer ever saw in here, it was hard not to make the association.

Just like the last three days, Rosalyn's jeans were down around her ankles, and her hiking boots were tapping the bathroom floor in a sad, quiet rhythm.

Today though, Jennifer also heard Rosalyn talking to herself. The cadence of the muttering was weirdly in sync with the tapping of her boots. After a few minutes, Jennifer realized that she hadn't heard any actual bowel action from Rosalyn's stall today. In fact, now that she thought about it, she hadn't heard anything the last few days either.

Was the doctor constipated?

The muttering was weird. It was honestly a little frightening. Jennifer had the horrible idea that Rosalyn had been sitting in here for *hours*, sitting here and tapping her feet and muttering through the night. A splash or two would have been strangely reassuring.

The first three mornings of this, Jennifer had just done her business as quickly as possible, trying not to inhale, and got the hell out of the bathroom. Any other course of action threatened to exacerbate what was already a deeply uncomfortable situation. Today though, before she could think through the implications of breaking their mutual silence, she asked:

"Are you okay?"

It took a moment for a response. Jennifer had a horrible thought: What if the doctor *wasn't* okay, and she had to go in there and help Rosalyn pull up her pants or something?

"Mmm?" Rosalyn finally replied airily. "Yes, fine. Thanks. How are you doing, Jennifer?"

The doctor sounded weirdly detached.

Jennifer struggled to say:

"Uh. I'm fine…"

"Have you had your period yet on board?"

Jennifer cringed. She'd been worried about how to deal with it when it arrived, but under no circumstances did she want to discuss this with Rosalyn.

"No."

"Mine should be next week… I wanted to let you know I have some tampons if you need. And once we run out, we'll figure something out. It will be okay."

Jennifer forced herself to say: "Okay."

Jennifer was done. She wiped herself with the crummy toilet paper on board–the kind that was like thin sandpaper–and pulled up her shorts. She got the seawater container from the mess, came back in and poured it over her shit. Every morning she had the same gross association: it was like pouring gravy over a Thanksgiving turkey. She gagged, pumped the levers as quickly as she could, and flushed. She went to the sink and used a little salt water and pink liquid soap from the dispenser to wash her hands and face. Then she rinsed her mouth out with plastic-tasting salt water.

In the mirror that hung over the sink, she saw Rosalyn's boots had resumed their light tapping.

Clearly something was wrong with the doctor, but Jennifer needed to get the hell out of this bathroom. She left the water container on the sink for Rosalyn and rushed out. Bahram was waiting in the dining room with a pen and paper. In the last few days, he'd been the one to initiate their meetings. His spirits had improved since he finally had someone to communicate with.

Jennifer, on the other hand, couldn't believe how slow their progress had been. She knew she wasn't the best teacher, but Bahram definitely wasn't much of a student. Probably because of his age. She'd heard learning foreign languages became exponentially more difficult after age thirty, and Bahram was at least double that.

By this point, they each knew probably twenty words of the other's language. His drawing skills were appalling. It could take a half hour for him to convey a simple fact to her, and even then she could never be sure she'd understood him correctly.

He smiled at her, a toothy grin. Despite his age, there was something childlike about his grin, flat nose, and wide eyes. He took off his jeff cap for a second and scratched his bald scalp. He looked back at the door to the bathroom, like to confirm he hadn't missed anyone leaving.

He pointed at his bare wrist, where a watch would be, then jutted his chin toward the bathroom.

Jennifer nodded in agreement. She pointed to the bathroom and then gave an exaggerated shake of her head, and two thumbs down, like to convey to Bahram that whatever was going on in there was not good, and taking too long.

Bahram nodded knowingly, pointed to his belly, and then hissed and moved his hands around wildly, acting out the frenzied state of Rosalyn's gastro system.

Jennifer gave him an over the top shrug like, *nothing we can do about it.*

Bahram made a series of gestures that Jennifer couldn't follow, and then laughed deeply. When he laughed his thorax seemed to serve as a kind of subwoofer, and he clutched his gut with both hands, as if the powerful laugh might explode through his stomach if he didn't contain it.

"What?" Jennifer said. "I don't get it."

Then she spread her palms wide like, *I don't understand.*

He made a sketch of something that was totally incomprehensible. It could have been an upside-down stalk of broccoli, or maybe just a hand with too many fingers...

The popular themes in their "talks" were: his son, Azzami, Adam, the ship, and the logo of the Daughters of January. Jennifer now recognized these four renderings. But anything new was a crapshoot.

She shook her head apologetically.

Bahram muttered something, rolled the piece of paper into a ball, and tossed it away.

He tapped his thick fingers on the table. They exchanged another smile. There was a lot of that. He glanced over to see if Rosalyn was leaving the bathroom. No luck.

"Mmm."

He took another sheet of paper and made a stick figure. He added a beard, a skullcap, and little strings hanging around the torso. Jennifer raised an eyebrow.

"Mel?" she asked.

"Mel," he confirmed.

Jennifer raised an eyebrow. Was he going to tell her that Mel had something to do with Adam's burns? Or the Daughters of January?

No. Bahram gestured to the drawn hat and beard and shook his head head quizzically: *why is he dressed like this?*

"Ahh," Jennifer smiled. It seemed he'd never seen a Jewish person before. Or at least, one who dressed like Mel. Of course he was curious; even Jennifer couldn't understand what would compel a person to devote their lives to a cult that was backwards, at best.

It wasn't just Jews, of course. It was any religion: Muslim extremists in Najaf shot and raped other Muslims for not being Muslim enough; Catholic priests molested little boys; the pastor of a Christian megachurch in Wyoming was discovered smoking crystal meth with a gay prostitute, and then apologized, said he'd been led astray by

Satan, and was welcomed back to the pulpit, revered all the more for overcoming the devil himself; Mormons conveniently allowed polygamy; there was a Jewish sect in Brooklyn that, when some prominent Rabbi molested a kid, tried to cover it up and protect him from the police, and even resorted to saying the kid had a mental disability and his testimony wasn't reliable.

To be a practicing member of a religion, Jennifer thought, you either had to be gullible enough to believe there was a man in the sky who did magic, or you had to be one of the assholes at the top of the pyramid scheme, getting money or sex from the gullible peons.

Jennifer took the pencil from Bahram and drew the logo of the DOJ, the two faces. Then under it, a bunch of stick figures kneeling to it. Beside it, she drew a bunch of people like Mel, with beards and hats, kneeling to a six-pointed star.

"Same," she said. "Same."

"Same," Bahram repeated. "Mmm."

She instantly regretted this. She didn't want Bahram to get the wrong idea. Mel himself, though gullible and brainwashed, was a decent enough guy. It was hard to imagine him hurting anybody.

"Mel is good though," she clarified. "Mel good."

Rosalyn finally emerged from the bathroom. She was pale, and her forehead was clammy with sweat. There were dark circles under her eyes. The doctor looked awful.

"Sorry to keep you waiting," she said to Bahram and Jennifer, as if she'd totally forgotten that Bahram didn't speak English, and that Jennifer had already been in there. Then the doctor quickly turned and rushed out of the mess, to the stairwell.

Bahram looked at Jennifer, shook his head somberly, and clicked his tongue. He pointed to the stairwell where Rosalyn had just disappeared and then touched his index finger to his temple, still shaking his head.

"Mel good. *Rose-aline–*" he rubbed his stomach and smiled mischievously. "No good."

Then he waddled eagerly into the bathroom and shut the door behind him. Not ten seconds later, the mess reverberated with Bahram's earth-shattering flatulence, and a groan of relief.

22

"Okay. I got bad news, good news, and better news," Art said. Sam Arnold shifted around on his chair until he found an angle where his hernia wasn't bothering him too much. "The bad news is we're still stranded on a boat in the middle of the ocean, and the world is destroyed."

Lily's face crumpled.

"Kidding, kidding," Art said. "I mean, I'm not kidding, obviously. Shit. I got off on the wrong foot here."

"Why is the door closed?" asked Vic. "You intend to kill us?"

Sam was also curious about the door. And why Art had only invited the three of them to his cabin. But it was the heat of the day–too hot to be opening containers–and it was Mel's shift on the radio.

"Jesus, you three are impossible," Art said. "Here. Here's the good news."

Art stood up, went to his closet, and pulled out two boxes, each the size of a loaf of bread. Vic was the first to recognize what they were. The Frenchman jumped out of his chair.

"*Oui!*" he cried, as Art plopped the still-sealed cartons of Marlboro Lites on the table between them. Vic rubbed the plastic wrap, as if trying to absorb some nicotine through osmosis. Sam felt a flicker of anticipation in his chest. He used to be a heavy smoker, and stressful situations still made him crave a cigarette. There had been few joys more profound than smoking behind the restaurant after a shift.

"Where did you find them?" Lily asked, eyes bright.

"Personal container. I guess someone moving overseas was worried they wouldn't have Marlboros where they were going."

"You smoke?" Vic asked Lily.

"I mean, I try not to," she said. "But you know."

"So that's the good news," Art smiled, "and now the better news."

Vic looked like he was going to explode from delight. What could be better than this?

Art pulled a wad of papers out of his pocket and spread them on the tabletop beside the Marlboros.

"I made a deck of playing cards. We finally have a currency on board, so we can play. Our hours of boredom are over!"

"Play what?" Vic asked, confused.

"Poker, obviously."

Vic furrowed his brow.

"Can we open the cigarettes, please?"

Art sighed, and opened one of the cartons. Vic snatched a pack, opened it, pulled out a smoke, and then, with horror, realized he had no way to light it. His eyes darted around the cabin, as if a source of fire might present itself. His face fell, as he wondered if God could really be this cruel.

Art grinned and pulled a yellow Bic out of his shirt pocket.

"Had this in my pocket when I came on board. You're welcome."

Vic immediately snatched the lighter, cupped his hand over the flame, and lit the end of his cigarette. He closed his eyes and inhaled. He held the smoke in for a long time, then let it stream from his nostrils.

"Ohhh," he sighed, in a way Sam found a little uncomfortably erotic.

"Well," Art said. And then lit his own. Sam and Lily couldn't resist either. The four of them smoked in silence around the table. Art put out a little hand-carved ashtray. Sam sucked in deep. The nicotine seemed to be spreading through his veins and arteries, healing him. His body loosened and he felt a goofy smile on his face. He hadn't felt this good in a long, long time. He could swear the smoke even made his hernia feel better.

Art shook his head, like in disbelief of how good it tasted. Vic still hadn't opened his eyes. Lily coughed at first, but kept on, undeterred.

Vic's burned down first, because he was sucking on it like a hungry calf. The rest smoked theirs down to nubs and tossed them in the ashtray. A haze of smoke hung in Art's cabin. Everyone's bloodshot eyes seemed to be shining.

"So… you didn't want to share these with anyone else?" Sam asked.

"You three are the only ones I can handle in mass quantity," Art said. "Besides the Rabbi, but he's working on something in his cabin day and night. And like I said, this is about more than just cigarettes. Here. There are eight hundred in total so we each get two hundred." He divided up the packs between the four of them. "Now I suppose you could just walk out of here with your smokes, but that would break my heart. I spent a long time making this deck of cards for our gaming pleasure." Art scooped up the cards and shuffled them so fast that his hands were a blur. "I'm not messing around here."

"You want to gamble with the cigarettes?" Sam asked, starting to understand.

"That's right," Art said. "We got nothing but time on our hands. Let's entertain ourselves."

Lily shrugged.

"I guess it was pretty nice of you to give us a share of the cigarettes. You could have taken them yourself. I'll play. I mean, you'll have to teach me."

"I've played before," Sam said. "Once or twice."

Vic clicked his tongue.

"What if I lose my cigarettes?" he asked.

Art laughed.

"Yeah, that's kind of the idea. Look, I'll teach you guys how to play, we'll just play for a couple cigarettes each, and see if you guys wanna keep going. Alright?"

"*D'accord.*"

Sam and Lily both nodded.

"Alright then. We'll start with five card draw. I think that's the easiest."

Art was an excellent teacher. Very patient. Sam thought he could listen to Art talk for hours without getting bored. When one of them asked a question, Art seemed delighted by the opportunity to answer. He kept the three of them totally engaged for twenty minutes, laughing, answering questions, until they all felt pretty confident that they understood the game. The quality of the homemade cards was remarkable. It was incredible that Art made these on board. His handwriting was perfect, and he'd even drawn kings, queens, and jacks for the picture cards. The ace of spades was a true work of art.

"Okay," Lily said. "Let's play for real."

Art raised an eyebrow.

"You sure? We can do some more practice hands."

"I'm ready," Lily said. "Are you two?"

"Alright," Sam replied.

Vic shrugged "*Pourquoi Pas?*"

"Okay, so everyone put one cigarette in the pot. That's the ante."

Art dealt everyone five cards. Sam picked up his hand. He had a pair of sixes, and trash.

"Dealer checks," Art said. "Madame? You to act."

"No bet," she said. "Check."

"Check," Sam said.

Vic stared at his cards intensely.

"I bet two," he said, tossing two of his cigarettes in the pot.

"I'll call you," Art said. Lily and Sam both folded. "Dealer takes three cards," Art said, exchanging three of his cards for three new ones off the top. "And Monsieur Victor, how many cards would you like?"

"One," he said. Art obliged.

"Okay," Art said, looking at his cards again. "I'll check. Vic to speak."

"I bet three," the Frenchman said.

Art shook his head and frowned.

"You trying to bluff me Frenchy? I think you are. I call. What you got?"

Art tossed three cigarettes into the middle and Vic showed his cards. Two pair: kings and threes. Art sighed and showed his lone pair of jacks.

"You win."

Vic eagerly scooped up the cigarettes in the middle, hands tingling with excitement.

"Nice one, Vic," said Lily.

Vic winked at her. "I learn rapidly," he said.

Art gathered up the cards and dealt another hand.

"Ante up, everyone."

They played for two hours, until Sam had to go up to the bridge for his radio shift. He and Art were the losers, each down about twenty-five cigarettes, and the winnings were split pretty equally between Vic and Lily. Sam stood up and winced. He'd been so engaged in the game that he'd forgotten about his hernia for a while. He had to give Art credit: that was easily the most fun he'd had since coming aboard. Sam gathered up his remaining packs of cigarettes.

"Good game everyone," he said.

"It has been a pleasure taking your smokes," smiled Vic.

"Yep," said Lily.

"When's everyone free next?" Art asked. "Should we play tonight after dinner?"

Vic and Lily nodded enthusiastically.

Sam sighed. He didn't want to lose more cigarettes, but at the same time, he was never going to smoke all hundred seventy-something that he had left. Art sensed his reluctance.

"We don't have a game without you, big fella," he said.

"Fine, fine," Sam said. "I'll be here."

"Okay everyone, see you after dinner. Frenchy, try not to smoke away all your winnings before then."

Sam left Art's cabin cradling his Marlboros. He stopped quickly in his own cabin and dropped them on a chair, then slowly climbed the stairs up to the bridge, a goofy smile on his face.

23

To the man He said, "Because you listened to your wife and ate fruit from the tree about which I commanded you, 'You must not eat from it', cursed is the ground because of you. Through toil you will eat from it all the days of your life."

Mel's writing was progressing slower than he'd thought it would. Every time he realized he'd made a mistake, he had to retrace his steps and correct it immediately, unable to proceed knowing there was an imperfection in his rearview mirror. They weren't necessarily big mistakes: the most common was the placement of the letter *vav*, which was a prefix meaning either 'and' or 'so' or 'and then'. There wasn't a lot of logic to which sentences and phrases began with a *vav* and which didn't, it was only a matter of memory, and when he suddenly realized he'd omitted a syllable three or four pages before, he rushed back and corrected it before the memory slipped away.

He worked all day, every day. Even on his radio shifts he wrote. He didn't help with opening containers anymore; this was more important. Art knocked on his door once to say hi, interrupting Mel's train of thought, and Mel had been so frustrated that he'd snapped at him.

"Please! I'm working!"

Art shook his head and gently closed the door, and Mel had immediately felt a pang of remorse. Much had been written about the pure state of mind required of a scribe while writing a Torah scroll.

But it was so frustrating, because Mel could only remember how to chant the first portion of Genesis if he started at the beginning of a chapter. So Art's interruption had cost him maybe twenty minutes, since he'd had to rewind to the beginning of the chapter and sing again from the start.

Also frustrating was that the more times he chanted a chapter of Torah, the less confident he was that he was getting it right–that his memory wasn't betraying him. The words became intertwined with other images, some appealing in their impurity, and he'd try to push these unholy thoughts from his mind, but they'd remain, and he'd clench his fists and shut his eyes tightly, as if he could physically block out these distractions.

"Please," he whispered into the still air of his cabin. "Please give me the strength to do this."

He thought of himself as a boy, in *cheder*, sitting on a hard wooden bench and studying for hours at a time. How much clearer his mind had been then!

He thought of his own son, Reuben. Ten years old, slightly portly. His son had been so much smarter than him. He'd asked questions that Mel had never considered, let alone had answers to.

Father, I don't understand. We eat Matzah on Passover to commemorate when the Israelites rushed from Egypt in such a hurry that the dough on their backs didn't have time to fully rise into bread, right?

Yes. That's right.

So then why, when the Israelites held the first Seder, in Egypt, before they left, did they eat Matzah? That was before the reason for Matzah even existed!

That night, after the Seder, when his family was asleep, he'd pored through dozens of books, looking for an answer. The whole time a little voice in the back of his mind whispered: Reuben is right... It doesn't make sense.

Mel and Reuben approached the Rabbi after prayers the next day to ask. Reuben was excited to repeat his question for the wizened man. Mel though, felt a prickle of something cold in his chest as he watched the Rabbi's face absorb this challenge to the canon . He had nothing but respect for the Rabbi, but he somehow knew his son was going to receive an inadequate answer. And Mel had wondered–is there any question Reuben could ask that would shake this holy man? Was there any inconsistency in the text that his son could point out that would make the Rabbi consider that there truly was something amiss?

The Rabbi nodded, smiled, and said it was an excellent question.

Time is not linear. There is even a Midrash *that the Patriarchs–Abraham, Issac and Jacob–themselves celebrated the Passover Seder, hundreds of years before the events it commemorated every occurred! The world, and time, were created by the Holy One, Blessed Be His Name, who has always known everything that was and will be. The Holy One, of course, knew that the Exodus would happen as it did, in a hurry, without time to bake bread. So He had the Israelites observe it in advance.*

Reuben was unsatisfied.

132   E.Z. Rinsky

Why would God command the Israelites to commemorate something that hadn't happened yet? And furthermore, doesn't that mean that nobody had any free choice about what would happen? What if Pharaoh had changed his mind and let them go freely? Then they wouldn't have had to rush and there would have been no Matzah.

There was a bitter taste in Mel's mouth as he watched the exchange. The Rabbi replied:

The Holy One knew that Pharaoh wouldn't change his mind and let them go freely. As I said, He knows everything that was and will be. He is beyond time.

Mel wanted Reuben to keep prodding the Rabbi; he was strangely disappointed when his son just nodded and accepted the answer. Mel wanted him to demand more. He wanted Reuben to challenge the Rabbi: you can explain anything away with these sorts of answers!

Time isn't linear.

This verse doesn't mean what it appears to mean.

Human beings cannot possibly fathom God's reasons for doing things

There's a higher meaning to things that we can't perceive.

He wiped sweat from his forehead with a rag. The cabin was so hot, but Mel would have had an even harder time concentrating in a public place, where anyone could–and would–interrupt him. On the page in front of him was the beginning of the story of Adam. The Garden of Eden. For the first time, he considered what meaning the origin story really held now that he knew the epilogue: how the world ended.

He thought of Shoshana. He thought about their first day and night as a married couple. That indescribable joy now seemed so silly. That the creation of life, his two children, would lead here. Nowhere.

He dropped his pen. He was thirsty, and if he didn't address this he'd get a headache and lose hours of work. He slipped on his loafers and walked out into the hall with the intention of finding Greg and asking for his water ration an hour early. His mission was sidetracked by a warbled voice.

"Excuse me?"

Adam was sitting on the floor of his cabin, door open. His maritime encyclopedia was closed, in its place a stack of loose papers.

"Yes?" Mel responded.

"Can you help me?

Mel hesitated. He wanted to get his water as soon as possible and return to his work. But what kind of Jew, or human, would he be if he ignored someone asking for help?

"Of course," he said, and stepped into the room.

"I don't understand… did you write these?"

Adam lifted the stack of papers, offering them to Mel like a burnt sacrifice. Mel took the papers. They were covered in handwriting: large, jagged letters which conveyed some sort of desperation.

"I found them next to me," Adam said.

Mel read the top page.

I am awake! The first time. I've been sleeping for a while, but don't remember my dreams. It's hot in here. The room moves. Through my porthole I see– porthole! Ocean! I'm on a boat! What is happening. You

The entry ended there. Mel turned to the next page.

Just waking up now from some kind of crazy sleep. Weird dreams but can't quite remember them. It's hot in here. Maybe because of the sun coming in through the porthole. Porthole. I'm on a boat. What's happening? Drugged? You've been taken against your will?

Mel looked up at Adam. The poor boy's face was pale. The burns on his chest, the faces, and the numbers seemed to have sunk deeper into his body over the last eleven days.

"Did you write these?" Adam repeated.

Mel quickly sifted through the pages. One after another had some sort of identical message, with slight variations depending on the time of day. He sat down on the floor, across from the young man, and set down the papers.

"You don't recognize your own handwriting?" Mel asked.

Adam fiddled with his right ear, twisting it as if to unscrew it from his head.

"I do," he said softly. "It does look like mine but… I didn't write these. I don't remember them…"

Mel declined to answer. He simply studied the boy, trying to understand.

"How did you arrive on this boat, Adam?" Mel asked.

The young man squinted at him, like Mel was an island on the horizon.

"You don't remember the bombs?" Mel asked. "The disease in the air?"

Adam stiffened, but said nothing.

Perhaps, Mel thought, he's forced himself to forget.

Mel thought of the trees he saw, a few days after the house where he'd found the Hawaiian Punch. He'd pulled over to sleep for a few hours. Sleep was fitful. He'd begun to sleep wearing mittens, fastening them to his wrists with duct tape; too many times he'd woke up choking, with his hands trying to pull off his gas mask.

He awoke with the sun, stomach growling as usual. He had amassed a collection of canned food but still didn't dare remove his gas mask to eat. Instead he sucked some apple juice through a straw. The sugar made him want to gag.

In the light of dawn he saw that he'd parked outside of a municipal court building. It was a sturdy building made of red brick, topped with spires. There was a grand walkway leading to the front entrance, an aisle lined on either side by a row of old trees. From the branches of all the trees, bodies were hanging from nooses. There were dozens, maybe hundreds, oscillating in the morning breeze like wind chimes.

The first days, he'd made an effort to bury some of the bodies he came across, but it was futile. Mel turned on the ignition and drove on, trying to ignore the voice in his head:

If you don't bury them, they'll hang there until the end of time.

That night, as he refastened his mittens, he kept forcing himself to remember that God had reasons for all of this, reasons he couldn't understand.

A dead Rueben questioned a dead Rabbi:

What possible reasons could the Holy One, Blessed Be His Name, have for creating a plague so heinous that hundreds of people chose to hang themselves just to escape the suffering?

I agree it's hard to understand on the surface, Rueben. But it's like an ant, in a home that's under construction, being remodeled. To the ant, all he sees is destruction. He can't possibly imagine that there is a human being improving his living conditions.

No! No! We are not ants! God gave us the Torah, we made a covenant. God said He'd make us a nation more numerous than the stars in the sky, He promised us that and He broke his promise! How can you defend such a God?

"Why are you dressed like that?" Adam asked. "With the hat and white strings on your shirt?"

"I'm a Jew," Mel responded weakly.

Adam nodded.

"A Jew," Adam repeated. "Why do Jews wear those little hats?"

"To remind us…" Mel's throat was parched with thirst. "To remind us always that there's someone above us. An almighty Creator."

"Oh."

And then Adam smiled blankly, and Mel understood that all was again lost.

24

For maybe the fourth day in a row, Rosalyn Carson was already wide awake as dawn seeped through the porthole in her cabin. Her hands were still shaking from some horrible dreams. She couldn't remember any images, but there had been a nonstop voice–maybe her own voice–narrating her dreams. Loudly. It got so loud inside her head that she'd jerked up out of sleep, expecting to find someone screaming inside her cabin.

At the first sign of light she rolled out of bed, onto the coarse carpet, and began her routine. Twenty-five sit-ups, fifteen pushups on her knees, child's pose, spring up for twenty jumping jacks, repeat. She finished the second set of jumping jacks and, feeling inspired, did some shadow boxing, maneuvers she knew from her Tuesday morning kickboxing class at the gym. The exercise was already making her feel better. She jabbed fiercely at the air, wearing only her yellowing bra and underpants, sweating profusely from the heat and exertion.

It was mostly word salad, what she could remember of that narrating voice. Random strings of words eliciting anxiety and horror, her subconscious considerate enough to skirt the actual issues. But her waking self had no such qualms. Already images of Scott were assaulting her. She whirled and punched the air, as if to keep them at bay.

Each time she ran through her loop of Scott it seemed staler, farther away, and evoked less of his essence, like her memories were an old film reel that was fading from overuse. She started to question little details. The over-the-top utopian memory of her out in her herb garden on an impossibly beautiful April day, down on all fours with a trough, putting in some oregano, when she hears the screen door slam. She turns to see Scott emerge with a tray holding a pitcher of iced lemonade and two glasses.

Give yourself a break, Rosalyn! My god. It's the weekend.

She wipes her sweat away with her sleeve and joins him under the awning, where he's reclining on a sun chair and sucking lemonade through a straw.

This is *my break.*

Just think about what people from a thousand years ago would think about that, Rosalyn. Peasant farmers. What would they think if they could see this: a doctor doing gardening on the weekend for recreation?

She takes her lemonade but doesn't sit.

I think they'd probably be less shocked by that than by airplanes, refrigeration, and your iPad.

Bob and Honey texted to see if we want to get dinner tonight.

So tell them no. I don't like them, and neither do you.

But they're our friends.

Why Rosalyn remembered that distinct afternoon, from probably three years ago, was a mystery to her. And the more times she replayed it, the more she worried that it hadn't even happened; that it was a totally plausible amalgam of several similar scenes. And the fact that there was no way to confirm or deny that it had really happened made her feel like an elephant was sitting on her chest. It was like that with all her memories. There was nobody alive who could verify any of them.

She's sitting in a coffee shop across from Prospect Park. It's dark outside and there's an inch of snow on the sidewalk. Textbooks and papers swallow her table. She's chewing on the end of her pen, reading about Prenatal Polyhydramnios, headphones injecting Goldberg Variations into her ears. It's late, too late to be here.

Excuse me?

She's pulled out of her textbook by a waving hand, attached to a short man with glasses and a bad haircut. She takes off her headphones.

Are you closing?

He frowns.

I don't work here… Can I sit down? All the other tables are taken. I won't disturb you.

Sure.

She pulls back on her headphones and tries to refocus on her textbook but his presence is making it difficult. He's not working on anything himself, that's the problem; he's just looking around the café, taking a sip of his coffee, examining the covers of her textbooks with interest, checking his clunky digital watch… Did he just come in here to get coffee and sit?

So you're a medical student?

She hears him through the Bach, but pretends she doesn't. He gestures for her to take off her headphones. She's annoyed, but sees no choice, short of being extremely rude.

So you're a medical student?

Yes.

At Downstate?

Yes.

You know, attention to detail is probably really important for doctors. All the baristas here are wearing matching red aprons and hats. It's a little worrisome that you thought I worked here. It means you didn't notice that. Imagine if I was your patient, and the matching aprons and hats were, I don't know, my messed up liver or something.

Rosalyn is losing patience.

I'm sorry, but I'm very busy. There's an empty seat over there, by the door.

He rubs the back of his neck. His courage is waning.

Yeah, okay, I mean honestly there was an empty seat there before too.

She still recalls, with pride, the neutral stare she returned at this point.

Like I said, I'm busy.

Can I just get your number?

When she doesn't respond, he adds, as if it will help:

I'm at CUNY. PhD. in classics. Greek stuff, you know.

Rosalyn considers giving him a fake number. Were it not for the fact that this is the closest thing to romance she's experienced in at least a year, she probably would have. But maybe it would be nice to have an admirer.

Here. And my name is Rosalyn. You should ask that.

He shakes his head like he's angry at himself for this misstep.

Nice to meet you Roz. I'm Scott.

Not Roz. Rosalyn.

Had it really been snowing outside as he walked out into the night, or was that a romantic detail superimposed by her memory? God, that little nerdy guy. She recalled distinctly that she'd had absolutely zero attraction to him that night. She'd told him that on their fifth date.

I immediately regretted giving you my number. I was kicking myself for being too nice.

Still regret it?

Undecided. You know, there's still a very significant chance this could all end in wasted time and deep unhappiness.

Where had their fifth date been? The memory of that conversation is without a setting. Just the two of them floating on barstools, the backdrop a generic restaurant or bar. File footage.

Rosalyn was wet with sweat. She commended herself on a great workout. Now it was time to pee, rinse herself off with salt water, and get to work. There were container locks to hack, and she needed to sit with Adam. She'd been spending time with him, what she thought of as therapy sessions. She was determined to help him. She believed he'd already made incremental progress; yesterday–although he didn't remember her name, and seemed to think she was a nurse–he did admit that, though he couldn't be sure, she did seem familiar to him.

She put on her linen shirt and jeans, then pulled on her socks and hiking boots and wandered out into the hall. Her mind was still cloudy with snippets of memories. Her boots carried her on autopilot to the end of the hall, down the stairs, and into the mess where Greg was sitting.

"What's up, Doc?" he smiled.

"Hello," she said, rushing past him into the bathroom where she shut herself in the middle stall. She tugged her pants down, sat down to pee, and suddenly went lightheaded. In an instant the euphoria from the exercise evaporated completely and she suddenly felt helpless and sick.

She lowered her sweaty forehead in her palms. Her vision was spotty; she was worried if she stood up she might faint.

She was probably just hungry. When was the last time she ate? Had she skipped dinner!? Yes. Horribly irresponsible, especially considering how much she'd been exercising. And now she was paying the price.

Give yourself a break Rosalyn! Scott said. *The world just ended.*

She folded her arms tightly across her chest. She was concerned that she might actually faint, even sitting down. The smell wasn't helping. Every day without running water it got worse. The air felt literally thick with the smell. She dry-heaved, and kept her head between her legs.

This was more than just hunger. She knew this feeling.

Seventh grade, Sadie Hawkins dance. What deranged mind decided that the cruel institution of middle school wasn't painful enough–hundreds of pubescent bodies crammed together in stuffy, windowless rooms for seven hours a day, all frustrated and confused, vying for dominance in a sexual hierarchy none of them understood in the least–

who decided that they needed to supplement this pain with four school dances every year?

For the Sadie Hawkins dance, girls had to ask the boys to be their date. She asked Joe Copela, a small, intelligent boy she sat next to in algebra. He shrugged and said fine.

The basketball court in the gym was converted into a dance floor: colored tissue paper hung from the rafters, the main lights were turned off, replaced by revolving colored spotlights that roved over clumsy couples with hands on shoulders and lower backs, swaying and gyrating like they'd seen people do on TV. Joe kept his mouth closed, probably to hide his braces. For a long hour they fumbled. When they noticed that some of the other kids seemed to know what they were doing, their steps a bit more confident, Rosalyn and Joe tried to imitate them.

After a series of classic disco tracks, the principal got up on the bleachers, beside the DJ, and took the mic. Rosalyn couldn't remember the principal's name, only that he was relatively young, and one of those adults who desperately wanted to be the cool one who "got" kids, the kind who wore sunglasses and playful ties.

The principal spoke into the mic.

Is everyone having a good time?

Like rowers on a slave ship under threat of the whip, the children responded in the affirmative.

And then the principal snapped his fingers at the DJ, who nodded like they were in cahoots, and immediately the gym was filled with that lurid synthesizer riff, that languid, throaty voice that conjured the scandalous scene from the film of the year, the merging silhouettes of Tom Cruise and Kelly McGillis.

All the boys dutifully grabbed their partners' hips and moved in close. Joe had eaten some kind of pungent fish for dinner, and Rosalyn wished someone would take *his* breath away.

Guys, I want you to enjoy yourselves tonight. You only live once, so take that chance.

The first couple started smooching. Then a second. It spread like a contagion, each couple yielding to the fear of looking like prudes. If the social pressure had been uncomfortable before, now the needle was in the red. Gaskets were threatening to blow. If memory served, the principal was fired not long after this dance.

The dominoes toppled all around them, until it felt like they were the only couple who hadn't yet locked lips. Rosalyn's pulse thumped in her ears. There might as well have been a spotlight on them, she felt, designating them as squares. Her eyes met Joe's, and it was clear that he too was in emotional turmoil. Something cracked. Joe could hold out no longer. He gripped her tight around the midriff and leaned in, expression almost apologetic. Rosalyn's blood went cold. She'd never kissed a boy before and had no desire for Joe Copela to change that.

She definitely didn't want this to happen, but it was happening. His dry lips parted and planted themselves on her mouth. She had the sense that he was trying to swallow her whole. His fish breath was overwhelming. His braces were sharp. The room was closing in on her. Her legs were shaking and she felt she might vomit or faint.

This isn't real. Nothing is real. The school, the dance, Top Gun. None of it's real.

"Are you okay?"

Jennifer's voice, in the stall next to her. Rosalyn gathered herself.

"Fine," she heard herself croak. "Thanks."

Jennifer finished, washed her hands and left. Rosalyn stayed.

Until three weeks ago, Rosalyn had been actively seeing a psychologist. He'd suggested to her that part of the reason she'd been drawn to medicine was the subconscious hope that it would give her the tools to master her *own* body and mind, so that she'd never again be a victim of these panic attacks. She'd dismissed this idea. If that was the case, why hadn't she gone into psychiatry or neurology? As a dermatologist, the most she could hope for was to master her own moles.

After maybe twenty minutes, Rosalyn realized she couldn't stay in the bathroom any longer. There were people waiting. Eventually someone would come into the stall and discover her in this state. And the possibility of being found like this–pants around her ankles, hugging her knees, head between her legs–was enough to finally spur her to stand up.

She braced herself against the toilet paper dispenser, and rose to her wobbly feet.

She washed her hands with salt water, splashed it liberally on her face and on the back of her neck, then left the bathroom. Yesterday Jennifer and Bahram had been sitting and waiting. This time she was thankful to find the mess empty; she didn't want anyone to realize how long she'd been in there.

She turned into the kitchen, opened a packet of yellow daal and poured it into a metal bowl, then turned on the propane stove to warm it. Somebody had left their dirty dishes in the sink. As her daal heated up she washed the dirty bowls and silverware, dried them with a dishtowel, and stacked them in the cabinet over the sink.

She sat down in the mess, and felt a little better after eating a few spoonfuls of warm lentils. In fact, she suddenly felt she had enough strength to do another couple sets of sit-ups, pushups, and jumping jacks. Or she'd do a few brisk laps of the ship on the perimeter walkway. Yes, a few laps and then she'd get to work hacking. Maybe Art or Sam—who couldn't be convinced to rest, despite his hernia— would be ready to join her by then. She mentally planned the day's itinerary: laps, hacking, polenta for lunch, radio shift, then maybe she'd do a few more laps before dinner. A fine routine.

She put down her spoon and rubbed her eyes. She thought again about Joe Copela's face as he inclined toward her, mouth open, ready to dock atop hers. Over Joe's shoulder, the principal on the bleachers beside the DJ, proudly surveyed his handiwork. The revolting, wet sensation as Joe latched onto her. The potent smell of his fish dinner.

Even thirty years later, Rosalyn was unable to eat any sort of fish or seafood.

25

"My pops was so cheap, oh man," Arthur Roselli said, laughing as he dealt the cards. "There was a hospital a few blocks from our house. He used to take me to eat there. In the hospital cafeteria. Because it was so cheap."

He remembered the red jello his old man always got for dessert. There was something evil and medicinal about its color. Art would watch his dad carve out each spoonful carefully, insert the dancing mound into his mouth and clamp down, biting the handle of the spoon with his front teeth, as if he was worried the jello might attempt an escape.

You want some kiddo? If you want some we can split this.

No, Art didn't want jello. That jello was foul. And his appetite was always ruined by all the sick and old people in the cafeteria with them. Art wanted a goddamn hamburger from McDonalds like a normal kid.

"Come on," Lily said. "The *hospital cafeteria*?? That's so gross."

Vic nodded.

"A revoltant tale. I bet four."

The Frenchman tossed four Marlboros into the pot. He had seven unopened cartons in front of him, which he'd brought back to gamble with, plus an unlit cigarette hanging from the side of his mouth. Sam and Lily both folded. Art smiled at Vic.

"How much currency did you smoke since yesterday?"

Vic wrinkled his face in confusion.

"He wants to know how many cigarettes you've smoked since we played yesterday," Sam explained.

"Ah," Vic shrugged. "I'm not counting. Life is short, you know. Shorter now."

Vic clearly had a hand. Whenever he had a hand, he put his cards face down on the table and covered them with his right palm. A common tell: protecting your valuables. Art called the bet anyway.

"I'm not your doctor or your mother," Art grinned. "I'm just worried about us running out of poker chips. How many cards you want?"

Vic shrugged.

"None."

Art laughed out loud.

"You got a flush, Frenchy?"

Vic winked at him. Art looked down at his pair of fives.

"Dealer takes three."

Art swapped out his three rags for three different rags.

Vic tapped his fingers on the table then silently placed an entire unwrapped carton into the pot. Twenty Marlboros.

Lily and Sam stared at Art, on the edge of their seats. This was getting exciting.

"My pops wouldn't even hand out candy on Halloween. He *hated* Halloween," Art said. He'd already decided that he was going to call Vic's bet, just to confirm his read for future games–that when Vic covered his cards with his right hand it meant he had gold. But in the meantime he'd let the Frenchman sweat. See if he could pick up any other useful tells. "It wasn't just the expense of the candy. That was just the start of it. It was more about having people on our property. He'd rant about it for the whole month of October. That's my strongest association with autumn, my old man at dinner, for weeks before Halloween, being like 'can you believe these people think that they have a license to trespass? To stomp over the lawn I mow every week, that I *pay* to water, to keep green?'"

Lily shook her head.

"But they're just kids."

Art laughed.

"Well that's exactly what my mom and I said!"

Art could see Vic was getting impatient. He was trying to act natural and listen to the story, pretending to laugh every time Lily and Sam did, even though Art could tell he couldn't quite understand everything. But every couple of seconds the Frenchman's eyes flitted back to the pack of Marlboros he'd bet–the twenty smokes in the communal pot a sort of Schrodinger's cat, belonging not quite to Vic, not quite to Art, the uncertainty clearly gnawing at the Frenchman.

"It's just tradition," Sam said. "Sorry to say, but if you don't like Halloween, you better move to another country."

"That's exactly right," Art nodded. "That's what my mom and I tried to explain to him. It's only one night, just deal with it. But the old bastard couldn't make peace with the holiday. Every year he'd try something new. I remember him buying crime scene tape, you know the yellow stuff? He wrapped it around our house and turned off all the lights. Spent the whole night of Halloween peeking out of one of our windows making sure nobody broke through the tape. But see, by the time I was twelve or so, Old Man Roselli had a reputation in the neighborhood. The crime scene tape worked the first year, but the second time he tried it everyone realized what he was doing. It wasn't just Halloween either, of course. You can be damn sure he didn't shell out for Christmas lights. I remember I asked him once if we could put up lights and he looked at me like I'd told him I wanted to be a ballerina when I grow up. He goes, 'Do you know how much our electric bill is? And you're asking me to put up lights *outside!?*' Then he goes, I swear to god, that he'll put up Christmas lights if I agree not to use any of the lights in my bedroom or the bathroom for all of December."

"No. Way," Lily said.

"Swear to god."

"Man," Vic's cheeks were pink. "The game, remember?"

"Right, right," Art smiled. "Sorry Victorino. You bet a whole pack there?"

Vic nodded vigorously. He wanted Art to match him so badly.

Art made a show of mulling it over, then tossed in his own pack.

"Call. What you got?"

Vic eagerly turned over his cards to show a full house.

Art nodded glumly.

"You win. Good hand."

This was their fourth session together. Art was now sure that he could determine Vic or Lily's hand strength with pretty reliable accuracy. When Lily was bluffing she sought eye contact with her opponent and talked even more than usual. But when she had a good hand, she turned quiet and found something else to focus on: fiddling with a cigarette or tying back her hair. Vic had the thing where he protected his cards when he liked them. He didn't bluff much, because he was genuinely terrified of losing cigarettes, and when he did bluff he bet too low. A big bet from Vic was almost certain to mean a made hand. Lily had tried a few big bluffs–and Art gave her props for gamesmanship–but she was usually unwilling to fully commit to the story, by taking only one or no cards after the first round.

For Art's purposes, these tells were more than enough. Once he started getting serious, there would be no contest.

Surprisingly though, he was having trouble with Sam. It wasn't that Sam didn't care enough about the cigarettes to get emotional and betray himself; the big fella had definitely been enjoying the marvelous return to a one-time addiction. Rather, Sam had some kind of freakish intuition for the game. Art had expected, based on the big fella's short fuse during group meetings that he'd be easy to get off kilter. That he'd make reckless, emotional moves. Nothing could be farther from the truth.

The giant's aura of calm would have been the envy of many professionals. While Vic and Lily's faces were like relief maps of the Himalayas–peaks and valleys of involuntary emotion–Sam's face was the ocean on a windless day. He never flinched, twitched, smiled, or grimaced. While they played, his voice was always level, and Art had yet to discern any correlation between his talkativeness and hand strength.

If they'd had all the time in the world, Art would have been more patient; sometimes it took hundreds of hours of playing with someone before you found a tell. But Art hadn't started this game just for entertainment. And he realized he'd soon have to begin escalating, even without feeling confident that he could beat Sam.

It was another hour and a half before an opportunity presented itself. Sam and Vic were up, Lily and Art were down, the latter by design.

Art looked down at two pair: kings and sevens. It was perfect: a hand just strong enough to be plausibly valued, while being vulnerable to a truly good hand. Now he had to hope one of them had something slightly stronger than he did. He bet five cigarettes. Vic folded, Lily folded. Sam raised.

"Fifteen," announced Sam, face as blank as always.

This could be it: the first escalation.

"Call," Art said, tossing in another ten. "How many cards you want, Sammy?"

"Two," the behemoth said, representing three of a kind.

Art himself took one card, which didn't change his hand.

Sam looked down at his new cards, stared at them emptily for a moment, then calmly reached to his cigarettes and threw in half a pack.

"Ten," he said.

"Thirty," Art said, quickly raising him.

Sam blinked once, twice, then put five cartons in the center.

"One hundred," he said.

Art's chest clenched in anticipation. This was it. The moment of truth. Art looked down at his cigarettes and made a show of counting how many he had in front of him. One hundred and eight left. He cracked his knuckles, and looked up at Sam.

"Tell you what, big fella. If I call you and lose I'm down to eight cigs. Basically, I'm toast. And I'll have nothing to smoke tomorrow. So here's what I propose: we all have those shifts at the radio. Three hours each. I figure that's kind of a chore. Nobody likes sitting up there. I think each of our shifts is probably worth about… twenty cigarettes? So what would you say to me calling your bet with sixty cigarettes and two shifts. If you win, I'll do two of your radio shifts. If I win, I'll just take those cigarettes in the middle."

Art knew Vic would be okay with this; he hated doing the shifts, and would love to have a way to weasel out of them. Art didn't know about Lily, but figured she could be swayed if the rest of them agreed to this rule change. Sam was his biggest concern. Sam and his principles.

"I don't know," Sam said slowly. "That doesn't seem right."

"Why?" Art asked. "You bluffing?"

"I mean…" Sam said, "we're just playing for cigarettes you know. It's just for fun. But it doesn't seem right that someone could have to take a bunch of shifts just because they lost at poker."

"Why?" Art shrugged. "Nobody's forcing you to bet *your* time. I'm just offering to cover yours because I want to make sure I have plenty to smoke for the next few days."

Sam blinked emptily.

"You think twenty cigarettes is worth one shift?"

Art threw up his palms.

"Was just my estimate. We can decide on a different value if you want."

"Seems correct," said Vic.

Lily nodded.

Sam stared at Art for a long moment. Art leaned back in his chair, locked his hands behind his head and assumed an expression of boredom. Sam's huge eyes seemed to be looking straight through him. For a second, Art was unsure whether Sam was trying to read the strength of his hand, or simply his overall worth as a human.

Lily's gaze swiveled back and forth between the two of them, like she was watching a tennis match.

"Alright then," Sam said. "You want to bet your shifts, go on."

"I do," Art said. "I call. I got kings and sevens."

Without smiling, Sam flipped over his cards to reveal three jacks. Then he wordlessly embraced the mound of cigarettes in the pot and pulled them toward him.

"Well," Art said. "Looks like that backfired."

"You're really going to do his shifts?" Vic asked.

"Of course. We had a deal."

"How does it work?" Lily asked. "Like, who chooses which of his shifts you take?"

Art shrugged, looked at Sam.

"I guess it's his choice."

Sam frowned.

"This doesn't feel right," he said. "Forget it. You don't have to do my shifts. It's not fair."

"Of course I do. We made a deal. You won fair and square. If I don't follow through, I mean… I guess our game is pretty much over."

The suggestion that their poker sessions might be discontinued seemed to horrify Vic. Lily too. They had worse facial control than the Muppets.

"Well alright," Sam shook his head. "I have a shift tomorrow at eleven in the morning, and the next day at ten at night. I guess you can take those."

Art made a big dramatic sigh.

"Alright."

They played another hour or so. No more shift bets; Art didn't want to push it. Finally the energy started to peter out. By the time they decided to end, everyone was a winner except Art.

"We're doing this again tomorrow!" he shouted after them as they filed out, grinning and shaking a fist at them. "I'm not going to let you crazy kids all fleece me again, believe me."

Now alone, Art looked down at his paltry supply of Marlboros. He'd lost all but forty of his initial two hundred. But he wanted a smoke. A couple. He took his yellow Bic and headed out into the hallway, then to the stairwell and up to the bridge. Elissa was currently on her shift at the radio.

"Good evening, miss," Art said, doffing a pretend hat.

"Hello Art. Come to keep me company?"

"I'm actually about to turn in pretty soon. Was just wondering if you had one of the flashlights up here… wanted to take a little stroll around before bed."

Elissa nodded, pointed to a cabinet underneath the communications panel.

"There are two in there. Just bring it back when you're done if you would. Don't want them to get lost."

"Of course."

Art took one of the flashlights and climbed down the slippery exterior stair to the top deck. He thought about what he'd try to carve during the extra shifts on the bridge. He wanted to make something practical–artistic pursuits felt a little empty these days–but didn't have many ideas.

The water was wild tonight, as he made his way toward the containers at the rear of the ship he nearly lost his footing a few times.

It took him a little while to find the container he was looking for. It was blue, and he'd scratched a mark on the front of it with the axe. He pried open the door with the butt of the flashlight. The contents were exactly as he'd left them: rubber car tires stacked from floor to ceiling. Nothing interesting–exactly what whoever packed this container had hoped the customs inspector would think as well.

Art knew he'd been lucky to notice something amiss a few days ago: mixed in with the familiar smell of rubber was an unexpected hint of soap. Maybe under different circumstances he wouldn't have thought twice, but the incredible monotony of ship life drove him to investigate even the most mundane curiosities.

He'd been right. The tires smelled of dish soap, and when he inspected them closely he could see that although they'd been washed and polished to give them that new-tire glisten, the treads were worn down on all of them. They were used tires. Someone wanted to make it look like they were shipping a crate of new tires. And the only reason someone would go through this whole charade was to hide something.

So Art had come back during siesta time with a step ladder, pulled a few tires off the top of one of the columns and tossed them aside. Another layer of tires, which weakened his hypothesis. But he'd come this far, so, dripping with sweat, he slid out one of the tires from the second row and tossed it to the ground where it bounced around a few times. He peered into the space behind the back row of tires, and realized he'd struck gold. At least ten cubic feet of still-wrapped cartons of Marlboros. Easily a hundred thousand cigarettes.

Tonight, just as he had when he first discovered the stash, Art pulled out a carton, unwrapped it, opened it, removed a pack, and had a lit cigarette in his mouth before he could even think about it, the whole act as automated as breathing itself.

26

Greg had been spending a lot of time starboard, about midway down the length of the ship, trying to make out what was happening on shore. He ran through the same numbers: the first night on board he ran the engine from five in the morning until eleven, when Rosalyn stopped him. He'd had it at low speed, average around eight knots. So that was forty-eight knots. None of the books in the captain's lounge addressed how to convert knots to miles or kilometers; either this was assumed to be common knowledge, or it was frowned upon in the maritime community to even acknowledge the nomenclature of the land bound. Elissa said according to the GPS they were about fifty miles from shore. Greg had inspected the atlas himself, and that seemed about right, but of course that atlas could have been doctored. Or the GPS could have been hacked.

The east coast was nothing more than a thin horizon line, sandwiched between the sky and the sea like a piece of bologna. Was it really true that at fifty miles you could hardly see the shore?

It was also possible that they'd been drifting. Or, that when he'd been sleeping, someone had turned on the engines for a few hours and sailed even farther away from land. But he probably would have awoken from the rumble of the engines, unless of course one of his companions was drugging him–a theory that was gradually seeming more and more plausible to Greg. Mel had cooked–heated up–polenta and daal for everyone two or three times and Greg had eaten it because the others would have been suspicious if he hadn't. If Mel had wanted to slip something into Greg's portion, he'd have no way of knowing.

But why would Mel do something like that? Did he have the motive? One thing was for sure: Greg wasn't going to trust him just because he dressed like an Orthodox Jew. There were plenty of "men of god" who were complete sickos. Mel could have drugged him because of Jennifer. Jennifer could have told Mel what happened that first night aboard; she would have lied and made it a big dramatic thing like 'Greg Pink assaulted me', and Mel would have agreed to put something in Greg's food to make him sleepy and docile, to keep him under control. Maybe something to cut his libido as well. Or hallucinogens.

That bitch, Jennifer. Greg gripped the slick railing tightly and stared down into the glassy green surface below. She was probably saying all sorts of things about him behind his back. That stupid little fucking girl. How old was she, twenty-one? Twenty-two? She didn't understand anything about the world. She was such a child that she didn't understand pain, the kind of pain that had come over him that evening. She'd never felt the kind of emptiness where you don't even know who you are, where you feel like you're a balloon, where you look down at your stomach and wonder if there's literally nothing under the skin. Every *adult* knew that feeling, and could empathize when someone else was feeling like that. But that dumb girl… she didn't understand that sometimes you needed someone to spend the night with–even if you felt absolutely nothing for them–just to help you forget that feeling for a while.

Greg spat over the railing. What was the simplest explanation for what was really going on here? It was obvious: a bunch of nutjobs had figured out a really clever way to kidnap a celebrity, without him even knowing he'd been kidnapped. And they all had really tight scripts to follow to make their backstory seem plausible. Right now they were probably demanding millions for his return. Or maybe it wasn't about money, it was just some kind of weird social experiment they'd concocted, and were filming the whole thing…

But how could that be? He couldn't figure it out because he'd seen the destruction himself, firsthand. That was what he kept coming back to the last couple days. He'd seen the highway, the family in the restaurant, the dog. It would have been quite an impressive production.

Much more impressive, certainly, than *Momma Bear*, the "heartwarming comedy for the whole family" he'd been working on when the world ended.

The set was a plantation-era mansion in rural Georgia. Greg sat on a wooden porch swing beside the kid who was playing his son. At the base of the stairs were a dozen PAs with lights and fans, sound and camera guys, and a miserable director. The smell of the citronella candles–set up around the perimeter of the set to keep mosquitoes at bay–was a little nauseating.

The script called for the swing scene to be shot at dusk, so they could only fit in about three chances a day. The past two days the kid had fucked up, either forgetting his lines or breaking character. Factor in the wet July heat, the flying bugs–each the size of a child's fist–for whom the candles were a laughable deterrent… tension was high among the staff.

Action.

The scene was with Greg's character, Lance MacIntyre and the kid who played his son, Freddy. Ever since Lance's wife died seven years ago he'd been having tough luck with women. Freddy had watched Lance strike out again and again trying to find Freddy a new mom. Well, now Lance had finally met someone he liked, and she liked him. The only problem was that she was a twelve hundred pound grizzly bear who'd escaped from the Atlanta zoo, and everyone could see that except for Lance.

This scene came about a third of the way into the movie, after Lance had gone on two 'dates' with 'Betsy', both of which happened to be walks through the park. The audience alternately saw Betsy as she was–a huge bear–and as Lance saw her: a brunette on the larger side, who grunted a lot, and always left an inexplicable path of trampled foliage in her wake.

Lance sighed and put his hand around his son's shoulder, and they both watched the sunset. The scene was a heartfelt lull in the action, sandwiched between visual gags having to do with Betsy's size and true nature (*Wow, Betsy, I can't believe we have the whole Starbucks to ourselves, again!*), and scenes in which Lance misinterpreted the Georgia PD Animal Control Division's fascination with his new girlfriend (*how many jealous exes do you have?*). The porch scene was meant to ensure that Lance was likable; that the audience saw him as helplessly lovestruck, not as a dangerous schizophrenic.

This was the third and final chance of the day. In fifteen minutes it would be night. Greg tightened his grip around the child's shoulders.

Love… You get a feeling like suddenly everything bad that's happened to you before with women is okay. Because it was all leading to this.

And you felt like that with Mom?

Greg sighed.

Oh yeah. The first time I met your mother… It was like all of life before that was a dream, and I was finally waking up.

The kid frowned

When I wake up I just feel groggy.

Hehe. Yeah, I guess when you're in love you're a little groggy too.

The kid actor didn't say anything. Some of the PAs shook their heads. Greg tried to prompt the kid again. They could cut it together in post.

Hehe. Yeah, I guess when you're in love you're a little groggy too.

The director tugged at her hair.

Cut! Goddamn it.

Greg pulled away his arm.

'So if love is so good why don't you do it again?' That's the line, buddy. Jesus Christ, can we get a teleprompter or something for this kid? Or just cut that line? Or get a different kid?

The kid teared up and rushed off the porch into the arms of his waiting mother, who shot Greg a horrible glare.

Greg climbed down the stairs to the mom and kid, and forced a smile.

Look, sorry, but we've almost wrapped all the daytime scenes. And if the crew has to stay an extra night here in the middle of nowhere, everyone's gonna be pissed, you know what I'm saying? Just make sure you run through the lines a few hours tonight.

Greg ruffled the kid's sandy hair.

You'll be fine buddy, but we have to *get this tomorrow, okay pal?*

Greg grabbed a sandwich off the buffet table and stomped toward his trailer. The crew parted to let him pass. He didn't make eye contact with any of them.

He slammed the door to his trailer and immediately filled a tumbler with ice. The actress who played Betsy (the human version) had given him a bottle of expensive scotch their first day on set with a note about how excited she was to be working with him. The bottle was buried under a pile of dirty clothes in his bedroom, and he now retrieved it and filled the tumbler to the brim.

He hated this movie. He'd told his manager Bobby to get him some more serious roles. He was sick of clowning around.

Greg, there's a dream role the Stone Brothers are casting in two months. The script knocked my socks off, and the lead is super complex. Depressed, but lovable. It's perfect for you.

Can you get it for me?

A hundred percent, but only if you do this one first. It's the same casting director. I talked to her last night, and she said if you agree to Momma Bear, she'll give you the inside track into the Stone Brothers project. Stack the casting lineup with a bunch of washouts.

Momma Bear?

It's actually hilarious. I think you're gonna love it. And two million bucks, plus executive producer credit and three percent on the backend doesn't hurt.

But what good was the money when he was stuck in the middle of some flyover state? He took a long drink. Then another, and another, until he finally started feeling pleasantly woozy. *Actually hilarious,* Bobby had said. This movie was a steaming pile of shit and everyone on set knew it. He called Bobby a few times to complain but he didn't pick up.

Greg awoke on his couch to harsh morning light, a pulsing headache, and his phone ringing, flashing **Bobby Fat Manager**. The chunk of lard was finally returning his call. As soon as Greg picked up, a familiar voice wheezed from the speaker; Bobby was always breathing hard, like he just ran up a hill.

Where are you?

Where do you think, fatass? Bumblefuck, Georgia. I'm stuck here until this kid learns his goddamn lines. I swear to god, Bobby. You've given me bad career advice before, but this–

Greg. Have you not seen the news?

Your wife is finally divorcing you? Good for her.

Jesus, Greg. Turn on a TV. The Russians bombed us. California is gone. Los Angeles, San Diego. They're vaporized.

Interesting… Who's directing?

Greg, fucking christ, turn on a goddamn TV. Check in on your mom. I gotta go. Be safe.

Bobby hung up. Greg stared at the phone for a second, confused about what had just come out of it. Had Bobby finally snapped? If so, it was gonna be a pain to find a new manager. Poor Bobby, Greg thought. He decided he'd pay for the rehab. He owed the guy that much, for the miracles he'd worked early in his career.

Someone knocked on his trailer door.

Fuck off! I'll be out in an hour!

Greg staggered from the couch to his bed and pulled the blanket over his eyes to block out the light. When he awoke a second time he felt a little better. He brushed his teeth and gelled his hair. As he studied himself in the mirror he decided he'd try to be less of an asshole today. He'd be professional. After all, he didn't want the casting director to hear bad things about him.

He pulled up the corner of the curtain covering the window next to his bed and looked out at the set. Sun, blue sky… but something was wrong. Everyone had disappeared, and in a hurry by the looks of it. They'd just abandoned hundreds of thousands of dollars worth of equipment.

He stepped out of his trailer and saw that someone had left a cardboard box for him. Inside was a rubber gas mask.

He swallowed. Something weird was definitely going on.

Greg returned to the couch in his trailer and tried to think. He took out his phone to check the New York Times homepage. It didn't load. CNN's site loaded, but didn't say anything about any disaster. The headline was still about some political scandal that Greg hadn't been following. He called Bobby. No answer. Before he could really think it through, he called his mom for the first time in maybe four months. It didn't even ring; her phone was off.

Greg pulled on a pair of khaki shorts and a purple polo shirt, snatched his RayBans off the counter and headed out, gas mask in hand. There were still doughnuts on the buffet table. He took a chocolate doughnut and cold coffee and went to sit on the porch. Greg called out. Nobody answered. Mosquitoes nipped at his arms–the citronella candles had long since gone out–but he didn't swat them away.

A whine somewhere in the distance turned into a sonic roar. Suddenly five fighter jets broke into the clear blue sky, flew over his head, and then disappeared as suddenly as they'd arrived. Greg scarfed down the rest of the chocolate doughnut and pulled the gas mask over his head. Someone had probably left it for him for good reason.

He left the porch and relieved himself against a tree. The mask was already uncomfortable. It was like his head was cooking in a little rubber oven, and the world was tinted green from the visor.

He zipped up and started walking. There was no fence delineating this property, and no other houses visible from here. Just a gravel road by which he assumed the crew had entered the property; he'd been asleep in his trailer when the filming caravan arrived.

He followed the road. The landscape was high grass forever. His Sperrys were paper-thin in the soles, and pretty soon his feet hurt from the sharp rocks. The exertion of walking, and maybe sweating out the whiskey, helped him think a bit more clearly. He was really alone. That was the main thing he thought about.

He rarely spent time alone in the evenings in his trailer, and when he did, he had his phone to distract him. And when he was home in LA he usually had some friends or girls hanging around by the pool, and even when he slept he kept movies playing on his plasma screen in the other room. The only sounds now were the crunch of his shoes on gravel, the pumping of alcohol-infused blood in his temples, and the rasp of his own breathing. No more planes. No traffic. No birds.

He didn't like this silence. To calm himself down he ran through some of his favorite lines from past films.

Yeah? Well you're turning this circus *into a* courtroom!

Honey... Yes I said she looks like a million bucks... but do you know what the inflation rate was last year?

What? I have no problem with racists—some of my best friends are racists!

God. All those movies were such shit.

Something caught Greg's eye. Maybe twenty feet off the dirt road there was a black marsh of brackish water. What attracted his eye was light-brown fur. A dog was lying at the lip of the marsh, as if she'd been washed ashore by the tide.

Greg left the road, walked through the tall grass to the marsh, and knelt beside the golden retriever. She wasn't dead yet, but it wouldn't be long. She was on her side. Her nose was clogged with yellow mucus and her breaths were shallow. The sight made him reflexively reach for his own nose, and when he did he felt only cold rubber and remembered he was wearing the mask.

He stood up. In the movies, this was where he would take a big rock and put the dog out of her misery, but he didn't have the balls.

The dirt road finally fed into a paved one, and that in turn to a two-lane rural freeway that seemed to stretch forever in either direction, totally empty. There was probably some way to use the sun to figure out which direction to walk, but he didn't bother. Instead he just chose the direction that seemed to grade slightly downhill.

His Rolex said it was five in the afternoon by the time he reached a proper highway. He could see the bumper-to-bumper traffic from a distance, and felt a surge of hope. He sped up, loping over hot black pavement toward the promise of humanity as fast as his throbbing feet would allow. It was only when he was maybe a half mile away that he realized it wasn't traffic in the conventional sense. Nothing was moving. Smoke curled up from the glinting mass.

The tangle of bent steel and smashed glass began even before he arrived at the highway. All along the entranceway, cars were backed up; wrecked before they could even reach the primary scene of destruction, like drunken party-goers collapsed on the lawn before even making it to the front door.

Greg squeezed between the wreckage, trying to avoid looking at the erstwhile passengers. Finally he climbed on top of a totaled Audi to survey the landscape more completely. The scene was unfathomable. A million-car pile up. And, based on the cars' contorted bodies, some of these accidents had happened fast. These weren't fender benders. It looked like people had been driving at normal highway speeds when something happened and suddenly everyone had lost control, slammed on the brakes to avoid colliding with the car in front of them only to be rear-ended themselves, the process violently iterating again and again... The sort of thing that in the hands of a light-hearted director could be framed as a sort of dark comedy of errors.

There were some cars facing west, but they were clustered much more densely going east, toward the water; some neolithic part of the drivers' brains telling them water was salvation. Maybe that's why the dog had died on the edge of the swamp.

Greg felt ill. The salty breeze off the ocean wasn't refreshing; it was heavy and foul. He stared down into the water and tried not to think about the golden retriever, her clogged up nose, sad eyes, and agape mouth.

Maybe it was a setup. Actually the more he thought about it, the more likely that seemed. What were the odds he found that dog *just* as she was about to die? It was just too perfect. Contrived. Bad script, that's what it was.

Greg laughed out loud. He needed to have a talk with whatever Jew writers were making a mess of things. Tell them it just wasn't believable that Jennifer wouldn't fuck him. Come on. It was the end of the world, baby! Lily and Vic needed a bit more substance–or at least one of them did. You didn't need two dumbasses on board. Actually three, if you counted big dumb Sam.

These fucking puppets. Greg laughed again, laughed at the murky sea and the orange sky. Elissa as an embroidered velvet sock puppet, someone's hand up her ass making her yap. It was so obvious.

Was Jennifer a puppet too? Allison Gregory had been, and they'd done a hell of a sewing job with her. Exquisite craftsmanship with those legs. The dog was a puppet with a drawstring coming out of her back, powering a series of levers and springs that made her chest rise and fall. Jennifer… he wasn't sure. But he would find out.

27

The most professionally gratifying moment of Elissa's long career was the week in 2008 that began with the Nasdaq dropping over ten percent in the space of a few hours. The 44th floor, her domain, was a lone island of sanity, sandwiched above and below by men in Italian ties and wristwatches the price of sports cars, who were currently going out of their gourds. She'd been foregoing excess profit for years in anticipation of a day like this, and it was impossible to not feel a little schadenfreude for those who'd ever questioned her methods. Her teams on the 44th were glued to CNBC with relief disguised as disbelief, watching their neighbors' houses burn down. Elissa's teams' net value today had actually increased slightly thanks to the puts– downside insurance–Elissa had mandated for anyone taking highly leveraged positions.

My brother just called me. Andy Ross poked his head into her office. A slender man with dainty fingers, who looked more like a classical pianist than a trader. *He heard Bear Stearns might be done. Bear Stearns.*

That week was gratifying only in hindsight. At the time Elissa was even more concerned than usual, for a risk even she had never anticipated: she'd hedged her own positions thoughtfully and meticulously for four decades. But what if a crash was bad enough to break down the entire structure of the market? What if an event was so catastrophic that the castles in the sky collapsed, that there was no trust left in the market, and the assets she'd protected were worthless bits of information on the screen? It could happen. A modern-day bank run. A self-fulfilling prophecy: everyone so terrified of their shares becoming nothing but a worthless deed, devoid of inherent value, that they'd sell them for pennies on the dollar until there were no buyers. No liquidity. The trust would be gone and nothing could ever bring it back.

Despite her own prudence, in the end she could be undone by her peers' utter lack of foresight.

Things had been happening on the ship without her noticing. She hated being the last to know, in fact she'd made a career out of being the first. She was visiting Greg in the engine room to get her water ration and check that everything was going alright. They'd looked at the water levels in the potable tank together, and it turned out they were being slightly more conservative than they'd decided to be. They were meant to have twenty-three days of water left at this point, and in fact had twenty-four.

"Have you had any issues with people asking for more water?" she asked him.

Greg Pink put his hands on his hips.

"Don't recall anything like that. Business seems to be pretty smooth."

"Great. Thanks again for taking care of this, Greg."

He saluted her.

"Ay-ay, captain."

She ignored his ironic show of respect. They left the engine room, Greg closing the heavy steel door behind them.

"Big plans now?" he asked her.

"I was going to go back to my cabin and read," she replied.

"Do you know where the lighter is?" he asked. She realized he'd had a cigarette tucked behind his right ear this whole time. "Is it on the bridge? We need to find another one. It's ridiculous, all of us sharing this one little lighter."

The appearance of the cigarette had a visceral effect on Elissa. She hadn't touched one for maybe twenty years. In the old days she'd smoked like everyone else. Once people stopped smoking in office buildings, it became a social and professional disadvantage *not* to smoke: you missed out on the key discussions that happened on the sidewalk outside the office, when traders were in their best moods of the day. And of course it hadn't taken long for her to begin enjoying the habit herself. The sight of Greg's cigarette triggered both a wave of nostalgia for those days, and a craving she hadn't felt for a very long time. Stress, she supposed, could do that.

"Where did you get that?"

"Lily gave me a couple. I guess she found a few packs on board or something. Do you smoke? I can trade a cigarette for a couple hours of the book."

Elissa's eyes narrowed. Sam had found a paperback copy of an old detective novel stashed in a suitcase inside of a shipping container. They were taking turns with it. Each person got a day with the book before it was passed to the next. It wasn't great literature by any means, but today was Elissa's day, and she had intended to savor the escape.

"You're not content with the sharing system we decided on?" she asked slowly.

Greg shrugged.

"It's fine. I just was thinking if you smoke, you know, win-win."

Without responding, Elissa turned and rushed up the steps to speak to Lily, who was supposed to be on shift at the radio now. But sitting in her place, on the swivel stool beside the radio, was Mel Glazer. He was writing something on a roll of double striated printer paper and tugging on his beard with great urgency. Of all the people on board who needed a haircut, Mel's situation was most dire: his *yarmulka* was lofted precariously atop a bird's nest of jet-black tangles, and his beard was growing sideways. He'd finally ditched the long-sleeve white shirt, and on his chest wore only the singlet with ritual white tassels tied on all four corners. Elissa realized she hadn't seen him in at least a few days, and he was the only person who seemed to have gotten paler since they'd climbed aboard.

"Where's Lily? This is supposed to be her shift."

Mel jumped at Elissa's voice. Evidently he hadn't heard her come in. He looked up, obviously irritated at the interruption.

"I took her shift for her."

Elissa took a deep breath.

"In exchange for cigarettes?"

Mel blinked, then nodded slowly.

"Do you even smoke?" Elissa asked.

Mel shook his head.

"No. But Victor does and he's the one with the tea."

"What tea? What are you talking about?"

Mel shrugged. His face was wet with sweat, and it dripped from the tips of his beard like melting icicles.

"I guess Victor found a box of Lipton tea bags. It's not coffee, nowhere close, but it helps."

"And he's charging for it?"

"I'm sure he'd give me a bit for free but I'd like a double portion. I need the caffeine."

Elissa could see the system she'd put in place unravelling before her eyes. Shifts were being exchanged for cigarettes… It was only a matter of time before water rations were traded too. And the next time something on board needed to be done–another round of searching the containers for food, running the engines in order to distill more drinking water, who knows what–everyone would try to pawn off their obligations on someone else. Once you had material stores of value without rule of law, you opened the door to theft. Violence. Chaos.

"Where's Lily?" Elissa asked.

Mel returned to his writing.

"No idea."

Elissa eventually found her in one of the lounge chairs at the front of the ship. When Elissa came upon her, she was just staring straight into space. It seemed a bit silly that Lily had traded cigarettes for the privilege of sitting here and doing nothing, instead of sitting on the bridge monitoring the radio.

"Lily," Elissa said. The younger woman looked up at her.

"Hi."

"Where did you get those cigarettes? The ones you gave Greg?"

"I don't have many more," Lily said. "But today's your day with the book right? Maybe we could swap?"

Elissa felt a vein throb in her forehead.

"Where did you get those cigarettes? Did you find them yourself?"

Lily Chen seemed to consider lying for a moment, and then shook her head.

"Art."

"He gave them to you?"

Lily folded her arms across her chest.

"No. I *won* them. We play poker with them."

"Gambling." Elissa said, not as a question.

Lily shrugged.

"It's fun."

In 2008, Elissa had been genuinely concerned about the collapse of the American financial system. If too many banks failed, it was over. The government couldn't bail everyone out without breaking their own rules and turning the whole thing into a joke. The government's power, like her power as a manager, was an illusion, only the status-quo by mutual agreement. If she set red lines, and her traders crossed them, she had to fire them; once she started making exceptions, the cracks in her veneer would expose that illusion. Group delusions only worked as long as nobody pointed out that the emperor had no clothes.

People were talking about the America illusion though, in 2008. Could the government really guarantee your bank account? What did those dollars really stand for anyway? What if AAPL and MSFT were worth pennies, and nobody bought them up because when a stock didn't pay dividends it didn't have any true value?

In the end though, as always, everything went back to normal for one reason: greed. That was the market: fear and greed. Fear sent the markets spiraling downward until the upside was just too enticing. A fire sale on assets, and as long as the world didn't end, you were going to make a boatload when the crisis blew over.

Arthur Roselli's cabin door was ajar. Elissa entered to find him lying in bed whittling with a fruit knife.

"What the hell are you doing?" she demanded. "Just give everyone an equal share of the cigarettes and be done with it. This is going to lead to problems."

Arthur set down whatever he'd been carving.

"Are you upset I didn't invite you? I didn't think you'd be into it. Judging by your facial expression, I'd say I probably thought right."

"People are trading shifts and tea for cigarettes."

Art was still reclining in bed. A show of disrespect, she thought. He made an exaggerated shrug.

"Of course they are," he said. "Free market. Capitalism. I figured if anyone can understand that, it's you."

Elissa took a step toward him.

"It's not *free*. You're a monopoly. Where did you find them?"

He waved a leathery hand dismissively.

"You're making a mountain out of a molehill. People are bored. Playing cards and trading and smoking is something to pass the time. That's why I didn't just give them the cigarettes. I made a game out of it to keep people from going numb with boredom."

"What you're doing is creating a culture of laziness, manipulation, and distrust."

Art chuckled.

"Look. I know everything has to be just perfect for you. Everything has to be *rules*. I understand that's how you operate. Only problem is that it doesn't work. People don't follow rules just because you make them. You gotta relax a little, Elissa, let people live. What's the harm? We're sitting here in the middle of the fucking ocean. It's the end of the goddamn world. Who gives a shit if people are trading cigarettes? God forbid we have a little fun before we all starve to death."

When Elissa didn't immediately reply, Art turned his attention back to his whittling. His hands moved with astonishing dexterity. She had a moment of admiration for Art. She took pride in being as sharp, at seventy-three years old, as she ever had been. She had friends who'd retired and moved down to Boca Raton, played tennis and waited to die while their brains turned to porridge. It disgusted her. Arthur was maybe a few years younger than her but it was clear he was cut from the same cloth. He was nowhere close to giving up on life. She supposed that was why he was here.

For the first time, Elissa considered that Arthur might be the most dangerous person on board.

"You're not planning on sitting here and starving to death any more than I am," she said. "You're trying to win these people over and send us on a suicide mission. Away from the coast. To that boy's imaginary island."

Arthur's hands stopped their dance. He set down the trinket, sat up in bed, and met her stare. He was silent for a moment.

"The Navy isn't coming for us," he finally said softly. "And there's nothing back there for us. We can sail down the coast. Mexico, the Caribbean… The air is carrying the disease there. You know that."

"There's no island at the coordinates on his chest. It's not in the atlas."

"Probably not," Art said. "I agree it's a long shot."

"The numbers were either put there by terrorists or the mentally ill."

"Like I said. A long shot. But once in a while you win the long shots."

Elissa scoffed.

"Think about what you're saying. You want to sail to the literal middle of the ocean based on some numbers on an amnesiac's chest?"

"The Navy isn't coming for us," Art repeated slowly. "There's nothing on the east coast or the Caribbean. So this is our only chance."

Arthur was a hell of a salesman, and for just a moment his reasoning and tender baritone washed over her. If they were on a used car lot, this is where he'd be holding out the contract and pen, whispering, *Do it for yourself. You deserve this car.*

"I won't let you lead us out into the middle of the Atlantic on a fool's errand."

Art smiled.

"We're going to that island. Whether you 'let' me or not."

28

Bahram sat in the mess practicing his drawing. It was so frustrating. He knew exactly how he wanted the image to turn out, but he lacked the ability to execute his vision. His sense of urgency though, was waning. *Yenfor*–the only one who had shown any real interest in sitting with him, hearing what he had to say, and trying to answer his questions–had grown distant. He'd sat in the mess all day yesterday hoping to catch her for a session. She came in once for the bathroom. When she came out she waved at him, gave him a weak smile, but then went back upstairs without sitting down.

Nobody else seemed likely to answer his questions. Why were they still just floating? Why weren't they heading back to America–or letting Adam navigate to the place Azzami had told him about? Maybe these people hadn't figured out how to operate the ship? If that was the reason, they didn't seem to be in any hurry to figure it out.

But Bahram had other questions that maybe the Americans could answer. Questions about that squat evil building where Adam was living before Azzami escorted him out at gunpoint. About Adam himself, who was certainly strange, but also sad and confused in a way that had made Bahram and Keti pity him.

The day after the evil building, they were on the road again, now four of them. Adam again sat in the front seat with Azzami. Even though they both spoke English, they exchanged few words. And when Adam asked something of Azzami, their son would hand the young man water or snacks wordlessly, without even looking at him. A few times Adam peered over his shoulder to look at Bahram and Keti in the backseat. Each time he'd turn the corners of his mouth up, in an approximation of a smile, scratch his cheek with his yellow fingernails, then turn back to face the highway.

Who is he?

Keti and Bahram had asked their son some variant of this question dozens of times already. And the answers were always vague.

He is one of fourteen Adams we have found, from around the world.

What do you mean?

Fourteen Adams, seventeen Eves. Beings unburdened by memory. They don't belong to this world. They're destined for a better, new world.

Yes, Son, but... where is Adam from? What about his family? Doesn't he miss them?

Don't worry about him. He is perfectly content. He may have once had a family, but he doesn't remember them.

Keti and Bahram exchanged a look.

That's very sad.

On the contrary, Mother. It is the most wonderful gift a person could ask for.

They drove all day, until arriving another motel. Again, Keti and Bahram took one room, Azzami and Adam another. Dinner was delicious: Azzami brought them a feast of flatbread wraps filled with oily beans, meats, and sticky orange cheese.

You took these from a restaurant?

Azzami laughed.

I wouldn't call it a restaurant. It's more like a food station. They give you food while you wait in your car.

Bahram didn't ask any more questions about the source of the food; he was too busy enjoying it. Adam ate with them and seemed very happy, despite being ripped from that white building at gunpoint just yesterday. He became more animated, smiling and laughing and talking between bites. Keti leaned forward.

What is he saying, Son?

It's a sort of nonsense. I can't understand most of it.

It's not English?

It's English but… I think these are places and people that exist only in his imagination.

Still, tell us about them. We want to hear.

Azzami hesitated. Adam continued laughing, soiling his corner of the hotel room with flecks of bean spittle.

He is confused. He thinks he is eating this meal in a different place, in a different time. He's speaking as if we are all children, including himself. He's asking about the toys that are supposed to come with the meal.

Adam stopped talking. He looked down at his carton of food and seemed to be studying it.

Son, ask him to tell us more.

Azzami fidgeted, then said something to Adam. The young man looked up from his food, his face suddenly drained of any trace of joy. He muttered something in response, then resumed eating, but with none of his prior enthusiasm.

He says the food makes him feel good.

They were on the road again early the next morning. Bahram had long since abandoned any hope of understanding where they were. He had a map of the United States that he'd bought at one of the petrol stations they'd stopped at, but he couldn't read the words on any of the signs they passed, and when he tried to match the numbers on the signs to the highway numbers in the map he only grew more confused. Adam was mostly silent in the front seat. Since that moment at dinner, he hadn't laughed or even seemed interested in conversation.

Today, Bahram sensed, was going to be different than the others. Azzami was talking on the phone a lot, and navigating more carefully.

Indeed, in the late afternoon they pulled into a parking lot the size of a football field–thousands of parking spots of which only a handful were occupied. At the edge of the parking lot was an enormous beige building. He'd seen dozens of buildings like this on their travels, and Bahram still couldn't figure out what purpose they served. They were one-story boxes that sprawled perhaps a half kilometer from end to end. The only structure Bahram had seen before this trip that was comparable in size to these monstrosities was the *Pul-e-Charkhi* prison, east of Kabul, which he'd seen from a distance years ago. It could be that these too were prisons, given that they were windowless and solid looking. But then why all the parking? Just for visitors? It could be. Though there were no guards outside, and no barbed wire on the roof. Azzami turned off the car, and turned to speak to his parents.

Someone is coming here to meet me in a half hour. You're not supposed to be with me. Go into that building, and stay there until I come in and get you.

Bahram's stomach dropped. Keti took his hand. She was frightened. Was their son going to threaten someone with a gun again?

You want me to bring your mother into that building? Is it a prison? Some kind of hospital?

Azzami laughed deeply. Something melted in Bahram's chest as he remembered the boy who, despite his intellectual and athletic shortcomings–or perhaps because of them–had developed a sort of brilliant style of humor. Often after dinner he'd entertain the family with jokes, either poking fun at his siblings or reading the newspaper and mocking politicians and clerics.

His son seemed, for an instant, to forget the serious, stressed man he'd become, and was himself again, laughing so hard he teared up.

*A prison! You won't believe it Father, but that entire building is a kind of market. Americans do their shopping here. In fact–*Azzami pulled out his wallet and handed Bahram some green American money–*buy some food for us while you're in there. And anything else we need.*

Bahram and Keti left the car and crossed the hot asphalt, toward the market.

Who do you think he's meeting?

Keti... I think we will both be happier if we stop trying to guess what is happening.

The glass doors at the entrance to the market slid open for them, beckoning them inside. They were hit by a wall of freezing air, and then Bahram's jaw dropped. He'd assumed that such a market would be filled with hundreds or thousands of vendors with individual stalls. But the products were just displayed on shelves like the snacks in the petrol stations. For a moment, Bahram forgot about his son outside in the parking lot, and staggered forward into this bright kingdom.

Bahram.

Just a moment.

He was in a row of nothing but televisions. Sleek, beautiful machines that made the small TV he had in his carpet store back in Afghanistan look like a toaster oven. And the images were so crisp, so hauntingly real... One displayed a waterfall in a rainforest, and it somehow seemed to be more real, in higher definition, than the landscapes he'd seen outside the car this morning. He stroked the frame that held this screen. If he could just possess this TV, he was sure, he could live out the rest of his days in pure bliss.

Bahram!

Keti was at his side.

Look at this Keti! Look!

You watch this stupid screen if you want. I'm going to stand by the glass door and watch our son.

Okay, okay.

He followed his wife back to the entrance. They kept behind the sliding door, so Azzami couldn't see them. But Azzami was too far away for them to see anything but the car.

Stay here Keti. I have an idea. I'll be right back.

He turned and rushed back into the bright lights, the rows of things. The people in blue uniforms were employees, he assumed. He stopped one by tapping her on the shoulder. She smiled and chirped something in English.

Bahram turned his hands into two cups, and held them over his eyes, then pretended to squint through them.

The employee smiled and nodded, beckoned for him to follow her. She led him down rows of outdoor furniture, past racks of children's clothing, past a sector large enough to be its own large toy store. They plunged deeper and deeper into the labyrinth, and Bahram grew worried he wouldn't be able to find his way back to Keti. Finally his guide stopped, and gestured to a wall, upon which hung dozens of types of binoculars. She said something. He grabbed a pair at random, looked through them, and gave her a thumbs up. These were good. Satisfied, she turned and left.

Bahram followed her at a distance, clutching the binoculars, hoping she would lead him back to the entrance where he'd found her. When he spotted Keti he sighed with relief, and rushed forward.

Here.

She took the binoculars from him and nodded, impressed.

Sometimes, Bahram, you're not as dumb as you look.

She held the binoculars to her eyes and looked toward the car.

Can you see him? What's happening?

He's still in the car with Adam.

What are they doing? Let me see.

Nothing's happening! I just told you.

They passed the binoculars back and forth for a while, taking turns observing, until a white car pulled up alongside their son. Bahram had the binoculars, and saw that the driver of the white car was a thin man with boney cheeks. The thin man left his car, holding a grey briefcase.

Bahram, what's happening? Let me see.

Just a second.

Azzami stepped out of the car, leaving Adam in the passenger seat. His son was holding the glossy photo that had Adam's face on it. Azzami and the thin man greeted each other with a hug. The thin man examined the picture, and then peered through the window to confirm that the photo matched Adam. They had a short discussion. The thin man looked pleased, or even impressed. He handed Azzami the briefcase and hugged him again,

Keti snatched the binoculars back just in time to see the thin man hop back in his car and take off.

What? What did I miss?

Keti refused to give him back the binoculars, until Azzami took Adam from the car, and the two of them approached the entrance where Bahram and Keti were spying on them.

Quick! We'll pretend we've been shopping this whole time.

Bahram tried to draw a picture of his wife's face, to remember her as she'd been as the two of them rushed back into the heart of the market to find the food area, his wife wearing the same mischievous grin as when she was a girl of seventeen. Perhaps that was the last time she'd ever smiled.

Bahram crumpled up his useless drawings and threw them to the mess floor. He stood up. His lower back and legs felt as stiff and delicate as fired clay. He walked slowly to the row of windows in the mess and looked out on the ocean. He should have taken a few minutes to drag Keti and Azzami's bodies into the water. Instead, in the madness of the moment, he'd left them on the dock as he pursued Adam and that woman.

His eyes welled up. He let his forehead rest on the warm glass and he closed his eyes, tasting tears as salty as the sea outside. What if in the market, he and Keti had just run away? What if he'd snuck into Azzami's room, taken the briefcase, and destroyed or hidden it? What if he'd untied Adam, and let him run free?

None of these possibilities had even occurred to him at the time. He often thought about people the same way he did his carpets. Some were more complicated, some more beautiful or expensive… But there was no such thing as a *bad* carpet; if a carpet covered the floor it was a good carpet. And if it didn't cover the floor, it wasn't a carpet.

Even until the end he'd held out hope that his son had retained some of the good sense Bahram had tried to hammer into his thick head. Countless times since coming aboard, Bahram had tried to console himself with the thought that he couldn't have done any better. That boy was born lost.

29

Lily Chen peered down at her hand. Terrible cards. Not even three of the same suit. She folded. She'd lost thirty-five cigarettes already tonight, and was getting a little frustrated with herself for playing poorly. No, she hadn't gotten good cards, but her bluffs had been picked off too. Mostly by Art. She still had over a hundred cigarettes in front of her, but each one she lost was one fewer to smoke or give to Greg.

Well, she figured, you win some and you lose some. That's just poker. At least she had something to look forward to now. When she lay in bed at night, before she fell asleep, she'd replay the past day's hands, and fantasize about winning more the next day. But it wasn't just the possibility of winning, it was the vibe. Smoking cigarettes, laughing, and gambling with her boys–that's how she thought of them–filled her heart with something warm and sweet. Yes, on an individual basis they had their flaws; it wasn't the same hanging out with them one-on-one. Sam was a bit of a square. Maybe 'stiff' would be a better word. He definitely enjoyed playing cards, but Lily could tell he still had some reservations. He always felt a little guilty that he wasn't working up on the deck opening containers instead. She'd sat with Sam once in the captain's lounge and tried to start up a fun conversation, the kind the four of them always had together, but it was useless.

Vic was… well, maybe it wasn't fair to say he was stupid, because some of it was the language thing. His English honestly wasn't very good and that was the reason he sometimes totally misunderstood what was going on. And he seemed to be pretty good at poker; he'd certainly picked it up faster than Lily. So what was it about him? Maybe that he *thought* he was so smart. The way he'd point his beady little black eyes at Lily when she was talking, one hand holding his cigarette in place, the other brushing a blond lock off his forehead… He observed her as an entomologist would a curious beetle. That's how she felt sometimes, anyway. She also didn't feel like Vic was particularly reliable. Like, if she started puking in the middle of the night or something and needed someone to hold her hair, she'd knock on Sam or Art's door. They'd help her *for sure*. Vic though… she could see Vic either pretending not to hear her knocking, or him going to wake up somebody else, so he wouldn't have to deal with anything messy himself.

So Art then, maybe he was the glue. He was what made this group so much greater than the sum of their parts. Art listened to Lily attentively and laughed at her jokes. He didn't treat her any differently than the other two because she was a woman, which set the tone for Vic and Sam to also treat her like an equal partner. Art was older than all of them, and wiser–it was indisputable. He'd lived a life Lily couldn't help but envy. He'd partied with celebrities on Miami rooftops ("Mark Wahlberg is an even bigger asshole than he looks"), had a solo exhibition of his paintings in a Chelsea Gallery ("I didn't sell a *thing*. People just stuffed their purses with cheese and took off"), almost been killed by the mafia ("Pro tip kids: never send back your clam linguini in Sicily"), sat at midfield during the Super Bowl ("Couldn't see a thing. Trust me, better to watch on TV"), and flown on a private plane with Elton John and someone named David Bowie, who she'd never heard of. ("Both great guys. Bowie scared me a little though").

There was just something magical about Art. Maybe it was his confidence. Lily started feeling more confident in herself just from being around him. She wished she'd met Art ten years ago, had had him and his confidence in her life when she lived in Lexington. With Art around, she would have told guys they better treat her like a fucking lady.

Thanks to Art's advice, she felt she'd already made a lot of progress with Greg. She still hadn't kissed him or anything, but she could tell he was starting to like her. Every time she went to get water from him now he asked her to stick around and have a cigarette with her.

"If you want to get Greg," Art told her last week, when it was just them in his cabin, waiting for the other two to show up for the game, "You have to understand that he's incredibly insecure. You need to aggravate those insecurities, and then make him feel like *he* needs *you* in order to prove something to himself. You get what I'm saying?"

"Yeah."

"Don't act like you're into him. Act like he's not good enough for you, because he's not attractive or smart enough–which by the way is probably true. I think you deserve better than him, but I understand that pickings are a little slim at the moment. Anyway. Imply that you think his movies and jokes are dumb and that he's getting flabby. Then he'll feel like he needs to convince you otherwise, in order to convince *himself* otherwise. Get it?"

That was the advice she needed years ago, when she gave in and joined SoulConnect. She'd heard good things. Cammie Parson had met her husband online. It was real people, Cammie had explained. The only difference between this and a bar is that you have your pick of the litter and you never feel forced to give your number to some creep just because he buys you a drink. Amanda came over to Lily's apartment, where they took bong hits of Northern Lights and did a photoshoot. In the end, Lily chose two pictures from that shoot: one of her in the kitchen cooking–both because it was an actual passion of hers, and because she knew guys liked women who could cook–and one that Amanda captured of Lily laughing really hard, high as shit.

She added a third picture that was a few years old, of her out with a group of girls. It was overexposed, but her hair looked good and it showed that she had friends.

Writing her profile was impossible. Lily wasn't much of a writer to start with, and this the highest pressure essay imaginable. You had to make yourself sound desirable, without making it sound like that's what you were trying to do. You also had to portray yourself somewhat accurately, because ultimately you wanted to attract someone who would like who you really were. She deliberated for days. Finally she began:

It's so hard to describe yourself in a few paragraphs... if you want to know more just ask!

She also put in a ton of her favorite movies and TV shows, and explained what she was looking for:

A genuinely good, pretty normal (but maybe a little crazy) guy. A MAN. No more boys please! If you're going to waste my time, forget it!

She got plenty of messages. Maybe two or three a day. That was nice. It made her feel like a catch. She didn't even answer anyone for the first few weeks and just savored this newfound source of attention. Worst case, if there was really a jewel in there, she'd respond later. Two weeks after joining SoulConnect, someone at the call center remarked that Lily seemed to have a pep in her step lately.

Finally she dug into the messages, and their respective profiles. A couple were really genuine:

You look so sweet! Would love to take you out to dinner if you give me the chance.

But those guys were disqualified for different reasons. Some were much older than her, a few were too fat, one was 'between jobs', one had bulgy eyes. Some messages were very crude, but that was to be expected. Cammie had warned her about that. One said he liked submissive Chinese girls. Lily actually responded to that:

If you're looking for a submissive Chinese girl, keep looking you FUCKER.

Then she blocked him, smiling into the glowing tablet screen with just a hint of sadism.

She got into message exchanges with a few guys on the site, and ended up going out for drinks with two of them. Both dates were scenario one–the kind where she left after an hour. After three months she was getting a little nervous. Going online had always been the last resort–if she couldn't meet her husband organically, she had always assured herself that if push came to shove she could just go online and pull a Cammie. After all, it wasn't like Cammie was so beautiful or funny. After a half year on SoulConnect she was starting to wonder if the problem was the site itself. There were a lot of options out there. Maybe she'd just chosen the wrong one? She was considering switching (or posting profiles on multiple sites simultaneously) when Michael messaged her.

Hey LChen194, I'm Michael. I'm not any good at writing these messages. I'll tell you that up front. But I think you're super cute and I also love love love LOVE Little Miss Sunshine. Tragically under-appreciated movie.

Lily's heart almost exploded when she saw that message. It was so perfect. When she went to click on his profile, she was praying: let him be cute. And he was. Not like, so gorgeous that he looked like a Ken doll. He just looked like a nice, sweet, good person. Great smile. Good hair. Three inches taller than her. Best of all, his pictures made him look like a super fun guy. The last one was a professional headshot in a suit, but the first four were awesome. One of him jumping off a cliff into some lake, one of him laughing while drinking a beer, one with a dog, one playing guitar. He was a real estate developer.

Lily called Amanda right away, and the first thing her friend said, half-joking, was: *make sure he's not married*. That pissed Lily off, because she felt it implied that something must be wrong if a stud like Michael was interested in her. Also, it freaked her out enough that after they'd been swapping messages for a day and a half, she just flat out asked:

You're not married are you? Just because I've heard crazy stories of guys on here…

Michael's reply did more than set her mind at ease. It made her feel like she might actually love him already:

HAHAHA. Married?? First of all, I'd have to be prettttty stupid to put my pictures on a public dating site if I was married. Second of all, I'm way too much of a loser for that. Two women? I'm just trying to get one good one… We'll go from there. Wait. Are YOU married???

Michael didn't ask her to meet until they'd been talking for three days, which was *perfect*. Less would be desperate, and longer was like, be a man already. And he asked her out to dinner, which was so much better than just taking her for a drink. French, which Lily found particularly romantic.

The day of their date she was so nervous and excited she could hardly function. She was supposed to have a call center shift from five in the afternoon until midnight, so she called in sick. Her manager sounded skeptical on the phone, but whatever. Lily woke up at seven from nerves, and by ten she'd already cleaned the entire house, including picking the hair out of the shower drain, which neither she nor Mona had done in way too long. She went for a run for the first time in months just to get rid of some energy. She went to the salon and got her hair and nails done. For lunch she made herself a really nice salad with blue cheese and almonds, but could only manage to eat a few bites. It felt like it took a week for evening to arrive.

She got off the bus twenty minutes before their date was supposed to start and decided to wait across the street from Brasserie Provence, because she didn't want to sit alone in there for fifteen minutes and have everyone look at her, thinking maybe she got stood up. Just thinking the words 'stood up' evoked a scenario so absolutely soul-shattering that Lily had to do a brisk walk around the block to calm herself down. As she bought mint gum at a Walgreens she checked her phone for probably, literally, the three hundredth time that day. Michael had texted. At first her heart froze in terror. Was he canceling?

Got us a table in the back. Take your time.

Her heart thawed from ice into a gushing river of joy. As she left Walgreens she tried to stop herself from getting too excited. By this point, of course, she was well aware of the pattern, and she knew the dangers of falling too hard. But somehow she was sure this time would be different.

Michael was in a booth, in a romantic corner of the restaurant. Usually on first dates guys would sit there pretending like they didn't notice or recognize her, forcing her to be like *Hi? Brad?* But when Michael saw her he immediately shot up from his seat to hug her, and ushered her chivalrously to the table. They sat down across from each other and both were silent for a moment, just staring into each other's eyes and smiling sheepishly. He looked exactly like his pictures, but only in person did she note that he kind of had a baby face. A double chin prickly with scruff that was actually sort of adorable.

Wow. I hope it doesn't make you uncomfortable for me to say this but... you're beautiful.

Lily felt herself blushing.

You can say that as much as you want.

The next five hours were so perfect. Lily thought back on those hours a lot. Since coming on board, she'd had a few dreams where those hours were happening exactly as they had, but everything outside the restaurant was utterly destroyed.

They both ordered fancy crepes and drank a few different kinds of wine. As he drank he grew flushed and giggly. They sat there until the waiter came over and apologetically informed them that they would be closing in fifteen minutes. Lily was sure that Michael was going to come to her place; far less amazing first dates had ended with that. But he just kissed her on the cheek and said he had a wonderful time. And then she asked him to come over, and he said he didn't want to take things too fast. After he turned away Lily almost wept from joy. He didn't want to take things too fast! He was thinking *long term*. Of course, he'd said as much over dinner. He said he thought a lot about *settling down* and *starting a family*. Lily couldn't take the emotion. She got home, put disco on the speakers, and danced around the living room until Mona came out and asked what the fuck she was doing. Lily hugged her and said, *it's happening.*

Michael couldn't go out again until the following week, but they texted all the time. The week between the first and second dates was maybe the happiest of Lily's life. The second date they went out for dinner again, this time to Jack's, which was a pretty fancy steakhouse.

Get whatever you want. Really.

She ordered filet-fucking-mignon, and drank a ton of amazing shiraz. The conversation was no worse than the first date. But the date didn't last as long, because about an hour in, Lily couldn't take it anymore. She was pretty tipsy when she leaned across the table, feeling a wonderful sort of empowerment brought on by the booze and his affection.

Get the check and let's get out of here.

Michael looked shocked by her forwardness, which was exactly what she'd been hoping for. She was in control. But he smiled and paid, and then they took a cab to her house because his car was in the shop.

The night was amazing. After all the preliminary stuff, he took her in his beefy arms, and made love to her gently, kissing her neck, licking her ear. It was so beautiful. But when they finished Michael said he had to run.

I'm so so sorry, he said, buttoning back up his shirt. *I have a presentation for a huge client early tomorrow morning that I have to prep for.*

Lily assured him it was no problem. She got on her tiptoes to kiss his cheek, and he promised they'd talk soon.

"Tell us more stories about your pops," Lily said to Art, as she folded another hand. She shuddered. She recalled the smell of Michael's anti-dandruff shampoo, the sandpaper stubble on his cheeks. Whenever she thought about that night she wished she had a machine that could just cut out all memories of the month that followed.

She had a nasty taste in her mouth and tried to rinse it out with a swig of tea. Vic had brought a big pitcher with him tonight. He was very generous with his tea during poker. Lily loved that. Her boys would do anything for her. That was how things worked now, in this new world. New reality, new Lily. Brasserie Provence and Jack's were both radioactive rubble. Michael was dead. Fresh start.

"Nah, I don't wanna think about that old bastard anymore," said Art, as he scooped in another pot. He had won at least a hundred cigarettes tonight, plus seven wood disks he'd carved with each of their initials, each of which stood for a three hour shift at the radio; if you had one with a 'V', for instance, you had the right to make Vic do one of your shifts, and then he'd get back his disk. They'd all started with ten disks a few days ago, but now Lily was down to four; if she didn't win some back she'd be sitting at the radio a lot, unless she could foist some shifts on Mel again.

"So tell us something else," Vic said. "Not about your father. Tell us one of the craziest things you've done."

Art mulled it over as he shuffled the cards.

"You guys ever been to New York?"

Lily and Sam shook their heads no.

"As an infant," said Vic.

"I always wanted to," Lily said.

"Well there are these ATM vestibules attached to all the banks. Bank of America, Chase, whatever. After a certain hour you can only get in if you swipe your bank card. Anyway, they're well lit. At night they're almost like little theaters on the street. So one night, after way too much tequila at my pal's opening, we got randy in a Chase ATM vestibule. People were walking past, staring, laughing, taking pictures. Someone called the cops obviously. Lucky my pal was the hottest artist in town at that point. Back when that was a thing people cared about. You couldn't get into his openings in Chelsea unless you knew someone. Anyway, he told the cops this was performance art," Art laughed deeply. "And they just shrugged and let us off."

Vic looked confused.

"You made love with… a man?"

Art winked.

"That wasn't really supposed to be the main takeaway from that story. But yes. Full house by the way–that good Sammy?" Sam shook his head, upset, and mucked his cards. Art collected yet more winnings. "What about you, Vic boy? Where's the weirdest place you've done the dirty?"

"Mmm," Vic took a long drag from his cigarette, as if he needed the time to consider all his sexual conquests. "I've made love once with this crazy girl. Very wild."

"Yeah but *where*," Lily said. "That's the question."

"Ah, in the erm, in the zoo."

"The zoo?" Sam repeated.

"Yes." Vic said.

Art guffawed.

"Now that's a new one," he said.

"Where in the zoo?" Lily asked. "And with everyone watching?"

"Erm…" Vic lit another cigarette and sucked it down fast. "The zoo was closed. It was night. She had the key to the zoo. She took me in the evening, and we walked into the monkey cage and made love. Very wild. Very sexy."

"What?? What about the monkeys?" Lily said, dubious. "Didn't they bother you?"

Vic licked his lips.

"No. The monkeys were, em, very peaceful."

This sounded like bullshit to Lily, but she didn't say so. It was Art's job to decide what was bullshit and what wasn't. And he was shaking his head and laughing.

"Victorino… you're nuts."

Vic grinned and took a long drag.

"Yes. I am crazy."

"Twenty," Art said. Everyone had folded except him and Sam. It was a big pot: forty Marlboros and one shift so far.

Sam looked down at his cards, sighed, and threw them away. Art gathered yet another pot. Lily looked down and was shocked to discover that she only had about thirty cigarettes left and two disks left. Art dealt another hand and bet. Vic raised, and Art called.

"Alright, fine. My pops," Art said, "he got mad one time because I took out the trash before the bag was totally full. Said I was 'wasting capacity'– How much you got there Vic boy?"

"Excuse me?"

"How many cigarettes and shifts you got left in your pile?"

Vic inhaled sharply as the implication of the question became clear, then slowly counted them out, like a man headed to the gallows.

"I have twenty-two cigarettes and three disks."

Art nodded.

"Then that's my bet. Everything you got."

Vic picked up his Dixie cup of tea, and tried to keep his hand steady as he took a sip. Lily wondered what would happen if Vic called the bet and lost. He'd have nothing left. Did that mean he couldn't play anymore? Would he be out of the game forever?

Vic looked down at his cards, then at the massive pot, then back to his cards, obviously weighing two horrible scenarios against each other: folding and surrendering this pot, or calling and losing everything. Vic was probably wondering the same thing, Lily thought. If he lost everything did that mean the game would end?

Art sat perfectly still, hands folded in his lap, smiling. Vic was in anguish. He smoked his way through two whole cigarettes before reluctantly shoving everything he had into the pot.

"I have two pairs," he said, voice trembling.

Art shrugged.

"I got three deuces. Sorry, Monsieur Fournier."

Vic looked shell-shocked as Art collected an armful of what just moments ago had been his Marlboros.

"You're on fire, Art," Sam said.

"I'm getting some cards tonight," Art admitted. Vic gazed longingly at the pile of what used to be cigarettes, as if imagining what it would have been like to smoke each and every one. The empty expanse of table in front of the Frenchman was jarring.

"So what–" Lily started.

"I'll do more shifts," Vic said, still staring at the mountain of cigarettes in front of Art. "I need an opportunity to recoup."

Art sighed.

"I don't think I'll have to do a shift for the next three weeks, Vicky. Afraid that's not a very tempting offer."

Vic turned to Sam and Lily.

"I have a lot of tea," he said. "We can exchange tea for some cigarettes?"

Sam frowned, like he didn't approve of Vic's desperation.

"I'll give you five," he said, giving Vic a handful of Marlboros. "If you win just pay me back I guess."

"Yes, okay thanks." Vic snatched the five smokes from Sam. Lit one of them, and puffed desperately as he gestured for Art to deal another hand.

"Alright," Art smiled. "Back in business."

Art dealt out the cards. Vic looked down, and immediately threw his hand away. Sam raised to three. Lily inspected her hand, and felt her heart jump when she saw that she'd been dealt a heart flush. Trying to remain calm, she picked eight cigarettes from her stack and dropped them in the pot.

"Raise," she said casually.

Art inspected his own cards, then called the bet. The action was back on Sam.

"I reraise," he said calmly. "Seventeen."

Lily's pulse pounded in her ears. Should she raise again? No. Keep it cool.

"Call," she announced.

"Call," Art echoed. "Sammy Arnold. How many cards you want?"

"One," he said, sliding a single card over to Art.

"Lily Chen–how many cards, dear?"

She sniffed.

"None," she said.

Art raised an eyebrow.

"Alrighty," he said, "and dealer takes two."

Vic had finished his cigarette and was clearly trying to resist the temptation to smoke a quarter of his remaining net worth.

"One shift and ten cigarettes," Sam announced, sliding the smokes and a disk into the pot. Lily felt her knees shaking under the table. Another huge hand, right after Vic had lost everything. The game had reached a new level of excitement tonight.

"Raise to three shifts," she said quietly, pushing three disks into the middle.

"Wow," Art said. "Things are getting serious now." Art thought for a long moment, took a drink of tea. "I have both of you covered, right? So… what can I say? I'm betting everything again."

It was Sam's decision first. He took a deep breath, and then pinched the bridge of his nose and closed his eyes. Opened them and said simply: "Alright."

He pushed his entire collection of cigarettes and disks into the center.

Now everyone looked at Lily. She had a hell of a hand. She hadn't even considered folding until just now. Her boys were looking at her, awaiting her decision. She had to admit, she didn't like the idea of folding. It was more manly to call the bet and lose than to appear scared. And if she won, she'd have triple what she'd had at the start of the hand… Probably a bigger stack than Art even.

Before she could really think everything through she said: "I call too. I have a flush."

She turned over her hearts. Sam's face fell. He stood up and threw his cards down angrily, showing three aces.

"Ah hell," he growled.

His cheeks were pink and his expression furious. For a second, Lily was scared he was going to upend the table or punch a wall. But he just stared at his losing cards and clutched his stomach. When it was clear that Sam wasn't going to do anything insane, Art slowly turned over his cards.

"Sorry Lily," he said. "Full house."

Her stomach dropped and she felt her face burning.

Art didn't even bother to gather the pot; everything was his now besides Vic's four cigarettes. Sam still hadn't sat down. He kept staring at the finished hand, the upturned cards, like a detective at a grisly crime scene hoping against hope that he misunderstood exactly what he was looking at.

"Well." Art shook his head sheepishly. He looked almost embarrassed at his abundance of riches.

Lily's face was still on fire, and her hands were shaking. She needed to calm down. She needed a cigarette. Reflexively she reached down to where her pile used to be, and then the reality hit her all over again. She felt like she might throw up.

"How can we get them back?" Vic said. "What do we do?"

"I..." Art looked flabbergasted at what had unfolded in the last fifteen minutes. "I don't know I mean, I guess I could just divide them back up again, but that doesn't really seem fair, you know."

Lily didn't even want that. Yes, she wanted a cigarette right now. But if Art just divided everything up again, gave everyone back their shifts and Marlboros, the game would in a sense be over. It wouldn't have any meaning. It wouldn't be exciting to win anymore, because you knew eventually if you won everything you'd just redistribute to the others and start again. And really what Lily wanted now wasn't the cigarettes and the shifts; she wanted the game itself, with its promise of emotional redemption and escape from their stark reality. In the minutes since the last hand, along with the gut punch of the loss, it was like she was sinking back into a very dark place: the place she'd been during the first couple days on board, when she'd felt stuck in one of those bad dreams where something horrible was chasing you but your feet wouldn't move; where every ten minutes or so she remembered that the unfathomable had happened, and she'd shatter all over again.

She wanted, *needed*, everything to be back to the way it was just a few minutes ago.

"Look, here," Art started counting out his cigarettes. "I'll give you guys each twenty back to play with–"

"No," Sam said. "That's not right. You won them fair and square. We don't want your charity."

Vic looked at Sam, pained, as if to say, *we don't?*

"You won, we lost. That's all there is to it," Sam said, sitting back down and placing his tea cup on the tabletop with a bit more force than needed. He wasn't mad at Art, she thought. He was just mad about losing and, like her, upset at the possibility that the game might be over.

Art nodded thoughtfully.

"Yeah, I hear you…" he picked up a disc emblazoned with the letter 'L', and twirled it between his fingers. "Well, maybe it's for the best that we're done here. I've got a lot of work to do tonight. Have to write a little speech."

"Speech?" Vic asked, still hungrily eyeing Art's heap of cigarettes.

"Yeah. Gonna call a meeting tomorrow morning and make a speech trying to convince you people to go to the island. The coordinates written on Adam's chest. I mean, how long are we gonna wait out here for the Navy to rescue us like a bunch of suckers?"

Lily cringed. She didn't like the way Art said 'you people,' lumping the three of them in with everyone else on board.

"You really think it's a good idea?" Lily asked.

Art shrugged.

"I just feel like it's our only shot of survival out here. I was speaking to Mel the other day, and I think he's starting to feel the same way. So I mean, I don't expect to get the votes I need tomorrow, but I feel like I gotta try." He cracked his neck and sighed. "I probably won't get to sleep for hours. I'm not much of a writer."

"I'll vote for you," Vic said.

Art raised an eyebrow.

"Yeah?"

"Why not. It's like you said, nobody is coming to rescue us. And I'm happy to support a friend, in any case."

Art nodded.

"I appreciate that."

"Of course," Vic rubbed a lock of blond hair out of his eyes, "I will want something small in return." He winked. "My cigarettes back."

Art laughed softly and twirled an unlit cigarette hypnotically between his fingers. "If you want my opinion, you should be voting to go out there anyway, rather than die out here," he shrugged. "But if that's what it takes, why not. Sounds like a fair deal. We started with eight hundred cigarettes each a few days ago, but I'm sure we have considerably fewer now. Vic, you count out the pile, and then take a quarter of whatever's there. And your shifts back, of course."

Art pushed his entire stash of cigarettes to Vic, and the Frenchman started counting.

Lily bit her lip. What Art was saying made sense: they'd been monitoring the radio for two weeks now, and not a blip. And nobody on board had yet made a convincing case about why the rest of the mainland, or Caribbean islands, shouldn't be just as infected as the places she'd seen with her own eyes. Plus she trusted Art's judgement. He just seemed to know about *everything*. Yesterday he'd explained how watches work, then they took a twenty-minute break from poker for him to open Sam's watch, show them the inner workings, and then reassemble it. An hour later, Sam mentioned something about what a mistake the Iraq war had been (trying to sound smart, Lily thought), and then Art–while not disagreeing–delivered what amounted to a thirty minute lecture explaining what the world looked like in 2001, economically and politically, and how hindsight could make you forget that sometimes in the moment bad decisions seem perfectly reasonable.

"I'll vote for you," Lily blurted out. "But I want my cigarettes too."

"Wow," Art said, and laid his hand on top of hers. "That means so much to me Lily, really."

His warm smile, twinkling eyes, and tender touch made her sure she was making the right choice.

Now if Sam agreed to do the same, they'd have a game again. Everything would be back to the way it was. But Sam's face was a stone statue.

"I'm not sure about this," he said in a low voice.

Art's mouth tightened.

"What do you mean?"

"It's not right. Things shouldn't work like this."

"Man, you just want to stay here in the ocean?" Vic said.

"It's not about that," Sam said.

Vic started to protest again, but Art held up a halting palm.

"It's okay Vic. Let Sammy decide for himself. We don't want to pressure anyone into doing anything. It's a big deal, what we all decide to do tomorrow."

Lily herself was silently praying that Sam would take the offer; it wouldn't be the same playing with just three. But she respected Art's wish to not pressure him.

Vic returned to counting the cigarettes. Lily crossed her arms and sat back in her chair. She wasn't sure what to say now. Sam had his hands clasped in front of him, face blank, staring at Art like he was in a big hand with him and was trying to figure out how good Art's cards were.

The silence became uncomfortable. Sam's gaze didn't waver from Art. The hairs on the back of Lily's neck pricked up. The only sounds in the cabin were the groaning of the ship–like a bear settling in for the night–and a sequence of whispered French numbers. Sam was hardly blinking. Art shifted his weight in his chair, obviously becoming a bit unsettled himself. Finally Sam dropped his hands and stood up.

"Goodnight," he said.

Vic's face fell.

"Man–"

"–I've had enough of this stupid game," Sam said. And lumbered out of the room, closing the door behind him.

Vic looked distraught. Lily chewed on her fingernails.

"What now?" she asked Art.

He lifted up his Dolphins cap to scratch his thin hair.

"Don't worry. We'll be fine."

<h2 style="text-align:center">30</h2>

Jennifer was pretty sure she wasn't suicidal. She definitely wasn't attracted to the idea of death. But after her shift on the radio she found herself at the railing again, peering over the edge, thinking about jumping. Not to kill herself exactly; just to get away from the boat and the people on it.

Part of what made this whole situation so hard to deal with was that she didn't have anyone to confide in, to debrief about how selfish or unaware or ignorant these people were. She didn't have Karen or Gear, from the task force, to help her understand how to deal with them. How to help them. What would Keren and Gear say?

For most people, it's really hard to care about those who look different than them, and live on the other side of the world. Usually to persuade them to join the cause you have to bring it back to them: *what if you were forced to marry at age fourteen, and could be killed for showing your face in public?*

At the same time though, you need to have empathy for people who have been so socialized by the military-industrial capitalist patriarchy that they never really had a chance–

–I disagree. Everyone knows what they're doing. It's a choice, whether or not to resist.

She was leaning over the railing–far enough to scare herself a little– when Greg sidled up to her, his approach so smooth that she didn't sense his presence until he was nearly on top of her. For the past weeks she'd immediately left a room whenever he entered and had managed to completely avoid any sort of interaction with him. This time she hadn't reacted fast enough.

"I like the view here too," he said, in his silky radio voice. "Looking back at the coast. Really makes you think, you know."

He was standing to her right, his elbows perched on the railing. She could smell lentil daal on his breath.

"What?" she said, hoping her tone was as bitter as she intended.

"Yeah you know. About everything. What happened. Life."

"Please don't talk to me."

He swallowed. Usually Jennifer just walked away anytime he was close, but this time she felt empowered by his silence. Her verbal body blow had landed. And anyway, where was there to escape to? Back to the stifling heat of her cabin to lie on her bed and stare at the ceiling? She was spending probably twenty hours a day in her cabin, which she was well aware was unhealthy behavior, but it was the only way to avoid running into people. She'd started to think of the people on board primarily as obstacles to be avoided, and whenever she was outside the cabin, she was mostly just thinking about how to get back to her cabin without being hassled.

Everyone wanted her attention. That was the thing.

Elissa always wanted to talk, and she wanted Jennifer to listen. She wanted to force her word vomit down Jennifer's throat. Elissa would start with small talk questions: *How are you doing? Anything you want to talk about?* But when Jennifer responded tersely and tried to escape, Elissa would literally corner her and just start ejaculating words, thoughts about the radio shifts, the weather or, most often, a follow-up on a previous conversation of theirs that Jennifer had also not wanted to participate in; this 'follow-up' tactic a particularly devious way of ensuring that by definition there would always be something for Elissa to talk about. The irony was, Elissa talked to her like she was a little kid or an idiot, as if she was doing Jennifer a personal favor by taking the time to explain things to her. If Elissa wanted to do everyone on board a favor, Jennifer thought, she'd ask Art to carve her a wooden ball gag.

Art also talked down to her, but that wasn't what really bothered her about him. Like Greg, he sometimes seemed to be taking their situation too lightly. But with Greg, Jennifer knew it was an act; Art actually seemed to be genuinely relaxed about everything. Sometimes he even seemed to be *enjoying* all of this. Jennifer didn't want everyone to act like Lily, to sob like a pathetic little child, but you had to have some kind of respect for everyone who died. When Art winked at her it wasn't the creepy possible sexual threat of it that bothered her, it was that he seemed to be saying that this was all funny to him, trivializing the fact that everyone Jennifer had ever known was dead. Her parents, her friends, everyone. There was nothing funny about that, and every time Art said something like *Well, looks like it's the end of the world*, she wanted to smack him.

Vic always wanted to talk to her. She ran into him in the mess usually. The few occasions when she'd felt she had no choice but to stop and say hi back, he'd given her a weird smile and said:

May I offer you some fresh tea?

Vic had said that exact phrase to her several times. The predictability of what he was going to say, the way he always said it in exactly the same way with exactly the same weird smile made her feel like time aboard this ship was stuck in some kind of cosmic hamster wheel.

Lily was obviously a nightmare. Fortunately the dislike was mutual, and when they bumped into each other Lily just gave a curt nod, mouth tight, and moved on.

Jennifer actually felt sorry for Doctor Rosalyn. She still heard her humming, tapping, and sometimes weeping in the bathroom, but since their one brief morning exchange neither had broached inter-stall conversation. Yesterday Jennifer ran into her in the kitchen. By the time Jennifer noticed her, it was too late to just turn around and leave. The doctor appeared to have poured one packet each of daal and polenta into a big metal bowl and was stirring them vigorously with a wooden spoon, while humming some deranged melody. She was stirring so hard that she had to grip the metal bowl with her entire off-arm, holding it in a kind of headlock to ensure that it didn't spill. Doctor Rosalyn heard Jennifer behind her and swiveled around. Her eyes were wide and yellow, the same color as the hideous concoction she was stirring. Like when she'd first encountered Rosalyn in the bathroom, Jennifer had the horrifying thought that the doctor had been in here stirring that bowl for hours.

"Oh hi there," Rosalyn said. She stopped stirring for a moment, but was still gripping the bowl and spoon with unsettling determination.

"Hi," Jennifer said, and ducked passed her to enter the pantry. She snatched a packet of daal, her main priority now just to get back to her cabin as soon as possible. But when Jennifer turned, Rosalyn was at the entrance to the pantry, partially blocking her escape. She had left the bowl on the counter, but was holding the stirring spoon; the doctor seemed unaware that the daal-polenta mix was dripping from the spoon onto the linoleum floor.

"How are you?" Rosalyn asked, cocking her head.

"Fine." And then when Rosalyn didn't budge Jennifer felt herself forced to add: "And you?"

"Fine, fine." Rosalyn gave a ghostly smile. Her hair was stringy and fraying. "How are you?"

"Fine."

Jennifer stepped forward and literally squeezed between the doorway and Rosalyn, rushing back to her cabin with her food packet. After that encounter, she stayed put for the rest of the day.

Sam wasn't too bad, actually. But whenever he saw Jennifer he tried to recruit her to help open containers, which meant she tried to avoid him as much as she did anyone else.

Adam wasn't dangerous. At first, Jennifer had assumed he was similar to the people who showed up at the protests for the women of Najaf without any real idea what was happening there, just wanting an excuse to get angry. Like Adam, they were unkempt and smelled bad. They'd wave their signs and shout so aggressively that Jennifer felt embarrassed to be marching with them. (Of course, you couldn't kick people out of a protest because they weren't protesting the way you wanted them to. That was actually one of the main challenges of organizing protests: selective advertising.) She'd assumed that Adam had a similar relationship with the DOJ's causes.

But after talking to Adam once or twice it became clear that he wasn't even with-it enough to be a DOJ zombie. Art had been right: Adam had suffered some kind of serious brain damage.

When was her last talk with Adam? Who could remember. Every day, she thought, was the same, and they blurred together in her memory like some puree of rotten vegetables. Whenever it was, she'd walked past his cabin sometime in the afternoon and saw him inside sitting on the floor looking at the pictures in the Italian maritime encyclopedia.

"Hi? Excuse me? Miss?" He sounded like a normal person. And without really thinking about it she came in and stood over him.

"Yes?"

"I think there's been some sort of mistake. I'm not supposed to be here."

"Where are you supposed to be?" she responded.

"I'm not crazy," he said. "I don't need to be institutionalized. If you bring a doctor in to evaluate me, I think you'll find that I'm totally healthy."

He sounded so sincere that for a moment she forgot about his supposed condition.

"What do you think this place is?" she asked.

He raised a tangled eyebrow, and looked around the cabin. It was night, so he couldn't see the ocean through the porthole.

"I..." he started, then gripped his oily hair with consternation. He turned back to her with a hesitant smile and asked when dinner would be served.

She felt bad for ditching Bahram, but sitting with him had just become so frustrating. She'd wanted to help him. Ship life must have been doubly miserable for him, since he couldn't talk to anyone, and he seemed to have things he was dying to tell her about the Daughters of January, Adam, and his son, Azzami. And she also wanted to hear about life in Afghanistan, especially if it was anything like Najaf, the region in Iraq she'd been working so hard to help.

But they just couldn't get anywhere. It was shocking how poor his memory was. It took at least forty repetitions for him to learn simple one-syllable English words, and often he'd lose his concentration or patience. His art skills were even worse than his linguistic ones. Sometimes it felt like every morning they were starting from a completely blank slate. Many of the simple words she'd tried to drill into him–'boat', 'food', 'sun'–seemed to just evaporate overnight. He'd draw the same inscrutable scribbles he'd done several times before, and get angry that she still couldn't understand. After five or six days of this, it was simply too frustrating to bear.

She hated Mel for reasons she wasn't entirely proud of. It was his continued optimism, buoyed by faith. She'd seen Lily and Art in his cabin a few times praying with him, and it made her blood boil. They were living in a fantasy land. It was such an obviously pathetic way of dealing with real life. "God" wasn't going to undo the bombs and the poisonous air, or replenish their water supply.

On multiple occasions she'd heard Mel say things to the effect of *Everything is for the best,* or *We just don't understand why things happen,* or *It's all part of God's plan,* and it made Jennifer want to choke him with those stupid white strings he thought automatically made him some kind of saint. Nothing was for the best, so stop pretending. That's all it was: a stupid pretend game to make themselves feel better.

Jennifer hated all the reverence people gave that game. Like even if they knew it was bullshit–as Jennifer was sure Elissa did–they still seemed to be happy that someone on board was praying. Jennifer happened to be walking through the mess the other day when Mel was delivering some kind of sermon to a few people: Elissa, Rosalyn, and Greg. Elissa invited her to come sit down. *Come join us*, was what she said, in a tone that made it sound like what she was really saying was, *Hey, stop being such a skeptic and come nourish your soul with us.* That smarmy, self-righteous, inviting smile on Elissa's face… it had been all Jennifer could do to just say *No thanks*, and rush back to her cabin.

And then there was Greg, standing beside her on the railing, smiling his million-dollar smile.

"Please don't talk to me," she said, which shut him up for a second.

"Look," he finally said. "I'm not trying to excuse my behavior–"

Jennifer swallowed.

"I'm going to go get something to eat," she lied, and turned to go. He stopped her escape with a hand on her shoulder. She could have brushed it off, but didn't.

"Please," he said. His green eyes were quivering. "Just let me say this. I won't try to excuse myself. My behavior was unacceptable. And I'm deeply sorry if I made you feel uncomfortable. But I think the way you're treating me is really unfair."

His hand on her bare shoulder was like a lead weight. She felt dizzy, and again the idea of jumping over the railing to escape him crossed her mind.

"Unfair?" Jennifer managed to croak.

"Yeah," he said. "Like, the way you ignore me, treat me like I'm not even a person. Do you know what I've been through? No. You have no idea. I'm trying to deal with my own shit here, just like you. I'm trying to deal with losing everyone I ever knew, and being on a boat with a bunch of crazy strangers, watching our food and water supply shrink every day. Just like you, I'm confused and freaked out and lonely."

Her chest seized. She turned away from him to stare down into the dark blue below.

Jennifer kept looking at the sea to disguise that her eyes were tearing up. She tried to concentrate on the small waves lapping at the base of the ship. She hated that she was crying now, in front of Greg, of all people. She hadn't cried even once while alone in her cabin. But here it was, and once the floodgates opened just a crack, the whole dam burst. She couldn't control herself. She was sobbing.

His arm closed around her shoulders.

"It's okay," he said. "It's alright."

He squeezed her into a tight embrace, and she put her face into his chest. She couldn't help it. It didn't matter that it was Greg, it felt so good to touch a real live person. The touching triggered more emotion. She was soaking the chest of his purple polo shirt with tears. He hugged her and rubbed her back while she cried.

"I know," he said. "I know. It's so lonely out here."

She clung to him like she would a life raft on a stormy sea, until he detached. He put his hands on her shoulders and pushed her away a few inches. He looked at her.

"I've gotta go give people some water," he smiled kindly, a little sadly. "But come talk to me whenever, okay?"

"Sure."

Jennifer retreated to her cabin, lay down and thought about the way it had felt to be held by him. She thought of something from her intro to psychology class: the Harlow Monkey Experiment. Baby monkeys latching onto a mother made of wool, just for the sensation. That was her, she knew it. And she wasn't stupid: Greg was obviously still trying to sleep with her.

But maybe, as he'd suggested, she *was* being too hard on him. Had he really done anything so unforgivable? It was like he said, he'd been through hell too. Who could blame him for acting a little weird in her cabin that night?

She wrapped her arms around her chest. What the fuck was wrong with her? She hated that she'd spent the better part of three weeks just lying here face up in her hot dark cabin. It was disgusting. How could a person do this? She'd been skipping meals. Once she'd slept for twenty straight hours. She'd woke up revolted by her own sloth, but still unable to will herself to her feet until Elissa knocked on her door to remind her about her radio shift.

She needed help. She had no faith in her own judgement. She needed someone to tell her what to do.

It all starts with gratitude. Every morning you get to open up two gifts: your left eye and your right eye.

Leave money out of it, Jennifer. If you could spend a year doing or studying anything, what would it be?

How do I do it? Every hour of every day I ask myself: am I making a difference? Could I be doing more?

I hate to say it but it's true: find a man that will take care of you. You'll thank me.

The monkeys in the control group were placed in an environment with a "mother" made of hard steel and wood.

The military industrial capitalist patriarchy operates by dehumanizing their opponents. That's how they stay in power: marginalizing the "other."

Don't tell me what you think you should be doing with your life, tell me what you want to do. What interests you?

If he thought he could get away with it, there isn't a man alive who wouldn't rape you.

You should keep a gratitude journal. Every day write down something you're grateful for. You're so fortunate it's disgusting.

Your father works very hard to make sure that we're comfortable.

Tons of stuff we're socialized to believe is just arbitrary or based on ancient superstition. Religion is used to justify archaic sexist views.

The monkeys in the control group had softer stool, trouble digesting milk, and were far more likely to suffer from diarrhea.

Jennifer opened her eyes. It was late, a few hours after dark. It had been hours since she spoke with Greg. She was starving. She pulled on her shorts and shirt and walked out into the hall.

She gripped the bannister. She was groggy from hunger and too much sleep. She reached for the door to the stairwell, but it swung open on its own. Vic was there, apparently coming back to his cabin after a late night bathroom trip. He studied her with his little black eyes.

"Hi," he said. "Good evening."

"Hi," she replied.

Vic had grown a blond beard over the last few weeks. It was the same color as his chest hair. He'd been pudgy when they'd climbed aboard, but had slimmed down and now his bronzed torso was tight. He was a bit shorter than her. His hands were meaty and strong, stronger than Greg's delicate ones.

They'd been standing there unmoving for a long beat. They locked eyes. Vic's chest was rising and falling quickly. He was obviously confused about what was happening.

"May I offer you some fresh tea?" he asked.

This small act of kindness made Jennifer feel like she might lose it again; start sobbing as forcefully as she had earlier today with Greg. Her pulse thumped in her ears.

"Yes," she said, through tears. "Please."

31

Sam couldn't sleep. Half of the reason was the pain in his stomach. There was a position he could lie in that was alright, but any small movement and the burning returned. Then it took a few minutes to shift around until he found the sweet spot again. The other reason he couldn't sleep was that he was craving a cigarette. He kept considering whether to wake up Vic, Lily or even Art to ask for one. He couldn't though, not after walking out on their game two nights ago. It would be too shameful.

Sam hadn't known his father well; his parents divorced when he was seven, and Sam and his sisters were raised by their mom. But one thing he had learned from his dad was to show yourself respect. It was one of the only clear memories Sam had of him: at dinner one night his father announced to the family that he had quit his job at the car garage that afternoon. His mother threw a fit. Sam remembered an explosion of broken glass as his mother hurled a plate against the wall, eyeshadow running down her cheeks. His father sat at the table calmly, while his wife went berserk, explaining himself to his only son:

That man disrespected me. I worked there for three years without a peep. And now he won't give me another dollar an hour? I can't work for a man like that. It's not about the money. I can't do that to myself.

Years later, Sam sat in the shadow of a reception desk, in the waiting room of an office on the 23rd floor of the Merrill Lynch building. The week before, he'd happened to strike up a conversation at a bar with a man named Grant. After an hour of schmoozing, Grant told Sam he could probably get him an interview at his company, Harvey & Leer, if Sam was interested. It was all Sam could do not to get down on the sticky barroom floor and kiss Grant's feet. Sam had been washing dishes at Café Roma for three years. His hands were permanently pink and dry from the hot water, and no matter how long he showered after a shift he could never wash off the smell of Italian spices. He'd submitted a few résumés a year and a half ago, and had been so discouraged by the rejections that he hadn't tried since.

I don't have any experience in, like, law.

That's fine, I didn't either. It's not really law, it's sales. And for sales all that counts is personality.

Even worse.

Ha ha. Listen I'll set this up. It's all about being able to talk on the phone. Sam, you talk to my boss the way you talk to me and you'll be hired on the spot.

Sam sat rigid in the expensive leather chair. He looked down at his notebook. He'd called in sick yesterday to Café Roma to do research on Harvey & Leer, but had only found enough information to fill half a page. The receptionist was a bored-looking platinum blond. Sam wore a suit he'd bought from Walmart for a hundred twenty bucks. It was an XXL, and still the sleeves of the jacket were too short.

Twenty minutes after his scheduled interview time, a man nearly as tall as Sam rushed into the waiting area. He wore a sharp Italian suit and blindingly shiny gold watch. He was completely bald.

"Hi Sam," he said, extending his hand. Sam rushed up out of his seat to grab it. "Sorry for the wait. Let's go."

Sam followed the bald man into the bowels of the office. They walked past thirty or forty people seated at a long table, mostly men, all wearing headsets and talking on the phone. He spotted Grant, and waved. Grant returned a quick smile and then returned his attention to whoever he was talking to on the phone. The bald man led Sam into a small conference room, and gestured for him to sit down. The bald man sat down across from him, and opened a laptop that was waiting for him on the table.

Okay, Samuel Arnold? he asked, staring at the screen.

Yessir.

He realized the bald man hadn't told Sam his name. Below the table, Sam gripped his thighs tightly.

Alright. I've got your résumé here. You're a friend of Grant's, is that right?

Sam hesitated. 'Friend' was a bit of a strong word.

Yes.

The bald man was still looking at the screen.

You're working as a waiter?

Sam's shoulders tightened. On his résumé he'd just put Café Roma as his place of employment, and been vague about his position.

I work in the kitchen.

The bald man nodded slightly and closed the laptop. Sam assumed this was the end of the interview and braced himself for rejection. But instead the bald man looked at him.

Grant says you've got charisma. He told me life has dealt you a tough hand, but that you've got skills, and could thrive if someone just takes a chance on you. Is that right?

Sam wanted to hug Grant. He was going to buy him a hell of a bottle of whiskey after this.

I don't know about the charisma. But yes sir, I can tell you man to man that I'm the hardest worker you've ever met. I may not know a lot about law, but I promise you I'll learn. You tell me the books, and I'll read them. Cover to cover.

The bald man smiled for the first time.

That's good. That's really good. I'm looking for hard workers. But you won't have to understand too much about the details of law—all that boring stuff. You have to understand people, you have to be able to talk to them, put their minds at ease and bring them in as clients. Do you think that's something you could do?

Sam kept his face dead serious.

Yes sir, I believe it is.

The bald man nodded, like he appreciated Sam's directness.

I'll give you the job Sam. But the question is, are you hungry?

Sam shrugged.

I could eat.

The bald man shook his head chuckling.

No I mean hungry. *Are you hungry to close deals? The job is commission based. The harder you work, the more you make. If you work half as hard as you say you do, you'll be rolling in it.*

Sam cleared his throat.

Well sir, I have to admit, I don't quite understand what you're selling. I thought this was a law office? I couldn't really figure it out from reading online. I guess I can't say or not whether I'm confident I can sell this product before I know what it is.

The bald man cracked his knuckles.

You're correct. We're a law office. And we're not selling anything. We're calling people and offering them money that they're already entitled to.

Sam didn't understand, but also didn't want to sound stupid.

So you're calling people and… offering to give *them money?*

The bald man rubbed his shiny head like he was polishing an apple. Sam feared that his interviewer was getting impatient.

Let me give you an example. Have you ever used Winston toothpaste?

Sam was confused.

No sir.

Ever? You've never been on the road, and it was what the hotel sold in their lobby? Or maybe your girlfriend uses it and you stole some once?

Sam shifted uncomfortably. He couldn't remember ever having actually used Winston toothpaste, but it was clear what answer this man was looking for.

I suppose yes, once or twice.

Well it turns out that about ten percent of all bottles of Winston toothpaste manufactured within the last three years contain trace amounts of lead. Lead, of course, is extremely unhealthy. It can lead to illness, birth defects, and even death. You think Winston didn't know this? Of course they knew it. But instead of burning millions of bottles of toothpaste and taking a big loss, they just said hey, fuck it, let's poison people. We'll get away with it. We're a big fucking corporation. Well guess what. A kid dropped dead last year in Houston. Ten years old. They found traces of lead in his bloodstream. Guess what toothpaste he was using.

A moment. Then Sam realized he was actually supposed to guess.

Winston?

That's damn fucking right. Winston toothpaste killed a kid. Now I don't know about you, but I'm sick and tired of these big corporations acting like they can do whatever the hell they want to little guys like me and you. So I'm suing them. I'm taking them to task for the evil they've done. And what those fellas out there are doing now, including your friend Grant, are calling honest folks like you and me who might be poisoning themselves every time they brush their teeth. And if the folks they call are using Winston, we're saying hey, climb aboard, we're gonna get you the settlement you and your family deserve.

Sam blinked.

And they just say alright, and then they're part of the case?

There's a trivial upfront fee, to cover administrational expenses. Usually just about thirty bucks a person. When we win a case for them, they might get back thousands.

But when you win a case, you also take a percent of that?

The bald man stopped rubbing his head and sat back in the chair.

It varies. But you don't have to worry about that. You just get folks signed up. In this case, for instance, every person you get signed up–full name, email, social–you get ten bucks. Think about that. If you can get them signed up in four minutes, that's a hundred fifty bucks an hour. That's more than a doctor makes. And we have an amazing script already written for you. All you gotta do is read the script–the script fucking works. It's automatic money. Now I'm willing to take a chance on you Sam. Are you willing to take a chance on me?

There were a lot of factors to weigh in that moment. But the only thing Sam could manage to think was: he would never have to wash a dish again.

I am, sir.

After three and a half weeks the bald man invited Sam into the same conference room he'd sat in for the interview. Sam knew he wasn't performing well. His average call length–always displayed in the top-right corner of his monitor–was twenty-one minutes. He'd already been warned multiple times to stop deviating from the scripts, but he just couldn't help himself:

I've been feeding Mama Mary's all-natural maple syrup to my children for years! Should I take them to a doctor?

Ma'am, your children are probably fine, but if it's going to bring you peace of mind then it's worth it, in my opinion.

How can they get away with this? Arsenic in Maple Syrup!?

Well to be honest with you, there's also arsenic in apple and pear seeds. It's a very small amount of arsenic in the syrup. Listen, ma'am I don't want you to worry too much about your children. The girl who died in San Francisco... listen don't spread this around but the truth is, yes her mother kept Mama Mary's in her house, but she was also hit by a car. So what I said at the start, that she ate Mama Mary's on a regular basis, and when she died they found above average traces of arsenic in her brain... while that is technically true...

The bald man sat down and cracked his knuckles.

You told me you were hungry, Sam. I'm disappointed.

Sam knew what this talk was. Already he felt the rich carpet beneath him was opening up and swallowing him. The girl he was dating, Leanne, had cried tears of joy when he told her about this job. And now what? He knew the face she'd make when he would tell her he'd been fired. It would be worse than anger. It would be something like pity.

I am hungry, sir. I'm the first one in every morning and the last to leave at night. I was here until eleven last—

But where are the results Sam? I need to see results. You're bringing in fifteen, twenty signatures a day. I need a hundred.

Sam's mouth was dry. His eyes were stinging.

I'm not letting you go, Sam. I think you're a hell of a guy. I just think the customer-facing role isn't a good fit for you.

Hope erupted in Sam's chest. It was all he could do to keep a sweet grin of relief off his face.

What did you have in mind, sir?

Let me show you.

The bald man led him back into the main office. Sam felt the gaze of his colleagues on him and looked away. They knew what was happening: he couldn't cut it.

The bald man unlocked a room Sam had never been in before. Inside were nothing but beige file cabinets. They spanned the entire perimeter of the large room, and then some; the wall with the windows was covered three-deep in filing cabinets, obscuring the view and most of the natural light. There were perhaps sixty cabinets, with three drawers each.

As you know all too well, we still gather signatures by snail mail, because sometimes the courts won't accept digital signatures. Here are about a quarter of our documents. We have warehouse space too. What I need is someone to digitize these. I'll buy you a scanner. You scan each document and save it on the computer, with the person's name as the file name, organized by which case they were a part of.

Whatever relief Sam had felt a few moments ago was gone. He hoped he misunderstood the job the bald man was describing.

Why do you need to put them on the computer? You just said physical is better for the courts.

The bald man sniffed.

A variety of reasons. So what do you say?

Sam's chest felt vacuous as he looked at the cabinets. The work, for all intents and purposes, was infinite. What he understood intuitively, but couldn't yet articulate to himself, was that as bad as dishwashing was, there was a certain very minor sense of accomplishment when you saw the dishes clean. A job completed. There would be no sense of completion here.

I'll pay you twenty cents per scan. So the harder you work, the more you make. What do you say? I think this will be a better fit for you.

He couldn't stop looking at the cabinets. The despair in his breast was absolute. How had it come to this? This was all the world thought he was good for: pulling papers from a file and placing them on a scanner. For months afterward he'd fantasize about this moment–imagine all the things he could have said, often accompanied by acts of violence so extreme that Sam felt guilty that these things even occurred to him. Many such fantasies ended with the bald man dangling out the window, face bloodied beyond recognition, only Sam's grip on his wrist preventing him from plunging to his death, pleading with Sam to spare his wretched life.

Instead Sam said:

Can I listen to my headphones while I work?

Of course.

Alright.

Someone knocked on Sam's cabin door. They'd been knocking for a while, he realized, while he'd dipped back into the well of some classic violent reveries.

"Just a sec," he said, unclenching his fists and sitting up slowly to minimize the pain in his abdomen. "I'm coming."

He flipped on the bedside lamp padded over to the door and opened it. Doctor Rosalyn was standing there, hands clasped behind her back. She had dark circles under her eyes. He was suddenly aware that he wasn't wearing a shirt, but if this bothered the doctor, she didn't show it.

"Hi there," she said. "Can I come in?"

"Sure."

Recalling their meeting a few weeks ago in the captain's lounge, he was careful not to close the door behind them. He didn't want to freak her out. She collapsed in a plush chair beside his bed. She looked smaller than when they'd come aboard.

"Close the door," she said.

Sam obliged, and then sat down across from her. She was quiet, staring into the empty space in front of her eyes. A few days ago she'd spilled daal on the chest of her linen shirt. It appeared since then she'd made a halfhearted attempt to wash out the stain, which only spread it around. Then the sun turned the stain a sickly shade of green.

"Do you know what rigor mortis is?" she asked.

Sam shifted in the chair to make his abdomen more comfortable.

"That's when, well," he cleared his throat, "it's when a dead guy's penis—"

"That's the comedy version, yes," she said. "But it can be any sort of post-death spasm. A movement in the fingers or something. Anyway. That's us. A spasm. The body around us is dead. We're dead. We just don't know it yet."

"That's not true, Rosalyn. We—"

"It is," she said, with a hard finality that discouraged further argument.

They sat in pained silence. Rosalyn tapped the tabletop in an erratic rhythm. Sam wondered why she was here. He'd assumed it was to inspect his hernia, but that didn't seem to be on her agenda. She suddenly stopped tapping.

"Almost certainly this is the end," she said. "But there's an infinitesimal chance we find someplace habitable. So I should get pregnant now, while there is enough food and water for the most critical parts of prenatal development."

Sam swallowed, unsure if he'd heard correctly.

"Get pregnant?"

Rosalyn nodded.

"I guess that makes sense," Sam fumbled for words. "But I mean.."

Rosalyn's expression betrayed nothing. She would have killed at the poker table, Sam thought.

"Will you help? You're my first choice."

Sam opened his mouth, but no words came out. He supposed he should be pleased by this development. But the businesslike way she was approaching this made him a bit uneasy. Still. He was a man, with needs, and suddenly his body was raring to go.

"Alright."

"Okay," she nodded. "Lie down."

Sam rose gingerly, and plopped down on his bed. She stood up and walked to his side.

"How's your hernia?" she asked.

"Same, I'd say."

She placed a cold hand on his lower abdomen and locked eyes with him. She applied a very slight amount of pressure to a spot about two inches north of the hernia.

"Does this hurt?" she asked.

"Yes, but it's not awful."

"Scale of one to ten?"

"Four."

Her small index finger traversed the expanse of his belly, heading south. His whole body clenched as she grazed the epicenter of pain. She pushed it very softly and he emitted an involuntary grunt.

"One to ten?" she asked.

"Eight," he wheezed.

She nodded thoughtfully.

"Probably best if I'm on top then, to start. Then we'll move to a spooning position at the end. That's ideal for conception."

She put her cold hand low on his bare stomach. Very low. His physiological response was immediate. Sam wanted to ask what was happening, clarify that he understood, but within seconds she'd tugged down his shorts and gripped him. She rubbed the dorsal side, then made a fist around his member and pumped a few times with clinical efficiency.

She released, and Sam watched as she peeled off her hiking boots and pulled down her jeans. Her underwear were the kind his high school friends used to call Granny Panties, once white, now grayish-yellow with wear. They disappeared as well and soon her hands were on his sternum, and she was bobbing up and down, like the ship on a choppy day.

Everything was unfolding so quickly and unexpectedly. Sam had a sensation of falling into a strong river, and warm water sweeping him away.

She moved up and down. Her eyes were closed tightly, and Sam thought she was imagining she was elsewhere, maybe the same powerful river. He took handfuls of her hips and helped her rise and fall. The movement was hell on his hernia, but for the moment he didn't care.

And then he was seized by the inevitable.

"No, no." She opened her eyes. "Wait no, not yet."

But he had no chance. He squeezed her butt hard and grunted. His whole body tensed and then exploded with such force that he got a charley horse in his right leg. She kept riding throughout, and even after, while he maintained some hint of rigidity. But they both knew the movie was over; they were just watching the credits because they weren't ready to stand up yet.

Eventually she rolled off him. There was enough space in the bed for them to lie side by side without really touching. She pulled her knees to her chest, something to improve the chances of conception, Sam assumed.

It was hard for Sam to wrap his head around what just happened. Reality loomed large. The cabin smelled like sex and, strangely, a bit like polenta.

Finally she stood up and pulled on her underwear.

"Next time we'll have to start with spooning, unless it's just too painful for you."

Her tone reminded him of a flight attendant instructing passengers to remain in their seats until the plane reaches the gate.

"Um, yeah. So. What about my hernia, actually?"

"You should continue to forego any heavy lifting," she said, buttoning her jeans.

"I meant like, is that okay to do? What we just did? There was some pain."

Rosalyn blinked.

"One to ten?"

"Six maybe?"

"That's fine."

Then she was gone, leaving him alone. He felt shaken. He was probably even farther from sleep now that he'd been before. He thought about what she'd said, about just being a spasm. Your body working automatically.

He closed his eyes and his thoughts drifted back to the file cabinets in that room. Hundreds of thousands of names, emails, and social security numbers. He'd given twenty-seven months of his life to those files and maybe gotten through a sixth of them. He finally fell asleep trying to calculate how many years of work the Daughters of January had saved him.

32

Elissa McClure awoke to Arthur's voice crackling through the PA system.

"Hey everyone. Rise and shine. We're having a meeting in fifteen minutes in the captain's lounge. If you don't show up your voice won't be heard."

She'd known something like this would happen, but his announcment still made her stomach tighten. Using her own rhetoric against her. She was begrudgingly impressed.

Elissa sat up in bed and put on her glasses. When she stood up everything creaked, and she had to steady herself against the wall for a moment until her clunky vascular system could catch up. She cursed her feeble body. Her mind, as best she could tell, was as sharp as ever. But the prison of flesh that held her was decaying. The whole aging process must be a lot easier, she thought, if your brain turned to mush along with the rest of you.

She pulled on her blouse and stepped out into the carpeted hallway. She walked slowly, and assumed she'd be the last up to the bridge, but

Vic was just leaving his own cabin. He looked unusually perky this morning.

"Good morning," he smiled.

"Hi Vic," Elissa said, embarrassed at how warbled her voice sounded. She needed a drink of water.

He opened the door to the stairwell for her and let her walk up before him. She was surprised to find that she wasn't dreading this meeting. On the contrary, she'd started dreading what would happen if nobody came for them: everyone slowly dying from dehydration, and her realizing that it was her fault; she'd convinced them to sit still in the middle of the Atlantic Ocean and die.

She and Vic were indeed the last ones to join the meeting. Even Adam was there, sitting at the head of the oak table next to Arthur.

Vic squeezed into a seat between Mel and Lily, across from Jennifer. The Frenchman smiled at the young woman, and she returned only a tight-lipped nod. Sam sat in one of the big leather chairs, back from the table. His huge arms were crossed over his chest, his expression hard to read.

It seemed that the chair at the other end of the table–near the door and opposite Arthur–had been saved for her. Elissa sat down. People were looking in her direction, waiting for her to say something.

"Okay," she said. "Then we're all here. What's going on, Arthur?"

Arthur nodded and stood up. He took off his baseball hat for a second, tousled his thin hair, then returned it to its perch.

"As you all know," he began, "we have two weeks left of potable water in the tank. More would be distilled, of course, if we fired up the engines to run the generator. With the amount of fuel we have, we could probably distill another three weeks of water. That's my estimate. I could be high or low on that. I called this meeting because I would like for us to reassess our situation, and decide on how to proceed."

Mel tugged on his beard. Greg kept pouring Dixie cups of water for people, an excuse to not concentrate too much on what Arthur was saying. Sam looked at Arthur with his arms folded, appearing concerned. Doctor Rosalyn stared at the tabletop; it was unclear if she was even listening. Lily nodded at every word Arthur said, as if to convey to the rest of the table that he was speaking for her as well.

"There is a general consensus on board, I believe, that we can't go back to the East Coast because of radiation, diseased air, and all that other shit. If anybody would like to claim otherwise, please speak up now."

Arthur paused for a moment. Nobody spoke. He nodded, and continued:

"That means we have three options. One: continue to sit here and wait to be rescued. Two: head down to the Caribbean islands, though I think there's also a general consensus that prospects there are very slim. I know some of us remember hearing about Cuba being bombed, and as I mentioned, it's close enough to the mainland that even if it wasn't hit directly, the spores have certainly been carried there by the wind. And then there's option three: go east, to the coordinates burned onto Adam's chest. Three weeks ago we decided to go with option one. Sit and wait to be rescued. Since then we've been monitoring the radio twenty-four-seven. Thanks Elissa for organizing that. Not a peep. With every day that goes by, the odds of someone showing up get smaller. We can argue about at what point we decide nobody is going to come. Some of you might say we should wait another week. Me, I say we've already waited long enough, and here's why: for starters we need to leave ourselves extra food and water in case we get lost or run into nasty weather or something. Two: if we *do* get to dry land where we can breathe, it will almost certainly take some time to find drinking water and food. The sooner we go, the bigger our backup supply of food and water will be when we get there."

Elissa felt herself being swayed by his *aw-shucks* voice, his down-to-earth mannerisms, his sad eyes. Part of her wanted to just give in to him. Let him lead. Let *him* be responsible for whatever came next.

"So we can quibble over whether to go now, or next week. But the bigger question is: option two or three. The Caribbean? Or the island–"

"We've had this conversation already," Jennifer interrupted. "Only an insane person would burn somebody–or themselves–like this And there's nothing in the atlas at those coordinates. *And* even Adam himself hasn't said anything about there being an island there. We're just going off one word, burned into his forearm. That's ridiculous."

If Adam realized they were talking about him he didn't appear to notice. He just seemed bewildered, like everything was happening too fast for him to follow.

"Sure Adam doesn't have much to tell us," Art said. "But Bahram does."

"I tried–" Jennifer started to protest, Art held up a hand to silence her.

"You didn't make it easy enough for him."

Art walked to the bookcase that held the Italian sailing books and pulled out something that looked like a wooden tray. He placed it on the tabletop.

"I carved this. It's roughly a bird's-eye view of the ship. Here's the deck. Here's the gangplank we all boarded on."

There were a dozen or so carved figurines resting on the tray, which Art placed upright. Many looked to be modified versions of chessmen.

"I let Bahram decide who these would represent."

"I spent hours and hours with him..." Jennifer said, perhaps a bit defensively. "I'm sorry but I really don't think he has anything meaningful to say."

"Look at his hands," Art said. "He's not a linguist or an artist. This man worked with his hands for many, many years. Bahram?" Art gestured to the pieces and the board. "Please show us. Adam. Bahram. Azzami."

Bahram looked at the people sitting around the table.

"Hello," he said.

He turned to the model, first choosing a knight, which he held up and displayed to the table. "Bahram," he said. Then he held up a crude stick man with a block for a torso. "Azzami. *Abnay.* My son."

"Note that his son, Azzami, has the insignia of the DOJ burned onto his chest," Art said. "Bahram was very clear about that."

Bahram nodded and repeated. "Azzami. Son."

Then he moved a similar figurine, that also had the numbers burned on his shoulder.

"Adam," Bahram said. Then, he put that figure down, and picked up another, identical figurine. "Adam." And another. "Adam!" Then Bahram picked up a figure that looked much like the others, though with crude breasts. "Adam...Vvv..." He looked to Art for help with the word.

"Woman."

"Adam *Voman.*"

"What is this?" Greg interrupted. "C'mon Art. Jennifer tried this already, like she said."

"Let him finish," Elissa said, though she was still trying to decide what she thought of this whole show herself.

Art cleared his throat.

"Bahram, I think it's clear, is saying there are many 'Adams'. This young man's name is not Adam. He never said his name was Adam, in fact, did he? We just started calling him that because of the burn, and because he never corrected us, we assumed it was his name. That's incorrect. He was labeled as one of many 'Adams.' And based on what Bahram is saying, there are female 'Adams' as well.' Bahram. Continue."

Bahram licked his lips, then selected one of the Adam figurines.

"Adam," he said, and pointed at the young man sitting with them in the lounge. He picked up the figure that represented his son, and showed him leading Adam up the gangplank, onto the deck of the ship. There was a piece of thread among the pieces, which Bahram now held up to show everyone, then he showed his son tying Adam's leg in the deck.

"His son, a member of the Daughters of January, was the one who tied up Adam here," Art explained.

Then Bahram showed his son jumping off the ship, leaving only Adam aboard.

"Oh, oh!" Bahram said, realizing he forgot something. "Bahram!"

He displayed the knight that represented him, and put it on the deck, off to the side. Then he pointed to his eyes. "Bahram *see* Adam."

Art nodded.

"Okay. Now what?" he gestured for Bahram to continue.

Bahram took a deep breath, and made a rumbling sound in his throat. The engines. Then he placed his hands on both sides of the tray and slowly pushed it down the width of the table.

Art rushed around to the side of the table, and leaned over between Jennifer and Doctor Rosalyn. He pointed to the spot the ship was heading.

"Bahram!" he shouted, unable to contain his excitement. "What's this place?" he made an exaggerated shrugging gesture. "Where was Adam supposed to guide this ship? What's here?"

Bahram stopped pushing the tray.

"*Nurld,*" he said. Then with some difficulty, "*Nu-orld. Nu-orld.*"

"New World!" Art yelled triumphantly, looking around the table, eyes ablaze. "The Daughters of January sent a bunch of people like Adam, men and women, to populate a New World. The island."

Everyone was silent for a moment while they contemplated this. Then Elissa shook her head.

"This doesn't make sense, Arthur. If there's really an island, why would his son, Azzami, abandon his father and Adam instead of sailing there with them?"

Art made a steeple with his fingers.

"I admit that part doesn't make much sense to me either."

"Furthermore," Elissa said. "Even assuming his son was part of the Daughters of January, the organization was very well funded. Why would they send Adam alone on a cargo ship–just hoping the autopilot doesn't malfunction? Why not fly him to this island by helicopter?"

Art deflated slightly.

"I'm not sure."

"And if Adam's purpose really is to repopulate the 'New World', don't you think they would have chosen someone a bit... healthier? As you said yourself, he can't even remember his own real name."

Art sucked his teeth, and said nothing.

Doctor Rosalyn spoke for the first time.

"Let's suppose, for argument's sake, the Daughters of January put Adam on this ship. That they wanted him to take this boat to those coordinates. And let's suppose there *is* an island there. It seems only logical that this island would be some sort of stronghold. Filled with them. Terrorists."

Art nodded.

"Could be, sure. At least that means they have more resources. Again, I'm not arguing this is an ideal course of action–"

"You've been wanting to go to the island for a while," Greg interrupted, smiling. His hand was tight around a Dixie cup. "And somehow you managed to get Bahram to say stuff making it sound like there's an island, eh? Quite a coincidence. In fact–how do we know that you're not one of them?" He looked around the room, shrugging apologetically as if he couldn't help but raise this possibility. "How can we know Art isn't part of the Daughters of January himself?"

Arthur glared at Greg Pink with such revulsion that Elissa shuddered involuntarily.

"You idiot," Art said, so softly he was nearly whispering. "I'm trying to save all of our lives."

Greg shook his head, to show he wasn't convinced, but didn't retort.

"I can't do anything but make suggestions," Arthur said, turning his attention to everyone else. In fact, Elissa was sure he was speaking directly to her. "And this is my suggestion. Set the autopilot to the coordinates on Adam's chest and go. Today. Right now. That's my proposition. I vote yes. Who else?"

Arthur slowly raised his right hand into the air. A long empty silence. But just as Elissa was about to say something, Vic raised his hand as well. Lily followed. Then Mel, with an audible sigh.

Elissa wasn't sure what she wanted. Arthur definitely made a certain amount of sense, and she didn't want to insist on staying and waiting for the Navy just out of a refusal to admit she'd made a mistake...

But at the end of the day there was *nothing in the atlas.*

"Well I vote against," Greg said, with a confidence Elissa hadn't seen from him in a few weeks. "I'm not sailing to the middle of the ocean because of this dude's puppet show."

"Not today," Elissa said, suddenly coming to a decision and raising her hand. "This is rash. We'll discuss some more. Maybe have another vote in a few days."

"I agree with Elissa," said Sam, raising his hand, and staring stonily at Arthur. "Not today."

Lily glared at Sam, evidently angry at his vote.

Jennifer raised her hand.

"Not today," she said.

Art looked exasperated.

"Folks, this isn't a leisure cruise. We can't just take a few more days, sip wine coolers, and schmooze about this. We're not expert navigators, we gotta leave ourselves some leeway to get to those coordinates. Rosalyn?" he pleaded. "You're the tiebreaker."

The doctor was rubbing her temples and shaking her head.

"I... I don't know. I'm not sure."

"What about Bahram?" Jennifer said.

"Art probably trained him to vote to go!" Greg shouted. "We have no idea what he actually understands."

Jennifer straightened, and turned purple, as if she'd been slapped across the face.

"You act like he's not even a person!" she said, "And you, of all people, should be careful making accusations, Greg. You're the one who 'discovered' Adam tied up, aren't you?"

"I guess you think Adam should get a vote too?" Lily said to Jennifer. "What about the chess pieces? Should they get to vote?"

"Stop this," Elissa said. "Stop."

"Greg found the food," Sam said. "If it wasn't for him, we'd all be dead."

"Another fantastic coincidence!" Jennifer yelled. "He found the crate with food, out of how many thousand–"

"Yes!" Rosalyn said, shaking her head a wild look in her eyes. "Yes. I vote to go. Today. So that's that. Five to four."

Sam looked troubled.

"Rosalyn," he said gently. "Are you sure you don't want to wait? Give us time–"

"No," she spat. "What's the difference? Today? Tomorrow? I vote yes. It's over."

Rosalyn stood up. Her gaze was cloudy; Elissa got the sense she wasn't quite present. "I'll go to the bridge now with Adam and enter the GPS coordinates. Sam, you go down to the engine room and start the engines."

"This is insane," said Jennifer. "This is totally insane. Vic," she said. "Why are you voting for this? It's madness."

Mel answered for him: "We have to do this eventually. If not now, when?"

"No," Jennifer shook her head adamantly. "No. I refuse to allow this to happen. This is my life. You can't make decisions like this that affect everyone on board. It's not like I have anywhere else to go–"

"Dear," Elissa said. "It's alright."

Jennifer turned to her, still flushed.

"It's alright," Elissa repeated, and a wave of calm washed over her. "The Navy isn't coming for us," she smiled sadly to Arthur, who nodded his head almost imperceptibly, thanking her for helping. "We have to take a risk."

Arthur turned to Adam,

"Alright then, kiddo. Go with the doc." He smiled. "Take us to the lucky numbers."

Part 3
Darkness, Upon the Face of the Deep

33

Mel read from his notes:

"And they said, 'let us build a city, with a tower that reaches to the heavens, so that we may make a name for ourselves,'"

Rosalyn Carson felt a lot better since the ship started moving three days ago. After weeks of just floating, there was something so uplifting about actually going somewhere. Mel also seemed reinvigorated. He'd started giving lectures, held every morning at eleven on the bridge, immediately after the daily navigation briefing from Elissa. Someone had to be here at all times anyway to play captain–although really there wasn't a whole lot to do besides ensuring the autopilot wasn't malfunctioning, continuing to switch through radio channels to see if anyone was broadcasting, and occasionally glancing at the radar to confirm there was nothing around but silent water.

When the ship had been stagnant, the bridge was a source of despair. The three glass walls offered a panoramic view of isolation; yellow sky and grey water as far as the eye could see. But now that the ship was moving the bridge had a totally different quality. You could see the bow cutting it's way through the grey sea, scaring the water into angry white froth. The feel of the ship was different now–the side-to-side rocking was replaced by a slight bobbing as they cut through the water head-on. Rosalyn had been sleeping better since they started sailing. This new motion of the ship felt like a mother's arms rocking her to sleep.

She'd been back to see Sam three more times. The last time they'd hardly spoken before or after; he knew the drill. She was considering sleeping with other guys as well; a man needed at least forty-eight hours to regenerate his sperm count, and so scheduling them on alternating nights would give her the best chance of conception.

Vic and Greg were the only possibilities; Art and Bahram were old enough that their virility was questionable, and Mel would surely refuse. She hadn't yet to approached Vic or Greg, but was planning to soon. She wondered how Sam would feel about that. He'd started coming to listen to Mel speak, and she was worried it was because he was growing attached to her, despite her being clear from the start about her motivation.

There was a constant breeze now that they were sailing, and it whipped through the open door of the bridge and made Mel's black hair dance like angels in a fire. His congregation this morning was only four: Sam, Lily, Bahram (only there to enjoy the company, presumably), and herself. Art came sometimes, ditto Vic and Elissa. But if Mel was disappointed with this morning's turnout he didn't show it. With his poise and power, he might have been lecturing to a crowd of thousands.

"The Tower of Babel was a blatant affront to the Holy One, Blessed Be His Name," Mel said. "A challenge to His sovereignty. He responded with vengeance. He–"

"Sent a flood," Lily interrupted. She was always interrupting. She was the only constant fixture at these classes, and sometimes it seemed to Rosalyn that she only came for the opportunity to interrupt. "Right? I remember this from Sunday school."

The corners of Mel's lips turned down. Or at least it looked that way; it was hard to tell exactly what his mouth was doing behind that tangle of beard.

Rosalyn accidentally made eye contact with Sam. He smiled weakly, a pleading puppy-dog smile. The empty conversations they had after sex were becoming automatic. Her asking how his stomach felt, him asking her if she'd been sleeping better.

She had zero attraction to him, was the truth. She got as much satisfaction from jogging laps around the ship for her evening workout as she did from the intercourse.

It had taken her a long time before she'd enjoyed sleeping with Scott, too. The first time they slept together was after eight dates. She'd found his eagerness and self-doubt revolting, to the point that she'd almost broke up with him immediately after they finished. She wasn't really comfortable with him sexually until, after a year, they moved in together and settled into a routine. Two times a week before bed he reached over and gave her a weak shoulder rub. This became the sign. After two perfunctory minutes he'd roll on to her and begin. Sometimes they kissed during it. The median duration of the act itself was between four and five minutes. Deviations were due to factors like stress, if they'd had wine with dinner, if they'd watched a film with sexually explicit scenes that evening, and so on.

"No," Mel said. "The flood was actually before this. In order to punish the builders of the Tower of Babel, the Holy One created different languages. Suddenly one person spoke Spanish, another Russian, and they were unable to communicate with each–"

"Wait," Lily said. "Before? But you started a few days ago at the beginning with God making the world and stuff. When did we talk about the flood? I'd remember. That was always my favorite story."

"With Noah," Sam contributed.

Mel tugged on his beard. Bahram laughed, deep and booming, for unclear reasons.

"I didn't, well…" Mel cleared his throat. "I transcribed the story of *Noach*, of course, but I didn't feel it was proper to discuss, in light of our current situation."

Rosalyn smiled.

"You don't think we can handle hearing a traumatic story about a boat? We're all adults here, Mel."

"No, no it's not that," Mel sighed, losing some of his momentum, a drooping hot air balloon sagging back to earth. "It's that the story has become somewhat problematic."

"What do you mean?" Sam asked.

Mel closed his eyes and rubbed his forehead. He clearly hadn't wanted this topic to come up.

"Well the whole point of the story is that the Holy One did a reset of sorts. A do-over of creation. He wiped out nearly everybody and started again from *Noach*–Noah–and his family. But then at the end, after the rains stopped and Noah and the animals returned to dry land, the Holy One showed them a rainbow. Does this ring a bell?"

"Yeah," Lily said.

Rosalyn and Sam shook their heads no.

"The rainbow was a promise from the Holy One. A promise that he'd never do a reset again. So you understand…" Mel spread his hands to call attention to their situation. "It's hard to square that with current events."

"Ah," Rosalyn said. "You're saying it looks like God broke His promise."'

"Well," Mel laughed mirthlessly. "It's like I said, I haven't figured out yet how to understand the story now, in light of what's happened. Because it's not possible that God simply 'broke His promise.' He knows everything that has been and will be. Knows the future, although more than that, since He doesn't even exist within the confines of time. So He wouldn't have promised something He knew He'd eventually have to renege on."

Rosalyn obviously didn't believe in God, in the same way that she didn't believe in the tooth fairy or karma. Yes, there was a richer, more profound lore surrounding the former, and a lot of good ideas had their origins in Judeo-Christian texts. Not to murder, for instance. But logically that didn't mean God was more likely to exist than the tooth fairy. Both were magical beings invented by people to serve their respective purposes. The tooth fairy's purpose was to keep kids from being frightened when their teeth fell out. God's purpose was to stop people from killing each other.

So the answer to Mel's "problem" was pretty obvious: people wrote these stories. People were comforted by the idea of a promise that they'd never experience a species-wide extinction event. People, apparently, were wrong.

There was no reason to say that to Mel. From the start, Rosalyn had only sat in on these lectures because they were the closest thing to intellectual stimulation available these days. They were insightful textual analysis, but she didn't consider them fundamentally different from a careful reading of Crime and Punishment.

"So God said he'd never wipe people out again," Lily said, "and then he did."

Rosalyn smiled to herself. Lily had a sort of intuitive attack engine, a subconscious knack for poking holes in concepts she didn't even fully understand. And Rosalyn's favorite part of these meetups was watching a Talmudic scholar struggle to defend thousands of years of tradition against a woman who was legitimately passionate about salad dressing.

Mel adjusted his glasses.

"Well. One explanation is that He was just promising He wouldn't wipe out humanity *in that way*. With a flood. But other options were still available."

"If that's the case, it would be a pretty weak reassurance, don't you think, Mel?" Rosalyn said.

Mel sighed.

"Yes. One could say that."

"If there's an island it means he didn't wipe us out," said Sam.

"What if we get to the island," Lily said, "and like, it's empty, but there's food and water and stuff. And we have kids with each other–" out of the corner of her eye, Rosalyn saw Sam blush, "–and one of our grandkids asks us about being here on the boat, and writes about it. About how we escaped and came to the island. That could be, like, the new Bible you know? How crazy would that be."

Mel peered at her over the top of his glasses, apparently deciding whether or not to indulge this line of thought. Sam, however, was sitting up straight. He was obviously inspired by this idea.

"That would be a book," Mel said. "A history book. The Torah is not a history book. It's the blueprint of creation, written by the Creator."

"Well," Lily shrugged. "That's your opinion."

"It's the opinion of many men–and women–much wiser than me," Mel said. "What I think is irrelevant."

"Jennifer told me the Bible says you should kill gay people," Sam said. "I talked to her at dinner yesterday. She said we shouldn't let you read the Bible on board because it says things like that. I told her I like listening, and you should be able to believe whatever you want. But is it true? Does the Bible say that?"

Mel stiffened. He obviously hadn't expected this kind of onslaught today.

"I… well… in theory, the act of a man copulating with another man is punishable by stoning, according to the Torah, yes. But to my knowledge that's never actually been enforced."

Sam looked stricken.

"Well Art told us he had gay sex," Sam said. "So the Bible says we should kill Art?"

"What? No. What?" Mel shook his head angrily. "Of course not."

Bahram leaned forward on his stool, intrigued by the drama.

"But the Bible says we should?" Lily pressed.

"I'm not a rabbi," Mel said. "But I feel quite confident when I say that no rabbi would ever suggest you should kill somebody for a homosexual act."

"So are you going to leave that part out then?" Lily asked.

Mel opened his mouth then closed it. He slowly rubbed an eyebrow between his thumb and forefinger.

"You can't just start picking and choosing," he finally said, a bit irritated. "That's the whole point. You can't say 'oh, I don't like this commandment. Let's scratch it out.' That's the whole point: the Torah is eternal. If you start scratching things out you're saying you're smarter than God. That's the whole point of the Tower of Babel, it's the story of hubris, of believing that *you* know best."

"I don't know, Mel," Sam said, folding his massive arms across his chest. "I think you should leave it out."

"Me too," said Lily.

Rosalyn said nothing. Bahram swiveled around in his stool to look out at the sea, apparently uninterested now that everyone had calmed down.

Mel pushed up his glasses. "Let's continue," he said.

34

"In four days, we've traveled just over eight hundred miles," Elissa said. "This is where we are, as of nine-thirty this morning, according to our GPS."

She pointed her pen at a spot on the atlas and made a careful dot, a tiny island of black ink. Art Roselli was relieved with Elissa's offer to give these morning briefings; it had more or less created a consensus on board that they were making the right move. It took the pressure off him to constantly defend himself, and the decision to sail.

"I also would like to announce," Elissa continued, "now that the engines are running, we're distilling water so efficiently that I think we're safe to turn back on the taps. And..." she paused for dramatic effect,"...I don't see any harm in us each treating ourselves to a short shower. Three minutes."

Lily squealed with delight. Even Jennifer couldn't maintain her stoic front in the face of this news. She didn't unfold her arms from her chest, but did crack a rare smile. Greg and Jennifer had been the main holdouts; the day they started the engines, the two of them both stated their refusal to help in any capacity, namely by taking shifts on the bridge to monitor the autopilot. Sam, on the other hand said that though he didn't agree with the results of the vote, fair was fair, and he'd do whatever was needed. Elissa had also been supportive from the get go.

Eventually though even Jennifer and Greg came around. Jennifer was still sour, but two days ago during the morning navigation meeting she'd declared that she'd take her shifts on the bridge, and would start helping more with crate hacking. Jennifer still seemed eager to clarify to anyone that would listen that she thought sailing to the island was a fool's errand, and was only helping under coercion, but Art was pleased not to have to worry about anything mutinous from her.

And Greg, too, had surprised everyone by doing a total U-turn; the day after the vote he'd become one of the most enthusiastic champions of the mission. At first Art had been sure it was an elaborate act to distract everyone from the unseemly accusations he'd made during the voting meeting; a way to get back into everyone's good graces. But with each passing day it seemed more like Greg Pink had experienced a real change of heart. He, not Sam, was the first one up in the mornings, doing the rounds to wake people up to go hack container locks: *We'll need supplies once we get to the island, that's for sure.* He took it upon himself to wipe the grime off the bridge windows with some cleaning solution he found in the engine room, even balancing on the narrow lip of molding to scrub the windows from the outside: *We have to see where we're going!* Last night he came upon Art smoking on the bridge and slapped him on the shoulder, laughing: *Enjoy it now—we're all going cold turkey once we get to the island right?*

Greg had also taken a keen interest in the logistical minutia of their journey, devouring the engine room documentation that, until now, only Elissa had bothered to read. Truthfully, Art found Greg's sudden enthusiasm somewhat unnerving.

"Why aren't we going in a straight line?" Greg asked seriously. interrupting the smattering of applause following the shower decision. He pointed at the atlas. "Every day the angle we're traveling at gets steeper."

Elissa looked down at the map, frowning.

"Curvature of the earth, I suppose," Mel said, twirling his *tzis-tzis* between his fingers. "The map is a flat projection of a sphere. I suspect that's why it appears we're not going straight."

Elissa nodded, satisfied with this response.

"Yes, I'm sure that's it," she said.

"And how are our fuel levels?" Greg pressed.

"I was getting to that," Elissa said. "The rate of fuel consumption yesterday was slightly higher than the day prior. Perhaps because of a headwind. But we have ten more days of fuel, easily. And we should only need six to get… there."

Art had never heard Elissa speak of the island as a certainty. This made sense, of course; it was the farthest thing from a certainty there could be. But she'd also stopped referring to their destination as 'the coordinates', which had sounded like an implication that those numbers represented nothing but more ocean. Whether she changed because of personal belief, or to inspire the crew, Art hadn't asked.

Art had found himself in a very strange mood ever since the vote. Melancholy spurred by boredom, interrupted by pangs of terror. He would never admit this to anyone, of course, but it had occurred to him that he'd only decided that traveling to the coordinates on Adam's chest was the right move so that he'd have a mission to occupy himself. That in that moment weeks ago, when Adam first took off that sheet to reveal a set of GPS coordinates, some part of Arthur Roselli had smelled a challenge: convince enough of these people to actually *sail* to those coordinates. That was the terror: that his subconscious, in an effort to give him something to do with himself, to keep him from one of those stagnant swamps of depression he'd stumbled into eight or nine times in his adult life, had deluded him into this idea–the best of our bad options–so effectively that he'd truly believed that the poker, the cigarettes, and the impassioned speech he'd given were truly life-saving measures.

These morning meetings, in particular, were difficult. The more everyone bought into the possibility of the island, the more deep his despair. It was like the morning after seducing someone twenty years your junior; turning over on the pillow to see the bliss on his face as he sleeps, and realizing that one night's greedy lust is going to mean weeks or months of misery for both of you.

Art now feared that–with the possible exception of Jennifer–he was the person on board most skeptical of the existence of an island. It was like he had no actual convictions except that popular consensus was always wrong. It was insane. And this stupid contrarian streak of his was leading ten other people to burn their remaining fuel, heading to some numbers burned onto an amnesiac's chest.

Obviously, it was far too late to say anything.

35

"Hi," Jennifer said, as Vic opened her cabin door, and quickly closed it behind him. Vic's heart jumped at the sight of her. She wasn't smiling, but that was pretty normal. "Did you bring cigarettes and tea?"

"Of course."

They sat down across from each other at the coffee table, and he placed the steaming cup of Lipton tea he'd just prepared on the tabletop. Then he dug three Marlboros out of his pocket, plus the yellow lighter he'd taken from the bridge. Jennifer lit a cigarette and sighed. Vic watched smoke curl from her nostrils. She was an exquisitely beautiful creature.

"God, I hate Greg. I hate him," she said. "And he's been worse since we started sailing."

"I think he's being quite pleasant," Vic said.

"No. Something's wrong with him. Believe me, he's not happy that we—well you—voted to go to the island."

Vic swallowed a reply. The day after the vote Jennifer didn't come to his room, and he'd assumed that would be the end of this, whatever it was. Since then she hadn't quite forgiven him, but also didn't seem to despise him for his vote. He didn't regret his vote, exactly, although he wasn't sure he'd do it again. At the time of the vote he'd been a bit more indifferent to his fate—die, not die, what was the difference? But in the days since, he'd finally found a purpose: to seduce this gorgeous woman.

He was getting close, he was sure. But for now he could hardly bear sitting so close to her without touching her. The beauty of her face was astonishing. He'd found her attractive the first weeks at sea, but lately his lust had crescendoed in a way that made him feel diseased. Now that they were spending time together there was hope, and hope made his insides wriggle; hope was turning him into a deranged animal foaming at the mouth. Not even the mythical Natalie Chandler had ever made him feel like this.

Jennifer helped herself to another of his cigarettes. This was a small price to pay for her company.

She had a blanket on her lap. The engines powered the generator, so the HVAC system was functional. Vic hadn't turned off the air conditioning in his own cabin for days. What a pleasure to be cold enough that you needed a blanket!

"When Greg looks at me I feel like he's a pitbull staring at a rotisserie chicken."

She talked about Greg a lot. A *lot*. Even though it was always in this way, about how much she loathed him, Vic wished she'd stop.

"Greg is like... he's everything that's wrong with men, you know? They create power structures just so they can be at the top, and force women to submit if they want to climb up to join them. Why do you think Greg became an actor? Because he has some love of the craft? It's the power."

"Yes."

Her throaty voice and harsh American accent were divine. This, Vic thought, was a real American woman. As with Natalie Chandler, the woman herself was only part of the appeal; there was also a kind of jingoistic eroticism when Vic fantasized about the act, a feeling that to conquer her would be to plant his flag atop America herself.

"By the way, I might say the same about Mel," she continued. "Well not Mel himself. I have no reason to think Mel has ever acted inappropriately with a woman–he's a thoughtful person, don't get me wrong. But the Jewish religion is just like any religion. It's all the same. Guess what the extremists in Najaf were using as an excuse to rape and honor kill women? Islam. God. Religion. It's the best excuse to form a patriarchy. And Judaism's the same, you know. Do you know there are neighborhoods where Jewish women have to wear skirts down to their ankles or they'll throw rocks at them?"

Vic realized she was waiting for a response.

"I didn't know this."

"Did you play poker last night?" she asked.

"Yes. A bit." he replied. "You should come sometime."

"I can't stand Art or Lily."

Vic didn't respond. There was no need to tell her that poker hadn't been the same the past few days. Sam stopped playing, which killed the group dynamic. Plus, Arthur hadn't been as funny and interesting lately. Not to mention they'd smoked through most of the on-board supply, and the game was a constant reminder of the looming specter of withdrawal.

Jennifer ground the nub of her cigarette into the table.

"I can bring an ashtray next time," Vic offered.

"What's the difference."

Jennifer smelled terrible, of course. They all did. Vic's own scent was so strong that it sometimes roused him in the middle of the night, like some rancid smelling salts. Jennifer's long brown hair was gross and oily. Still, from across the table, he thought he caught a whiff of something fruity from weeks or months before.

He still remembered the peachy smell of Coco's hair and neck, and the cigarette breath that had been a bit strong, even for him.

It had been a long day at the Walmart Superstore. Some woman came to pick up her baby photos and berated Vic because her spawn wasn't sufficiently smiley in the pictures, and now this developmental stage would forever be documented sans the cartoonish ecstasy that made for the fondest deathbed memories.

Madame, our photography department cannot be responsible for making your child oblivious to the perils of this life.

What? What!? Let me talk to your manager.

She is at lunch. May I offer you a coupon for a thirty percent discount off another photography session?

No! I don't want a coupon. I want a full refund for these shitty pictures, and an apology.

When Vic's manager returned, she chewed his ear off for being rude to a customer, and then practically groveled at the mother's feet, begging for forgiveness. When the mother left, the manager told Vic that he was never to speak directly to customers again. Just take the pictures and develop them. That was his job.

Back at his apartment he had two beers, finished half a bottle of Shiraz, and then flopped onto his bed and opened his laptop. He found a video of a young woman giving a full body massage to a large tattooed man. What began as a nominally therapeutic session quickly escalated. Vic pulled down his pants and groped for the vaseline in his nightstand. But by the time his hands closed on the tub, he'd already grown bored of this video. He searched for another: *massage sex film.* Soon he was contemplating a scene shockingly similar to the first. He liked this massage avenue though, it was a new direction for him. He searched for: *massage sex video very naughty butt.* A third clip. This video didn't do it for Vic either.

Inspiration struck.

He searched for: *Charleston NC relaxing massage for men,* and found Bubble Dreams Spa on page two of the results. It was obvious from the pictures of the masseuses that they weren't exactly licensed professionals, but there was just enough vagueness as to the precise services they offered that he managed to convince himself he was just going to get a massage from a pretty lady.

It was on the south side of town, a twenty-five minute walk. The Shiraz numbed him from the icy wind. He stopped at an ATM. There were no prices on the website, so he pulled out nearly his entire account balance–four hundred dollars–to be safe.

He arrived at the address, but it took him ten minutes to find the place. There were no signs, and the entrance was in an alley between a nightclub and pizza restaurant. He only knew it was the correct door because of the name on the buzzer. He ascended four flights of poorly lit stairs, his hands trembling in anticipation. There was another buzzer at 4B, which he pressed, and then the opaque door swung inwards.

Hi come in.

An older Asian woman–probably fifty– took him by the forearm and led him inside. The lights were dim and someone had strung Christmas lights from the ceiling, which reminded Vic that he had to mail his sister a gift, something from the Superstore probably, by Monday if he wanted it to arrive in time for Christmas.

They were in a sort of waiting room which smelled of mold and bleach. Another Asian woman was dozing on a couch that was so worn you could see stuffing coming out of the cushions. The older one barked something, and the sleeping woman sat up. The woman on the couch was slightly younger than the one currently holding his hand. She wore a tight black dress that stopped at her bruised thighs. As soon as she saw Vic, she smiled warmly.

First time Bubble Dreams?

Yes.

You want massage?

How much is a massage?

Sixty dollar one hour. Full body. Special massage more sixty. You want special?

Vic nodded. Yes. He wanted special.

The younger woman stood up from the sofa and approached him, smiling widely. She was handed off to him by the older, and she led him through a door into a dilapidated room where the treatment was to happen. The floor was stained brown with water damage. There was a toilet in one corner without a seat, and a hose coming out of the wall with a spray nozzle attached to the end. In the center of the room was a massage table covered in tissue paper. She beckoned for him to sit down on the table and smiled again at him.

I am Coco. What your name?

Uh. Dave.

Hi Dave. Nicetomeetchu. How old you?

Thirty-two. How old are you?

Thirty-two also. You pay now? One twenty special.

He opened his wallet and she saw the wad of twenties. He selected six bills and handed them to her. She was still looking at the contents of his wallet.

You want sex? More sixty.

He swallowed. He was suddenly aware of how cold it was in this room. Was he really going to get undressed in here? There was a creaking radiator, but it was no match for the draft piercing the thin walls. He considered just leaving. Even letting her keep the money. He just wanted to be out of here. Her tight black dress was too shiny, and for some reason he found this detail revolting.

So one hundred eighty?

Yes. One eighty hour massage sex.

He handed her three more bills and she smiled a little wider. She pointed to the nozzle and hose.

Want shower?

No, thank you.

Okay. I come back.

She left him alone in the room. He pulled off his jeans. Then hung up his coat, peeled off his flannel shirt, white undershirt, and finally his boxer briefs. Naked, he sat down on the edge of the massage table. As predicted, he was freezing. He felt very sorry for himself.

Coco returned to the room and closed the door behind her.

Lie down on stomach.

He obeyed, fitting his face into the slot at one end of the massage table. He was looking down at the peeling linoleum floor. He heard Coco shuffling around, and then she squeezed some freezing oil onto his back and spread it around without clear purpose.

Relax.

Her voice was like a ghost cooing in his ear. He felt the Shiraz had left him, and wished he'd drank more.

Coco's cold hands rubbed his shoulders aimlessly for a few minutes, and then she moved to his inner rear thighs, stimulating his erogenous zones in a pale facsimile of massage. Once it was clear to her that he was at least physiologically aroused, she tapped on his shoulder.

Turnover.

He flopped onto his back. Coco had turned off the overhead bulb, leaving the room illuminated only by a string of multicolored Christmas lights. She undressed. Vic studied her body. Her nipples were big and brown, and her stomach was flabby; nothing like the women in the videos he'd watched earlier that evening. When she caught him staring she smiled widely, and he tried to smile back.

She pulled a condom from her purse, opened it up, and rolled it on to him with some difficulty. Again she smiled at him. She then opened a second foil packet and smeared the contents between her legs. Vic somehow felt both excited and completely numb simultaneously.

In a well-practiced motion, Coco boosted herself up onto the table and straddled him. She smiled down at him. He thought again about how he had to send Christmas presents to his sister. He thought about the mother who'd been upset with him today. He thought about his manager, who'd told him he was forbidden to speak with customers. Coco's smile seemed totally incompatible with every aspect of this situation. Without losing her smile, she emitted a gasp.

Oh. So good.

He realized that since they'd started, she hadn't looked at him squarely in the face. She was staring at the door behind him, as if the promise of eventual escape was the source of her pleasure.

He left Bubble Dreams as fast as he could, let the alley door slam behind him and rushed back to real life. He'd crossed a line, he thought, as the cold wind slapped his face. He could never undo the last half hour. The memory of his sin would never leave him.

"Let's say there is an island," Jennifer said, sipping the tea. "I don't think there is, but for the sake of argument, let's say there is. Are these people on board going to keep listening to Mel's sermons every morning? Are they going to decide all the women on the island have to cover their elbows and knees? You get what I'm saying? It's a very dangerous road."

Vic nodded. He wasn't sure he agreed with her–this seemed like a pretty trivial concern–but he was scared to disagree and alienate her. Every cell in his body was screaming for Jennifer Presley. He wanted her to stop talking and lock eyes with him. He wanted her to take the blanket off her knees…

He had to be very careful not to offend her as Greg had. But he could take this no more.

"I think I'm going to enjoy a shower," he said.

"Okay," she said.

The muscles in his face tightened.

"Perhaps I'll use your shower?"

She frowned at him. Had he phrased that clearly enough? Damn his English!

"Mmm," she said. "No, mine actually isn't working so well. You should use yours."

He forced a smile.

"Of course," he said, and stood up.

"Close the door," she said. "Keep in the AC."

He rushed out into the hall and shut the door to her cabin behind him. He leaned against the wall and tried to collect himself. His heart was racing. He replayed the interaction. Had she rejected him? Or was her shower actually broken? Or was there some linguistic subtext he'd missed all together?

He needed some air. He rushed up the stairs and was delighted to find Greg Pink sitting on the bridge, at the controls. He'd be a great change of pace. Maybe he'd tell some jokes to distract him from Jennifer.

"*Bonjour!*" Vic said, sitting down beside his pal. "How are you Greg?"

"Vickity Vic!" Greg replied weakly. "Never better. What's cracking?"

"No respect," Vic said. "I'm getting no respect!"

Greg laughed and clapped him on the back.

"You're getting it."

Vic motioned to the control panel, the autopilot system.

"I'm hoping you're navigating us to somewhere with a beach," he joked, and was delighted when Greg rewarded him with a smile.

"You and me both, brother."

"You're not still upset about the vote?"

Greg's left eye twitched.

"Nah. It's great, actually. Not having to ration water."

"Can I offer you a fresh cigarette?"

Greg grinned.

"Would love one."

Vic took the communal lighter from his pocket. He lit his own first, then handed the yellow Bic to Greg.

Vic inhaled, then blew out a rich plume of smoke. His vision got a little brighter and pleasant warmth spread through his body. What a pleasure.

"Thanks for the smoke, Vicky. What's new with you? Everything alright?"

Vic shrugged.

"You know. Women."

Greg broke into a wide grin and he smacked Vic so hard on the back that he nearly lost his cigarette.

"Women! My man! Spill the fucking beans already! You and Lily Ching Chong finally doing the dirty?"

"*Non, non*," Vic shook his head. "Not her. She's not for me. I am…" he searched for a vague enough way to describe what had been happening, "…being with Jennifer."

Vic expected Greg to be thrilled with this news, but instead the actor froze, the unlit cigarette dangling from his dry lips. Greg looked like he'd forgotten how to breathe.

"Greg?" Vic asked, concerned. "You're alright?"

"Yes, yes," Greg's smile had completely evaporated. "Just, wow. A bit surprised. You and Jenny eh? How'd you… How'd you manage that one?"

Vic took a casual puff of his Marlboro.

"In truth, it was her idea."

Greg seemed to be in some sort of gastronomical distress. The cigarette almost dropped from his mouth, like he'd forgotten it was there. He managed to grip it with trembling fingers just before it fell.

"You sure it's Jennifer?" Greg croaked. "The young one. Not the Chinese one."

Vic frowned. Greg wasn't reacting at all how he'd hoped.

"Yes. Jennifer. The truth though is she's a bit driving my nuts."

Greg made a sound like a donkey braying, and stood up.

"Listen, Vicky, would you mind taking the bridge? I gotta run down to the little boy's room. Emergency."

"Of course."

Greg dashed out without ever lighting his cigarette, doubled over. Must be a real emergency, Vic thought.

36

Lily found Elissa in the belly of the engine room. There was air conditioning now that the generator was running, and they could also run all the lights without fear of draining the battery. They were on the lowest level, which was well below the surface of the ocean. Hard to say how far though. The whole chamber vibrated with the growling of the engines. Elissa was hunched over a console, studying an ancient monitor.

"How's it going?" Lily shouted over the din.

Elissa didn't hear her. Lily moved closer and repeated herself even louder. This time she got the older woman's attention.

Elissa shrugged like, *everything seems to be fine.*

Lily pointed up at the metal catwalk above their heads.

"Can we go outside and talk?" she shouted.

Elissa nodded and followed her up through three levels of steps, past intermediate catwalks and rows of monitors and dead buttons. At the top level of the engine room Lily put her shoulder into the heavy iron door–the only entrance to this cavern–and they emerged into the soft light of the stairwell.

"Don't know how you can stand it in there," Lily said. "It's so loud and dark."

"What did you want to talk about, dear? There's a lot of work to do."

"Let's go to the bow," Lily suggested. Elissa acquiesced. They walked in silence to the frontmost point of the ship, where the massive anchor lay brooding like a stone gargoyle. Below them the water frothed, protesting angrily before relenting to the sharp metal stern. There wasn't much noise here since the propellers were in the rear. Just a pleasant breeze.

"What's going on, Lily? I shouldn't leave the water system for too long."

"Oh. Well. I just wanted your advice," Lily said.

"Sure."

"Well, it's probably only four days till we reach those numbers you know, see if there's an island right?" Lily said. "And I've been thinking about what you said. About making babies. So it seems like, well you know, who knows what will happen if there's an island. Maybe there will be other people there you know? Other women? I know Greg probably wants to take things slow. I usually would too. But it seems like we should get together you know. Before the island. So we'll be together already. You know?"

Elissa's mouth was tight. She turned away from Lily and watched the churning water below.

Lily had already been taking Art's advice: not acting like she was into Greg, teasing him a little. In short, playing it cool. She was pretty sure it was working, and that Greg was getting really interested in her. But it was time to take it to the next level and she wanted Elissa's advice on how to proceed. She wanted to make sure she didn't do anything stupid. With a twinge, she thought about Michael.

"Lily…" Elissa breathed out, a long weary breath. "I know this isn't what you want to hear, but I mean it: forget Greg. You're too good for him. You deserve better."

Lily laughed.

"*I'm* too good for *him?*" she shook her head. "Elissa, he's *Greg Pink.*"

"He was," Elissa said. "Now he's just Greg. And you're just Lily. And I know you can't see it, but you're too good for him. You're a sweet, caring woman. He's… well."

They both stared straight ahead, at the sea. Every morning was bluer than the last. That was promising.

"There aren't exactly a lot of choices," Lily said.

Elissa sighed.

"Well that's certainly true. But I think Sam, Vic, or even Mel would treat you much better than him."

Lily frowned. Sam and Vic were just friends. Her boys. She wasn't interested in either of them. And Mel? Gross.

"On the other hand it's hard for me to give any advice to you," Elissa continued. "This whole ordeal… I'm sure it's much harder on the younger people. Me and Art, Bahram too I suppose, we've already lived long lives you know. For us this is just an interesting epilogue. But for you, I'm sure, this whole thing feels very unfair. Of course we're all grateful to be alive but…"

Lily put her elbows on the edge of the railing and let her cheeks sink into her hands.

"Yeah," she said. "That's why I like listening to Mel talk. Makes me less upset sometimes."

Elissa reached over and brushed Lily's shoulder. The maternal gesture triggered some primordial flutter in Lily's chest.

"Do you think there's gonna be an island?" Lily asked.

Elissa sucked her teeth.

"I made a career out of admitting that I wasn't wise enough to see the future. I always hope for the best but make preparations for the worst."

Lily frowned. She didn't like answers like that.

"So yes or no?"

"Maybe. But I'm leaning toward no."

"But what about Adam's burns?"

Elissa shook her head.

"I'm not sure exactly what to make of it all. But why would someone leave Adam–a confused, helpless and possibly brain-damaged individual–with directions to this island, but not come aboard and save themselves as well?"

Lily didn't like hearing this stuff. She wanted to be reassured.

"So then how did it happen?" she argued.

"Someone totally insane did it. It's all just nonsense."

"You think the numbers are just random?"

"Lily, I don't know." Elissa sounded weary. "I should get back to the engine room."

"So just say that's the answer then," Lily said. "Don't say 'probably not'. Say you don't know."

Elissa looked at her, seemed about to say something, then just sighed.

"Fine. I don't know. I'm going back to keep an eye on the distillation process."

Elissa left her alone at the bow. Lily sat down on the lounge chair. She had a cigarette in her pocket, but didn't feel like walking all the way back to the bridge just to get the lighter.

She believed there was going to be an island. That's why she'd voted to go. Well, Art had made a really good argument too. Really good logic. But also she knew there was an island. Yeah, it was optimistic, but she just *felt* it. She'd even started having dreams about it, the eleven of them pushing out the gang plank and carefully descending to solid ground. God, she wanted that island so bad. She was pretty sure it was there. She could feel it. But she wanted answers.

Lily left the chair and strode around the walkway, climbed to the top deck, and then the steps to the bridge. Art was sitting on a swivel chair smoking.

"Hey sweetheart!" he grinned at her. "Want a smoke?"

She smiled back.

"I'll be back in a bit. If you're still here I'll have one," she said.

He cracked up.

"I'm not going anywhere too far, that I can promise."

Lily climbed down the stairs to C-deck, went straight to the door of Adam's cabin, and knocked. Everyone said he had some sort of brain damage and couldn't remember a thing, but Lily had never really bought that. Everyone remembers things. Otherwise it's like you're not even a person.

"Yeah?" he said from within. She opened the door. Adam was sitting on the carpeted floor. He was staring into the Italian maritime encyclopedia and holding a pen. Beside him was a huge stack of loose leaf papers.

He looked up at her and the sudden movement caused a light flurry of dandruff to float, snowlike, down onto the carpet.

"Hi, I was actually wondering, when's lunch?"

"You can get food whenever you want," she said, sitting down on the floor facing him. "Just go down to the mess."

He absorbed this information, nodding.

"Right right, the mess."

He peered over his shoulder out the port window.

"Do you know my name?" she asked.

"I…" he looked back at her, pained. "You do look familiar… remind me where we met?"

"We've been on this ship together for almost a month. You really don't remember who I am?" She was skeptical. She didn't think he was lying, exactly, but maybe embellishing.

"I'm sorry. I'm not good with faces and names."

"Adam," she asked. "Can you tell me more about the island?"

He was tight lipped. His brown eyes swiveled back and forth quickly.

"Um. I'm sorry?"

"The island. I thought maybe you could tell me what to expect when we get there."

He gripped his hair, stirring up another blizzard of dandruff.

"What is this, the Spanish Inquisition?"

"Don't play your stupid games. The burns on your chest are the reason we're going there," Lily said, then poked her finger in his face. "So tell me what you know."

His eyes went wide. Lily thought of a moment from her childhood when she caught a raccoon digging around in the trash at night; the way the rodent froze when she caught it in her flashlight beam.

She finally had him, Lily thought. Busted.

"Um, the island," he said. "It's well, um. The island. It's surrounded by water."

"So it's there?" she said. "It's definitely there?"

"Definitely."

"Who put the numbers on your chest?"

His face contorted in a way that seemed to defy both anatomy and physics. It was like his mouth was a black hole sucking his face in on itself.

"What?"

"Don't play dumb with me."

He looked around the cabin, back out the porthole, at the four walls, his surroundings suddenly inducing mild panic.

"Nurse?" he cried to the door. "Hello? Nurse?"

"There's no fucking nurse here," Lily said.

"Can you please leave me alone?" he whimpered.

"Who put the numbers on your chest?"

For the first time, Adam looked down at his own chest. When he saw the scars he emitted a horrible squeak. It sounded like his windpipe was a stiff accordion.

"What did you do to me?" he said, tracing first the burns with his index finger, and then the two-faced logo. He looked up at Lily, pale, jaw slack. Then he studied the contents of his cabin: the bed, the coffee table, the chairs. Each object seemed to confuse him more than the last. "Whatever I did," he sputtered. "I'm sorry. I'm sorry. Just tell me where I am and what's happening."

Lily stood up. She was wrong. This was no act, it couldn't be. Nobody could feign the raw look of anguish on his face, the pleading emptiness in his eyes.

"I'm Lily," she said. She approached him and put a hand on his shoulder, willing herself to ignore his sour odor. The touch seemed to settle him down a bit. "You've just been having some trouble, but we're going to get everything sorted out real soon, and you'll be back to your old self."

He sighed in heavy relief.

"Great," he said. "That's great. Yeah I can tell something's a bit off. Also, Mi– Lily. I don't want to be rude but I'm starving. Is there any way–"

"Yes," she said. "Follow me. I'll get you some polenta and lentils."

He frowned.

"Are there any other options?"

37

It was getting harder and harder to play their games. They were all against him, Greg now understood. He suspected they were all terrorists, likely members of the Daughters of January. He was sure they were having secret meetings while he slept, discussing how to deal with him. It was a miracle he'd survived this long, a feat he could only attribute to his wit and guile. He'd convinced them that he'd drank their Kool-Aid and joined their group psychosis. For now, they seemed content with that. As long as he stayed in line, they seemed willing to let him live.

"Well, I have good news and bad news," Elissa said. "I'd thought we'd be arriving at the coordinates in two days. And since today is, um–"

"Thursday, I think," Rosalyn offered.

"Right. Thank you." The old hag pushed her glasses up on her nose. She was the ringleader, Greg thought. Elissa McClure. It wasn't Sam, the brute. It was her, this withered old cunt. They worshiped her like a goddess, hung on her every word. It would have been amusing if it wasn't so horrifying. "So, I'd anticipated arriving on Saturday," she said. "But I've revised my estimate to Monday morning."

"Can't wait!" Greg said, and grinned. It was important to show that he was eating up all their bullshit. It would buy him some time until he figured out his escape. "How are our fuel levels?"

"We have about eight days of fuel right now."

He didn't believe a word the old bitch said. Eight days. How convenient that they wouldn't have enough to make it back to the East Coast once they arrived at their "destination" and found jack shit.

What was their endgame here? Ransom, he assumed. Kidnap a famous actor and convince him the world has been destroyed to keep him subdued. But there was more to it than that, and he hadn't quite been able to piece it all together. Adam was the key to something. Adam and those numbers. His working theory was that Elissa–if that was even her real name–burned the numbers onto the poor fella, then drugged the shit out of him so he wouldn't remember. Why? He couldn't figure it out yet. Maybe that was just how she got her kicks. Maybe Adam had been their previous victim. They'd kidnapped him, and he hadn't played ball–and nobody would pay his ransom–so they turned him into a vegetable so he couldn't rat them out.

"Why the delay, Elissa?" Art asked.

"The sky has gotten a lot clearer," the Chinawoman announced, apropos nothing. The very sound of her sing-song ching-chong chirping was agony to Greg. He struggled to keep himself composed. "So that's good?"

Greg pitied her. She was obviously drugged herself. She'd knocked on his door last night and come in before he could say no. She flipped on the light, leaned against the door frame and, plate in hand, went, *Hey there, I brought you some food I whipped up.* His eyes narrowed. Clearly, she'd been sent to poison him. As she took a step toward his bed he groped for some kind of blunt instrument to use as a weapon, and his left hand found the reading lamp on his nightstand.

He told her he wasn't hungry, but thanks. She took another step toward him. His grip on the lamp tightened. She told him she'd spent all afternoon working on this "recipe". He found this unlikely. From where he lay, her creation appeared to be a pile of yellow polenta mixed with steaming garbage. Was it lethal poison, or something more sinister: sedatives, hallucinogens, or, worst to consider, whatever they'd given Adam? She'd done something with her hair, tied it in some way after her shower. He'd told her not to come any closer. That he was feeling sick, and he didn't want to contaminate her. He faked a cough, without taking his left hand from the lamp; if she didn't relent she'd leave him no choice. But she retreated. No doubt scurried back to the queen, told her she'd failed in her mission and groveled for forgiveness.

"I awoke this morning to find that the GPS led us somewhat astray, while Lily and Mel were on duty–sorry that's not an accusation, I should be clear," Elissa said. She took off her glasses and wiped them with the edge of her black blouse. "It had been working so well until now that we all got complacent. I should have thought of this. GPS is dependent on satellites orbiting the planet, which have to be constantly monitored and course corrected. So, you know, if nobody is managing those satellites... If the military bases housing that equipment were destroyed, then it's no surprise the GPS is somewhat unreliable. So last night the ship nearly did a U-turn. We're about seven hundred miles west of where we should be. The GPS isn't dependable. We'll have to navigate manually, using the compasses, from here on out."

Shocking. They weren't going to arrive at the "island" on time. It was all Greg could do to not roll his eyes. This was why they'd all shrugged him off when he'd pointed out that they weren't sailing straight. It was deliberate. They were buying time.

"If I'm comprehending," Vic said calmly, as if this whole thing only mildly interested him, "This means that we're not having fuel for a return?"

Greg had underestimated the Frenchman. Greg had considered him a fool, which was exactly what Vic wanted. Greg studied him from across the bridge. The short man fiddled with an unlit cigarette with one hand, and rubbed his hairy stomach with the other. Vic's silence was deceptive; he was cold and calculating. He'd been telling the truth about Jennifer; Greg saw him duck into her cabin, and emerge only hours later. Elissa was the ringleader publicly, but Vic was pulling the strings behind the scenes. And Jennifer was probably scared that if she didn't give Vic what he wanted, she'd end up just like Adam. Even from the start, she'd had to resist Greg's advances, out of fear. All the pieces were falling into place.

"North America would be out of the question," Elissa said. "Not that any of us think going back there is a good idea. The Azores or Portugal would still be feasible."

The Frenchman caught Greg staring at him and smiled. Mouthed: *No respect, I'm getting no respect.* Greg shuddered. It was some kind of coded threat: *Keep dancing, Pink.*

Greg had been studying the course of the ship, measured against the sun in the sky. They were indeed traveling mostly east. They couldn't fake that. But now he understood that they were reversing course, retracing their steps while he slept. And if his sleep had been drugged, and he was sleeping days at a time (during which they came in and reset the date and time on his Rolex) they could be absolutely anywhere in the world. He'd always suspected the GPS was rigged, and now Elissa had all but admitted that. She'd spent hours reading about the systems and she could easily manipulate the measurement tools. Even before this confession, Greg was studying all on-board documentation himself, trying to figure out how she could have gone in and changed their GPS location without leaving a trace. He felt he might be close to understanding, but was several steps behind her. She was crafty, the old bitch.

"So that's the situation," Elissa said, folding up the map to prevent Greg from getting a good look. "I don't see that it changes a whole lot, to be honest. So let's not overreact. Anybody want to add anything?"

Everyone on the bridge was quiet. They were all thinking something, the same thing, something Greg wasn't privy to. His chest tightened. There must be some sort of problem with the ransom. It was getting risky. The Feds were closing in and they were considering whether to throw him overboard. Eliminate the evidence. He was breathing fast. He had to play their game. Show them he was gonna be a good boy. He'd jump through their hoops. He wouldn't testify against them if he was caught.

"Sometimes the anticipation is the best part," Greg said. "I'm getting really excited. For the island."

This was met with a few grim nods.

"Let's all keep our expectations low," Art said. "Don't forget, it was always a long shot."

"Right," Greg nodded. "Of course."

Keep dancing, Pink.

38

Sam had finally surrendered to the pain of his hernia. He'd stopped hacking at crate locks–it's not like they were finding anything useful anyway–and was resting as much as he could. He preferred resting on the lounge chairs on the bow so he at least had some fresh air.

After this morning's travel briefing, he skipped Mel's lecture, came straight to his spot, and eased himself as slowly as he could onto the plastic straps. The frame buckled and moaned, like it was unhappy to see him again, but ultimately held. He folded his hands on his lap and exhaled slowly. The pain wasn't so bad when he reclined like this. Beyond the winch that held the anchor were miles of wide blue. A few clouds in the sky today. Sam wondered if it might finally rain soon.

He'd kill, he thought, for a Sports Illustrated to read right now.

He also wanted to talk to Doctor Rosalyn about what had happened three times, on alternating nights, and then stopped abruptly. The whole situation was bothering him more and more. He didn't like how afterward she'd just zip up and walk out. And he didn't like how it had only happened when she decided it would happen, and now, it seemed, she'd decided it was over. And how when he tried to catch her eye in the light of day she would barely even smile back at him. The one time he'd said something to her, asked what she was doing later, she shrugged and said she didn't know, then asked how his hernia was.

Each time she left him alone in his cabin he felt like he'd disappointed her somehow. He hated that she was causing him to be so angry. He hated the word 'bitch', he'd never *ever* call a woman a bitch. But that's how he felt she was acting. Like a bitch.

Sam rubbed his eyes. It felt like he never got to decide how things were gonna be. Not with any of his exes, certainly not at the stockyard or Café Roma or Harvey & Leer. And now here, on board. It didn't matter that he didn't want to sail: here they were, sailing. That's how the world worked. There were people who got to decide how things were gonna be–people like Art and Elissa and Doctor Rosalyn–and there were the people like him who just had to go along with it.

He lay there on the lounge chair for maybe an hour, getting himself more and more worked up about this. The unfairness. Doctor Rosalyn acting like a bitch to him. The pain from his stomach anytime he shifted in the chair wasn't helping his mood. Finally he sat up and, gripping a damp rail for support, pulled himself to his feet. He groaned in distress; his hernia felt like someone was stabbing him from the inside.

It was time to talk to Doctor Rosalyn. He also wanted a cigarette. After they spoke he'd get one from the dwindling stash in his room; they hadn't been playing much poker but he'd been smoking like seven or eight a day.

Mel's class had finished, and only Jennifer was on the bridge, glumly doing donuts in the swivel seat. She was so hot, Sam thought. She really was. Great smile, on the rare occasion when she let one escape. Amazing legs, albeit pretty hairy. He wondered what she'd be like to have sex with. He wondered if she would want to. Then he'd tell Doctor Rosalyn about it. The thought brought a smile to his face.

"Hey," Jennifer said.

No, no, no. Sam mentally slapped himself. She was much younger than him, for one thing. And moreover, it wouldn't be right to try to sleep with her in this situation, in the middle of the ocean. She might perceive him even asking as an implicit threat, and might say yes just because she was scared. See? he told himself. See how thoughtful I am?

How respectful of other people's feelings? Is it too much to ask for a little bit of respect in return?

"Hey," he said. "Do you know where Doctor Rosalyn is?"

Jennifer snorted.

"Probably either in the mess, her cabin, or the captain's lounge."

"Right," Sam said, feeling stupid he'd even asked the question. "Right."

He headed down the stairwell to C-deck, the impact of each step causing a flare of pain in his gut. Doctor Rosalyn wasn't in her room, and he would have headed straight down to the mess if he hadn't heard thumping and grunting coming from a closed door at the end of the hall. The gym. He hobbled down the blue carpeted corridor and opened the door to the gym. He hadn't been in here since his first day aboard; more physical exertion was the last thing he needed.

Doctor Rosalyn was fully dressed in her linen shirt, jeans, and hiking boots. The gym was a pitiful space, really only comfortable for one person at a time. She'd cleared the machines and dumbbells out of the center of the room to make some space around a mat she'd leaned against the wall, upon which was was currently directing an impressive slew of jabs and kicks.

She saw him come in, but didn't break her routine. Sam sat down in the corner, on an adjustable bench.

"Hey," he said, over the smacking of the makeshift punching bag, the constant stream of thumps, and her heavy breathing.

She glanced over at him. "How are you?" she said, panting, hopping from foot to foot. "You shouldn't do any sort of exercise. You'll strain yourself further."

"I know," he said. "I didn't come here to exercise. I came here to talk to you."

"Can we speak in an hour?"

Sam bit his lip.

"No," he said. "No, I want to speak right now."

She seemed mildly annoyed, but also sensed he wouldn't be easily dissuaded. She took a step away from the upright mat and lowered her arms, demonstrating that she was taking a break from her workout, but that it would be brief.

"Okay," she said.

He took a deep breath.

"I'd like to talk about what's been happening. In my room."

She nodded neutrally.

"Okay," she said. Then gestured impatiently with her hands for him to continue.

"Well, I..." Sam suddenly felt unsure of himself. Was he being ridiculous? Was he being a drama queen? "I just don't think we can keep doing that and not talk about it. Like see each other the next day and pretend nothing happened." The words were flowing out before he could measure their judiciousness. "Let's just talk plainly. We had... Well. We had *sex* with each other."

Doctor Rosalyn's face remained impassive. Sam was regretting going down this road.

"Yes," she said. "That's what happened."

"And... and..." Sam struggled to find the words. "And actually, when I see you around now, you're just *ignoring* me."

She exhaled slowly, studying him with her brown eyes.

"Well okay. I apologize," she said hollowly. "I think what happened was probably a mistake. I think I was being too emotional when I made the decision. It was a mistake to try to conceive before we're sure we have a place to land. So. I made a mistake. I'm sorry if you feel like I wasn't respectful to you."

Sam wished she'd stop saying the word 'mistake.'

"Was it bad or something?" he said, immediately wishing he hadn't. "I hadn't, you know, done it for a while. That's why it was so–"

"No," she said sharply. "It was fine."

"So–"

"I miss my husband terribly," she said. "And I allowed that to cloud my judgement. That's all. It's no fault of yours. I thought if I was pregnant... I don't know. Maybe it would fix things somehow. It was stupid. We'll probably die here, and having an unborn child when that happens would just be horrible."

She turned back to her mat, like to indicate that this conversation was over. But Sam wasn't satisfied.

"But you didn't realize that before?" he asked. His stomach was really hurting; when his blood started flowing from anger or excitement it made it throb, which in turn just aggravated him further. "You didn't realize that you missed your husband terribly *before* you came into my room last week? Is that what you're saying, Rosalyn?"

She turned back to him, eyes wide in exasperation, like she couldn't believe this conversation wasn't over yet.

"What do you want me to say?" she said, her calm totally infuriating to Sam. It made him feel even more like an idiot. "What? What could you possibly want me to say?"

"I–"

"Tell me," she said. "I'll say it. What? What answer were you hoping for?"

Sam felt heat on his cheeks and the back of his neck. He couldn't even bring himself to meet her gaze. He shrugged helplessly.

"I don't know," he muttered. "Forget it."

He pushed up off the bench and walked to the door of the gym gripping his side, maybe exaggerating the extent of the discomfort a bit. His face was burning as he opened the door to his own cabin, slammed the door behind him, and then collapsed on his bed.

Why did he have to open his stupid mouth? He buried his head in the pillow, balled his hands into fists and punched the mattress. Why did he have to be so damn stupid?

39

"I always say everything is for the best," Mel said. "And our unexpected delay is no exception. We were supposed to make landfall today, Saturday, the Sabbath, the day of rest. But instead the Holy One, Blessed Be His Name, has given us a day of calm and peace at sea, to gather our strength for the week ahead."

He'd had to relocate his classes to the mess, since the manual navigation now required three people working on the bridge at all times; actually working, not just occasionally glancing over to make sure there were still numbers on the GPS screen, but actually constantly confirming they were headed in the right direction.

"You really think it's a good thing?" asked Lily. She and Sam were his only students this morning; Doctor Rosalyn and Elissa were working on the bridge. Art was probably hacking crates.

"I do," Mel said, and smiled. Lily smiled back.

Mel then looked down and flipped through his homemade Torah to find the day's passage. About a week ago, his transcription had suddenly taken on new life. He'd sat down to write, but instead of the usual struggle the words seemed to be coming from above, gliding through him effortlessly, directly to his pen. It was a joy he'd never known. Finally he understood what it meant to be a vessel for the Holy One's light. He'd transcribed verse after verse in a kind of trance, spilling holy ink until finally his rumbling stomach ripped him away from his work. It was dark outside; he'd been writing for six hours.

He'd feared that this session would be a one-time phenomenon. That he'd never again be filled with *Ruach Ha-Kodesh*, the Holy Spirit. Despite being utterly exhausted by the experience, he'd been too wired to sleep that night. Nothing could compare to the sheer ecstasy he'd felt that afternoon. The first time he met Shoshana, had gazed into her eyes and known that the two of them had been placed on earth for each other; standing with her under the *chuppah*, and sliding the ring onto her finger; their first night together; when Rueben was born; when Tsipora was born... None of these had filled him with the same light.

Well before dawn he slid out of bed, returned to his desk, and picked up his pen with trepidation. Would it return? He stared at the last verse he'd written. His frenzy had carried him all the way through the chronicles of Abraham, and he'd left off in the middle of the story of Jacob and his brother, Esau. What came next? He gritted his teeth. What was the next line? He closed his eyes and whispered.

Please. Please fill me again with–

He was in a trance until midday, and when he emerged he saw that he'd written another five chapters of Genesis. His eyes watered in joy, studying his work. At this rate he'd complete the entire five books of Moses within a few weeks.

Yes. That was it, he realized. The Holy One was giving this to him, as He'd once given the Torah to Moses atop Mount Sinai, over forty days and forty nights. It wasn't hubris. Mel was doing nothing himself. He was only clay in the hands of the Creator.

But why, he wondered? He didn't have the impudence to think he could comprehend the Holy One's intentions, but surely He wouldn't transmit his word to Mel, only to have him die in the middle of the ocean. And wouldn't it have been easier for the Holy One to just put a copy of the Torah in Mel's car for him?

And that was when everything clicked. The destruction, the pain, the loss, and the boat. Mel Glazer understood the divine plan. Warm relief washed over him. It was all so perfect. It was a key sliding precisely into its lock. It was the way a man fits into a woman.

He turned back to inspect his work, already knowing what he would find. The ancient letters seemed to be alive on the page, shouting to him. The cabin was filled with their singing. He turned back a page and the melody changed.

"*Noach,*" he whispered to himself, blood pumping in his ears. "*Noach.*"

He flipped to the story of the flood, the ark, the animals two by two. The rainbow after, when the Holy One made his promise to never again destroy humanity.

But that's not what Mel was reading:

"Behold," the Holy One said, "this rainbow is a covenant. As long as my people obey my commandments, I will provide. But when the time comes..."

It was different from the original. Mel had written something different; the *Holy Spirit* had written something different. Mel was breathing very fast. Yes. The Holy One was updating the Torah. The Torah was the blueprint for the world, but the world needed to change, and now the blueprint was changing too. Changing by Mel's hand. This is why he was put on this boat: to transcribe it, and teach it. From this *new* Torah would come a more perfect Jewish people, a more perfect mankind. What better proof was there than his diligent students, hanging on each verse like they were sopping up liquid gold?

And the new version was perfect. Even more perfect than the original. It was clouds parting to reveal the sun in all its glory. It was a chorus of angels in divine harmony.

"*Esau returned from the hunt, tired and very hungry,*" Mel read, in the mess, to Sam and Lily. "*He came upon his brother, Jacob, who was cooking a stew of lentils. 'Quick, let me have some of that stew! I'm famished!' And his brother Jacob replied 'first sell me your birthright.'*" Mel took a sip of water and explained: "Because Esau was the firstborn, normally he would be the spiritual heir to their father, Isaac. Of course, we all know that Jacob was the true spiritual heir, the one who embodied the values of the Jewish people. This was Jacob's opportunity to fix this. Esau replied, *'I'm about to die! What use is my birthright to me?' And Jacob said, 'swear an oath to me, selling your birthright.' Esau agreed, and so Jacob gave him bread and lentil–*"

"Whoa!" Lily interrupted. "His brother was about to *die* from hunger, and instead of just sharing his lentils, Jacob made him give up his rights? That's terrible."

Sam nodded slowly.

"Took advantage of him, seems to me."

Jennifer burst through the swinging door, into the mess. She scowled at the three of them.

"Art and I are opening containers. Trying to find more food, if any of you three would like to join." Her voice was sour. "Honestly, now that three of us need to navigate at all times, I'm not sure we have time for this," she waved her hand dismissively in their direction.

"Man cannot live on bread alone," smiled Mel.

Jennifer shook her head and walked into the bathroom.

"Maybe she's right," Sam said. "Maybe we should be helping with the containers."

Mel shook his head adamantly. "We'll have all day to search," he said. "We can afford to take an hour from our day to study the words of our Creator."

Lily nodded and reached across the table to put a hand on Sam's shoulder. "This is important too. It's okay."

Mel poked through his beard to scratch his left cheek. All this sweat was making him break out.

"So. Taking advantage. I understand why you two would say that," he said. "But from Jacob's point of view, he was correcting an injustice. And think about this: Esau didn't even protest! Apparently he didn't even care about his birthright, if he was willing to trade it for a pot of lentils."

"But you just said he was *dying*," Lily prodded. "He didn't have a choice."

"Well, this is why it's so important to have the written word of the Holy One," Mel said. "To clarify. Because it's written..." Mel peered down into his handwritten Torah, turned the page and raised an eyebrow. Interesting. He was quite sure that originally, the verse concluding this story had been **Thus Esau despised his birthright**, removing any moral ambiguity about what had really transpired. But that's not what he'd written. Instead it said: **Thus the descendants of Jacob were cursed, for Jacob forced his kin to swear an oath under duress.**

"Well," Mel cleared his throat. "It seems you're right, actually Lily. And Sam. It seems this *was* a moral blunder on the part of our forefather Jacob. Even though his intentions were pure, and he really was destined to be the spiritual heir to Isaac, you're right, he came upon the birthright in a backwards way."

Jennifer walked out of the bathroom and made a bit of an exaggerated show of clomping through the mess, and then letting the swinging door slam shut behind her. Mel suddenly felt the need to relieve himself as well.

"Excuse me," he said, leaving his makeshift lectern.

In the stall, he unzipped, pulled the strings of his *tzis-tzis* back with his left hand, and used his right to guide his stream into the filthy receptacle.

Thus the descendants of Jacob were cursed.

He tried not to think about it; it was improper to consider anything of holiness in the restroom. It was said that the Goan of Vilna, a Torah prodigy from the 17th century, kept his entire library of secular subjects–math and science–beside his toilet, and only then would he take time away from his Torah study to read them.

Mel shook, zipped up, and went to the sink to wash his hands. He studied his reflection in the mirror. He'd lost weight in his face. His thick black beard was filthy with oil and dandruff. His velvet *yarmulke*, once black, was grey from the sun.

Thus the descendants of Jacob were cursed.

Like most of his transcription, he had absolutely no recollection of writing those words.

"Mel?" Sam opened the door to the bathroom and poked his head in. "You alright?"

Mel realized he'd been rinsing his hands, lost in thought, for a long time.

40

Lily was sleeping when someone knocked on her cabin door.

She'd been having a dream that they arrived at the island. It was lush and filled with squawking rainbow-colored birds. There were palm trees, mountains, and a beach with crystal-clear water. It wasn't exactly the eleven people on board in her dream. Her boys–Art and Vic and Sam–had definitely been there, but the rest she hadn't recognized.

She sat up in bed with a smile on her lips. It had been a beautiful dream, and for a moment, she was sure it would happen. They'd reach that island.

The knocking came again.

"Just a second!" she said, turning on the reading light beside her bed, pulling on her shirt and rushing to the peephole. She was sure it would be Vic or Art trying to recruit her for a midnight poker game, and was shocked instead to see Greg.

It was happening. It was happening!

She'd been taking Art's advice and ignoring Greg a little bit, or mocking him, to try to make him feel self conscious. She couldn't believe it worked! But here he was at her door in the middle of the night. What else could it be?

She smoothed down her hair, puffed out her chest, and opened the door.

"Hey," she said, trying to act indifferent to this development.

"Hey Lily," he said, smiling widely. "Can I come in?"

She pretended to think about it a moment, then shrugged.

"Sure."

He stepped into her cabin and slammed the door behind him. Then grabbed her around the waist, leaned in, and kissed her neck.

"I can't stop thinking about you," he murmured. Then one of his hands crept up her shirt to find her left breast, which he squeezed like it was a squeaky dog toy. He kept kissing her neck. He licked her ear. Then he pushed her gently in the direction of the bed.

Lily's heart hammered in her chest. She could hardly process what was happening. She was on her back, and Greg was on top of her. Somehow he'd already pulled his own shirt off. She pulled away from his kisses for a moment and looked up at him. Even in the dim light his green eyes glowed with some kind of wild fire.

Whatever words she'd wanted to say got stuck in her throat.

He moved in closer, until their noses were practically touching. His pupils were too large.

"Lily…" he whispered. "What are they planning?"

She shook her head.

"What do you mean?"

His grip on her shoulders tightened.

"Are you even real?" he asked. But before she could answer this strange question he broke into a wide grin. "I'm just kidding. God you're so beautiful," he cocked his head and smiled sweetly. "You're a hell of a catch, Lily Chong."

Then he exhaled pleasantly and leaned in to resume kissing her neck. One of his hands slipped down the front of her shorts and caressed her.

She felt rigid and cold.

"You're so beautiful," he cooed in her ear.

Michael texted her fifteen minutes after leaving her house that morning, saying what a wonderful time he'd had, and already asking if they could go out again next week. Lily asked if maybe they could do it even sooner, and immediately kicked herself for sounding desperate. He said he would love to, but he was just so busy with work. Next week on Monday, though, he was all hers.

This week wasn't as great as the one before, because Michael couldn't text much. He'd drop her a line occasionally to apologize for not answering, but he was just so buried with work. Lily understood. He worked like twelve hour days pretty regularly, he said. And now, especially, he was trying to put a huge deal together. Then on Saturday he texted her to say they'd have to postpone just a couple days because he had to fly to Cincinnati for work. Thursday, he promised. Lily texted him asking, jokingly, if he was sure he wasn't married. He responded in the best way possible:

Lol. Not yet ;)

Thursday he texted at five that he was gonna have to work late, but still really wanted to see her… Was there any way he could just come over after work and they could share a bottle of wine at her place and just chill? Lily thought that actually sounded amazing.

He showed up at ten. He looked a lot more tired than he had during their dates.

Where's the wine?

Oh, sorry, I assumed you were getting it…

Lily, I've been working all day, did you work today?

No…

And you didn't have time to go get a bottle? Did you expect me to pay for it again, is that it?

Oh my god, I'm so sorry. I have beer, is that okay?

Michael then collapsed onto the couch and buried his head in his palms.

No, don't apologize Lily. I'm taking it out on you. That's not fair. Beer is great.

Lily was secretly loving this interaction. People were always talking about how healthy couples had fights. It was never easy. Here they were, having their first fight!

Taking out what?

Just work stuff. Super stressful.

What is it?

It's boring. I promise babe.

No! I want to hear. Really.

He told her about work: all the details of his day and little problems. Lily loved it. It was almost more intimate than sex. And after talking for a while he was back to his old self. The guy she'd had two amazing dates with.

They kissed for a while.

I'm so wiped… I need to unwind. Do you wanna go to your room?

Yeah of course.

The fooling around started nicely enough. Gentle, affectionate, beautiful. But suddenly something changed in Michael. It was as if he was seized by a demonic spirit.

He abruptly moved the encounter to an unfamiliar place. Lily's chest tightened. She tried to catch his eyes, to communicate to him this was uncomfortable, but he wasn't looking at her. He was looking straight ahead, mouth slightly agape, eyes glazed. Lily was scared of pulling away and upsetting him; he'd had such a hard day at work and was trying to relax, and her starting some kind of argument now and stressing him out was probably the last thing he needed.

Still though, she wished he would meet her eyes. Because when he didn't, she felt she might as well be a toy. She closed her eyes and pretended she was somewhere else. Eventually he released his grip on her head and collapsed back on her bed.

Oh wow Lily. That was great. You're incredible.

Lily brushed off her concerns, her brief moment of terror, and cuddled up to him. He spooned her and all felt right. He was like a big hairy bear.

I'm sorry… I'm just so stressed out about this deal. I'm so wiped.

Michael slept over that night but took off early in the morning. Lily texted him a few hours later:

Great time last night…When are we going out again? Xoxo

She met Amanda for lunch and gushed. She omitted the kind of unpleasant part, because today she felt like it was an overreaction to be upset about that. Like, what did she really have to complain about? Michael hadn't done anything wrong.

Oh my god. So yeah, last night he came over and we just drank beer and talked. He's so funny, but he also takes his work really seriously. He's really passionate about it, which I think is so hot. It's important that someone is passionate about what they do, you know. You're gonna love him Amanda.

When are you seeing him next?

Dunno. He hasn't texted me back yet. Hopefully I won't have to wait a week again... I mean I get it he's bus–

What?? A week? He made you wait a week between dates??

Uh... Yeah I guess. I mean, let's see our second date was on a Wednesday . So let's–

Wait. How many times have you seen him?

Three.

It's been like three weeks Lily! You've only seen him three times in three weeks!? What the fuck. That's not *okay.*

Trust me it's fine. He's just super busy.

Uh. No. Listen. I don't care how busy he is, he has to make time for you. Tell him you're not waiting a week this time. He's not married right?

NO! Dude you don't get it. You don't know him. He's just super, super busy and stressed.

Lily checked her phone as she left the restaurant. He still hadn't replied. She suddenly felt ill.

On the bus to her night shift she kept thinking she felt her phone vibrate in her purse, but when she pulled it out there was nothing. It had been six hours now since she'd sent the text. He was probably just busy at work. Maybe he was even on a plane, traveling somewhere. Unless... Had she done something wrong last night? Could he tell that she'd been uncomfortable? He'd said at Jack's that he loved how chill she was... What if she'd been too stiff? Self-conscious?

She pulled out her phone and texted him, hitting send before even reading what she'd written.

Sorry if I was weird last night. Just really excited about everything. I want to do that again btw. Next time will be even better ;)

She stared at the words on the screen, now feeling really sick. Where the hell did that come from? She slammed the red button to tell the bus to stop even though she was two miles from the office and rushed out into the damp night. She sat down at the bus stop bench. It had been four minutes since she sent that text and... Oh god. There were check marks next to the text, indicating that he'd seen it. He wasn't on a flight. He'd seen the text and was making a deliberate decision not to respond. She texted again.

Ignore that. Lol. I just meant I want to see you again soon that's all. Let's not wait a week this time ;) Xoxo

She stared rapt at the screen. Her heart thumped against her ribs, like it was trying to escape her body. Check marks suddenly appeared next to this text, and her vision went sideways. She tasted bile in her throat. She was vaguely aware that she was meant to be at work five minutes ago. She called her boss and just barely managed to explain that she was sick again–bladder infection from last week that hadn't gone away. Then she got off the phone as fast she could so she could to see if Michael had replied back yet. He hadn't.

She texted Amanda.

Omg omg omg omg. I think I fucked up. Omg.

Her best friend replied right away.

What happened????

Sent him some more texts and he didn't reply.

Hmmm. What did u say send me screenshots.

Nothing rlly…just that i didn't want to wait a week again this time!!

Sure it's fine. Just be patient.

Lily couldn't be patient. She took a cab home because she couldn't bear to get back on a stuffy bus. By eleven he still hadn't responded, and she had to take three Advil PMs to fall asleep. She woke up at three in the morning and groped for her phone. Nothing. The antihistamine in her bloodstream pulled her back into merciful sleep. When her alarm went off at nine she opened her eyes and lunged for the phone. Initial hope at seeing she'd received texts, but they were from Amanda, plus one from her dad. She felt she was in free fall. She wanted to die. Before she could really think it through, she texted Michael again.

Hi, just seeing if everything's okay cuz I didn't hear back from you. Are you alright? Anyway can't wait to see u again. Sorry about the weird texts before. Haha. I had such a nice time though.

An hour later, check marks appeared next to this text. Lily was feeling feverish. She tried calling. He didn't pick up.

Hey you're not ignoring me right. Lol. What are you doing tomorrow night?

She never heard from him again, and she'd had years to pick apart every minute detail of their affair, try to pinpoint the moment where exactly she'd made a mistake.

So in her cabin, pinned beneath Greg Pink, she closed her eyes and pretended to enjoy what he was doing. She'd messed up once before and it had nearly destroyed her. This was her last chance at love. She wouldn't mess this up too.

41

There were many foods Bahram was craving, but chief among them were eggs. Fresh eggs. He'd grown up with boiled eggs; usually you'd put them whole into a stew you were slow-cooking, then you'd peel them and eat them along with the stew. Bahram liked eating eggs like that just fine, but those weren't the eggs he was craving. He wanted the kind he'd had that morning with Azzami. At that restaurant, they fried the eggs for just a minute or two, so the whites stayed white, and when you poked the soft yolk with your fork it fell apart and coated your toast like cream.

He emptied a packet of yellow lentil stew into a plastic bowl, and joylessly shoveled spoonfuls into his mouth, swallowing without even chewing. It was peasant food. The first thing he'd do when they docked at *Nuworld*, before even trying to catch a flight back to Afghanistan, was to go to a restaurant and order five fried eggs. He hoped they'd have strong coffee too, like they did in America.

It would be their last real meal.

Mother, Father, come. We're going to go have a classic American breakfast.

They left their motel and walked down the boulevard of some small town. They must have looked a strange foursome: the three Nasims and Adam, the latter wearing the jean shorts, t-shirt, and plastic sunglasses Azzami had bought for him at the huge market. Azzami led them into a restaurant. The floor was fine blue carpet, and there were pies and cakes behind covered glass.

They sat in a blue leather booth, Bahram and Keti facing Azzami and Adam.

Don't worry. I'm going to order the whole menu.

Their son smiled. Today was the first time since he'd picked them up at the airport a month before that didn't seem to be in a hurry to get anywhere.

A waitress arrived and Azzami dictated two pads worth of requests. Adam had his hands folded on the table, and smiled at Bahram and Keti.

Moments later a second waiter came by with a pitcher of steaming coffee, and Azzami ordered him to fill up their mugs.

Be careful, Americans like their coffee very strong.

Keti took the warning to heart, and sipped cautiously. But Bahram scoffed.

My son, I've drank coffee with the Taliban. I think I can handle this American luxury drink. Look, they've even filtered out the grounds.

Bahram downed his cup. Three minutes later his heart was filled with so much joy his body couldn't contain it: his hands were trembling and he was breathing hard.

Then the food came. Golden cakes topped with cream and berries; buttery omelets filled with cheese, vegetables, and meat; fried potatoes… Then the waiter brought each of them a tall glass filled with some kind of frothy mud.

What is it?

Don't you trust me by now, Father? Just try it.

Bahram slurped some up through a straw and his eyes went wide. It was silky chocolate cream. It reminded Bahram of a poem he'd read long ago, about the delicacies the angels dine on in heaven.

Then the waiter came and refilled Bahram's coffee.

Throughout the meal, Azzami kept turning to look out the window of the restaurant.

Bahram ate and ate, long after the other three sat back in the booth clutching their stomachs. Finally Bahram reached the point where he could simply eat no more. He loosened a belt buckle and leaned back against the booth. He was suddenly exhausted.

Wow. These Americans know how to eat…

Azzami was suddenly alert, staring out the window. Bahram looked too. Across the street, a crowd was gathering outside a laundromat. They were watching a TV mounted on a wall inside.

Oh no.

Azzami was on his phone, cheeks flushed. He was watching a video on the screen. Then he shoved the phone in his pocket and stood up. He looked ill.

Come on. Come on. We have to go right now.

Bahram realized that the restaurant had gone silent in the past few minutes. Everybody, even the waiters, was staring down at their phones, mouths slightly agape.

Don't you have to pay?

It doesn't matter.

Azzami rushed Bahram, Keti, and Adam out the front door of the restaurant. Indeed, nobody seemed to notice or care that they hadn't settled the check. The city outside was also strangely silent. All the drivers were pulled over to the side of the road, now either looking at their phones or making calls on them. The four of them seemed to be the only ones not frozen in place. As they walked past a barbershop, Bahram saw that the barber and patron alike had abandoned their warm shave to stare at the TV.

Azzami, what's happening?

It's started too early.

Keti's hand slipped into his, as they hurried after their son. Azzami screamed into his phone in rapid English. His other hand was around Adam's waist, half-dragging the confused young man along.

They arrived at their motel and followed Azzami to his room. He rushed to his suitcase and dug through it madly, like a dog following a scent. Finally he found what he was looking for: a plastic bag with a zipper seal.

Mother, Father. Go to your room. Change into long pants and long sleeves. Put any medications you need in this bag and close it tight. Meet me back here in five minutes.

Azzami's phone rang and he answered it with a furious flurry of English. He took a handful of his hair and pulled it so hard it looked like he might rip it out by the roots. He screamed something into the phone, and the reply seemed to knock the wind out of him. Then he realized his parents were still standing there.

What are you doing? Go change! GO!

Bahram and his wife crossed the hall to their own room. Confused and frightened, they followed their son's instructions. Bahram changed into a long-sleeve button-down, and then took their medicines from the bathroom. He put his cholesterol and heartburn pills in the bag. Keti didn't need any medicine.

When he came back to the bedroom, Keti was sitting on a chair, a shirt wrapped around her head like a shawl, reading from a book.

Keti?

She held up a finger. He saw she was reading from a travel-sized *Salat*. She was praying.

He'd only seen her pray once before, when their daughter, Andisha, was in the hospital for a burst appendix. Like most the families in their village, they fasted for Ramadan and had family meals on *Eid Al-Fitr* and *Eid Al-Adha*, but rarely went to mosque or studied holy texts.

Keti finished her prayer and closed the book. She looked up at him.

We're never going to go back to Afghanistan. You understand that, right?

Bahram swallowed.

Get dressed, Keti.

Back home, Keti wore a long skirt every day. But last week Azzami took them shopping, and treated her to a pair of blue jeans. When she slid into them now, Bahram forgot about the mess outside their room for just a moment, and laughed.

You look like an American cowboy!

Keti managed to crack a soft smile herself.

Azzami was knocking hard on their door, and shouting.

Mother, Father, come on!

Keti quickly folded up the *Salat* and fit it in the back pocket of her jeans, then opened the door. Azzami had changed into a black turtleneck shirt, blue jeans, and black boots.

Come. Come.

He led them back to his room. Adam had been changed into the same outfit as Azzami. He sat on the edge of the bed, looking as bewildered as usual .

Azzami handed Bahram and Keti each a hunk of black rubber that Bahram initially took for some kind of diving equipment.

Pull them on over your heads.

Azzami then took another piece of rubber from his suitcase and fit it onto Adam's head. The young man was transformed into a man-sized insect, with opaque grey windows for eyes. Azzami tightened a strap at the base of the mask, creating a perfect seal around Adam's neck.

Growing up, Bahram had a friend whose father raised goats. Mostly they were used for dairy, but once or twice a year, usually for a wedding feast, he'd slaughter and roast one. Bahram had been there once, in the pasture, when the father chose a goat to kill, and led her down the hill to the butcher. Before he separated this goat from the others, he put a black hood over her head and tied it tight around the animal's neck with string. It was a kindness, he explained. Once they got close to the butcher there would be the smell and sight of dead animals. This way the goat wouldn't be frightened, or realize what was going to happen to her.

Bahram tried to put on his mask, but struggled to pull it wide enough for his head. His son saw him and groaned. He was getting very anxious to leave.

Let me, Father.

His son grabbed the mask, stretched it, and rammed it down over Bahram's head, damning him to the most intimate of prisons: the grey half-light permitted by the visor; the pressure and heat from a second skin pressed against his face. Then Azzami tightened the neck strap, constricting the flow of air. Bahram immediately had to cough but didn't feel like he had the space.

Someone took his hand. Keti was at his side, wearing her own mask. Neither could see the other's eyes. He wondered what her face was doing beneath the rubber monstrosity.

Azzami hurried them out of the hotel room. He was wearing a bulky camping backpack, and pulling an overstuffed black suitcase with one hand, holding the grey briefcase he'd gotten from the man in the parking lot with the other. They took the elevator down and rushed through the lobby. Bahram thought they'd get looks for the masks, but the only two people left in the lobby were huddled in the corner sobbing.

Azzami popped the trunk to their car and threw in his baggage, then the four of them got into the car. He turned on the ignition with a kind of violence. Azzami gunned the engine and they shot out of the hotel parking lot.

In the back seat, Keti again took Bahram's hand. There wasn't much else to do.

There were no cars on the road, and Azzami sped down narrow streets, taking each turn with such force that Bahram and Keti were slammed against the windows. With the mask on, it was easy to forget that this was his son driving, and not some kind of djinn sent down to Earth to wreak havoc.

The sidewalks were empty. Where was everyone?

It didn't take long for an answer. The logjam of cars started maybe a kilometer before the highway itself. They were stuck. From Azzami's mask came a muffled shriek, and he punched the steering wheel over and over, his honking drowned out by thousands of others. In the car next to them, Bahram saw a family: two parents and two children. A girl was staring at them, obviously frightened. It took Bahram a moment to realize it was because of his mask.

The forehead of Azzami's mask was on the steering wheel. His shoulders quaked. His son was sobbing silently, and for some reason this—more than the masks, the empty sidewalks, or Adam's deranged smile—frightened Bahram. A wave of terror washed over him, a crest as tall as a building. His legs felt like they were made of the same rubber as his mask. His normally steady hands were shaking uncontrollably.

Azzami turned off the ignition right there in the middle of the road.

Get out. We have to walk.

Walk to where?

In response, Azzami only reached across Adam's lap to collect his pistol from the glove compartment, then popped the trunk and ran around to get the luggage. In the car next to them, Bahram saw, the girl was blowing her nose.

42

Vic swiveled around to face Art.

"Go and fetch the cards, man," the Frenchman said.

"Just mind the autopilot," Art said. "We can't afford to fuck up again."

Vic groaned.

"Nothing is happening with this," he gestured to the panel in front of him.

Beside Art, Sam was hunched over the radar, massive forearms on either side of the screen, staring down expectantly at the display like it was a dinner plate he couldn't yet touch. There was light rain outside. Periodically a splatter of water emerged from the night to slap the bridge windows.

Art was exhausted. They all were. It was about four in the morning. The strangest hour. Art once knew a guy who said his only rule in life was that he was never awake between four and five in the morning. Said it was unnatural.

The swivel stools were murder, and Art tried to alternate sitting and standing up, just to keep his back from tightening up too badly. He'd take hacking the locks off shipping containers over this any day. At least hacking was *doing* something. On the bridge he just sat like a robot, watching the numbers, dreading tomorrow morning.

What was going to happen tomorrow–when the autopilot announced that they'd arrived at the coordinates and there was nothing but open water? Or, even if there was something… What if it was just a sandbar?

What next? They'd try for the Azores he supposed. Though the population of those islands was probably enough that someone had thought to bomb them as well.

"Man," Vic said. "Get the cards."

Art looked up at him. What the Frenchman really wanted was cigarettes, of course. And in his nicotine-starved mind, there was some

Pavlovian link between cigarettes and the cards themselves. But the supply on board had dried up, as far as they knew, and there was no way for Art to give them more Marlboros without revealing that he'd been holding out on them for weeks.

Over the last few days, Frenchy had been noticeably irritable and impatient. Similar to how he'd behaved during the first week on board. Art attributed this to withdrawal.

"We can't play cards," Sam half-snapped, not looking up from the radar. "We have to navigate."

Vic snorted.

"For one hour now I'm sitting with my hands on my cock. And once we arrive at the island, Elissa will make us march and explore like mules. This is our last chance to relax."

Art was also craving a smoke, real bad. But he'd have to get the lighter from the cabinet next to Vic, and sneak out to the container where the Marlboros were, which he hadn't done for a week. It was risky, and also he felt guilty about what he'd done. He felt like he deserved to be jonesing along with them. It was a small penance for his sins of deception.

Art had developed a fondness for a lot of the folks on board. Vic and Sam especially. Not the sharpest, but good guys. And their hope was a fucking dagger in his heart. They were only sure about the island because of him; because he'd sold it to them. He'd pictured the way it would play out many times. The awful moment wasn't when the crew, waiting expectantly on the bow, realized that the horizon was empty. It was after that, when they all turned to Art, disappointed. Realized what a mistake it was to put their faith in this silly old fool.

He looked down at the compasses, both the magnetic and gyroscopic. The boat was headed 14.3 degrees Northwest. Unwavering. Headed toward nothing, he was sure.

When he was working as a bookie, Art had a client kill himself. Art still remembered the guy's face distinctly: the sad hanging jowls, eternally flushed cheeks, thick lips that he always smacked in distaste after a sip from his perpetual glass of seltzer. His name was Carl. They had a standing appointment every evening at eight at a sports bar on the corner of Essex and Houston. Presumably Carl worked close to there, but Art never asked. He was always there by the time Art arrived, watching the games, drinking seltzer, frowning. In retrospect, it seemed inevitable that Carl would kill himself.

Carl only bet on basketball games, and he was terrible at it. As a bookie you didn't want your clients to go belly up; you wanted to cultivate a consistent enough clientele that for any given bet you'd have a party on either side of the action, ensuring you'd collect a risk-free vig regardless of the outcome. Art was just starting out at this point, so he was playing the house for Carl; taking the other side of any action Carl wanted. Still though, Art often found himself trying to talk Carl out of bad bets.

The Hornets played last night, Carl, and they're on the road. Walker isn't 100%. They're exhausted. At least take the points.

I know what I'm doing.

Carl didn't know what he was doing. He lost mostly, but won just enough to keep false hope alive, to preserve the illusion that he was a good bettor on a bad streak. Art didn't know where Carl got his money and didn't want to. The less he knew about his clients the better. He figured it was a family fortune he was squandering on road underdogs and terrible prop bets.

I want the Spurs to win the series in exactly five games. What odds can you give me on that?

Fifteen to one is what Vegas is offering, but come on Carl. Sure the Spurs will take it down, but could easily be a sweep, or go six. Take the easy money.

The Spurs are gonna take it in five, I know it.

Art was making a fortune off the poor guy. The NBA season ran nine months of the year, and there was at least one game every night for Carl to lose on. Art was making enough from Carl's losses to payroll a collection agency–two poorly-tempered Ukrainian men–and a decent office space in Bed Stuy.

When Carl didn't show one Tuesday evening, Art was only mildly surprised. Carl was in the middle of a particularly bad week. Even the bets that Art had thought somewhat prudent ended up losing. Art had made so much money off Carl over the past month he was seriously considering buying the guy a really nice Christmas present to thank him for his patronage. Art ordered a tequila and soda.

You see Carl tonight?

Who?

The guy who always sits right here, drinks seltzer, and glares at the basketball game like it just personally insulted him.

Oh. No didn't see him tonight.

Carl's phone went straight to voicemail. His outstanding debt to Art was considerable, but not more than usual. Not enough to skip town over.

Art came back the next night. Still no Carl.

If he told the Ukrainian guys about this, their eyes would light up. They'd track down poor Carl like wolves and wring every last penny out of him. Art decided to let it go. He knew it was no way to run a sportsbook–you had to be fucking ruthless, protect your margins like they were your children–but the thought of pitiful Carl getting smacked around was just too much to stomach.

That would have been the end of it, had another client–Brad White, the guy who'd given Carl Art's number in the first place–not said something a month or so later when Art was collecting his Super Bowl bets.

Hey did you know Carl? Carl Waxman? Did he ever bet with you? He asked me if I knew a book like a year ago. Was he betting with you?

Art's gut tied itself in a knot.

I know Carl. He bets with me here and there. Why?

Oh man. You didn't hear?

No…

You serious? He offed himself man. Tied one end of an electric cord to the corner of his bedpost, and the other around his neck, then hopped out his apartment window. His kid came home from school, and was like, why is the window open in the middle of January.

His kid?

Yeah. That's what I heard from Robert, anyway. Maybe the most fucked up part is he mortgaged his apartment. A fucking orthopedic surgeon. Took out a mortgage without telling his wife, and nobody knows where the money went. So his wife and kid had to move in with their sister. It's nuts. That's why I asked if he was betting a lot with you.

Art had to sit down.

Just here and there, like I said. Shit. Do you have the wife's number?

Jesus. The body's still warm, Art.

Give me the goddamn number.

In the end he couldn't bring himself to meet her face to face. He mailed her a big toy bear stuffed with hundreds, and tried never to think about it again.

Art's hands were shaking on the compass. He needed a smoke.

"Boys, I'm gonna go get some air," he said.

"Go get the cards, man!" Vic pleaded.

Art walked over to the Frenchman, sitting at the autopilot. He put one hand on his bare shoulder, and with the other reached into the drawer to grab the flashlight, simultaneously snatching the yellow lighter.

"Okay. I'll get the cards," Art smiled. "But don't take your eyes off the autopilot for too long. Sam, check the compass periodically. I'll be back in five."

He slid the lighter into his pocket and then slid open the forward door of the bridge. Despite the rain, the night air was warm. The light drizzle was actually refreshing. He kept one hand on the wet railing and eased down the slippery steps carefully. The staircase and upper deck were lit up by the powerful lights mounted atop the bridge. When he looked back up, Vic and Sam were lost in the glare. On the deck, he flipped on his flashlight and walked to the edge of the ship, where he descended the few steps to the perimeter walkway.

Could he come back with a full carton and plausibly convince them that he'd just now stumbled upon another stash of Marlboros? It was sketchy, but maybe they'd be happy enough to have the smokes that they wouldn't ask any more questions.

He was torn and still undecided as he climbed back up to the main deck, now at the aft of the ship. He'd left scratches on the colorful containers, and now followed the breadcrumbs to the blue container marked with his X.

He pried it open with the flashlight, and was relieved to see his step ladder leaning against the stacks of rubber tires, just where he left it. He climbed up, pulled out the top tire, and tossed it down to the container floor. Then he moved a tire from the second layer to the side to reveal the hidden treasure. His nose was filled with the rich scent of unburnt tobacco, and already he felt himself settling down. He reached in and groped until his fingers closed on plastic-wrapped cardboard. He descended the stepladder with a sealed carton of sixteen packs in hand.

He ripped off the plastic. He could hardly open a pack and get a cigarette out fast enough. He stuck it in the side of his mouth and whipped the Bic to life. The walls of the container insulated him from the wind and rain, and on the first try the flame caught the tip of the Marlboro, bursting into wonderful orange. He took a glorious lungful of smoke. Warmth spread down through his legs, and tickled his toes. Even his lower back felt better for a moment. He felt like he was twenty years younger.

"I thought everyone was out of cigarettes."

Art turned to the flashlight in the direction of the voice, illuminating Sam standing outside the entrance to the container, face dripping with rain.

Art swallowed.

"I had a couple left," he said. "What's going on Sammy? You left Vic alone on the bridge? Let's go back and keep him company."

"I saw you take the lighter."

Sam now noticed the stacks of tires and stepladder. Wordlessly, he entered the container, walked past Art straight to where the tire had been shoved to the side to reveal the payload. Art could hear Sam's heavy breathing as the ogre reached his hand into the darkness. A crinkle of plastic. And then Sam pulled out another unopened carton of Marlboros. Sam looked down at the cigarettes in his hand. Art's heart thumped in his ears.

"What is this?" Sam asked.

Art's mouth was dry.

"Turns out there were more than I thought."

Sam dropped the carton onto the wet floor and turned back to the stacks of tires. He grabbed a tire and, with a pained grunt, turned and tossed it behind him, out onto the deck. Then another. And another, until he'd cleared an entire column. Then he moved to the second row, and pulled these out one by one, each tire he removed revealing more of the wall of cigarettes, stacked to the ceiling of the container.

Sam turned back to Art. His cheeks were flushed, and he was breathing very fast through his nose.

"You lied to us."

Art forced a laugh.

"You're all healthier this way. Think about how much you would have smoked if you'd had all of these. Vic would be–"

"You *lied*," Sam's chest rose and fell. Art was suddenly aware of how close they were. He realized he should have tried to run while Sam was moving the tires. "You kept these to yourself."

"Hey, I didn't *make*–"

"We're going to the island because of you," Sam was looking down at him, eyes wide and bone-white in the glow of the flashlight. "You convinced us. But you're a *liar*."

"Sammy, c'mon, don't be dramat–"

Sam's right hand shot forward, clamping onto Art's throat and shoved him against the interior wall of the container. The impact shook Art's vision and sent a wave of pain radiating throughout his back and shoulders. The man's strength was unbelievable. Art was still holding the flashlight, but it was aiming down at the ground, so Sam's face was now nothing but shadow.

"You thought we were *stupid*," Sam growled, pulling Art toward him then slamming him back against the wall. This time the back of Art's head smacked into the cold steel. He could hear the trembling in the giant's voice as he was overcome by rage. "You thought I was too stupid to understand."

Art tried to respond, but his voice came out only as a weak croak. Sam was cutting off his air.

"You can't treat people like that!" Sam said.

Sam's fist tightened around Art's neck. Sam was ten times stronger than him. He smacked Art against the steel wall repeatedly, like a chimp angry with his doll. Art smelled blood, his own, from the back of his head, and realized that, intentionally or not, this man was going to kill him. Art had only one option. He'd managed to retain his grip on the flashlight throughout this ordeal. It was a hefty piece of equipment, but Sam was a hefty piece of meat. The giant had only one vulnerability.

"You *liar*," Sam said.

Art swung the butt of the flashlight as hard as he could into Sam's gut, and it met with something sickeningly soft. Sam's grip went slack and he made a terrible noise that was both shrill and impossibly guttural. Sam released Art, and staggered backwards, clutching his stomach, making a gurgling sound. Art's knees were wobbly and he was lightheaded, leaning against the wall for support.

Sam sank to the damp floor of the container, struggling to breathe, both hands gripping his stomach.

"Sammy," Art dropped to his knees and crawled to the mountain of man. "Sammy, I'm sorry."

Art shined the flashlight in Sam's face. His eyes were milky with pain.

"Oh my god. It burns," Sam wheezed. "Oh god."

Art turned down to inspect the damage. Sam's hands were groping around his lower belly, as if he was a leaking barrel that needed to be plugged up, if only he could find the hole. There didn't seem to be any blood, but somehow Art found that even more worrisome; everything bad was happening on the inside.

Sam's face was bright red.

"Something's wrong," he croaked. "It's not right. It burns so bad."

"Okay, Jesus. Shit. Hold tight. I'm gonna go get Doctor Roz."

Art dashed out into the light rain. He was bleeding himself, from the back of his head, and his throat was on fire. The horizon was a thin strip of pink. Soon it would be morning.

43

He awoke, as if from a long sleep.

He'd had so many dreams, but couldn't remember any with clarity. Actually, it seemed likely that this was still a dream. He was in some kind of labyrinth, each wall a stack of colorful boxes. He was surrounded by strangers.

It was very early morning but the sun was already hot, and a faint mist rose from the wet floor. He was confused to find he was wearing a makeshift shirt; a white sheet with a neck hole cut out of it.

A huge man with paprika hair was lying flat on the metal deck. A brown-haired woman with a linen shirt sat over him, periodically touching his stomach, shaking her head in either frustration or despondence.

"So try the surgery," said an older man with skin the color of burnt sugar. He was wearing a turquoise baseball cap.

"I can't," the kneeling woman said. "We don't have any tools or anesthetic, and I haven't even thought about abdominal surgery since I did my rotations twenty-three years ago."

"What is it?" shrieked a woman with plump cheeks, wearing a red shirt. "What's happening to him?"

"It could be extreme inflammation, that's what I'm hoping," the doctor said. "But if the hernia has turned gangrenous or ruptured, there's not much I can do."

"For god's sake," the older man was nearly sobbing. "We have to at least *try*."

They all just watched the huge man who was sprawled on the deck, breathing slowly.

"You just found him like this, Art?" The woman in red asked. "I don't get it. What was he doing out here? And what were you doing here?"

"Putain… c'est quo ce bordel?" A shirtless man with a mop of yellow hair held a wrapped carton of Marlboro cigarettes in each hand. "Arthur, you knew about these?"

"I'm going back to the bridge," said an old woman with limbs like dead sticks. "We're sailing blind. I need at least one person to come with me."

Yes. A boat! This whole time there'd been some kind of growling beneath his feet, and the wet floor was swaying ever so slightly.

"I saw it!" a young, attractive woman suddenly appeared from behind a row of cartons. She was out of breath but smiling ecstatically.

"What?"

"I saw it. It's there. The island."

Everyone looked at the young woman.

"I'm serious."

The woman in red was the first to abandon them. She sprinted into the labyrinth in the direction from which the young woman had appeared. And one by one, everyone followed. The brown-haired doctor said something to the huge man, and rushed off herself, leaving the giant alone, prone on the deck, clutching his gut.

The huge man looked up at him and smiled.

"It's okay, Adam. Go with them," he croaked. "Go see if it's true."

He nodded and ran himself, following the brown-haired woman past column after column of colorful boxes, until emerging into the full glory of the morning. They were indeed on a ship, and everyone was at the railing looking out onto the sea, which was sparkling beneath a purple dawn.

"I see it!" said the woman in the red shirt. "I knew it! I knew it!!"

He squinted and could make out a small break in the horizon, what must be an island.

Beside him, the old woman's eyes were wet with tears. A man with a bushy beard and skullcap gripped the railing so tightly that the veins in his forearms popped out, as if he was drawing power from this metal bannister. Beneath his beard, his mouth emitted utterances too soft to make out.

A portly man wearing a golf hat said, with a thick accent:

"Nuorld. Nuorld."

It was a quiet and beautiful dream

"Adam's island," said the doctor, smiling at him strangely.

It was then that he noticed the burns on his forearms. The one on the left that read **Adam**, on the right, **Island**, followed by a line that led up his bicep toward his shoulder.

He inhaled sharply. Could this really be a dream? It seemed too vivid: the yellow pit stains on the bearded man's undershirt that nearly stretched to his midriff; the tactile sensation of rubbing his index finger along the raised flesh of the words burnt onto his arms; the hazy spectrum of pinks, oranges, and yellows in the dawn sky; the gentle rocking of the ship; the smell of brine…

It couldn't be a dream. It seemed much more likely, in fact, that he was dead.

The yellow-haired man suddenly turned away from the glistening panorama.

"The engines are off," he said.

The older man with the green baseball hat then abandoned the horizon to take stock of the eight other people around him.

"Where's Greg?"

Part 4
Daughters of January

44

Six of them sat in the captain's lounge, all chain-smoking.

Sam was down in his cabin; if they'd left him on the deck face up, he would have died of exposure before anything else. It had taken four of them to help him down to his bed. Sam was delirious. The pain was so bad that he'd passed out every few seconds as they hauled him down the stairs, awakening just long enough to groan in agony and vomit.

Lily was taking care of Sam, which just meant giving him water and applying compresses to his burning forehead.

Adam could be anywhere.

Vic was in the stairwell outside the engine room, hoping Greg would finally want to talk.

And Greg was killing them. He'd barricaded himself in the engine room twenty-four long hours ago, and hadn't even come to the door to talk.

The exuberance of spotting the island had quickly turned to unspeakable frustration. They could *see* it. They were so close, perhaps forty miles away. But they had no way to turn the engines back on.

The air in the captain's lounge was hot, stagnant, and wet; once again they couldn't run the air conditioning without depleting the battery. And because the ship was stationary, there was none of the fine breeze they'd all become accustomed to. Jennifer took a tentative sip from a Dixie cup. They were also back to closely monitoring their water supply; Greg had switched off the plumbing along with the engines, so the only potable water they had was in a few plastic containers that Elissa had stashed in her cabin for a situation precisely like this.

Damn Greg, she thought. Damn that bastard.

"Obviously, our options are limited, and becoming more limited by the hour," Elissa said, from the head of the table. Over the past day, she seemed to have aged several years. She seemed feeble, drained. "The lifeboat is a horrifying prospect, I agree. But increasingly, it's our only choice."

Jennifer agreed: the lifeboat was horrifying. They would have to abandon their water and food supply and cram in, ten of them into an inflatable craft built for five, then hope it could sail forty miles. And what if the island was desolate? They'd have to cram back in and hope they could make it another forty miles back to the waiting boat… and that was assuming Greg didn't just resume sailing once he had the boat to himself.

And of course, Sam's condition made the whole proposition even more unappetizing.

Next to Elissa, Art held his weary head in his hands, staring blankly at the tabletop. He, too, seemed broken.

"We shouldn't be afraid," said Mel. "The Holy One will provide."

Jennifer took a spoonful of polenta to hide her disgust. Here they were trying to make the most difficult decision of their lives, and Mel was talking about fairy tales.

'There has to be something we can do," Rosalyn said.

Her pathetic comment lingered in the air like a foul smell. Nobody responded. Even Bahram seemed to sense the doctor's hopelessness.

"We do have enough drinking water for at least a few days if we ration well," said Art. "And after that it's going to be very hard to get ocean water we can distill without access to the engine room. We'll have to figure out an easy way to draw it up in one of those metal bowls."

Elissa shook her head.

"It's not just about that. It's about Greg. Most likely he has no food in there. And I mean. If he hurts himself…"

She didn't have to finish the thought: if Greg killed himself, the engine controls and water tanks would be sealed off until the end of time.

"I've been looking for another way in," Art said. "There must be ventilation shafts to the engine room. Otherwise you'd suffocate in there."

Jennifer padded her sweaty forehead with a piece of torn-up cotton sheet.

"I think we should go silent for a few hours at the door," she said. "And then I'll speak to him alone. He might be responsive. He tried to sleep with me several times."

Art perked up.

"Yeah. Go silent," he echoed. "Pique his curiosity. That could work. Then maybe pretend that we're hurting you. That you need his help."

"Why didn't you mention this before?" Rosalyn said.

Jennifer glared at the doctor.

"Because it wasn't anyone's business."

"Swallow your pride, you sad little girl," Rosalyn snapped. "Sam is dying."

Jennifer felt her cheeks burn.

"Jesus, how about blaming the guy who shoved the flashlight into his hernia?"

Art winced.

"I made a mistake…" he said softly. "A big mistake."

"Yeah, a big fucking mistake," Jennifer said. "Lying about the cigarettes for two weeks. I suppose that was an accident?"

Art sat up straight.

"I wouldn't have had to do that if you'd agreed to sail to the island in the first place. Oh, and you're welcome, by the way," he suddenly raised his voice to a trembling roar, "If it wasn't for me, we'd still be sitting on our asses waiting for the Navy to rescue us!"

"Arthur is right," Mel looked at her, eyes were wide and sad. "If it wasn't for him we wouldn't have gotten this far. I know it may seem strange to us, but it's all part of the Holy One's plan."

Rage swelled in Jennifer's breast. These people talked to her like she was a stupid little girl, when *they* were the fools. *They* hurt each other, *they* lied and manipulated, *they* warped justice, kneading it like dough until it suited their needs. *They* believed in fairy tales to distract themselves from what was happening right in front of them. And suddenly the thought of actually getting to this island and spending the rest of her life with these monsters seemed like a more heinous punishment than just dying out here on the open water.

Bahram was looking at her from across the table, holding his jeff cap to his chest. He was the only one she could tolerate. The only person on this boat who wasn't deranged, deluded, or simply pathetic. And she'd grown frustrated and abandoned him.

She looked down at her hands. Her nails were cut at crude angles from trying to clip them with a kitchen knife. Her palms were calloused and pink from gripping the axe. Her fingers were nicked with cuts from the splinters of the wooden crates, and bloody from long cuticles she'd plucked off in her sleep. Every part of her hands was covered in grime and toasted by the sun.

Staring at these hands, unrecognizable to her, she felt a hint of madness. She sensed there was an emergency ripcord she could yank on if she needed to flood her mind with nonsense and delusion, as these people obviously already had. The unreality would bring sweet, cool relief.

"Jennifer?' Art asked. "So you'll try to speak to Greg later?"

She retreated from the ripcord. Left it dangling in some dark corner of her mind and closed the door behind her. She wouldn't tug on it, not just yet.

45

When Sam was awake enough to feel anything, he felt like he was a pig skewered from anus to mouth, slow-cooking over a fire, his lower stomach directly over the flame. But most of the time the pain and fever pushed him in and out of dreams, and he hovered in a hazy purgatory.

Usually when he opened his eyes, Lily's face hovered above like an autumn moon. He could tell she was smiling only for his benefit, as one would for an infant. She held Dixie cups of water to his lips, wiped sweat off his forehead, and swapped out the mixing bowls he used when he vomited.

The air conditioning was gone. In one of his dreams, he was a mound of dough being baked in a convection oven.

"What happened to the island?" he asked Lily.

"Technical trouble. Don't worry," she answered.

"Got a cigarette?" he asked weakly. Every syllable cost him drips of precious energy.

"I don't know if you should…"

Sam would have laughed if it wasn't so painful.

"I don't think it can hurt at this point," he said, before closing his eyes and again submitting to the pain.

He thought about the night of his high school graduation. Most of the graduating class ended up at the same house party. Must have been two hundred kids there. The party was fine, but at some point Sam and three of his close friends went outside and sat on the cement curb that was the border between the lawn and the smooth asphalt cul-de-sac. One of his friends, Paul, handed out cigars he'd brought. Not cheap Swisher Sweets. Real Dominican cigars wrapped in dry black leaves, the tobacco smelled like what Sam imagined was the rainforest.

Paul passed around a fancy cigar lighter and thin sticks of cedar wood.

You light the wood, then use that to light the cigar. Otherwise the cigar gas can spoil the taste.

When it was Sam's turn he cupped the flame from the summer breeze and lit the wood.

Hold it to the tip and puff hard.

He complied, and was rewarded with a mouthful of fruity smoke so thick that it burned his eyes and made him double over coughing. All of them struggled at first, but soon got the hang of it. Each boy silently puffed and pretended to savor the rich aroma.

Behind them in the party, the raucous youth shrieked and laughed. Sam felt that the four of them had transcended this nonsense; were out here enjoying the finer things in life. One of the other boys, a jovial guy they called 'Bean' for reasons Sam never understood, held up his cigar and toasted them.

Congratulations guys. We made it.

The fourth boy clapped Bean on the back and raised his own half-gone cigar. He was a small boy with braces, who didn't play sports like the rest of them. Sam couldn't remember his name.

This is the beginning Bean. Now the good stuff starts.

Seven years later, Sam would ask Bean for a job at his marketing firm. He believed Bean made a genuine effort to find something for him, but it didn't pan out. He lost touch with Paul shortly after graduation. The small boy, Sam heard, became a psychiatrist.

Sam opened his eyes. Mel was sitting beside the bed. One leg was crossed over the other, supporting a stack of papers.

"Hi Sam," Mel said.

Sam could only form a gurgle in response.

"He's awake?"

It was Lily's voice somewhere in the distance.

"He is." Sam felt Mel's hand on top of his. "Are you feeling any better?"

Sam took a moment to form the word, then gasped: "No."

Mel nodded, as if he'd expected this response. Then he leaned in very close, maybe so Lily wouldn't hear him.

"Aaron, the brother of Moses died, in the wilderness, before the Israelites entered the promised land." Mel was speaking very fast, and it was difficult for Sam to follow. "The Holy One told him his time had come, so Aaron climbed mount *Hor*. At the lip of the cave, he undressed and entered. Inside the cave was a bed, and a candle. Aaron lay down on the bed face up, closed his eyes, and died. It's said for great men, death is as smooth as a hair pulled from warm milk."

Sam's eyes lost focus, then reformed Mel's pink face inches away from his.

"You're a great man, Samuel," he whispered. "Our children will know your name."

Sam blacked out again. Unknown hours passed. He saw the small boy with braces again holding his glowing cigar up against the night sky.

This is the beginning Bean. Now the good stuff starts.

He couldn't remember that boy's name.

Lily padded his forehead with a lukewarm compress. He wished the rag was colder. There was no ice on board.

"How are you feeling?" she asked.

Sam's throat burned from reflux, so he just smiled and gave a weary thumbs up. What he really wanted to ask was where Rosalyn was. If she'd come to visit, he hadn't been awake to see her.

"I thought I should tell you," Lily said, "it's not technical trouble. It's Greg. He locked himself in the engine room and turned off the engines. He doesn't even want to talk. It's horrible. He's so horrible…"

Lily trailed off and returned to mopping Sam's forehead.

"A few nights ago he came into my room and it feels really… well I don't know. I don't know."

She was trying to focus on sponging him off, but Sam could hear her shallow breaths as she tried to swallow something awful. With some effort–every movement was agony–he extended his hand and rubbed her forearm with two fingers. That was all it took. She dissolved, falling back into her chair sobbing.

Sam watched her cry for a while. Finally she wiped her eyes and smiled a little.

"You know what's weird? I was thinking about it, but I'm kinda jealous of Adam. If he makes a bad decision, he doesn't have to keep thinking about it you know?"

Sam wasn't sure he followed, but he did his best to nod.

The next time he came to he was desperately thirsty.

Art stood next to the bed, clutching his Dolphins hat to his chest with both hands. Sam noticed for the first time that Art had grown a thin grey beard.

"Sammy," Art exhaled, seeming relieved that Sam was awake. "Sammy boy…"

Sam didn't have the energy or wherewithal to think about anything but water.

"I'm so, so sorry buddy. I never meant for this to happen."

"Water," Sam croaked.

"Jesus. Sure, sure."

Art filled up a Dixie cup and held it to Sam's lips. Only about half the water actually got in his mouth. Then Art pulled over a chair and sat.

"I don't know what else to say except sorry. For everything. If there was any justice, I'd be the one lying there. I know that. I just hope you can somehow forgive me–though to be honest I wouldn't blame you if you didn't."

Art filled up another Dixie cup and took a sip.

"When it comes down to it, Sammy, I'm a real piece of shit."

<h1 style="text-align:center">46</h1>

Rosalyn sat on the steps outside the steel door to the engine room. Jennifer sat beside her, dutifully on hand in case Greg ever got close enough to the door to talk.

Vic had his ear pressed to the door, listening for any sign of Greg's footsteps.

Rosalyn had never trusted or liked Greg, she decided. From that first morning, when she'd thought it might just be the two of them on the ship, she'd found his smiles and jokes disconcerting, the recourse of an unstable mind.

Vic held a finger to his lips and strained against the door. Then shook his head.

"Never mind," he whispered.

This waiting was awful. Water was dwindling, and Rosalyn was fairly certain Sam had a ruptured hernia. If so, the only cure was surgery. Otherwise he'd be dead in two days, and that was generous. But to operate herself would be insane. Even if she could remember the required incision, they had no tools besides kitchen knives, and no means of sterilization save fire–totally insufficient for an invasive surgery.

Eventually, though, she'd have no choice but to try. She'd have to cut some skin from his back to use as a patch on the rupture. Someone would hold a warm saltwater compress on the wound to minimize bleeding, and Art's hands might be nimble enough to sew on the patch, and then help cauterize the incision shut.

The risk of infection would be sickening. The blood loss would be staggering. There was, she supposed, an infinitesimal chance that there would be more advanced medical equipment on the island. But even moving Sam to the life raft would be nearly impossible, and also likely to widen the rupture enough to just kill him on the spot.

So if nothing changed, she'd do the surgery here on board, in his cabin. It would fail, and Sam would die. Then she'd crawl into the life raft with the others, coated in Sam's blood.

The thought made her hands shake. Yes, Art would have to do the actual sewing.

Vic sat down on the metal grating, leaning against the door.

"I said from the start: we should have just relaxed."

Rosalyn stared at Vic. He truly was a fool, this sunflower-haired Frenchman. Was he trying to impress Jennifer with his bravado, even now?

"You're welcome to go jump in the sea," Rosalyn said.

Vic pursed his lips as if mulling this offer.

"Mel has said it's a great sin to take your own life," he said. "Unless the alternative is to slander God."

Jennifer laughed bitterly.

"It's so transparent. Religion is a virus."

"*Non, non–*" he waved his hands, trying to undo his mistake.

"It even programs the host organism to self-destruct rather than cure itself," Jennifer continued. "And Mel brought that virus on board with him. And he even wrote down his sick algorithm, so if anything happens to Mel, his virus will have a chance to survive." She raised her voice "Don't you *see* that Vic?"

Poor Vic was shriveling and squirming like a worm in the rain.

"Jenni–"

"Don't you see how stupid you are to listen to his dangerous lies?"

Just when Rosalyn decided to intervene. Vic perked up, turned, and smashed his ear against the door. His eyebrows flew up and his voice dropped to an urgent whisper:

"He's coming."

Rosalyn quickly moved to the side of the door, out of the range of the peephole.

Jennifer took a deep breath, and approached the door. She held a screwdriver behind her back. If Greg opened the door, she'd jam the screwdriver into the grated metal floor to prevent the door from closing again, while Vic and Rosalyn rushed in to tackle him.

Rosalyn held her breath. She could hear the footsteps nearing. Closer, closer. Then the footsteps stepped. He must have been standing right on the other side of the door.

"Greg?" Jennifer said.

Nothing. Vic was crouched, ready for action.

"Greg?" Jennifer repeated.

A long pause. Then Greg's muffled voice:

"Hey."

Rosalyn tried to will her hands to stop trembling.

This isn't real. None of this is real.

"Hey Greg," Jennifer said, as sweetly as she could manage. "Listen. Do you think I could come in? I wanna talk to you."

Rosalyn's heart was in her throat.

"What do you want to talk about?"

"Well I..." Jennifer's hands were curled into fists. "I'm just feeling really lonely. Remember how you said to come to you if I needed anything? Well... I want that now."

"Are they out there with you?" the voice from the other side asked.

"What? No. It's just me..." Rosalyn saw Jennifer clench the screwdriver even tighter. "I'm just feeling lonely. I want to be with you."

Silence.

"You have to be careful," said Greg, through the door. "The Chinagirl, she's fake. She's some kind of silicon bot."

Rosalyn motioned to Jennifer: *Keep talking.*

"I know," Jennifer said. "Lily is fake."

"Which others? Tell me."

Jennifer tried to hide her impatience and confusion.

"Vic," she said. "Mel–"

"Yes!" Greg cheered from inside. "I knew it. *I knew it.*"

"Yeah," Jennifer continued. "Listen, that's something I want to talk about. I'm getting scared of them. Can I come in? I think I'll be safer in there with you…"

Vic lowered his shoulder, getting ready to charge.

"You can't believe anything you see," Greg continued. "None of it is real."

The hairs on the back of Rosalyn's neck pricked up at hearing her mantra come from Greg's mouth.

"Wait. How do I know *you're* not one of them?"

Jennifer swallowed.

"I saw how it ended for Sammy," Greg continued. "He got out of line, so you put him down." Greg's muffled voice shot up an octave. "You wanna come in and finish me off too, you sneaky bitch? You want to drug me again don't you? Give me some of those hallucinogens? Well I got news for you: Greg Pink is *seeing clear baby.* The Feds are on their way, you know. You won't get away with this. The buck stops here! Aha! Get it? Buck! Because it's a deer! No? *No respect! I get no respect!*"

"Greg. Can we just talk face to–"

The voice behind the door devolved into histrionic laughter, and then they heard his footsteps again as he retreated from the door, his shrieks fading out.

"No respect! No goddamn respect!"

Silence. Vic rose from his crouch.

"He's gone completely mad," he said, his small black eyes still trained on the door.

"I shouldn't have asked to come in," Jennifer said, breathing hard. "It spooked him."

Rosalyn sat back down on the stairs and put her head in her hands. The silence was somehow more oppressive than the growl of the engines. It left space to hear your heart hammering blood into your ears; your teeth clacking against each other–stalactites and stalagmites grinding each other to dust; your impossibly loud thoughts. The cacophony of voices in her head, some hers some unidentifiable, all tried to shout over the others in a mutually assured destruction, all the voices pureed and swirled into something like the yellow mush of the polenta and daal mixture which, for weeks now, had just tasted like mud.

47

Bahram still couldn't figure out what was happening to all the sweat his face was pouring into the rubber mask, as they trudged through this oppressive heat–where did it go? Did he exhale the water, leaving his cheeks caked in organic salts? He was baking in this rubber oven. He spent most daylight hours fantasizing about ripping off this sick contraption, but every few minutes they passed another morbid reminder of why he couldn't.

They walked for an hour at a time, then took ten-minute rests. They hardly talked, because the masks made it so difficult.

Azzami was loaded down like a pack mule: he pulled the overstuffed black suitcase with one hand, and held the silver briefcase he'd gotten in the parking lot with the other. His big backpack must have burdened him another twenty kilos. He refused to let Adam or his parents help with any of these.

At the end of the first day, one of the wheels broke off the suitcase. Azzami resorted to dragging it on the ground, but eventually the fabric itself ripped apart, and they had to leave the suitcase. It was mostly loaded with food and water, and Azzami stuffed as much as he could in his backpack.

Their food supply was packets of white powder, which Azzami mixed with water until it congealed into the texture of watery pudding. They sucked up the yolky slurry through straws in their masks. It tasted like some kind of generic fruit, and left a revolting aftertaste in Bahram's mouth.

The highway was too congested with stopped cars, so they walked parallel to the road, through fields of high grass. Once they passed perhaps fifty dead cattle sprawled like a blanket across the land. Azzami had tied Adam's wrist to his own with steel cable so he wouldn't wander off, and the way the young man trotted dutifully in tow he too seemed like some kind of livestock.

Around noon on the third day they passed an orchard. Bahram noticed something wrong with the trees. The fruits were swollen and bloated, like they were puffed up with air. He let go of Keti's hand and wandered closer to the nearest of the trees. Even through his dirty visor he could tell the colors of the tree were all wrong. The leaves were turning purple around the edges and oozing something that looked like syrup. Azzami grabbed him by the shoulder.

Don't touch it!

The sky grew cloudier each day, until the sun disappeared completely. The air became so hazy that objects just ten meters in front of them became blurry.

Each evening they camped somewhere in a field, somewhere far enough from the highway that they didn't have to see the bodies in the cars.

They sat in a circle and slurped down the vile drink as the sun set. Once it was night, the darkness was absolute. The first two nights, lights from a plane occasionally broke through the sky, illuminating it for a moment, but by the third night there were no more planes. There was no moon or stars; they were probably hidden by the thick clouds. They had two flashlights, but Azzami instructed them to use them only when necessary.

There wasn't much talking; the masks muffled their voices and also made it hard to hear unless you were really face to face. So as Bahram and Keti curled up together on the soft earth, they communicated with their bodies; nothing of real meaning, just reassuring squeezes and caresses. As hard as all the walking was on his hips, he knew Keti was having the hardest time of all. Her legs were short and her feet were small. Still, she never slowed down the group or showed any sign of weakness.

Their son always slept far enough away to give his parents some privacy. Azzami kept Adam tied to his wrist, even while they slept. Bahram wondered what was going through Adam's head. He thought about the way Azzami had stolen him from that white building with a gun, and essentially kept him as a prisoner since. At least he and Keti had each other. Adam was with three strangers, two of whom he couldn't even speak to, being dragged through a nightmarish hellscape by his wrist. How could he not attempt escape? How could he be so docile? He really was like some kind of well-trained animal.

Five days after they left the car, they saw the ocean. It was morning, but the sky was dark and brooding. Azzami stopped and consulted a map and some huge green highway signs. He spoke for what seemed like the first time in years, voice muffled by the mask.

We're only a few kilometers north of the ship.

They picked up the pace, buoyed by the prospect of this miserable march finally coming to an end. But the closer they got to the coast, the denser the mass of cars and bodies, and soon they couldn't avoid walking directly through the heaps of corpses. Bahram tried not to look, but there was a kind of primal curiosity that kept him glancing down at the gaping faces that stared up at him wide-eyed, as if asking him to explain what had happened to them. He was thankful that he couldn't smell anything through the mask. But still the sight of children, in particular, made him sick. He tried to think of other things; he didn't know what would happen if he vomited with the mask on. The thought was unspeakable.

Azzami led them past a once-beautiful lawn. They kept to the walkway, avoiding plots of wilting violets and tulips, a stagnant fountain on which floated greying lily pads. Bahram glanced up and discovered that the lawn belonged to a towering building right off the coast. Their son led them inside.

The lobby was still mostly intact. Dead chandeliers hung from the high ceilings. The body of a young man in a suit was slumped forward over the concierge desk. Azzami searched for a staircase, then rushed them up three flights to a dark hallway. They padded over soft carpet until Azzami found an unlocked room. He jerked Adam inside, and Bahram and Keti followed.

The room was far nicer than any they'd stayed in over the past weeks. One wall was a glass door that led out onto a spacious balcony facing the sea. Azzami leaned in close enough to speak through his mask, first to Adam in English, then to his parents:

Sit down for a second and rest.

Bahram and Keti collapsed on the bed while Azzami dug around in his backpack until finding a pair of binoculars. With the hand not fastened to Adam, he held the binoculars to the visor of his mask and scanned the horizon through the glass door, slowly revolving, until he stopped suddenly, apparently finding what he was looking for. He stared for a long moment, then dropped the binoculars and slumped down in a cushy chair, perhaps troubled, or deep in thought. Adam was still staring in the direction of the sea, motionless.

Azzami finally stood up, and approached his parents on the bed, dragging Adam along with him.

Mother. Father.

His voice was wrong, and not just from the mask.

I know I've misled you at every turn. I know you don't understand what's happening. But I need you to do exactly as I say one more time, or else all is for nothing.

Bahram looked at Azzami, hoping for a glance of his son's eyes behind the opaque visor. He saw only the reflection of his own mask.

What would you like us to do, Son?

I'm taking Adam now to the port. There is a ship docked there. And... a woman waiting for us. You need to follow me and Adam, but far behind. You can't let her see you.

He handed Keti the binoculars.

Once we go onto the ship, wait a few minutes, then follow. Go below deck and find a cabin. Soon the engines will start. Stay in the cabin. Keep your masks on for at least two hours after the engines start. Then you can take off your masks and go up to the control tower, where I'll leave this food for you. You will see Adam there. Don't touch him, or the navigation equipment. All you have to do is wait, and the ship will take you to a safe place.

Bahram shook his head.

I don't understand. Where will you be? Where is the ship going?

The mask of his son was silent for a moment.

You and Mother will be the only ones who get to enter paradise. In English we call it the New World. You're not supposed to. They think that anyone besides the Adams and Eves will taint it with their memories of this filthy world. They're mostly right. I would, certainly. But they don't know you. Father, Mother. I was a disturbed, broken child, but neither of you ever raised a hand at me. Instead you taught me how to find meaning in working with my hands, how to have compassion for animals, how to deal with the anger that I felt at God for making me... You taught my brothers and sister to accept and love me...

He trailed off. He had more to say, perhaps, but stopped himself. Instead their son unholstered his pistol and handed it to Bahram.

If you see anybody else on the way to the ship, kill them.

Azzami stood up from the bed, pulled on his camping backpack, and picked up the grey briefcase. Bahram and Keti slowly returned to their feet.

The few minutes of rest had made Bahram's legs and knees lock up, and when he stood, fire shot down from his butt to his toes.

Azzami put his hand on Adam's shoulder and led the young man out of the hotel room. Bahram and Keti followed the two young men back the way they'd come, down the stairs, out of the lobby, back to the lawn and fountain.

Follow us, but from a distance.

Then Azzami led Adam down the walkway, passed the lawn, in the direction of the sea.

Bahram and Keti waited, holding hands, then when the two figures were just out of sight, followed.

They followed them down a boardwalk that ran parallel to the coast, again trying to ignore the bodies. Eventually a white mass became the hull of a ship. This was where Azzami and Adam were heading. They followed.

There was a figure sitting beside the gangplank. Keti stopped and looked through the binoculars. Whatever she saw shook her, and she gripped Bahram's hand and urged him closer to the action. They crouched low, keeping an eye on the scene, and stopped maybe twenty meters away, behind a car.

They were now close enough to see that the figure was a woman, dressed entirely in black, wearing a gas mask identical to theirs. She was holding a large automatic rifle.

As Azzami and Adam neared she raised the rifle, and in response their son quickly lifted the grey briefcase high in the air. Her whole demeanor shifted once she saw the briefcase. She put the gun on the deck and pulled up her black shirt to reveal a burn just above her belly button. Azzami rolled up his shirt to display his own corresponding burn. Then she rushed to them. She embraced Azzami like an old friend, and then turned slowly to Adam. She sank to her knees and prostrated herself at Adam's feet, clutching the young man's ankles.

That was when Bahram noticed the bodies spread out all around the dock. He'd seen enough bodies that had died of sickness to know this was something different. The awkward angle of their limbs showed that they'd died in action. Some of them were wearing gas masks themselves. The wood beneath the bodies was stained with blood. They hadn't died of disease or gas. All of them had been shot as they tried to approach the ship.

The woman finally released Adam's ankles, rose to her knees, and gazed up at Adam's masked face for a moment. Then stood up and led Azzami and Adam to her camp at the base of the gangplank.

Bahram took the binoculars from Keti.

The woman had her own grey briefcase, identical to Azzami's. They pressed the two briefcases against each other, and each clicked open. Bahram had never considered before how strange it was that Azzami's briefcase had neither a keyhole or a number combination lock.

They carefully placed the open briefcases down on the wood dock. From their respective briefcases, each delicately removed a syringe filled with gold fluid, and a digital watch. Azzami and the woman each put on the watches. Bahram focused on the syringes. What was this? Were they going to drug Adam?

The woman rolled up her sleeve and Azzami did the same. He injected her, she injected him, then they each immediately hit buttons on their watches.

There was some kind of deeper compartment within each briefcase. Azzami and the woman each worked on the other's briefcase; they each only knew the code to the other's, Bahram figured.

The trapdoor to the inner chamber swung open in each briefcase, and they pulled out two pieces of shiny fabric, each about the size of a pillowcase. No, not fabric. The material was shiny and heavy. It was metal; it looked like chainmail. They held the two textiles together, as they'd just held together their briefcases, and Bahram saw that together they completed a garment, approximately a long-sleeve shirt, though with precise shapes cut out from the chest and arms.

Keti grabbed his wrist. She wanted the binoculars back. Bahram slapped his wife's hand away, but she didn't relent. She yanked the binoculars from him with astounding strength.

Even without the binoculars, Bahram could still mostly see what was happening. The woman had Adam pinned on his back against the wood dock. She had her own supply of steel cable, and she used it to bind his hands and feet to four rivets at the foot of the gangplank. Azzami and the woman kneeled and fastened the garment on Adam's chest, even as the poor man struggled and squirmed.

The woman was now holding a silver tube. She held a lighter to the nozzle, and a stream of blue flame shot from the tip. A blowtorch. She held the flame to Adam's chest.

Even from twenty meters away, with his ears wrapped in rubber, Bahram heard Adam's muffled scream.

Keti dropped the binoculars. Her slender hands were tensed like claws. Adam screamed again, and his wife recoiled like she'd been punched in the stomach.

Again Bahram thought of the goat, hooded and bound. The kill is supposed to be instant, a flash of blade against the jugular vein. But on one occasion his friend's father made a mistake and missed the mark by perhaps half a centimeter. The goat flailed and made the worst sound Bahram had ever heard, a bleating cry that Barham felt in his spine. It seemed the goat was crying out not for her own suffering, but for the sad, cruel ways of the world that led to this moment–

Keti wasn't at his side. Bahram looked up and his heart stopped. She was running toward Azzami, Adam, and the woman, waving her arms and yelling through her mask.

Stop! Azzami! Stop!

Bahram tried to call out to his wife, but his voice was stuck in his throat. The woman and Azzami stopped their work, both momentarily frozen by the sight of this small woman rushing toward them.

Azzami!

The woman calmly reached for her rifle, and took aim. Azzami lunged at the gun but wasn't fast enough. Four loud cracks filled the air and Bahram's wife crumpled to the deck.

Azzami wrenched the rifle from the woman, only for her to unholster a hunting knife and lunge at him. Azzami swung at her with the butt of the rifle, catching her in the shoulder.

Bahram felt he was watching this whole scene on television, from a couch on the dark, silent bottom of the ocean. Keti's left leg was folded backwards beneath her. One of the eye holes of her mask was shot out. Bahram found that he was draped over the hood of the car and unable to will himself to move.

The woman straddled Azzami's chest, trying to stab him. Her jabs were wild and fierce, and one cut through his black shirt and found purchase with something firm underneath. She raised the knife again. Azzami grabbed her wrist to prevent a death blow. Unfazed, she kneed him in the groin, once, twice... Beside them, Adam thrashed silently against his restraints.

What was all of this, Bahram thought. What was all of this?

With her free hand, the woman reached for Azzami's neck. Not to strangle him. Instead she undid the neck clasp of his mask, and pulled it off his head.

Azzami instantly lost his grip on her wrist. His body convulsed like he was being electrocuted. The woman, satisfied, climbed off of his chest. Azzami's hands groped emptily toward the sky, then fell to his sides. He spasmed once again and then went still.

The woman checked her watch, the one that had been in her briefcase, then quickly returned to Adam. She reignited the blowtorch.

Adam's howling, as the woman picked up where she'd left off, barely registered with Bahram. He was on the hood of the car, unmoving, a deep weariness like he'd never known before seeping into his bones.

The woman finished. She unfastened the chainlink garment from Adam's chest and tossed it into the strip of brackish water between the deck and the ship. Then she untied Adam from the pegs and dragged him to his feet. The young man could hardly support himself, so the woman kneeled and pulled him over her shoulders in a fireman's carry. Teetering beneath Adam's weight, she started up the gangplank, supporting his limp body with one hand, dragging a duffel bag behind her, her steps rhythmic and brutally efficient, as if her legs were pistons being cranked by an internal combustion engine. Finally she disappeared over the lip of the ship.

Even from the dark bottom of the ocean, Bahram saw that this was the moment he had to decide whether to continue living. It was only the thought of his children and grandchildren in Afghanistan that made him shove off the car and stagger toward the gangplank, forcing himself not to look down at his wife or son; he didn't want those memories.

He climbed the slippery ramp slowly. He felt like his blood had been replaced by cold jelly.

At the top, he grabbed the railing and carefully lowered himself onto the deck. Then he saw the woman climbing a metal staircase, still carrying Adam and dragging her bag.

This woman was surely going to kill the boy.

Bahram closed his eyes for a moment. This wasn't what he imagined anguish would feel like: complete and utter exhaustion. He opened his eyes, hoping to find himself in a different place. But alas, there was the woman nearing the summit: a glass control tower. Bahram stumbled after her.

The steps were very slippery and he nearly tripped several times, saving himself only by holding fast to the hot railing. At the top of the stairs, he came to a sliding glass door. He saw that the woman had put Adam on the floor next to a swivel chair, and tied his ankle to the base with steel cord; the same kind Azzami had used. Adam was unconscious, but breathing. The burns on his chest had the consistency and color of chewed bubblegum. They were letters and numbers, Bahram saw. The metal garment had been a kind of stencil.

The woman worked with astonishing speed. She pulled a framed mirror from her duffle bag and secured it to a window across from the stool with four pieces of putty. Then she dashed to one of the panels.

She consulted her phone for reference, turned a dial, pushed a button, then suddenly fell forward onto the dashboard. Her chest heaved. She struggled to pull herself upright. She looked at her watch and rubbed the spot on her arm where Azzami had given her the injection.

Bahram was too exhausted and confused to do anything but just open the door and walk in.

She didn't even notice him as he walked toward her; her hearing was muffled by the mask and also it seemed something was very wrong with her.

When she finally turned and saw Bahram standing there, she didn't even go for her weapon. Instead she shouted something at him and pointed at the control panel. Then she gestured to the floor–or something below the floor–and screamed something urgent that Bahram, of course, couldn't understand. She convulsed again, and doubled over. Bahram got a glimpse of her watch. It was a countdown timer, with only three and a half minutes left. When she recovered, she pointed at the burns on Adam's chest and again yelled something while pointing to the controls.

Then she lurched out of the glass room.

Bahram watched her climb down the stairs, all her poise gone. She swayed like she was drunk. And with a few stairs left, she lost her grip and tumbled down to the deck, landing in an awkward heap. He realized he was still holding the binoculars, and from his vantage point he watched as she flopped up to her hands and knees and crawled to the railing at the edge of the ship. She used the railing to pull herself upright. She leaned halfway over the ledge. Bahram watched as she unfastened her mask at the neck, tugged it off and let it fall. She had beautiful red hair and clear white skin. She looked in his direction, but Bahram could tell she couldn't see him. Anyway, her eyes were looking somewhere far away; she was inside of a memory. Then with her last remaining ounce of strength she leaned out just a bit more and toppled over the railing, plunging into the murky water of the port.

Bahram turned back to Adam. The wounds on the young man's chest were already starting to harden into raised pink wounds. He remembered Azzami's instructions: his son had said the engines would start, and they were to wait until they'd sailed at least two hours before they took off their masks. But the woman hadn't been able to start the engines. He spoke to the young man, lying on the floor of this room:

I will save us, Adam.

But his optimism soon faded. There were hundreds of buttons and dials in this room, and he couldn't read any of the labels. He left Adam tied to the swivel chair, bearing in mind what Azzami had said:

Like a blade of grass. If it's not connected to the earth, it will just blow away.

Bahram walked around the ship. The engines were below; maybe there would be some way to turn them on down there.

He found the engine room, but here the cause felt even more hopeless: row after row of machines and buttons, all labeled in an alien tongue.

He slid down onto the rubber floor. He felt like he'd been opened up and emptied out. Everything was in vain. Keti and Azzami were dead, and soon he would be as well. At least he'd had a good life. Keti too. Death was only a tragedy if it came too soon. In any case, his fatigue was so complete he didn't even have the energy to mourn or eulogize. He wanted only to submit.

He sat there for hours, until finally climbing back up the metal stairs. He teetered down a hallway, and pushed into the first door he came upon. There was a bed, his deathbed, but he tripped over the leg of a chair and tumbled to his knees. He sunk into the carpet, and was asleep in an instant.

At some point Bahram thought he heard someone enter the room, close the door, then collapse onto the springy bed beside him, but in his state he couldn't be sure if it was real.

48

Elissa McClure sat with Lily and Doctor Rosalyn on the bridge about an hour after sunset. Until the last moments of daylight they'd been looking at the island on the horizon, hoping for who knows what... Smoke? A rescue helicopter? There'd been nothing, and the longer they stared at the little blob, the more pathetic yesterday morning's ecstasy seemed. What was the difference whether the eleven of them were on this ship, or standing on dry land?

A renewable source of food, perhaps, if the island was large and fertile enough. Maybe water too if, again, the island was large enough, and they could set up some kind of tarp system to catch rainwater. They'd soon find out. Dwindling potable water and Sam's deteriorating condition meant they would be forced to all cram into the lifeboat in the next day or two, with as much food as they could carry and what little water they had.

Elissa wiped her glasses. Sam would probably die if they tried to move him to the lifeboat. Though, truthfully he'd die soon anyway. Everyone knew it, but didn't dare say it out loud. She imagined them arriving at the island without Sam or Greg, all desperately thirsty, but the island would be nothing but a sandbar. And they'd collapse from thirst and die baking alive.

Lily looked very tired. Doctor Rosalyn, too, seemed to have crawled inside her own head since darkness fell, breaking only for the occasional, cursory compass check, to see if the ship was rotating. Not that it particularly mattered at this point. Elissa watched the dark sea through the glass window. It was raining a bit, and little drops tickled the windows of the bridge.

Lily, mindlessly fiddling with buttons, accidentally turned on all the external lights. For a moment the whole bow of the ship and all of the brightly colored containers were bathed in a ghostly glow. The black frothing sea, too, was illuminated for maybe thirty feet ahead of them. Beyond the range of the lights was absolute black stretching all directions.

"Oops," Lily said sheepishly, quickly flicking the lights back off. With the engines off, it was important to save the battery. "Sorry."

Lily hadn't been her usual chatty self for days. Obviously it could have just been the trying circumstances, but Elissa suspected she'd also finally been rebuffed by Greg. It was obvious that that would happen, and this was half the reason Elissa had tried to talk her out of pursuing him. The other half though was the truth: Lily was too good for him. But Lily Chen would never believe that.

Lily's eyes were misted over, disengaged from her surroundings. She'd stopped tending to her hair entirely, and the black oily mass hung off the side of her head. Each time she moved, it flailed like an angry octopus. Lily's once-red shirt was filthy and bleached from the sun. It was also too big for her now, given how much weight she'd lost—she'd withered away everywhere but her cheeks—which only added to the pathetic spectacle.

But Lily hardly looked more pathetic or wretched than the rest of them, Elissa thought, turning her gaze to Doctor Rosalyn. Holes on the doctor's jeans had widened to the point that she was basically wearing rags from the knee down. Her cheeks, nose, and forehead had gone through so many iterations of sunburn that they seemed to be stained a permanent burgundy. For weeks now, the doctor seemed unable to keep her eyes at rest; they darted constantly from side to side, like she wasn't sure from which side the inevitable attack would come.

They were so far from home. Looking out on the dark water, Elissa thought about her apartment in Soho. Her softly-lit bedroom, her cozy bed, covered in a huge down comforter and fluffy down pillows. The grotesquely large TV facing her bed that she almost never watched. Her walls and walls of bookcases filled exclusively with–she was proud to say–books she'd read cover to cover. That was the rule: she wasn't allowed to use a book as decoration until she'd read it. Her art deco, stainless steel kitchen where she'd been trying a new recipe every night from her Flavors of India cookbook.

She'd bought her Soho apartment for a pittance forty-three years ago, and today it was worth at least four million dollars. Without meaning to, she'd built a pretty valuable estate. It was only at one of her employee's insistence that she finally met with a lawyer to write a will.

She'd been getting Halal with Jake Flanders, who'd traded oil equities on her floor for twelve years. He was a skinny, conscientious man who she enjoyed eating with because he didn't talk to her like she was his boss.

Anna and I were at the lawyer yesterday. Updating our will. Crazy thing, really. Hard to wrap your head around.

Would you believe I don't have a will?

Jake nearly choked on his chicken shawarma.

You don't have a will!? Elissa are you insane?

What. I'm not planning on dying anytime soon.

How could you, *of all people not have a will. You understand risk better than anyone I've ever met. And well, to be frank, you're in your seventies. I don't want to insult you, but it's just plain old statistics–*

I know.

A month later Jake brought it up again. Again she demurred. A few weeks later, Jake told her he'd made her an appointment with his estate lawyer because he knew she wasn't going to take care of it herself.

That was some serious chutzpah, Jake.

Just take the appointment. And be careful crossing the street on the way there.

Begrudgingly, Elissa put it in her calendar.

The lawyer was a small woman who seemed too young and healthy to work in this field.

It's good you came. Nobody wants to do this, I know. It's like making an appointment with the grim reaper. But it's the right thing to do, for your loved ones.

It shouldn't take long. Just write something up that says that everything goes to my sister and her kids. That's it. 25k to each of her kids and the rest to her.

The lawyer sifted through Elissa's tax returns, bank statements, property deeds.

What about charity? You have a lot of assets. Maybe you'd like to consider apportioning a couple percent to a charity? I can recommend some organizations that I know well, where your money will be used efficiently.

Sure. Five percent to wherever you think. Good idea.

The lawyer kept sifting through the papers, like to stretch the appointment to take up the whole hour.

Elissa pushed her glasses up on her nose.

It's a lot of money, isn't it.

The lawyer blushed.

No, I–

It is. It's way too much for one old woman. I don't even use it. I still take the bus to work sometimes.

The lawyer seemed uncomfortable.

I'm sure you work very hard.

Yes. I work extremely hard. Insanely hard. Seventy-hour weeks are pretty standard for me.

Have you considered retirement? You certainly have enough to live on comfortably.

And what? Move to Boca? Learn to play tennis? Travel to Paris and eat rich food and take pictures of the Eiffel Tower?

I–

I'd kill myself. I'm not even exaggerating. I'd literally kill myself.

The lawyer nodded, and shuffled the papers mindlessly.

So everything goes to my sister's family. Do you need any more details?

The lawyer seemed relieved to be back in familiar territory.

Your sister's information, and her childrens'. Social security numbers, address, and contact information. That should be it. I'll write this up within a week and you can come back and we'll sign and notarize it.

That evening, Elissa hadn't been able to concentrate on the Austen novel she was rereading. The meeting had stirred up exactly the feelings she'd feared it would.

She was supposed to go back the following Tuesday to sign the will, but on Friday the first bomb fell on Los Angeles.

Elissa closed her eyes and listened to the soft rain drum against the bridge windows. She wondered how she would have gotten along with any of these people if she'd met them in New York. She smiled at the thought of Vic stepping into her office for an interview. Or Lily. Or Greg. Or Sam. She would have known none of them were hirable after about twenty seconds, but would have granted them fifteen minutes just to be cordial, and for the sake of her reputation. She liked to think she would have given Art, Mel, or Doctor Rosalyn more of a chance, but honestly doubted it.

Elissa pulled herself out of this trance.

"Any updates on Sam's condition?" she asked Rosalyn. No answer. The doctor was gazing at the rain on the glass windows, her brown eyes unfocused. Elissa cleared her throat. "Doctor?"

The dermatologist jerked to attention, and smiled dreamily at the two other women.

"Oh," she said. "I… guess I just lost myself there."

Elissa wondered

"Were you thinking about your husband?" Lily asked.

"Lily–" Elissa started.

"Yes, actually," Rosalyn replied, not seeming to be bothered at all by the intrusive question.

"What was his name?" Lily asked.

"Scott."

"You miss him?" Lily pushed.

Elissa wanted to stop this line of questioning, but bit her tongue; she was the one who was uncomfortable, she realized. Not Rosalyn.

"Yes. I miss him a lot. I thought maybe it would get better with a little time but it isn't. Getting better."

"What was he like?" Lily asked.

Rosalyn hesitated.

"Very, very smart. Very sarcastic. Extremely sweet, but you had to dig a lot. He cared a lot about other people, but was self-conscious about showing it. I never knew why."

Elissa, resigned that this conversation was going to happen, took a seat between the two women.

"That's so amazing." Lily's voice was breaking a little. "Was he romantic? Did he bring you flowers and chocolates? Did he ever just kiss you for no reason?"

Rosalyn was silent for a moment, thinking.

"No," she finally laughed. "No, he never did any of those things."

Lily nodded and went quiet. Elissa was getting restless. It was time to go keep Jennifer company while she waited for Greg next to the engine room door, and then to stop by Sam's room to check on him. She needed to feel like she was doing something.

She was about to head down the interior staircase when she heard a clang outside. She looked out. Someone was rushing up the external metal staircase to the bridge, holding the flashlight. Art came in, damp and panting.

"Evening gals," he said, sitting down to catch his breath. "I've got good news and bad news."

"What's the good news?" Lily asked.

"What's the bad news?" Elissa asked.

"The good news is I found a ventilation shaft that I'm pretty sure leads into the engine room. The bad news is it's narrow."

Elissa frowned.

"How narrow?"

"I can't fit, that's for sure," Art hesitated, looking at her. "I think you're the only one who has a chance."

Elissa nodded.

"Alright."

"Also," Art cleared his throat, "there's a smell."

49

There were ten ventilation shafts that opened onto the deck. Each had to be connected to the HVAC system, which serviced the living quarters, bridge, and the engine room. Each shaft could well be a maze, branching and delivering air to dozens of endpoints across the ship. A limb that terminated in one of the cabins wouldn't be passable–the vents in the rooms were much more narrow than the openings above deck. But the vents in the engine room were, if Art's memory served, roughly the same size as these above-board openings, necessary because it could get so damn hot down there.

At least one of the crawl spaces would lead to the engine room, but trial and error wasn't really an option. Besides the wasted time, and Elissa's limited strength and energy, it was quite possible that a wrong turn would be lethal: if she ended up in a branch that led to a cabin, it would be too narrow to squeeze down, but likely too steep to retrace her steps.

Art had worked through the night, prying the fans off every vent on deck. Under the morning sun, they gathered around the shaft he felt was their best shot.

"The sewage smell is the strongest for this one. The pipes and system must be backed up since the engines are off and our waste isn't being processed, " he explained to Elissa, Lily, Jennifer, Rosalyn, Vic, and Bahram. Mel was sitting with Sam. Adam was unaccounted for. "This vent is also, by my reckoning, directly above the bow side of the engine room. I figure it's as close as we'll get to a straight shot down there."

"You are sure?" Vic asked, puffing hard on a Marlboro.

Art wiped cold sweat off his forehead. It was hard to blame this tone-deaf comment on Frenchy's poor grasp of English. It was more like a lack of situational awareness, subtext, body language, etc.

"Sure? No, I'm not sure," he sighed. "Of course not. I can only see so far down with the flashlight."

"What if she gets stuck?" asked Lily.

Art took a deep breath. He was exhausted and irritable.

What do you think will happen if Elissa gets stuck, Lily? She'll die one of the worst deaths imaginable, slowly dying of thirst while suspended in a hot, dark shaft that smells like sewage.

"Maybe we should just take the lifeboat," said Rosalyn. "It's not worth the risk."

"The lifeboat is also a risk," Elissa reminded her. "An enormous risk. We'd abandon our water supply and most of our food supply. And we don't know the boat's range. No, it's okay. I'm the one taking the risk. I said I'll go."

Art nodded, tight lipped, feeling less and less confident with this plan.

"We can also wait another day," Rosalyn said. "See if Greg gets hungry enough to come out."

"We're running out of water," Elissa said.

Rosalyn rubbed a hand through her hair, and said nothing. Next to her stood Jennifer, silent, arms folded across her chest. Something was brewing behind those cold eyes.

"We'll use this rope," Art said, indicating the coil at his feet, several lengths tied together. "It's synthetic. It was keeping a deconstructed grand piano from shifting around in a container. It's definitely strong enough, and we should have enough slack to lower Elissa all the way down."

He handed her the Phillips screwdriver, a small needle-nose pliers, and a flashlight. He hoped everyone was distracted enough to forget what he'd done with the flashlight just two days ago.

"I assume any vent covering in the engine room will be screwed in from the outside, as they are up here. So you'll probably need the pliers to take off the nuts, and won't need the screwdriver. But best take it, just in case."

"What about a kitchen knife?" Jennifer finally broke her silence. "For Greg."

Jennifer's locked jaw and folded arms seemed to be challenging someone to argue with her. Art didn't disagree at all. He'd considered the knife too, of course, but thought it would be best for someone else to raise the possibility.

"He may be dead already," Vic said. "We've not heard from him in a full day."

Lily seemed physically jarred by this suggestion. Art wondered how her crush on Mr. Hollywood was holding up these days.

"Yes, but he might not be," said Rosalyn. "I agree you should bring one, Elissa. To protect yourself. He's obviously unstable."

Elissa pulled off her glasses and wiped the lenses with the fabric of her blouse. Without the glasses she looked older, and Art's heart shuddered as he again thought through what was happening here: sending a seventy-something year old woman down a ventilation shaft, and hoping she could overpower a young, fit–albeit very hungry–man.

"I'm not bringing a knife," she said. "What's the point? I'm not going to stab him."

"Why not?" Jennifer asked. "He's effectively going to kill all of us."

"Because we are civilized people," Elissa said, returning her small glasses to their usual perch. "And we don't stab the mentally ill. Now," she turned to Art, "show me what to do with the rope. Should I tie it around my waist?"

"Definitely not," Art said, relieved that the conversation had moved on from passenger-on-passenger violence. "Around the waist could be bad." He picked up the end of the rope and tied it in a sort of harness that wrapped under Elissa's boney armpits and around her upper thighs. "Sorry," he said, apologizing for the intimacy of looping the rope through her groin. She just smiled, as if the insinuation of intimacy between two old fogies, especially at this particular moment, amused her.

Art undid his belt and tried to fasten it around Elissa's waist, but she was too skinny. After he made a new hole with the screwdriver, the belt nearly looped around her twice. Then he tucked the screwdriver and pliers between the belt and her hips.

"I suggest the following system," Art continued. "Hopefully we'll be able to hear your voice, but in case we can't: one tug means give you more slack, two tugs means something's wrong and to pull you back up."

Elissa nodded dutifully, and flipped the flashlight on. Her lack of hesitation was shocking. She was the most gung-ho of all of them.

Lily stepped forward, and offered Elissa a Dixie cup of precious water. Elissa took it and shot it down like it was an energy drink; like Olive Oil with a stolen stash of Popeye's spinach. Then Elissa put her feet into the shaft and dropped her torso through the opening. She dangled, Art and Vic holding her up with the rope. It was very, very tight. Even with her elbows tucked into her chest she didn't have more than a few inches on either side. Art and Vic prepared to lower her into the darkness. For a moment Art wondered if he would have had the balls to go down this vent, and then quickly decided the answer was, obviously, no.

She looked up at the six of them. "If I'm not back in two hours, take the lifeboat," she said, and then disappeared.

50

There was very little for Lily to do besides hold Sam's clammy palm and speak gently to him. From time to time his eyelids fluttered, and she thought maybe he was looking at her. But he hadn't been responsive since she'd swapped out nurse duty with Mel.

She thought about Elissa in the dark ventilation shaft. And then she tried to imagine Greg after two days without food, barricaded in the darkness. What the hell had he been doing this whole time?

Lily remembered Greg's face, staring down at her with such intensity it was like he was trying to bore holes in her with his eyes. She'd initially taken this for some extreme form of intimacy, known only to the elites–actors, rock stars, billionaires–and this was her initiation into this secret world of pleasure. But as the act continued, unexpectedly mechanical, she saw in the dim light that he wasn't in pleasure at all. His gaze was more like he was standing at the mouth of a dark cave, peering into the abyss with dread. Then she thought he wasn't so much looking at her, as looking through her. Or trying to.

His face looked like a ball of clay being mashed angrily by a potter. He shuddered, gnashed his teeth, and then went limp.

Wow, that was tremendous.

Lily said nothing. He stood up and smiled, even as his left leg jittered uncontrollably. She was suddenly frightened of him.

I'm just gonna hop up to the deck and get some air for a sec.

He closed the door gently behind him, and left her alone in silence. She was too stunned to sob; that would come later. Instead for an hour, maybe more, she just stared at the blank wall across from her bed, shaking.

She squeezed Sam's cold hand.

"How are you feeling?" she said. His eyes remained closed. His face was the color of boiled beets.

It's important in life, Lily thought as she lit a Marlboro, to have something to look forward to. It didn't have to be a lot, just a kernel of an idea of something good that could happen next month or next year. After the Michael debacle, she'd doubled the hours she was putting in in the kitchen, trying out new salad dressing recipes, imagining growing her business until she could quit the call center. She decided she'd have her bottles in every Whole Foods in the country: Teriyaki-Carrot-Sesame, Tahini-Orange Blossom, Dijon with Honeycomb Infusion, Maple-Habanero, Guatemalan Cocoa-Vinaigrette. And every bottle would have a drawing of her smiling face on the label and written in cursive: *Lily's Luscious Liquids*. Well. She'd never quite settled on a brand name.

The little reverie dissipated, like the cigarette smoke curling from her nostrils. There was only her and Sam in this hot, damp cabin. Sam's mouth was an O, and his breathing was raspy.

She puffed on her cigarette. She thought about herself, two days ago on the railing, staring at the island on the horizon. How pathetic she imagined she must have looked, misty-eyed with her dreams of a tropical paradise. How strange, actually, that her memories were in third person. In fact, her memories of the night with Greg were also in third person, as if taken from a camera opposite the bed. When she replayed the night, she wasn't looking up at Greg, she was watching herself holding her knees to her chest as he flopped around on top of her like a seal. She zoomed in on her face, and was sickened by what she saw. A stupid little Chinese girl, with fat cheeks, contorting herself into a loading dock.

Sam squeezed her hand back. She put out her cigarette, and leaned over. Was he waking up?

"Sam?" she said. "Can you hear me? Are you okay?"

He opened his eyes and looked at the ceiling, made a phlegmy sound, and wheezed.

He gargled, and then stopped. His eyes were wide open and his hands were totally limp. He'd stopped breathing.

Lily ashed her cigarette onto the carpet and went up to the deck to tell the others.

51

Sam's body seemed to be even larger now than when he'd inhabited it. It was the first time Vic Fournier had seen a dead body, not counting his grandmother's open-casket funeral when he was eight. Mel told nobody to touch the body, that it was impure. He cut off Sam's clothes, keeping a blanket over the groin for modesty. He then washed the corpse's feet and hands with grey water from the sink.

Lily watched the ritual, stone-faced. Art was tearing up. It was hard to tell what was going through Doctor Rosalyn's head; she sat next to the porthole window holding a cigarette with trembling fingers, looking back and forth between Sam and the ocean.

Jennifer was standing next to Vic, and he was surprised to see that she was crying softly. He considered putting an arm around her hips or shoulders. He was ashamed that, even in these morbid, desperate conditions, he was still thirsting for her. Maybe even more than before, in fact. The proximity of death, and the increasing likelihood of his own, combined to form a surprisingly strong aphrodisiac.

They'd left Bahram up on the deck with the rope, but Elissa had untied herself an hour ago.

Mel finished washing the body, and drew up the blanket to cover everything but Sam's face.

"We'll bury him at sea, I suppose. Though the logistics..." Mel was clearly gauging the corpse's weight, "are daunting."

A hard silence.

"Anybody want to say anything?" asked Art, weakly.

Rosalyn inhaled sharply on her Marlboro. This irked Vic; even he was refraining from smoking now out of respect.

"Sam was a really good person," Lily said. "I think... maybe better than any of us. He didn't deserve this."

Art cringed. Vic wondered if someone was going to say something about the circumstances of Sam's injury.

"I agree," Jennifer said softly. "He was a very good person."

"He was," Mel nodded and closed his eyes, then began to chant something in Hebrew, a stirring melody that made the hairs on the back of Vic's neck stand up. When he finished, Lily asked:

"What did you say?"

"It's the traditional prayer for the deceased. *El Malei Rachamim*. Holy King of mercy, who lives above, give true rest on the wings of your Divine Presence, amongst the holy and pure and brilliant who shine like the heavens. The everlasting is his bounty, and he shall rest peacefully at his lying place, and let us say: Amen."

"Amen," mumbled Art, then Lily and Rosalyn. Jennifer said nothing, and so Vic too stayed silent. He'd never been so full of lust. The very sight of Jennifer's shoulders, peeling and cracked from sunburn, made his heart jump. As with the sun, he only dared glance at the curve of her breasts beneath her tank top peripherally, for fear of being overwhelmed by their radiance.

"Elissa has been gone an hour and a half," Rosalyn said, finally putting out her cigarette, "and has untied herself. Let's prepare the lifeboat in case she doesn't come back. Vic, Jennifer: go collect maybe a hundred food packets from the Red Cross container–the supply in the mess isn't enough for us to bring. Art, go back to the engine room door in case Elissa unlocks it and needs help. Mel, find Adam. I'll go wait with Bahram at the rope–"

"We need to carry the body up to the deck," Mel said. "We can't leave him unburied. Otherwise his soul will never find peace."

"He's dead," said Jennifer. "Under better circumstances, sure, it would be nice to give Sam the respect. But we need to conserve our strength."

Mel shook his head, laughing bitterly, as if amused by this girl's naiveté.

"You *can't* leave a body unburied. His soul will wander for eternity–"

"Enough with these fairy tales!" she shouted. "Christ, we're trying to survive here, and you're talking about *nonsense*. Let's get off this goddamn boat before we all die from thirst!"

Mel stared at her for a moment, then simply turned away.

"Arthur, Victor," he said, "help me move the body up to the deck–"

"Mel," Rosalyn said. "Let's compromise. First let's get the lifeboat ready, okay? Then we'll come back and take care of this."

Mel was silent for a moment.

"Very well. But I will need to stay here to guard the body. You can't leave a body unattended before it's interned."

Jennifer turned away in disgust.

"Okay," Rosalyn stood up. "Let's go."

"I don't think Art should come with us on the lifeboat," said Lily suddenly. Everyone turned to look at her. She was flushed. "He's a murderer."

"Lily, there's no time for this," said Rosalyn. "Everybody is thirsty."

"He killed Sam," Lily said, voice shaking. "And I don't want him to come to the island. What if we have kids? We're going to let him teach and take care of them? He's a *murderer*."

Art flinched, as if physically struck by this word. He tried speaking a few times and failed. Then finally managed to say:

"Lily, it was an accident."

"No it wasn't," she said. Art moved his mouth like he was chewing fiercely on a piece of gristle. She gestured to the body on the bed. "Look what he did. He shouldn't be allowed to come with us."

Everyone looked pained.

"So," Rosalyn said emptily. "Let's vote."

"C'mon," Art said, shaking his head. "C'mon. We wouldn't even have gotten this close if it wasn't for me."

Rosalyn studied the others with dead eyes.

"Raise your hand if you don't think Art should be able to come on the lifeboat."

Lily raised her hand.

Vic wiped his forehead. Sam was dead, and Greg wasn't coming. Of the men, that left Art, Mel, Adam, Bahram, and himself. Art, he felt, was the only one that the women could potentially prefer to him. Even though Art was older, he was so smart and smooth. With Art out of the picture, it seemed all but certain that he'd be the prize stallion. Vic raised his hand.

"Lily? Vic boy…?" Art's eyes welled up. For a moment Vic pitied him. "You'd really leave me to die?"

"It's like Lily said," Vic whispered, unable to meet Art's gaze. Guilt, or something, was making the back of his eyeballs itch.

"Okay, well I vote to bring Art," said Rosalyn, and raised her hand.

"Me as well," said Mel.

"Jennifer?" Rosalyn asked, and Vic steeled himself. This would be the moment of truth. If she chose to bring Art it meant maybe she'd want to copulate with him, right? Did it? He was so weak from thirst it was hard to follow any cognitive thread to its logical conclusion.

"I'm guessing my vote doesn't count?" Art forced a smile. Everyone ignored him, looking at Jennifer.

"I don't know," she said, shaking her head impatiently, as if this whole situation was just a big nuisance to her.

"You must decide," Mel said.

She closed her eyes.

"This is all ridiculous. All these stupid… *games*. Figure it out yourselves. Vic, let's go get food and load up the lifeboat."

Yes. This was going well, Vic thought. She obviously wasn't interested in Art. Jennifer took a sheet from the linen closet to use as a satchel for the food packets. Vic walked shoulder to shoulder with Jennifer down the hall.

"Sam is dead and they want to play stupid games," he said to her.

She looked at him, jaw half-cocked.

"Those people are all insane," she said, as they walked out to the top deck. "They've lost their minds."

The intimacy of this statement, the way she referred to 'them', stoked a fire in Vic's loins. And suddenly he had a fiendish, unspeakably horrible, but delicious idea.

"Perhaps we should just go in the lifeboat ourselves," he said, then added with some reluctance: "And we can bring the Arab as well I suppose."

Jennifer didn't immediately reply. She was in front of him now, leading him down the perimeter walkway toward the food container in the rear of the ship. He was disappointed to note that her butt, once so full and bulbous, had withered from malnutrition. Still, his eyes were riveted to her swaying rear, the tension in his limbs becoming unbearable.

"Jennifer?" he said. "Did you hear–"

"Just stop," she turned around and snapped at him, something lean and lupine in her face. "Stop."

They didn't speak again until they arrived at the Red Cross container.

The two of them looked up at the opened container, stacked on top of three others. One of them would have to climb up to get the packets. Until now, only spry, wiry Greg had done it. Jennifer probably lacked the upper body strength.

Vic sighed. Rosalyn had obviously expected that he, as the strongest person left on the ship, would be doing the dirty work.

"*D'accord,*" he said to Jennifer, as he stepped into the mouth of the bottom container. "I will climb and throw them down to you."

The climbing wasn't easy. It was essentially a series of three pull-ups in a row–jumping to grip the lip of the container floor above, cranking yourself up, then repeating. He stopped to rest after the first one. He was a bit dizzy from the heat, the thirst, and the exertion. Jennifer seemed antsy as she watched.

"Just do it two more times," she called up to him.

Suddenly his attraction to her evaporated. Instead he wanted to slap her.

He ignored her and sat down to catch his breath. Then attempted the next pull-up. This one was harder, and when he collapsed on the lip of the third container from the bottom, his biceps and forearms were shaking uncontrollably.

"One more," he heard Jennifer say from below.

God, he thought. She was actually sort of horrible. He thought about making her submit to him. Yes. That was how he wanted her. He didn't love her at all. He hated her. He wanted to simultaneously please and punish her.

"Vic? Come on!" she shouted. She only talked to him when she wanted something. Cigarettes. Food. He imagined him and the women on the island. Lily, Rosalyn, and Jennifer being kept in cages. They'd reach out to him, desperate to be his chosen concubine for the evening.

One more reluctant pull-up and he jerked himself up to the threshold of the hallowed cave. Cardboard boxes filled with glittering foil packets of polenta and lentil daal were stacked to the roof of the container. Enough nauseating food to keep them alive and miserable for months.

52

Even after an hour and a half, Elissa hadn't gotten used to the smell.

She'd gagged as they first lowered her into the shaft, the hot air laced with olfactory malice from the sewage tanks below.

It was a very tight fit. Art's homemade rope harness squeezed her thighs and torso like a boa constrictor. Craning her head back with some difficulty, she saw the square of sunlight shrinking as she descended. She shined the flashlight at her feet and failed to make out any landing beneath her.

She'd never considered herself a claustrophobe, but of course she'd never been jammed down a dark mine, blasted with hot air reeking of what was, at least partially, her own excrement. It was impossible not to think of herself as a metal coil being snaked through a backed up sewage pipe.

The shaft was much deeper than she'd thought possible, and soon the voices from above were too distorted by echoes to make out properly. She resorted to the tug system, giving them a jerk every ten seconds to indicate they should continue lowering her.

When her feet finally found purchase she felt no relief. The shaft split into two horizontal crawl spaces. She had to put her legs through one opening to lower her stomach down to the metal floor. Now she had to choose a direction.

She shined the flashlight ahead and saw nothing but more corridor. There wasn't enough space to see behind her, so she had to stand back up in the shaft and then lie down facing the other direction. Here too, no end in sight. She tried to orient herself, building a 3D layout of the ship in her mind to figure out which direction made more sense. But then realized she wasn't even entirely sure she wasn't mixing up her bow and stern direction... In fact was she even sure the two horizontal shafts ran parallel to the ship's length, and not perpendicular?

Her heart was beating fast. She shined the flashlight up through the shaft, following the length of rope with her eyes until it disappeared. She could still tug twice and be lifted back up. As long as her rope lasted, though, she could also be pulled back through a horizontal crawl space.

She gave the rope a tug for some slack, chose a direction at random, and started forward. It was excruciating to crawl through such a narrow space. She had to keep her arms straight in front of her, one hand holding the flashlight, while her legs did all the pushing work. Her frail calves and quads were soon burning with exertion. She pushed the pain from her mind by concentrating intently on what was in front of her, namely, length after length of uniform steel ventilation shaft.

The rope went taut, preventing further progress. She closed her eyes. The smell seemed to have grown more potent. A good sign, she supposed. Someone on the deck above gave her rope an inquisitive tug.

She'd need to untie herself. And to do this, she'd have to let go of the flashlight. The shaft seemed flat but the thought of losing her flashlight was somehow even more frightening than that of disconnecting from her safety harness.

She carefully loosened her grip on the flashlight to test if there was a slant that would carry it away from her. It seemed pretty stable.

"Please, God," she whispered.

She left the flashlight ahead of her, pointing back at into her face and squeezed her arms and hands down the length of her torso, to her hips. Blindly she fumbled with the knots, ignoring a series of quick tugs from above, desperate, she guessed, for an update. She loosened the harness enough to crawl out of it. A sudden clank behind her made her jump, and she banged her head hard against the top of the shaft. As the echo died down she realized it was just the screwdriver and pliers falling out of the belt now that the harness had come loose.

She needed to give them some kind of signal, but no convention had been agreed on for this scenario. She gave the rope five slow, patient tugs, then fumbled around at the ground near her hips until finding the tools. She slid them up in front of her, next to the flashlight.

Back in her groping zombie position, one hand on the flashlight, the other holding the tools, she continued forward without her safety net.

The corridor forked eventually, but the decision was easy: the shaft to the left was flat, while the right one slanted down. Before the descent she took a minute to rest. Her progress had been so slow that it was impossible to tell how far she'd crawled away from that first vertical shaft. But to return to the rope she'd have to retrace her steps. And if this down-sloping shaft turned out to be a dead end, she'd have to crawl backwards, uphill, to get back to this fork. The angle wasn't that steep, but the metal was slippery and there was nowhere to get a grip.

This shaft would be an unpleasant place to die. She'd probably linger for two days until surrendering to thirst, trapped in her steel coffin, wrapped in a hot blanket of shit fumes.

She took the downward shaft. It was a bit steeper than she'd thought, and a few times she actually had to press her knees out against the walls to stop herself from sliding too fast. The smell was so thick and heavy it seemed to be burrowing inside her nose and mouth. And then she saw the vent at the end of the shaft. She scurried forward eagerly to see where she'd arrived, and breathed a nasty sigh of relief when she spotted the red glow of the engine room emergency lights.

There was a fan in front of the vent, but it was off because the engines weren't on. Through the fan and the grate, she saw the vent opened about four feet above a catwalk, the middle of the three levels. For a moment she watched silently, to see if Greg popped into view. Nothing. Was he dead? Highly unlikely–starvation wouldn't have killed him after two days. But if he was still alive, what was she going to say to him? She hadn't even had time to properly think this through.

She stuck the flashlight down the neck of her blouse so it was aimed at the fan and vent, then got to work with the pliers. The angle was awful. She didn't even have space to lift her elbow for leverage, so it was all wrist and forearm. First she unscrewed the nuts on the bolts holding the fan in place. But there was no place to put the fan until the vent too was opened, so she had to reach through the blades of the fan with the pliers to access the nuts on the bolts holding the vent in place. This required an unspeakable contortion. She worked on the first nut, pain coursing through her elbows and shoulders. The screw itself started turning along with the nut. So she had to switch to using the pliers to hold the screw in place while she twisted the nut loose with her bare hand. Her face was mashed into the fan. She grasped and strained. The screw was greasy, and kept slipping through the jaws of the pliers. She was close to crying with frustration.

Elissa froze. There were sloshy footsteps ringing up the catwalk staircase, approaching. Had Greg heard her? She squinted. Through the fan blades and grate she saw his long shadow cast against the red light on the far wall. Then his shape, swaying as he trudged down the catwalk toward her. He was breathing hard and mumbling. Before he arrived at the vent, he turned and lumbered up another staircase. His footsteps were slow and purposeless.

Once his footsteps retreated, she returned to the nuts. It took her an eternity to remove the first of the six bolts holding the grate in place, and her arms were cramping horribly.

She pulled her arms back to rest for a moment and listened for Greg. She considered what would happen if she just shouted for him. Was there any way she could convince him to actually help her with the screws? With someone holding them from the outside it would just take a few minutes. For that matter, what exactly *was* her plan? She'd either have to talk some sense into him, or just sneak around and unlock the door, and hope he was too hungry or unhinged to notice.

Failing either of those… Was she even capable of hurting him? The idea of attacking someone was so ludicrous she almost laughed out loud. Instead she took a deep breath and resumed her work with the nuts.

She tried not to check her watch as she worked; it was too disheartening. Only when she finally unscrewed all six nuts that held the bolts holding the grate in place, all the skin on the pads of her fingers rubbed away as if by sandpaper, leaving blood and pink flesh, her arms and hands shaking uncontrollably from exertion, did she allow herself to check the time. Two hours and ten minutes had passed since she entered the vent.

Surely, *surely*, they'd wait a bit longer before taking the lifeboat.

Greg had passed by maybe ten times as she worked; up the stairs, then down the stairs, all the while talking to himself. Sometimes he laughed hysterically, sometimes he seemed to be taking one or both sides of a violent argument. She waited until he passed, going down, then pushed the grating and fan forward, hoping she'd be able to gently lower them to the floor below. But they were far heavier than she'd expected, and her grip was so weak that she immediately dropped them. The metal pieces crashed into the metal floor, and the echo seemed deafening.

She quickly crawled forward until she was hanging halfway out of the vent. She heard his footsteps from somewhere below, perhaps a bit faster than usual. She scrambled forward, groping for the floor, and then just tilted forward, unable to avoid a hard fall. She lay there for a second, dazed. His footsteps were approaching, and he was talking. Without the grate and fan muffling the sound, she could hear every word, the three-story engine room magnifying his monologue like a theater hall.

"Now that's what I call a *sticky* situation. Haha! Not a word about this to your mother, buster..." his register suddenly shifted from strained-uproarious to grounded-baritone. "So tell me a little about yourself–what do you like to do besides nature walks and fishing for salmon in the river?" His voice shifted again, to affected ebonics: "Yo, pass the damn rock, son! You out here trying to beat them guards one on five. But we're a *team*, son. Now you pretend that ball's a hot potato okay? You catch it and it's too hot to hold onto, you move it, swing it around the perimeter..."

Elissa got to her feet as he jangled up the staircase toward her. He stopped in his tracks, gaping at her.

Greg's eyes were as red as the emergency lights, and his face was bony and pale. He had dried food–yellow filth–all around his mouth, and coating his hands. He must have brought food packets down here with him. Why had nobody considered that possibility?

"Hello Greg," she said.

He suddenly relaxed. He grinned at her and smoothed back his brown hair.

"How the hell are ya?"

"I've been better," she said. "How about you?"

"A million bucks. I feel like a million bucks!" He leaned in and winked conspiratorially. "But do you know what the inflation rate was last year?"

She forced a smile.

"What have you been doing down here? Aren't you getting bored?"

He walked past her and sat down on the stairway that led up to the top floor and the locked door. He closed his eyes and again rubbed his hands through his hair. She wondered if he'd heard the question. Finally he looked back at her

"I figured it all out," he said, and winked again. "Took me a while. They put a lot of effort into the set and special effects. They must have had a *hell* of a budget."

Elissa wondered whether it was more prudent to let him ramble, or try to steer the conversation to someplace constructive. Again she considered the scenario where the others escaped in the lifeboat, leaving her and Greg alone together on the ship.

He was blocking her way up, and besides, unlocking the door to the engine room would require her sprinting up a long flight of stairs. He'd be much faster than her. Maybe instead, she could pull one of the many fire alarms in here. At least then the others would know she'd gotten in, and keep waiting.

Greg dropped his voice to a whisper.

"It's a test, see. They took me to a controlled environment, where they could observe and prepare me. But prepare me for what? See that's the question. And then I saw the island and I realized. It all adds up: all the filming–it wasn't for movies. I mean, yes they'd turn it into movies, but just for cover, so I didn't catch on. But mainly they were studying me, my every movement, to capture the essence of Greg Pink. So they could *replicate* me. See? We know they can build flawless silicon humanoids–they've been using them as agents for years now, in fact I figured out there are several here on this very ship. Have you noticed? Lily Chink doesn't need to eat. She just does it for show when I'm around, so I don't catch on! The French dude hasn't lost a pound since he got on board. He should have lost weight right–we're all eating less–but he's exactly the same! See they don't have technology yet to make the humanoids' bodies *change*. That's very advanced tech."

Pulling the fire alarm would be a bad idea. It might freak him out–break his trance–and then where would she be? She had to get up to unlock that door. There was a second staircase she could climb, on the other end of this catwalk. She kept facing him, trying to keep her expression one of deep concern for his theories, and delicately eased her feet backwards toward the far staircase.

"See, once they replicate me, on that island, they won't need me around anymore. In fact, I'll be a liability right? Because I'll know the truth. Aha–I see you're confused. Why the big scheme? Why do they want an army of Greg Pinks which can reproduce asexually, to avoid contaminating the Pink genome?"

Greg's grin stretched so wide it looked like his face might rip apart. He stood up suddenly, startling Elissa. She gripped the railing to avoid tumbling backwards.

"And that's when I realized!" he was positively giddy, wild-eyed, a manic professor deriving a magnificent formula for a theater of awe-struck students. "The destruction I saw. The dog, the cars... they were *real*, but they happened a hundred years ago! From birth they hid the destruction from me, creating elaborate sets where my mind and body were honed for the ultimate role. The *ultimate role*. But I was too smart, see. I figured it all–where are you going?"

She froze. They locked eyes. And then she turned and sprinted toward the second staircase with as much speed as her fragile knees and legs would allow. She reached the stairs and started up, but they were too steep for her to take quickly. She heard him rushing up behind her.

When she glanced back he was nearly on top of her. Both hands extended, zombie-like. Which meant he wasn't holding onto the railing...

She stopped, gripped the railing tightly with both hands, and kicked backwards. Her heel found his chest, and he immediately lost his balance and tumbled back, arms flailing, eyes wide.

Greg landed on the catwalk below her with a sickening crunch, followed an instant later by a shrill guttural shriek that echoed so deeply it sounded like the engine room walls themselves were screaming.

He'd landed with his right leg pinned beneath him at a freakish angle. His foot was pointing the wrong way. It looked like his ankle had turned to rubber and his foot had simply been rotated one hundred and eighty degrees until it was facing backwards.

He emitted a haunting howl, like something from the crypt. Finally he found words.

"Help me!" he screamed. "Help me. God help me!"

She stopped for a moment to catch her breath. She was feeling faint. Then she carefully climbed down to join him. The damage was even worse than she'd thought. A shard of bloody bone jutted from just below his knee. His whole body convulsed, like he was having a seizure.

"Help," he moaned. "Help."

Elissa took a deep breath. She knew what she had to do. Yes, somebody this badly injured would be a liability. But that wasn't her primary concern.

They couldn't have him on the island. His mind was poisoned. It didn't matter whether this state was his fault or not. He should be treated like he had a lethal, incurable disease. A contagious one. And it wasn't fair to bring the others in on this decision. She needed to deal with this herself. Her conscience alone would bear this burden.

"Help me..."

She hurried down the stairs to the bottom floor, where the sewage tank and most of the engine controls were. Here the smell was so potent that it could have only come from a broken pipe; Greg must have done some feverish smashing down here over the past days.

There was a heavy lead socket wrench that protruded from the sewage tank; it was in case you needed to open the tank for repairs or, god forbid, manually drain it. The wrench was removable.

She was surprised how calm she felt as she climbed back up to the catwalk where Greg Pink was flat on his back, convulsing in agony. The weight of the wrench was strangely reassuring. She felt a vibrant warmth in her limbs, a distinct sensation she could only remember ever feeling while watching a well-researched option trade pan out exactly as she'd anticipated.

Greg was still partially conscious, and seemed to understand what was about to happen as she gazed down at him, taking the heft of the wrench. She'd have to do this quickly, before she lost her nerve.

She raised the wrench over her head with both hands.

Greg Pink's cerebral hard drive held more bytes of data than there are stars in the universe; high-definition memories recorded and encoded since he was a toddler. Elissa brought down the wrench on Greg's temple and wiped the hard drive clean.

53

At the stern of the ship, Mel and Rosalyn had figured out how to deploy the lifeboat.

The yellow craft was positioned on a downward sloping ramp, and held in place only by a few long pegs. Inside the boat was a lever to retract the pegs, allowing the lifeboat to slide down the ramp and fall thirty feet into the ocean.

To smooth the descent, there was a heavy telescoping crane which unlocked from the wall. The pole guided a thick nylon painter which branched into four hooks. These hooks were meant to be clipped onto the top of the lifeboat, and the ropes would slow the fall, and keep the boat upright. Once the boat landed, you could unscrew the hooks from inside, and sail away untethered.

Vic and Jennifer arrived with the second round of food packets, and tossed them into the open door of the lifeboat. Art packed in his distillation equipment, for the off-chance there was some kind of freshwater lake or river on the island.

The heat seemed unusually punishing this morning, as if with the unfettered wrath of the Holy One. Mel sucked on some daal juice to wet his mouth.

It was the last morning they'd be on his ship. If death came, Mel was ready. But he knew this wasn't his moment. He was too close to bringing the Holy One's plan to fruition, delivering his flock to the New World, teaching them the new path.

The most magnificent temples are built on fields of ashes.

He gathered the strings of his *tzis-tzis* in his right hand and thought about what they represented: the six hundred and thirteen commandments given to the Jewish people at Mount Sinai. He had sewn a fifth tassel to the front of his shirt to indicate the fifty-seven new commandments the Holy Spirit had imparted to him over the past weeks. He would lead his flock to new spiritual heights. They would have children who would be raised purer and more pious than any generation before; from the cradle they'd be in the loving hands of the Holy One, Blessed Be His Name.

"How much longer should we wait?" Rosalyn asked him. "Elissa has been two and a half hours."

"We still need to carry up Sam's body," Mel reminded her.

At the moment, Lily was down in the cabin supervising the unburied corpse.

"I understand why it's so important to you," Rosalyn said. "But it's a huge expenditure of energy."

Mel didn't respond. Sometimes he grew frustrated with his *chevrai*, his community of students. But he had to remember that if they sinned, it was his fault as a teacher. Such was the burden the Holy One had pressed upon him.

Mel sat down on the deck with his Torah in his lap. Art had helped him bind the pages together with a bit of twine. He recalled a passage from Old Exodus that told of the sin of the golden calf–the greatest stain on the Israelite's history. He closed his eyes and sang the words to himself, as best he could remember.

"When the people saw that Moses was so long coming down from the mountain, they gathered around Aaron and said, 'Come, we'll make our own gods who will go before us. This man Moses, who brought us from Egypt, we don't know what happened to him.'"

According to the commentaries, the delay was a result of a misunderstanding. Moses was meant to be on the mountain for forty days. The people started counting the day he ascended, while Moses started counting only the *next* day, his first full day on Sinai. So on the thirty-ninth day, the people panicked. One day.

Rosalyn, Vic, Jennifer, Art, and Bahram were at the door of the lifeboat.

"Give Elissa more time," Mel said to them. "We should be patient. Let's all rest a few moments, then we'll go and retrieve Sam's body."

"I'm sorry Mel, but we should go get Lily, find Adam, and go," Vic said. "We're all so thirsty."

Jennifer nodded in agreement.

Art took off his baseball hat and scratched his scalp.

"Afraid I agree, Rabbi," he said. "I hardly have the strength to stand up."

Mel looked from face to face. Would his stubborn, wayward flock really leave the body of their friend rotting on this boat?

A stiff-necked people.

It was his fault though, he reminded himself, for not adequately instilling the value of the Commandments–both the old and the new.

"Do you know why Moses died?" he asked them. "The greatest prophet the world has ever known died before entering the promised land. Do you know why?"

Rosalyn looked a little exasperated. The Holy One was pushing her to her limits.

"Mel…"

"The island is right there," Vic pleaded.

"Impatience," Mel said. "He was impatient to get his water."

Jennifer turned to the others. "If Mel doesn't want to come, let's leave him. I'm not going to die here because of his nonsense."

"I don't mind waiting another fifteen," Art said. "But then we gotta go."

"I'm going to go get Lily," Jennifer said. "Bring her here. We'll see what she wants to do."

Mel stood up too fast. He was lightheaded for a second, and his legs wobbled.

"We can't leave the body unattended," he said, coming to join the others beside the lifeboat, "and we are not leaving this ship without burying Sam at sea."

"So carry him up yourself," Jennifer snapped.

"My child," he said, growing impatient with her. "You have a lot to learn."

"Guys, cool it," Art said. "We're all tired and irritable."

"We all liked Sam," Vic said, "But please—"

"'*My child?*' What the hell is wrong with you?"

Mel smiled at Jennifer. She was a difficult case, but ultimately as much a child of the Lord as any of them. And no matter how disagreeable she could be, after she was bathed in the ritual waters and converted, her loins would bring forth the holiest generation, the children of the redemption, and for that she should be treated with the utmost reverence.

And this situation with Sam's body was an important instructional moment: Mel would show them that if you had the will to perform His commandments, the Holy One would always provide you with strength.

"Arthur, Vic, Bahram, come help me with Sam's body," Mel said, patiently. "The women can stay here and rest. As you know, the women shouldn't touch the body since they haven't been purified since menstruation."

Jennifer tensed up.

"What the fuck did you just say?"

Mel smiled

"Women must be purified in a *mikveh* after menstruation," he said, flipping through his Torah for a verse that might help elucidate the concept of ritual impurity. "Once we're on the island you can just go into the sea of course. Don't worry, I will instruct you on the proper blessings to—"

Jennifer took a step toward him, ripped the Torah from his hands, and ran to the railing. Mel rushed after her, but he wasn't fast enough. She tossed it over the edge into the sea.

He slammed into the railing just in time to watch the word of God flutter down, and be swallowed by the waves. His legs suddenly buckled beneath him and he had to brace himself to stop from passing out.

Jennifer turned to him, a look of hideous triumph on her face.

"Sorry," she said.

Mel's vision narrowed until all he could see was black. His Torah. His Torah. The Holy One had *transcribed that to him directly*. Mel could hardly breathe. She'd destroyed the new word of God. The only copy on the face of the earth.

Jennifer turned and Mel barely heard her address the others.

"That had to be done," she said. "Okay, so who's going to get Lily?"

Mel was truly, violently sick. It felt like his insides had been drained and replaced with boiling acid. The others were talking, but he couldn't understand a word. She'd destroyed the word of God and… A new wave of dread washed over him as the implications of her actions exploded, one by one, a chain reaction of psychic bombs vaporizing the ground beneath his feet.

This could have been the great redemption, but it had happened again. Some five thousand years ago, the Holy One had wiped the world clean of sin, leaving only Noah and his family, but it hadn't worked. The next generations had fallen back into sin and stayed there until now.

And man had failed again.

All the destruction and suffering was for nothing.

His wife and children hadn't been martyrs to the Holy One's cause.

Tsiporah, Reuben, Shoshana.

He felt dead. Slowly, his sight returned, filtered through sheets of red.

"What have *you done*," he growled, not recognizing the fury in his own voice. Jennifer was only a dim outline, a crimson form on a scarlet screen.

And then, as if of its own accord, his hand shot out and slapped her across the face.

She fell to the ground clutching her cheek and he was on top of her. He smacked her again.

Vic pushed Mel off of her, tackling him onto the hot deck. Vic raised a closed fist and Mel felt a blow land on his cheek. He tasted warm blood. The pain didn't bother him.

"Vic!"

Arthur, Doctor Rosalyn, and Bahram tried to peel Vic off of Mel's chest. But the Frenchman was in the frenzied grip of rage. He lashed out at the others, indifferent to who he was attacking. He caught Art in the neck with a wild fist, and scratched Rosalyn across the cheek. Bahram finally caught Vic in a headlock and drove him hard into the deck. Vic flailed, pinned beneath the Afghani's substantial weight, until exhausting himself.

Mel was still on his back. Despite the brutal sun, he felt cold.

Bahram eased himself off of Vic, leaving the Frenchman face down a few meters away, weeping softly.

Rosalyn's cheek was bleeding. She sat in the shade of the lifeboat, knees tucked to her chest.

Jennifer stood up, looked around, and said nothing.

Art kneeled beside Vic and rubbed his shoulders.

Bahram sat on the deck panting from the exertion of his takedown. His usual grin was gone. He was looking at Adam. How long had Adam been standing there watching? The young man had taken off his sheet, exposing his burns. His expression was flat. He seemed to be simply trying to make sense of the people sprawled, sobbing, bleeding, like he was tracing the scenes of an elaborate fresco.

Mel might have simply lay there until roasting under the punishing sun, had Elissa not returned.

She was holding a blue plastic water container. She looked somehow even smaller, more delicate, than she had when they'd lowered her into the shaft.

"What happened?" Jennifer asked.

Elissa was silent for a moment.

"Nobody is waiting with the rope," she said, voice quivering. "What if I'd needed to be pulled back up?"

54

The nine of them watched from the bridge. The approach would take only a half hour or so.

Their faces were filthy, bloody, peeling, gaunt. They sipped on Dixie cups of water as they watched the island grow gradually larger on the horizon. There was a sense of awe and trepidation, what the first astronauts to land on the moon must have felt: the perpetual orb that had seen them through childhood, that had shone down on their first kiss, had glowed through the nights they toiled on their university work, had offered a romantic backdrop for their wedding... that in just moments they'd *walk* on this looming luminary. The first people to walk on ground that wasn't earth.

The sailors imagined all sorts of terrible possibilities: The island would be nothing but dirt. The island would be as poisonous as the land they'd left behind. The island would be some sort of mass grave.

But there were hopeful scenarios too, and no less vivid: waterfalls and lakes of fresh, saltless blue. Trees bearing tropical fruits, brightly-colored birds living in their branches. Bulbous, delicious eggs...

But the most precious fantasy was other people; hundreds of other survivors inhabiting this tropical paradise who would rush the ship as they docked to celebrate the newest additions to their civilization.

A woman let out a shout. There was another ship docked on the island. And then they saw another, and another. One was a cargo ship like their own. The others were much smaller. Deep sea fishing boats maybe. None of them knew enough about boats to identify them with any certainty.

They just knew that other boats indeed meant other people. Possibly living people; people who were nothing like those currently on board.

A new kind of tension descended as their visions of what lay in store adjusted to this new information. A man tentatively reached for a woman's hand, hoping to leverage the emotional charge of the moment. She hesitantly accepted. A man took off his baseball cap and held it to his chest. A man who had been huddled in the corner in near-catatonia now rose and cautiously approached the glass wall. When he saw the other ships with his own eyes he wept.

A woman wrung her hands, this anticipation obviously a kind of torture for her. Unable to just stand there idly, she left the bridge, climbed down the exterior stairway, rushed to the railing, and leaned out halfway over the ocean, as if relenting to the magnetic tug of the growing landmass.

They were close enough now to see trees. It was clear the island was fairly large, at least two miles across. The woman at the railing inhaled deeply, and swore she could smell the foliage.

The woman at the controls reduced the engine speed. The man clutching his baseball cap smiled sadly and said something to her, and she cracked the tiniest smile herself. A woman standing apart from the others mashed her face against the glass window and muttered something to herself. She was crying but would be hard-pressed to explain why. A grinning man kept pointing and shouting, as if the others hadn't yet noticed the island.

The woman at the controls cut the engines entirely. They needed to approach slowly, so that when the hull hit sand it wouldn't rupture.

They were maybe fifty yards from the shore. Everyone but the woman at the controls rushed down to join the woman at the railing for a better view. The spot they were approaching was thick with palm trees. Someone noted that this meant coconuts. A man pointed a stubby finger at something and shrieked; there was a flock of bright yellow birds perched on a branch.

The deck beneath them suddenly shook, tossing two of them to the ground. The ship had struck land. They helped the man and woman who had slipped up to their feet. The boat was still. The woman who had been at the controls climbed down the exterior staircase and joined the other eight at the railing.

None of them could tear their eyes from the scene. They were no farther from the beach than spectators in the lower stands of a football game from the field.

But there was a strange hesitancy to lower the gangplank and wade to shore. Maybe they were worried this was some kind of communal mirage, and the moment they approached it would dissolve. Or maybe, like infants in the womb, they simply weren't ready to leave their familiar surroundings.

A woman saw something flash behind a tree. Had she imagined it? And then a figure emerged from the protection of the foliage and took a few steps over the sand toward them. It was a near-naked man. He shielded his eyes from the sun and gazed up at the ship. The woman waved to the near-naked man, and he suddenly tensed up, frightened, and retreated back into the brush.

The sailors exchanged worried looks. They waited at the railing to see if the man would return. There was no sign of him. Finally, a few of them got to work extending the gangplank into the sea. From the way the bottom dipped into the water, it looked like it was shallow enough here to wade to shore.

There was some discussion about the man they'd seen. Someone suggested they should carry kitchen knives with them, in case the man turned out to be dangerous, but nobody really had the appetite for violence.

A woman volunteered to go down first, alone if necessary.

No, no. It wasn't necessary. They'd all go together.

But before they could, the near-naked man appeared again on the shore. This time he was joined by two other men. They tread over the sand toward the ship, and then waded into the sea. They stopped maybe ten feet away from the base of the gangplank, and stared up.

The sailors were silent. All three of the men's chests were covered in burns. From this distance, they looked to be identical to the burns covering the chest of one among them, a ninth sailor who had been silent for a very long time. Maybe days, in fact.

This close, they could see one of the savages was wearing a pair of athletic shorts. The other two wore some kind of crude loincloths. Their expressions were of deep confusion.

More people appeared from behind the trees. Maybe two dozen. They moved as a silent mass toward the ship, first over the hot sand, then splashing through the water. Roughly half were male, half female. None of them wore anything more than shorts or loincloths. Some were nude. All had the same burns on their chests. One woman's belly and breasts were swollen in what was surely early pregnancy.

The burned savages didn't talk amongst each other. They just looked up at the ship with bewilderment, like it was an alien craft that had dropped from the sky.

Long, silent minutes passed. In the distance, some of the yellow birds chirped. Then the man with the baseball cap took the elbow of the ninth sailor, the one with the burns, and led him to the gangplank.

"Well then," he said. "Go on down and join them, kid."

Acknowledgments

An enormous debt of gratitude to: Eric Alterman, "Unca" Mark Rinsky, Noah Rinsky, Polina Fradkin, Becky Strapp, Oliver Worth, Annabelle Herzog, Yishai Seidman, Shira Schindel, Adam Chandler, Abigail Singer, Chana Gantz, Joe Gelman, and Arielle Kushner.

Lior Zwasinger, in addition to being an early reader, was a trove of unsavory medical insights.

Esther Naamat for translations.

Sophie Strajnik for a beautifully designed book

And Mom and Dad, for everything.

E.Z. Rinsky has worked as a bagel maker, statistics and economics professor, product marketing manager and–for one misguided year–a street musician. His first novel, *Palindrome* (2016), was short-listed for the International Thriller Writers award for best debut novel and translated into Czech. The sequel, *The Binding*, was published in 2017. *Daughters of January* is his third novel. He is currently working on a new book and a TV pilot. He lives in Tel Aviv.

More at ezrinsky.com

www.ingramcontent.com/pod-product-compliance
Lightning Source LLC
Chambersburg PA
CBHW021102110726
47900CB00007B/1986